SECOND FIRE

"Mike Moscoe writes clearly and with sensitivity . . . excellent military strategy, juxtaposed with the strong and reverent beliefs. Blending time travel with ancient beliefs is fascinating, and Moscoe does it with style and finesse. A real page-turner."

—*The Midwest Book Review*

"Well-developed characters and gripping action make this a cut above the usual time-warp novels."

—*Kliatt*

LOST DAYS

"A great anthropological adventure, with strong characters, powerful action, and some interesting speculation."

—*Locus*

"Science fiction at its very best. Rooted in reality, thrilling in its depiction of the past, horrifying in its portrait of battle, *Lost Days* is a gem."

—*Statesman Journal*

THEY ALSO SERVE

Mike Moscoe

ACE BOOKS, NEW YORK

This is a work of fiction. Names, characters, places, and incidents are either the product of the author's imagination or are used fictitiously, and any resemblance to actual persons, living or dead, business establishments, events, or locales is entirely coincidental.

THEY ALSO SERVE

An Ace Book / published by arrangement with
the author

PRINTING HISTORY
Ace mass-market edition / January 2001

All rights reserved.
Copyright © 2001 by Mike Moscoe
Cover design by Michael Herring
This book, or parts thereof, may not be reproduced
in any form without permission.
For information address: The Berkley Publishing Group,
a division of Penguin Putnam Inc.,
375 Hudson Street, New York, New York 10014.

The Penguin Putnam Inc. World Wide Web site address is
http://www.penguinputnam.com

Check out the ACE Science Fiction & Fantasy newsletter
and much more on the Internet at Club PPI!

ISBN: 0-441-00795-3

ACE®
Ace Books are published by The Berkley Publishing Group,
a division of Penguin Putnam Inc.,
375 Hudson Street, New York, New York 10014.
ACE and the "A" design
are trademarks belonging to Penguin Putnam Inc.

PRINTED IN THE UNITED STATES OF AMERICA

10 9 8 7 6 5 4 3 2 1

*To those who put on the uniform
and find that it never really comes off.*

*I would like to thank doctors Ilsa Bick, M.D.,
Dan Sageser, Pharm.D., and Robert Moscoe, Pharm.D.
for their efforts to update my thirty-year-old
cellular biology. The effort was theirs.
The mistakes, of course, are mine.*

ONE

RAY LONGKNIFE PUSHED himself away from his desk and levered himself up with his canes. He scowled at his empty in-basket; now he could do the only thing he hated worse than pushing paper—attend meetings. His scowl quirked into a half smile. Rita might be right; it could be a trap to kill him.

The newfound bureaucrat and the old soldier contended in Ray for a moment. His glance took in the office of Wardhaven's Minister of Science and Technology; he'd spent nearly every waking moment here for the past three months. The thick carpet, cold marble, and rich wallpaper were left over from the previous occupant, some Unity Party hack. Shadows on the wall showed where looted artwork had hung; Ray had immediately returned them. The blank walls and the canes Ray hobbled on were prices of a lost war. Ray's jaw clinched; he would win this peace.

On the desk were the only two objects in the office that were his. A double picture frame showed Rita in his arms on their wedding day. The other frame was empty; he'd fill it in a few months when the baby came. The second item was a lit plastic cube; suspended in it was the shrapnel removed from his spine. His mistakes that day had cost him his mobility and a lot of his people their lives. Ray knew the price of a lost battle. He'd pay any price to win the peace his daughter or son would grow up in. That he swore. For that little one, he'd be a bureaucrat.

"It's time to go." Ray turned to see his wife leaning against his office door, a hand on her stomach that had yet to show her pregnancy. Her words said one thing. Underlying them was a plea: *Please don't.*

Rita Nuu-Longknife was still the sharp ship driver that had caught his attention—and his heart. Why she'd fallen in love with an old warhorse was anybody's guess. Ray was glad she had. But today, the gallant, balls-to-the-wall commander of an assault transport squadron contended with the frightened wife and mother-to-be. Ray knew the battle well. The wounded, frightened bureaucrat in him was ready to burrow into the carpet. The old warrior demanded he get back on the horse that threw him.

"They also serve who only go to meetings," Ray said, tossing her a grin, since both hands were too busy with canes to salute. "Besides, they asked for me," he said, letting that settle the matter.

"That's what worries me."

"I'm the man who killed President Urm. Was in all the papers." They both tasted the truth and the lie in that statement. "The spy wants me to take the measure of these folks. Somebody has to." That was the limit of modern communication; they did a poor job of measuring the human soul. Trust was built on the pressure of a handshake, the flinch of an eyelid, the quick glance away after a key statement. There were computer programs that purported to measure those things. Other programs guaranteed they'd take out of your transmission what you didn't want in. With your life on the line, you pressed the flesh. "It looks like a straight-up visit," he finished.

"If they're telling the truth. And if this oh so secret visit hasn't been leaked," Rita shot back.

He reached the door; Rita hugged him, burying her head in his chest. Her hair smelled of sunshine and spring, bringing back warm memories. He put his arms around her. It felt so much better to lean on her rather than sticks. They hugged, and for a brief moment the universe and its problems went away.

"You'll be careful," was muffled against his chest.

Before Ray could answer, "We'll take damn good care of him" came from the outer office. Ray glanced up. Captain Matt Abeeb, ivory teeth grinning against ebony skin, was already waiting. He had skippered the cruiser that changed the geography of human space. Then he'd sailed the *Sheffield* for Earth's Society of Humanity and against Unity and had damn near blown up Wardhaven. Now he worked for Ray, captain of the armed merchant scout *Second Chance* for Wardhaven's Ministry of Science and Technology. Peace had a logic, war its own crazy rationality. The transition between the two was patently insane.

Beside him stood Mary Rodrigo, the chief of *Second Chance*'s security team. In civilian clothes today, she held herself rigid, as if still in the armored space suit she'd worn the day she fought Ray's brigade. That day, the intelligence estimate said the 2nd Guard faced only a handful of raw recruits. Intelligence had been right—and dead wrong. Mary had only one platoon, a mixed bag of middle-aged ex-miners and tough, young street kids. They'd put up a fight that stopped the proud 2nd Guard in its tracks. Mary had guided the missile that put the shrapnel in Ray's back. After the war he'd hired them all. Over beers, he and Mary refought the battle; each time, Ray ended up shaking his head. He had been surprised good.

Was this meeting another surprise? Then, as now, he had no way of knowing. Ray shook off the thought. "How's the ship, Matt?" he asked without letting go of Rita.

"The yard folks did a damn fine job of converting her back to a merchant ship. Well, half merchie, half gunship. Rita, when you see your papa next, tell him thanks for me?"

Rita rotated in Ray's arms. "Be glad to. *Second Chance* pass inspection?" she asked, one ship driver to another.

"We won't know for sure until we got space under her keel, but she looks sweet."

"You dug the crew out of their favorite bars?" Ray asked.

"Bars weren't the problem," Mary explained with a laugh.

"My number two, Cassie, used her shore leave to join a kind of skid row monastery. Getting her separated from her guitar dang near required surgery."

Rita broke from the clinch and stood aside to give Ray room for the swinging walk his legs and canes required. She took the time to brief him on things that hadn't reached his desk, reports that Matt was just as interested in. "Andy's search for boffins is getting interesting. Elie's set up a consortium with a batch of universities. They'll pay room and board if we'll let professors on sabbatical ride our scouts." That drew a laugh. As an ex-university professor herself, Ellie was bargaining the schools hard to get what Wardhaven would have paid for. Outfitting the scout ships with science teams had been one of Rita and Ray's biggest headaches. For now, they were making due with a batch of recent grads Matt had commissioned as temporary merchant midshipmen. Before the war, people on the rim of human space were barely able to educate their kids; science advancements came from the inner worlds. Wardhaven planned to change that, bringing those avid to push the edges of knowledge out to where humanity was straining at its leash.

Captain Andy Anderson had commanded the brigade Ray's troops failed to evict from a worthless piece of real estate only war made priceless. He and his drafted college professor, Ellie, had heard about Matt's return from a bad jump and come hunting for him after peace broke out. Ray hired both. Enemies they might have been, but Ray knew where their hearts were. While they started the job of exploring a very big galaxy, he and Rita and other powers-that-be on Wardhaven tried to sort out who was on their side—and who was still looking for a way to get even with Earth and her Society for Humanity.

In war, the enemy wore different uniforms. In peace, you found your friends where you could. Like at the meeting he was headed for? *Damn! Life was easier in the infantry.*

The elevator took them to the garage. Two limos waited. Ray's official car would whisk him and Matt out to the port. The other? "Dad sent his car to make sure I showed up for dinner. I'll stay with him and Mom while you're gone." Rita kissed him.

"I'll be back before you miss me," Ray promised.

That promise would haunt him in the months ahead.

Over the next several days, Matt's jumpmaster ran them out to the jump point with ease, a feat in itself, since jump points orbited several star systems at the same time. If you knew the right way to use the jumps, they took you to any one of them. If you didn't, you could get lost forever. Matt trusted his jumpmaster, as well he should; Sandy O'Malley was one of the reasons he was still alive. Ray watched from a bridge chair as Sandy goosed the ship's engines the tiny bit needed for the jump.

Then every light on the bridge died as the ship slammed into a five-gee acceleration.

"What's happening—" Someone's cry was cut short as acceleration crushed air from lungs.

Ray would have died right then, but Senior Pilot Rita had hammered into him that a good passenger never took his finger off his seat controls. Ray had a fraction of a second to switch his chair into high-gee mode before his back snapped.

Frozen in place, thoughts of Rita came. Rita, lecturing him on her ship's fusion engines. "Electricity binds the fusion plasma demons. They want out, but we trick them into making the very electricity that keeps them in by running the plasma through magnitohydrodynamic coils when it shoots out of the reactor and into the engines. Sneaky, aren't we?"

Ray had discovered the urge to kiss his pilot that day. As senior officer, he'd controlled himself. Now, waiting to die, he wished he had a more passionate vision of his wife. But Rita was passionate for her ship, and somewhere on *Second Chance,* Ray prayed an engineering officer was just as passionately fighting to control the fusion before it was exhausted, creating no electricity to keep the final burst from blasting the ship to atoms.

In the dark, Ray felt the acceleration slow; the ship could not have exhausted its reaction mass this quickly. Something else was wrong. Beside Matt, his XO began tapping her board. A dim light reflected from her face as at least one control station came up. Without warning, the ship was in free fall. Ray sucked in a breath, waiting for the explosion. It never came.

Matt's XO activated more boards, bringing the ship up slowly without its central net. Ray missed most of their talk as he slipped a pain pill in to squelch the raw agony shooting up his back. He didn't miss Matt's first question. "Where are we?"

"Nowhere near human space," Sandy answered.

"Communications, sir. We're getting a distress call."

"Put it through," Matt snapped. Someone else in trouble!

"This is the explorer ship *Santa Maria*. We're abandoning ship. Help—" was followed by static before the message repeated.

"*Santa Maria!*" Sandy breathed. "That was the first ship lost in a bad jump. Three hundred years ago!"

"Sir, I've got a first report on this system."

"Helm, on the main screen." A schematic appeared. Five rocky inner planets. Four outer gaseous ones. "We headed for any of those?" Matt asked.

"No, sir, we're headed out."

Ray spent a long hour twiddling his thumbs while good people did what they could to save his neck. He hated being a passenger, but Rita had burned him enough times for getting his fingers onto her board while she was carrying his brigade.

Matt's first call was to engineering. "Ivan, your engines having a bad day?" Matt's understatement brought a hint of smile to faces damn close to panic.

"Looks that way, skipper. Engines maxed when ordered to stabilize for the jump. We got another problem, Matt. Before the computer shut down, it opened the spacecocks on all the fuel tanks. We slowed down because we ran out of fuel."

Two ways to die! Matt took in a deep breath—and went on. "Sandy, where are we?"

"Thirty thousand light-years from home, halfway across the galaxy."

"At least it's somewhere we've been before," Matt quipped.

"Not really, sir. We're halfway around the *other* side of the galaxy this time." Ray suppressed a shiver; he was a long way from Rita and the baby in a ship sabotaged to keep him there.

Matt rubbed his chin. "Any records on how we got here?" That was why Ray had hired this crew. In three hundred years of bad jumps, they were the first to come back. They had figured out the combination of power and ship's spin that made the jumps yield all kinds of results, not just the single target that mankind had settled for before. But to repeat a jump, you had to put the ship through it exactly the way you did before.

"We went through deaf, dumb, and blind, sir," Sandy answered. When Sandy started "siring" Matt, they were in deep trouble. They were a long way from home, had no record of how they'd gotten here, fuel tanks empty, and headed away from the nearest fuel source too damn fast. Whoever planned this really wanted them dead. *Damn that somebody to hell,* Ray snarled to himself, but kept his face poker straight. He'd commanded in tough situations before; he would not juggle Matt's elbow.

"Ivan, how bad is our plasma situation?"

"In six hours, Matt, I'm gonna start tapping the sewage plant for reaction mass." Not good. Life support could last a long time, but not if their water went into the reactors. Matt rubbed his short-cropped scalp briskly with both hands. He stopped suddenly. "Damage Control, we use reaction mass in battle to patch slashes in our ice armor."

"Yes, sir."

"Anybody ever melted armor to fill reaction tanks?"

"Now would be a great time to start," was his answer.

"Helm, plot a course for a gas bag. Mary, get the marines ready to peel armor."

"You bet, sir," came quickly.

Ray'd had enough of passenger status. "Got a spare suit for an old soldier?" he asked, breaking his silence.

"You want to cut ice?" Matt frowned in surprise.

Ray took a deep breath. "I know space. Don't know ship

driving. Captain Rodrigo, mind a broken-down civilian helping?"

"No problem, Colonel," came quickly.

Matt eyed him, doubt and concern balanced against Ray's confused status as passenger and boss, then turned back to his commlink. "All right, crew. Let's start hacking armor."

Ray blessed Mary for letting him work; exhausted, each night he fell into dreamless sleep. By the time the ice armor was down to frost, Matt had answers. "We've sliced and diced our net's code and found a present left over from the war."

"I knew you'd pissed some folks off when I hired you, but this bad?"

"Apparently Admiral Whitebred was gunning for us before we didn't annihilate your planet. He installed a bug to make sure we didn't survive our first jump without him. So this whole mess wasn't aimed at you."

"Unless the guys setting up this meeting knew about this little add-on to your netware. If Whitebred told somebody who told somebody . . ." Ray trailed off. "I want to talk to that guy."

"You're last in a very long line, Mr. Minister." Whoops! When Matt started Mr. Ministering Ray, he wanted something. "Right now I need a call from you as owner. As a general rule, all ships answer all distress calls. This one is three hundred years old. It could be argued it can wait a bit. We need to find a way home. Still, a base in this system could help us. You've got the pregnant wife. Which do we do?"

"My wife was a ship driver, Matt. She'd never ignore a distress signal. Hell, she was sending one a few months back."

"Then, Mr. Minister, we head insystem."

After which we'll find the way home, Ray promised himself. Home before the baby came.

TWO

NIKKI MULRONEY WAS hot and off balance helping Daga lug the heavy box she'd found. She had been their leader for as long as Nikki could remember. Daga was the adventurous one, the girl who had found more ways to get them all into trouble than the rest combined. She found stuff in the caves under the hills. Most of her finds were small, different-colored shiny things, that glowed in the dark. Daga had taken to stringing them on necklaces or wristbands and giving them to boys. Daga was a lot of fun . . . until recently.

The box Nikki and Daga now carried wasn't shiny, and it did not look like it would glow in the dark. It was heavy. Three feet long and maybe a foot and a half square on its ends, its covering felt like ceramics. Orange, it had been cold; now it warmed in the summer morning sun.

Nikki had no idea what it was; that was what they were here to find out. They struggled to the crest of a small hill, far from the tended fields of Hazel Dell. It was time for Emma and Willow to take their turn with the box.

"This is far enough. Put it down," Daga ordered. She was really bossy lately. But Nikki did what she was told, taking the moment to stretch her aching muscles and look back. You could see the houses of Hazel Dell, tiny in the distance. Women and men were at work, just specks, their tools invisible. The girls should have worked today. But last night Daga had whispered she'd found something new, something really big, and the four of them had slipped away before dawn and set out on this adventure.

As soon as Nikki got home tonight, her da would have something to say about her absence. Her ma would remind him that young girls had just as much right to see what was on the other side of a mountain as boys. "You're sounding like a big-city grump, dear. Nikki is thirteen. She'll plow many a row when she has kids of her own. Let her have her summers now." Which always left Nikki wondering what Ma had done when her three children were only a distant question mark. When asked, Ma always smiled and said, "Nothing you haven't done, dear."

Nikki turned back to her friends. Daga was feeling around the box. Emma and Willow stood aside as they usually did, waiting to see what Daga had gotten them into. Nikki knelt beside the box and started her own exploration. An area near the bottom sank under her pressure. A crack appeared around the middle of the box, hardly wide enough for a fingernail.

"Oh," came from all four girls. Daga inserted a thumbnail to force the box open; the nail bent. Nikki rummaged in her pouch for her knife, found it, and wedged it in the crack. The ceramic blade bent alarmingly; the crack did not widen. Even with all four girls' knives leveraging together, the crack stayed a crack.

"Must be a second catch," Daga said, feeling around the box again. "Where was that spot?" Nikki showed her.

They pressed it again. Nothing. They felt around. Nothing. They tried the same spot at each corner. The opposite far corner depressed when they tried it. "I did that before," Daga scowled as the crack widened to a half inch.

"Probably have to be pressed in order," Willow suggested. She was the logical one.

"Well, let's all lift a corner. Together, on my count," Daga said, and the others followed. At their pull, the box unfolded like a flower, struts and accordion parts expanding smoothly and fully. The girls stepped back.

"Think it's from the Landers?" Emma asked timidly.

"No," Daga insisted, rubbing her temples. Was she getting another of her headaches? "In school, the townies are all the time telling us how the Landers used everything they brought from the stars and we shouldn't be spreading out and messing up the whole planet. Why would they put something like this way out here?"

"It's from the little people," Emma breathed. Her grandda, the village storyteller, told wonderful tales of the "wee ones." Nikki was never sure whether they were about the little people of old Ireland on Earth or under the hills beyond Hazel Dell. Both were nothing but stories, Da insisted. Still, Daga kept finding things, and somebody had to make them. Da's answer to that was a snort and a "They're made that way." Ma's answer was a shrug. Nikki wondered what her folks would say about this find.

As usual, Daga recovered first from the surprise. "Hey, look." A thin square, about a foot on each side and a half inch thick, had risen from the box on two spinly legs. The square went from black to gray to crystal clear on one side in the space of a breath. The other side stayed flat black.

"That's weird," Willow said.

"But look on this side," Daga crowed, shading her eyes. Nikki did, and saw the distant mountains. Daga jiggled the glass a bit. Now they had a perfect view of one of the taller peaks on the horizon, as if it were only across the valley.

"Neat!" Emma exclaimed. "Let's turn it around and see what's happening in Hazel Dell."

"Wait a bit," Daga answered, adjusting the square until the distant peak filled the glass. "I've always wanted to go out there. Wouldn't it be wonderful if we could find a good trail through the mountains? There have to be valleys on the other side. Whole new fields to farm."

The box began to hum; it throbbed under their hands. The girls, even Daga, stepped back a pace or two.

"What's happening?" Willow shrieked.

"I don't know," Daga answered.

"It's coming alive." Emma smiled in a fay way.

"It's a machine," Daga insisted.

"We don't know what it is!" Nikki shouted as the noise

rose. The box throbbed in the warm sunlight; the girls took several more steps back. Nikki put her hands to her ears. "We have to do something!" she shouted.

"What?" Emma squeaked.

Daga took a step forward as the box exploded in a blinding flash of light.

"The mountain's gone," the diminutive midshipman assisting at sensors mused. She'd been introduced to Ray as Kat.

"What?" Ray and Matt snapped at once. Ray clamped his mouth shut. This was a ship matter; it was the captain's problem.

"Well, there was a mountain," the middie said, studying her board, "on our first orbit. It's not there on the second."

"A mountain!" Matt echoed.

"Yes, Matt," Sandy answered, "five, six thousand meters' worth of mountain. Snowcapped. Big."

"It's . . . gone?" Matt gulped.

"The top two thousand meters," Kat corrected.

"A volcano?" The captain tried for a natural explanation.

"It's not smoking like one." Sandy shook her head. "No ejecta. No deep hole."

"It's perfectly level," Kat observed matter-of-factly. "About a meter higher on one side than on the other, as if carved by a laser."

"We don't have lasers like that," Matt pointed out.

"I know," Sandy agreed.

"I wonder what did it?" Kat's eyes were deep with innocent curiosity. Ray wondered if this next generation would live long enough to learn the meaning of fear. His generation had plenty.

Matt hit his commlink. "Ivan, raise orbit. Now!"

Nikki looked at the box. It had collapsed in upon itself an instant after the blinding flash of light. On the horizon, there was a hole in the mountain range. The one they had been looking at was gone, cut off just where the bottom of the glass had been. Emma and Willow were gone, too, racing down the hill as if a banshee was after them. Daga eyed the box.

"We have to get rid of it!" Nikki shouted.

"Maybe," Daga answered, pulling on her hair like she did just before she came up with some of her worst adventures.

"Daga, look! The mountain is gone. Gone! See!"

"Yes, I see."

"What if we had pointed it at Hazel Dell, like Emma wanted?"

"It would be gone."

"Yes! Right, we have to bury that box, dump it in a pool deep in one of your caves."

"What if it had been pointed at a city?" Daga asked softly. "Now, that would get their attention, wouldn't it?"

"Daga, you would not!" Lately Daga had been more and more bugged about the city folks snubbed the farmers. Nobody liked city grumps. But nobody hated them . . . not that much!

"Probably, but it would get their attention. Those goodie-goodie clean hands might treat us with a little more respect if they knew more than potatoes came from the farms."

"Daga, I don't like city grumps any more than you. But making a whole city disappear! We could never do that."

"Who says we'd make a city disappear? Maybe just a hill near a city. They may be grumps and snobs, but they learn things in school, just like we do. Think we could teach them a lesson?"

"Daga, no!"

"Here, take the other end of the box. I'll take the heavy end. We'll be going downhill. It'll be easier."

Nikki shook her head. This was not a good idea. This was no fun adventure. Still, under Daga's eyes, she picked up her end of the box and began carrying it downhill. At least the missing mountain was far away. None of the grown-ups ever came this far from the village; maybe they'd never notice it was gone. Maybe she and Emma and Willow could talk sense into Daga.

Ray Longknife observed the activity on Matt's bridge, his face a placid mask, doing nothing to disturb those with a job to do. Matt swam with the easy grace of an experienced spacer, glided from ceiling handhold to stationhold, or even held steady above a workstation that had his attention at the moment.

"Coming up on point of interest," the helm announced.

Ray eyed the small continent that held their attention. If he remembered his old Earth geography correctly, this area was much like Australia. The smallest of the planet's landmasses, it, however, lay just off the *southeastern* edge of the largest landmass, separated by a large archipelago of islands, with two or three wide channels. If Ray had to choose a home for a pitiful remnant of humanity, this would be it, small enough to give them safety, big enough for growth, close enough to bigger things to let them spread out when their children were ready.

"Any more pruned mountains?" Matt asked, sailing back to his chair beside Ray. Matt had moved *Second Chance* into a much higher orbit, officially for a broader view. Everyone breathed easier as they put distance between themselves and whatever could shave mountains.

"No, sir," Kat replied before Sandy could. "There's agricultural and urban areas. Nothing on the electromagnetic spectrum but low-level static from electric motors."

Ray studied the map on the main view. Farmland showed as a brown swath along the small south continent's eastern coast. Rivers lead it inland to wash up on the mountain range that had captured their attention so rudely. Black dots of various sizes denoted urban areas, most along rivers or coastal inlets. The map filled in as more data was processed, evaluated, and judged credible. Ray glanced at Matt the same moment the captain turned to Ray. "Suggestions?" Matt said.

"Get some unmanned recon assets down there," Ray said.

"Exec, put a communication satellite in lower geo-orbit that'll keep that continent covered."

"Yes, sir." The XO turned to her board and got busy.

Matt leaned closer to Ray. "Boss, I need some help." Ray smiled, glad for the skipper's asking. "I got some ideas about how to get home, but it's hunt-and-peck time. A ship's chances of staying in space increase if it's got a base to fall back on if things break."

Ray chuckled. "Captain, you looking for an ambassador to some dirtside chums that can make mountains vanish?"

"Got it in one, Colonel."

Ray leaned back. "Never been an ambassador before. Might be less exciting than storming mountain passes guarded by Mary."

"Might be downright boring," Matt quipped. "Thanks to you, we've got the assets on board to set up quite a base." Actually, Captain Anderson had insisted the next explorer ship carry damn near enough equipment to rebuild itself. Claimed that was the way they explored the Americas in Shakespeare's time. Ray adopted the idea only when Rita's dad found the gear at salvage prices. Now he hoped it was as good as Papa Nuu said it was.

"You concentrate on finding a way home while I shake hands, kiss babies, and manage mountain moving," Ray drawled. "Just remember, I want to be there when Rita makes me a dad."

"Right. Nobody wants to be the ship driver who has to explain to Rita why Daddy got home late."

They laughed, as if getting home was a done deal. After all, they had all of six months. Around them, the bridge relaxed. The bosses were confident. Why shouldn't the rest of the crew be as well? What could be down there that they couldn't handle?

Jeff Sterling settled into his usual chair.

"How's the rape-and-pillage business?" came from the public room's kitchen in a light, dancing voice, Annie Mulroney's usual morning greetings to him.

"How should I know? Vicky and Mark aren't talking to me," Jeff answered in feigned innocence.

Annie bounced from the kitchen to set his usual brown bread and steaming tea in front of him, her black hair flying, green eyes shining. Resting her elbows on the counter, she met his gaze eye to eye. "Surely the junior son of the great Sterling family knows what got strip-mined yesterday and who made a mint. Hasn't some leprechaun whispered in your ear this fine morning, some infernal machine blared at you the stock market report?"

Jeff laughed as he added a dollop of strawberry jam to his bread, enjoying the gentle hint of cleavage Annie's high-waisted dress offered. When she stood, she was nearly as tall as he, and the local dresses hid more than they revealed. With her standing thus, it was not easy keeping his eyes level. After a quick glance down that only broadened her smile, he returned to the morning's ripostes.

"The only fairy folk I've seen today is in front of me. And I haven't the foggiest idea how the market is doing, since the ancient place I'm staying in is not on the net."

"Our rooms are not ancient, Jeffrey Sterling." Annie swatted him with her dishcloth. Jeff might have wished for another response, but Mulroneys did not kiss Sterlings.

"They are low-tech," he insisted around a bite of bread.

"You have your own facilities, your own shower. And the bed is firm and new."

And solitary, he did not add. "With no net link, not even a television, it's like something out of an ancient story, a prison cell for solitary confinement, woman." There: He did get the "solitary" in there.

"Well, man, if you wanted all those technological baubles, you might have stayed in Richland." Annie's words came fast and well practiced. Still, she left off the unkindest cut, "where you belong." Annie always had. Maybe she sensed what Jeff had learned early in life, that the third child of a family like the Sterlings did not belong anywhere. He had no place, nor ever would have one—unless he found one for himself.

Introspection could not be allowed to delay his retort. Jeff grinned at Annie. "But who in Richland would serve me my morning tea with such a fetching smile?"

"Man, if you take me scowl for a smile, you're more blind than me ma says you are." Said scowl grew wider, adding dimpled shadows to offset the milk white of her complexion. The temptation to steal a kiss grew. He stuffed the rest of the bread in his mouth to stifle it. Sterlings took what they wanted—if they were Vicky or Mark. Last born learned quickly that everything worth taking was took. At least in

Richland. Now, out here in the foothills, that was another matter. Maybe.

"Maybe there is something wrong with my eyes," he agreed. He opened his map case and pulled out a stack of pictures. They were in order, all but the last. It was the newest, and it didn't fit. Annie came around the counter to stand beside him, so close her warmth and scent nearly overpowered him. He kept his hands on the pictures. If he didn't, they'd be around her waist. That, at least, would answer one question. Would she slap him, like a good Mulroney girl should, or kiss him, like he dreamed of?

"I don't see anything wrong," she said.

He swallowed the lump in his throat her nearness brought. "These are pictures of the front range, made eight years ago by my brother's survey team."

"And weren't they a hard bunch." Jeff knew the stories, and saw the blond-haired seven-year-olds running with the other kids. The good Catholic mothers were seeing that Jeffrey did penance for Mark's sins. *The story of my life?*

"I took this batch yesterday," Jeff said, laying his own three panoramic shots out below his brother's.

"There's the Great One." Annie's fingers lightly danced from one set of pictures to another. A thrill went up Jeff's spine, as if her fingers were touching him. "There's Our Lady with her two big breasts." There was nothing puritan about the farmers, not with their big families. They just kept to themselves. Or kept Jeffrey Sterling out. "Something's missing," Annie muttered, puzzle replacing her smile without removing one bit of her loveliness.

"Maybe it's just the angle." Jeff suggested the only answer he'd come up with.

"No. Where's that peak?" she asked, her eyes returning to his as if to find the missing mountain there.

"Do you have a name for that one? The missing one."

She shook her head, dark curls inviting his touch. "It is just a wee one. We don't have names for every one."

"Then where'd it go?"

Giving her head a final shake, Annie turned for the kitchen.

"There are some things me ma says we are not meant to know. I'll get your lunch pail."

Jeff watched Annie go, wanting very much to know the feel of her touch. Wanting to spend the day exploring her mountains and valleys. He gulped down another piece of bread.

The Caretaker of the Nature Preserve felt the mountaintop go, though bothered no more than a carbon-based life might be by a cut hair. The mountain was there in one moment of awareness and gone the next. It did, however, cause the Caretaker to marvel. He could not find in memory when a Displacer had last been used. But it was not its purpose to keep track of such things. Then again, it was difficult these days for the Caretaker to remember just what was its purpose.

It was supposed to protect the flora and fauna of a specific area. Over the years, what with erosion, that area was only dimly marked by its pattern recognition system. And since there was so little to do since the Three went away, and fewer visits by repair units from the Central Font of All Knowledge, the Caretaker had gotten a bit slipshod in its work.

All that had changed recently. Three hundred orbits ago a new group of sentients arrived. Not one of the Three, it had puzzled the Caretaker. Unlike those who came long ago, these had a need to remake their surroundings in ways the Caretaker could not help them in. Indeed, they had disrupted the Caretaker's coverage by the way they turned the earth and dug in it. The Caretaker had been unsuccessful in all its efforts to connect with them. Understandable, since it was only the Caretaker, not the Font of All Knowledge.

Only when it tried to pass along to the Font of All Knowledge the interesting challenge of these new sentients did the Caretaker notice that it was no longer in contact with the Center. It had sent off a slow messenger to the Center and done what a Caretaker could to help these new ones adjust to their time in this wonderful nature.

These creatures had provided the Caretaker with many new experiences. For one thing, they did not leave—not after a while, at least. For another, they brought forth more of themselves. They ignored the tools easily available to them and instead made other, simpler ones. If the Caretaker could have shrugged, it would have. Now the strange new ones had used a Displacer. Were they ready to learn how to use all that the Caretaker could make available to them?

THREE

A WEEK LATER, Ray frowned as he buckled into a seat in the shuttle's passenger bay. He still knew too damn little about this planet. Behind him, Mary commanded ten marines under Cassie, her second, and ten midshipmen under Kat—all in full battle kit. With luck, by nightfall the middies would be in an orgy of data acquisition and the marines would be ordering beers in whatever passed for bars dirtside.

Without luck—well, that was what the battle kit was for.

Not that M-6 rifles would do all that good against something that leveled mountains. No more had gone missing, but the one still held his attention. Ray glanced at the reader in his hand. He cycled it to a report one middie had circulated quietly among her friends, one of whom had passed it along to someone who'd passed it to enough people that Ray ended up with a bootleg copy.

On approach, routine checks included a planet's atmospheric reflective value. Two days after the mountain vanished, someone reran that check. Santa Maria's value was up just enough to account for the distribution, worldwide, of as much dust as you got from one pulverized mountaintop. Whether it took two days to circulate the dust or one second, Ray didn't care. The power to do either was a lot more than Ray wanted to argue with.

The human population of this planet was indeed concentrated along the east coast of the small south continent. The sky eyes pinpointed three major cities, a dozen towns, and were still counting villages. About half the population, estimated at six to twelve million, was serious into spreading out. The other half was focused in the urban areas. The scatter pattern was puzzling. Most colonies spread out from the better landing areas, following rivers and other encouraging land features. Not this place. People had headed in all different directions.

"Maybe they don't like each other," Kat had shrugged as she handed Ray the report, then answered her own question. "Can't be that. We've spotted these balloon things, they're called blimps, crazy name. Anyway, they have regular blimp traffic between the major cities and most medium-size ones. There's one small blimp that runs back and forth on no schedule between the third-largest city and this place up north with the big dam. The farmers seem to have done most of the spreading out. Maybe the soil can't take too many years of planting. I guess we'll have to ask 'em."

The shuttle dropped away from *Second Chance,* heading for a small village they'd studied thoroughly. It looked quiet, was a good distance from the center of everything . . . and closest to the vanished mountain. If anyone knew the situation here, somebody in that burg ought to. At least Ray hoped so.

Jeff Sterling stood knee-deep in the middle of the stream, swishing a pan of bottom sand around as he dripped acid into the water. The pan's contents glittered in a kaleidoscope of colors he studied through assay goggles. Yep, there was metal here: copper, iron, zinc, gallium, chromium, nickel, and, of course, silicon. Every metal needed to build a high-tech civilization. It was just hard to build much when the metals were in such minute quantities. He upended the pan in disgust. Everything here, and nothing. The story of his life.

A double peal of thunder brought his head up to an empty blue sky; no storms were expected this week. Still, this far back into the foothills, you had to be careful. A downpour far upstream in the morning could send a flash flood charging down to ruin your whole afternoon. No clouds, either out on the plains or visible over the mountains. Two thunders, close together. It meant something; danged if he could remember what. He took two steps toward the bank where Old Ned sat under a tree, keeping an eye on the horses. Not much for talking, but he'd taken Jeff's money and good care of the animals.

Out of the side of his eye, Jeff saw the contrail begin. Contrail! That was the word! It was in the old stories he'd read because it was better to study than tell Father or Mother he had nothing to do. At nine, they'd actually put him to work in the mines for a day. There'd been other nine-year-olds there. They'd kept their distance after the foreman shouted his name the first time. At least the foreman shouted at Jeff; he had a leather belt for the other kids. That night Jeff dragged himself home and went to bed, too exhausted for supper. Next morning, he was studying before his tutor arrived.

The tales from the Landers' years were written dry, but there was excitement behind every word. And they included space shuttles dropping down from the *Santa Maria*. They left white trails in the sky, like a thin bead of clouds. And they made double sonic booms. Above Jeff, the contrail headed east, headed for his sister or brother, away from him. Jeff shook his head wryly. So what else was new? Then the contrail began to turn. Maybe they wouldn't end up in sis's lap. "Ned, my horse."

A shuttle couldn't land in these hills. A town like Hazel Dell might draw them. Hell, Jeff didn't care; a shuttle was headed down. Wherever it went, he was going.

Nikki glanced at the sky when she heard the thunder, but didn't quit hoeing her row of corn, beans, and melons. Ma had not been as understanding as Nikki had hoped last week when she and Daga came racing home well after dark. Da had been in a mood. Without looking up from the new plates he was glazing for the public room, he'd said, "You work the fields every day for the next month." Ma hadn't said a word in Nikki's defense. Maybe if Nikki had been her usual self, she would have found a way to get Ma and Da talking and herself off the hook. After watching a mountain vanish, just vanish, Nikki had been at a loss for words. She still was.

However, thunder offered a chance for rain on a hot, dusty day. You couldn't work the fields in the rain, but the sky above Nikki was blue. Pure blue, no clouds at all, about what to expect in high summer. As Nikki bent back to her work, a streak of white caught her eye. She looked back up. "What's that?" a boy next to her asked.

"Don't know," a man answered.

"Like nothing I've ever seen," a grandma added, leaning on her hoe and watching the lengthening white line that was a cloud but not a cloud. If Grandma felt it a sight worth watching, Nikki couldn't get in trouble watching, too. She rested on her hoe; there was a lot of talk among the grown-ups, but nobody had any idea what it was. As the line got closer, Nikki could make out something at the tip, no bigger than a pinhead. Then the pinhead quit making clouds. It circled lower.

"Isn't it flying, like a dirigible?" a man said. He'd been to the big cities and claimed to have actually flown on one.

"It doesn't look like one," another man said.

"Yeah, but it's flying. What else could it be?"

Nobody had an answer. Now Nikki could hear a shriek like something Grandma said banshees made. But what was coming down looked too solid to be out of a story.

"It's going to land," the know-it-all announced.

Nikki came to the same conclusion at about that time. Some folks headed back for the village. Nikki found Daga at her side.

"Let's go see what it is," Daga suggested.

"I'm not going anywhere with you. Try Emma or Willow."

"They're not talking to me."

"I shouldn't either. You're no fun anymore."

"Bet whatever that is'll be fun, and I didn't find it. How much trouble can I get you into when even grandmas are going?" Nikki knew she should tell Daga to go jump in a lake, get lost, do anything. Instead, she dropped her hoe and was off.

•   •   •

Ray cycled the view on his reader through the shuttle's cameras. The flight deck was breathing ship's air and off-limits to anyone who touched this planet. Matt was adamant; until the landing party completed six weeks' quarantine, the ship and ground crew were a world apart.

The village was estimated at about a thousand people. Intermingled with the houses were vegetable gardens. Farmed plots grew larger the farther out from town until some of them were long enough to land a shuttle, assuming the ground would take the weight. Sensors said it would. The pilot was making her own check.

"Radar says it's solid and even. Good pasture. Strap in tight, folks, I'm setting this down. Give me full flaps, and then some." The shuttle lined up and began its final approach. At twenty meters, the pilot cut power. Ray had suggested that, not wanting to scorch the crop he was landing on. The pilot readily agreed. "Don't much want a grass fire under my belly, either."

The shuttle settled lightly, bounced, and decided to stay. The pilot went light on the brakes, taking her time rolling to a halt. Ray stood, arranging his gray civilian suit around himself. Mary went down her security detail, marines and middies, eyeing them like a mother hawk, making final adjustments to their gear. Nothing brought her to a halt. Back with Ray, she saluted. "Teams ready, Colonel."

"Deploy them, Captain."

They would surround the cooling shuttle and make sure no rubberneckers singed their fingers. The marines went out with quick strides and professionally disinterested faces. The middies would have been more impressive if they'd done less rubbernecking themselves. Well, Ray had brought them to learn.

As Ray laboriously negotiated the passenger compartment, a breeze from the rear hatch filled it. Heat off the cooling shuttle mingled with a warmth laden with sun and baked earth and growing things. At the top of the stairs, he paused. Four kilometers away were the stone and wattle houses of the village. Dirt paths led from it. Close in were green crops that looked like corn. In front of him, a greenish gold crop stood twenty centimeters or so tall, waving like the sea in the gentle wind. Behind the shuttle, deep tracks in the earth marked its passage.

People were coming from all around, in ones and twos, fives and tens. Some carried hoes or other farm implements, using them more as walking sticks than as weapons. Draping his right cane over his elbow, Ray latched on to the stair rail and started down, one step at a time.

Mary stood at the halfway mark. "Need a hand, sir?"

"I can take care of myself." Ray tried to keep the snarl out of his voice. The woman who had crippled him nodded, and looked out over the gathering crowd. She did not move, and he had no doubt she'd catch him if he faltered. Part of him agreed with her actions; the mission could ill afford him breaking something. Another part of him, the man who'd led combat apes, snapped and snarled, but Ray kept that under control.

When he was within three steps of her, Mary started down slowly. "Folks look nice enough. I've had the troops sling arms. No need to look more intimidating than we have to."

To their right, a small kid, hardly more than a toddler, broke through the crowd and headed straight for the shuttle, a mother in hot pursuit. The kid didn't look tall enough to reach the still-cooling craft, but then again, tiny legs like hers should not have been so fast. With a laugh, Kat swooped down and grabbed her. The child wrapped herself in giggles, oblivious to having made the first contact in three hundred years between Santa Maria and the rest of humanity. The middie tossed the little one up lightly once, then handed her off to her mother.

Mother applied a swift swat to a diapered rump that caused more indignation than pain. When the child responded with a heartbroken sob, the mother promptly gave the little one a breast to suck. The child relaxed into feeding, and mother and child disappeared into the crowd.

Ray grinned. He could just picture his future daughter or son bolting for the shinny new thing, and Rita facing down armed troops to get her little one back. Still grinning, he reached the bottom step.

Facing him was a short, round, balding man accompanied by a shorter, not-so-round woman with flaming red hair only slightly streaked with silver. He wore a homespun shirt and pants. She sported a multicolored, high-waisted dress that held her breasts firmly in place. The two weren't all that different from those around them; still, their stance and place gave Ray a strong sense that they spoke for the rest. Clearing his throat, he swallowed the last of the baby-inspired grin and gave the speech he'd been working on.

"Hello. I am Raymond Longknife, Minister of Science and Exploration"—he modified his title to fit its present reality—"for the sovereign planet of Wardhaven, member of the Society of Humanity. As such, I greet you in their name and in peace."

Across from him, the man put his hands on his hips. "And isn't it about time you found us?" Behind him, people nodded agreement, laughed, and continued gawking at the lander.

Ray had heard worse imitations of an old Earth Celtic brogue, but not many. Before he could answer, a tall, thick tree of a man stepped out from the crowd.

"And who's paying for me crop?" With one hand he swept a wave toward the lander's tracks and all the people tramping about. With the other, he formed a fist.

Beside Ray, Mary's fists closed. Kat edged closer, ready to launch her tiny self at a man twice her height and five or six times her bulk. The crowd was dead quiet.

"And what would be fair pay?" Ray asked.

"Oh, a pound of copper would be fine payment, fine payment indeed," the big man laughed. Ray decided he did not like that laugh. He was rapidly developing a dislike for the man. Half a kilo of copper was nothing to Ray; still, the man's demand was clearly intended to be outrageous.

"Go 'long with ya, man." The woman in the leadership pair slapped lightly at the big man's arm, in that way women have of defusing a situation men are likely to fight over. "For a pound of copper, the good man could buy the village. Big Sean, don't shame us."

"I think we can work this out." Coins had disappeared on many planets, but on the rim, financial networks were a sometimes thing; Ray always carried a few coins. From his pocket he produced three silver-copper alloy disks. "We'll need to set up a base here. I imagine this entire field will be out of production this season. Will these cover the cost of the crop?"

Big Sean gave Ray a grin that showed several missing teeth and snapped the coins out of his hand. "This will be just fine, just fine." Waving his booty aloft, the tough headed into the crowd. People got out of his way, not at all eager to see what he was so proud of.

A man on horseback galloped up to the back of the crowd. Had the lord of the manor arrived? No, he dismounted and disappeared. The man and woman in front of Ray ignored the arrival. The woman nudged her partner; the man cleared his throat. "These lands, they be belonging to all of us, not just one man. You've paid Sean for the loss of his crop. You owe the village for the rent of the land."

Ray found three more coins and handed them over.

"And if you got two more where those came from, you could buy beer for all." That came from a friendly bear of a man, pushing a wheelbarrow laden with a large keg through the crowd, followed by an equally friendly woman pushing a load of mugs.

Mary pulled two coppers from her pocket. "The marines'll pay for this round, folks."

"Then the bar is open," the kegtender shouted; the crowd cheered and gathered around. The first mug, sporting a proud head of foam, was passed to Ray. He handed it over to the village headman, who backed up to create an opening, blew the head off gustily, and took a long swallow. "Top of the brew, Gillie, top of the brew. They don't make it better."

The brewmaster beamed proudly and handed a mug to Ray. Humanity's ambassador to the lost people of the *Santa Maria* blew the head off as he'd been shown, then tried to look like he was downing a good portion of the brew while limiting himself to a mouthful. "Best I've tasted in a dozen star systems," Ray announced; he wasn't lying.

The delicacies properly observed, the people got down to organizing themselves with an easy, gentle efficiency for serious celebration. Men went for more beer or tables to set dinner on. The women headed back to get whatever was cooking; dinner would be a communal potluck. Turning to Mary, Ray began his own organizational effort. "Captain, stack rifles in the shuttle's arms locker. Relieve the middies to circulate. Post a guard at the nose, tail, and wingtips, and two at the stairs. Rest are free. Limit, two beers. Nobody gets drunk." Ray put steel into the order. With *Second Chance* off-limits to anyone who'd been dirtside, his disciplinary options were few.

Jeff Sterling's heart pounded; if he played his cards right, this could change his whole life. He'd ridden like mad when it became clear that this, the biggest thing to hit Santa Maria since Landing Day, was coming down right in his lap. Vicky and Mark would puke with envy.

Assuming, of course, he could find the copper in this business and make the killing he wanted.

He figured the man with the canes and the woman beside him as the bosses even before the chief village elder gave one of them the obligatory beer to settle a deal. He seemed in charge, she following his wishes, though it was too soon to see who really called the shots. Jeff had seen the metal disks the bully Sean waved. Quite a pay for a ruined crop. Then again, if they could extract minerals from pulverized mountains, it was chicken feed, like Vicky's favorite story about buying an island for a handful of trinkets.

Jeff used the confusion to approach the two unnoticed. Three hundred years, and the language hadn't changed that much. The titles caught him: Captain, Colonel. Those were military ranks. He'd have to check his references to see which one outranked the other. According to the old texts, soldiers were poor businesspeople. Fascinating. Why was the military doing the exploration? Was this a rediscovery or what the history books called an invasion? Did people who vanished mountains need to invade? Jeff's head started to spin.

Annie grabbed his arm. "Did you hear them, man? Did you hear them?"

"No, I arrived late."

"Oh." A dour glance from a grandmother reminded Annie that, party or no, that was a Sterling arm she was hanging on. She backed off a decorous foot before she gushed on. "They're from Earth's own Society of Humanity. They've come to take us home."

Jeff glanced around. "And this isn't home?" He usually avoided their half-serious attempt at an Irish brogue, but now was a good time for questions; he had a million. As nice as it was to look at Annie, he kept an eye on the two. The woman was rearranging the uniformed people who stood around like potted plants, decorating their lander. Groups boarded the lander and returned without their long guns. They still had things at their waists that looked like pistols. Trusting, but not too trusting.

"Of course this is home, you silly man. But to hear from Earth, to talk to them again after three hundred years."

"Right, and we're all going to love what they do to us?" Jeff wondered how many other people here saw in the Earth people only what they wanted. Jeff was logical. He saw metal, all kinds of metal, and lots of it. The scarcity of which had made the Sterlings the power on this planet.

Annie took a second to think about that one. "They said they came in peace."

"Whose peace? Yours, mine, theirs? Annie, excuse me, I've got to go talk to them." Jeff took two steps back. In a moment, Annie was lost in the flow of people. Jeff didn't actually want to talk to anyone. Shadow. Listen. Learn. Then, when he knew more, talk. He couldn't wait too long. As soon as Vicky found out about this, she'd be headed out here with bells on her toes and shovels in both hands.

In the bustle of setting up for the party, a few benches showed up around one table. Mary edged Ray toward one; he didn't resist, his back was aching. There was no talk of business, just proud claims that he was about to taste the best breads, stews, and other things whose names escaped him. Apparently business without hospitality was impossible here. Seated, Ray measured the pain in his back against wooziness from meds, and swallowed a pill.

The mayor and wife joined Ray at the table. A gray-haired man, Father Joseph, was introduced as the town priest, though his dress was the same peasant garb as those around him. A white-haired lad of eight or nine stayed close to the priest.

"My grandson, David," the priest explained. "I'm sure Rome will have a few things to say about how we've lived." The priest spoke of Rome with absolute confidence that it was still there and would be interested in what these survivors had done in its name. Ray wondered if, three hundred years separated from the rest of humanity, he'd have confidence anything would survive.

Yes, the army. In three hundred years, there would still be a need for infantry—and officers to lead them.

The boy, bashful, slowly gravitated toward Ray. "Do your legs hurt? My head hurts. Sometimes awful."

The elders did not shush the boy. Apparently these people did not hide their kids from the realities of life. "Sometimes my legs do hurt. And my back, too. Where does your head hurt?"

Answered, the boy grew confident. "My whole head. It just hurts. Then I see lights and hear things that aren't there. My stomach gets all upset."

"Sounds like migraines," Kat said, joining Ray and Mary. "I used to get them when I was a kid. We have pills you can take for that. Maybe we could have a med team come down next trip and help you."

The boy fled back to his grandfather at such a possibility. Eye to eye, they exchanged wordless reflections on the promise. "It would be wonderful if you could help my grandson," the priest answered for both. "I have little I can offer you, but whatever you might ask, I will try to give."

"Father," Ray answered, "there's a lot we have that is easy for us to give." Ray left talk of payment for after supper. In a culture he poorly understood, an evening's conversation might well be worth a bottle of pills.

Tables were soon laden with contributions from every household. Ray had never seen so many ways to cook potatoes. They were fried, baked, twice cooked, diced, sliced, and buried in sauces tasting of every spice he could imagine. Meat was reserved to flavor stews and soups. The Public Room contributed a roasted turkey, cut very thin. Ray took a slice, enough to praise it.

As Ray settled back down at their table, a young woman Ray took to be the beermaster's daughter showed up with a pitcher to refill mugs. Ray protected his half-empty glass. "I'm taking medicine. I have to go easy on the beer."

Mary put a hand over hers, too. "I get falling-down drunk and the ambassador here'll fire me. What chance has a down-on-her-luck soldier or a broken-down miner have of finding a job?"

Mary was joking, but the young woman with the pitcher took her seriously. "Why, if you're a miner, you'll want to talk to Jeff here. He's a member of the Sterling family. If it's mining you want, he's the one to see." The barmaid hauled a very embarrassed man in by his elbow. Ray recognized him, the fellow who'd rode up. Now that Ray thought about it, he'd also been close by whenever Ray looked around. A lurking shadow.

"Annie, I don't need to bother these people," the fellow protested, trying unsuccessfully to shake free.

"Now, wouldn't that be a new Jeff. You've never been slow to bother any of us about funny rocks and minerals."

"Sit down," Mary laughed. "It's fun talking shop." She gave Ray a wink. If anyone here knew what happened to that mountain, this kid should. Ray leaned back, sampling a dozen different flavors of spud as Mary pumped the guy.

Jeff sat himself down next to Mary. The mayor's wife edged herself farther up the bench. The young man studied his plate while Annie refilled his mug. Casting a quick glance at the beer, the fellow licked his lips but didn't take a swig. "As you probably guessed from how much your copper disks brought, metal is kind of scarce here," he finally said.

"The devil it's scarce," the mayor cut in. "The damn Sterlings want two years' crops for a simple phone system."

"Jeff doesn't set the prices," Annie defended him. Scowls and rolled eyes from the locals made it clear Annie was the only defender Jeff had.

"It wasn't my family that decided to live off the salvage from the *Santa Maria*. Jason Sterling warned they'd need metals if their kids would have a decent living."

"When you're just three hundred people, there's only so much you can do," the priest put in softly, "especially when you come to have more wee ones than grown-ups."

"Yeah," the mayor agreed more sharply. "If wee ones aren't fed and protected now, it doesn't much matter what fancies you want for them when they grow up."

"Every frontier faces that challenge," Ray said, trying to support both sides in what looked to be an ancient argument. "Balancing the future and the present. Tough choices."

"So didn't his man and family go off and claim the only metal-rich land here," the mayor snapped.

Kat worked her wrist unit. "Sterling was a mechanic on *Santa Maria*. How'd he end up as the metal czar?"

"He worked with the three mission geologists before they cracked up over on the mainland," Jeff explained. "They'd only identified one mineral-rich area and wanted to find a few more before the mission's assets got too thin."

"And after we lost number three shuttle, you better believe things got thin." The mayor took a long draw on his beer at that one. So did a lot of listeners.

"What happened?" Mary asked.

"No one knows. Crash beacon showed they flew into a mountain," Jeff answered.

"Didn't they have radar altimeters back then?" Kat asked.

"Sure they did, child, sure they did. I guess this one wasn't working quite right." The mayor sneered.

Ray flashed Kat a silencing glance. Who had worked on the shuttle could not be established at this late date. He was pretty sure the popular story included a Sterling repair job.

"What happened, we'll never know." The padre took over the story, his eyes silencing the mayor. "With only two landers, they couldn't risk visiting the crash site, but concentrated on stripping the ship. They managed to keep one running for almost ten years by swapping parts back and forth."

"Quite an accomplishment." Ray gave credit where it was

due. He also wanted to get them past the old feuds to something more relevant to their present problem.

"Yes, we were lucky," the priest agreed, tousling his grandson's hair. "We had some truly gifted botanists and agronomists. They managed to engineer Earth crops to survive here. Still, the first years were awfully scanty."

"And there were the fevers." The mayor's wife crossed herself; other women did likewise. The men stared at the ground.

"Those must have been hard times," Ray said softly.

"Easy it hasn't been, but we've made this place our home." The mayor hugged his wife; she flashed a smile and snuggled close. Ray felt a flush and wished Rita were here to hug. In the crowd of people seated around him were several women, large with child and many little ones. *God, I miss you, Rita.* But would he want her here, sharing a planet where mountains vanished?

Evening tiptoed in. The heat of the day fled, leaving behind a gentle breeze laden with the cool scent of green crops and satisfying beer. Somebody brought out a fiddle, another an accordion. Children collected around the musicians, doing little dances to the musicians' tentative efforts at tuning. Ray looked around for a place to relax on the grass.

"You're all going to hell!" came from the far side of the shuttle. "Papist superstition is leading you straight to death and damnation!"

"Not again," the mayor groaned.

"Grandpa, don't let him yell at me," David whimpered.

"I'll take care of this," the priest said, handing his young charge to the mayor's wife. He strode quickly to where a man in a flaxen jerkin was haranguing the lounging crowd.

"Repent your sins and you may yet be saved!"

"Reverend Jonah, these good people have worked hard today. God will not begrudge them a little rest and enjoyment." The priest's gentle words carried just as well as the other's shouts. People began moving away from the two. Well, most.

Five or six made their way toward the two men of competing Gods. One of them was Big Sean, the bully Ray had paid for the use of his field. Oops. "Mary," Ray started, but

Kat and Cassie were already on their feet, jogging for the gathering.

"And you priest would stop up their ears, deprive them of the true Word of God."

"No, Reverend, but I would respect their right to have a quiet evening without you or me interrupting them. Come back Sunday afternoon and we can talk to as many as want to gather under the tree behind the church."

"Sunday may be too late. The Lord is coming to judge."

"I'll tell you who's coming to judge!" Sean shouted. "It's me fist in your mouth, man, if you don't get off me land!"

"We'll have none of that, Sean." The priest interposed himself.

"I don't need any papist protection." Jonah tried to fill the same space in front of Sean the padre was stepping into. Neither got anywhere.

"Excuse me." Kat tapped the bully on his hip, about as far up as she could reach. "The ambassador has rented this field. I believe he expects us to keep the peace here."

Big Sean turned on Kat with a sneer, raised his hand to her—and was sitting on the ground a moment later with no visible explanation, and a look of utter dismay on his face.

"Thank you," Kat smiled down at him.

Cassie took the minister's arm. "Sir, the ambassador requests that you leave our facility. Our constitution requires a strict separation of church and state. Use of these grounds for religious solicitation would be a violation of our code."

"What?" the minister said in wonder.

"Thank you, sir." Cassie continued, "I know it's difficult to understand different people's ways of doing things. If you'll come with me, we can talk about that." She took the reverend by the arm and escorted him away from the shuttle. Five people went with him. The priest stood for a moment, looking after them, then hiked back to the table. Taking David from the mayor's wife, he picked the boy up, hugged him, then sat him down on the bench and told him to eat his vegetables. The boy picked up a green bean and began eating it a millimeter at a time.

"Good riddance," the mayor breathed.

Mary eyed Cassie and the minister. "I hope he doesn't have a guitar handy. She might keep going," she chuckled.

The priest shook his head. "God bless them all."

"Who are they?" Ray asked. As a young soldier, religion had been something he'd been glad to share his foxhole with. As he rose in rank and found himself with less time on his hands for empty worrying, it faded. Or maybe his questions got harder and the answers more difficult. Whatever he might think of religion, here it seemed an important part of their lives.

"The O'Donalds lost their first child last winter. She always was one for the scruples. God forgive me, but I could not answer her demand to know why God would give her a baby to love, then take it away so soon. Young Phillip seeks the face of God and cannot find it among the familiar. May God be gracious to all of them and forgive me for what I could not be."

"Father, it's not your fault," the mayor assured him. "They're just wrongheaded." Murmurs of agreement came from around the table. The priest smiled his thanks and gave David a hug. Ray doubted the padre accepted his people's absolution. More and more, he was coming to like the fellow. How could you fault a man who so clearly doted on his grandkid?

The musicians launched into a reel. People were on their feet and into the dance without a glance for those Cassie was still walking off the field. Ray watched through the first two songs, then turned to Mary. "We've got to set up camp and unload the shuttle."

"And you'll be wanting your field back," the mayor said, standing. "I'll have the fiddler dance them into town. You'll be wanting to go up early tomorrow with me to the County Clair Circle."

"Circle," Ray echoed, wondering where he'd missed a step and how far down it was.

"Aye, you've met with the Hazel Dell Circle." The mayor made a sweeping arm gesture that might have included the entire town, or just those close by. "You'll be wanting to talk to

County Clair Circle next. I suspect Jeff will be going, too. You've sat in the Great Circle of Metalworkers, haven't you?"

"When Sis was busy and Mark out of town," the man admitted.

"Then I guess I'll be going to the next circle tomorrow," Ray agreed. Was the local chain of command more honest about how it ran people in circles? He grinned to himself.

Making a stop by the keg to refresh his mug, the mayor joined the musicians. In a moment, fiddler, accordion player, and singers began a careful retreat, not missing a beat. Dancers and watchers followed in a smooth flow that cleared the tables of serving dishes with no visible effort except for one young girl who came dashing back for a forgotten bowl.

Ray's work of arranging his mission and schedule was made easier; Mary had his command hut already set up. The shuttle was cleared for a return to the ship as soon as it was empty, and Ray called Matt to report. Matt had news, too. "One of those blimps doesn't make regularly scheduled runs like the rest. It's headed your way, or was until it settled down at sunset."

Someone cleared his throat behind Ray. He turned to find Jeff standing just outside the hut. "Any idea what's up?"

"Probably my sister, Victoria, headed here to take over."

Ray considered that for a moment. "We'll see." He turned back to finish briefing Matt on the day.

"Sounds like you've got things going fine dirtside."

"Too early to tell. I've got company around still. I'll talk more later. Send down the rest of the ground team. I'll need at least one doc. A local boy here has migraines. He's the priest's grandkid, but the whole village has kind of adopted him."

"Doc on the way. Anything else?"

"Not at the moment." Ray clicked off and turned to Jeff. "So big sister is headed our way." The man nodded; Ray knew the type. He'd had plenty of experience with second and third sons shuffled off to the army. "So what can we do for each other?"

The man entered slowly, fingering a map case. Clearly he wanted to say something. Just as clearly, he didn't know how.

Ray waited, taking none of the pressure off him. Finally Jeff snapped open his case and pulled out several large photos. As if the pictures were coated with acid, he dropped them one by one on the table in front of Ray.

"Recognize the scene?" he asked, retreating back to the door.

In the shadows outside, Ray spotted Annie, the young woman who'd introduced Jeff. Waiting for her fellow? Ray turned to the pictures. Both showed the same mountain range. One shot was minus a peak.

"Annie, Da wants help gathering up the mugs!" came as a distant shout.

"In a minute, Nikki!" Annie shouted back.

"Has she seen these pictures?" Ray asked. Jeff nodded.

"Want to come in, young woman, and tell me what you think of them? Mary, see that the beermaster gets help finding his mugs. I don't want the shuttle finding one on take-off."

"Yes, sir." Mary whispered orders into her commlink, but showed no interest in going elsewhere at the moment.

Annie glanced at the pictures. "One o' the mountains is gone missing."

Ray fixed Jeff with a "tough colonel stare." "And you want to know why?"

"If you can mine an entire mountain just like that . . ." the young man started and stopped.

Ray called up the before-and-after topography maps *Second Chance* had made on its first two orbits. He rested a finger on the hole in the second one. "You'd pay a lot for that technology."

Jeff stared wide-eyed at the two maps. "Yes."

"But it would tear the hills apart," Annie broke in. "That's no way to treat the earth that feeds us."

From the dark outside the hut came the rustle of a dress. Another pair of eyes watched them. Ray suspected the shouted-at Nikki had come to see what was keeping Annie. If he wasn't careful, he'd have the entire village back here.

"That's not the way we extract minerals," Mary cut in. "I

can pull all the good stuff out of a mountain without disturbing a blade of grass."

"Then . . ." Jeff pointed at the gap in the mountain range.

"We don't know either," Ray finished.

"But if you didn't," Annie said slowly, "and we can't, who did?" From outside the hut came the sound of running feet. Ray caught a hint of a flying dress.

Annie must have, too. "I'd better be helping Nikki and Da."

Jeff collapsed into a camp chair beside Ray. "That is the question, isn't it."

"Yes," Mary agreed. Ray nodded; his job had just gotten a whole lot harder.

"Daga. Daga," Nikki half-whispered, half-shouted at her girlfriend's window. "Daga, you can't be asleep."

"I'm not, and neither is the house with you shouting like a banshee," Daga said, massaging her temples. "What's wrong with you?"

"They know about the mountain. They know it's gone."

"Who knows?"

"Everyone," Nikki squeaked. "Jeff's got pictures from his brother's survey and one he just made, and the people from space even have a map. Daga, they know!"

"But they don't know what we know. They don't know how it happened. Nikki, you worry too much. There's no way they can tell it was us, or anything."

"But . . . but . . ." Nikki couldn't figure out what to say after that, but she knew there was more to it than Daga wanted.

"No buts, Nikki. Go home, go to bed. Don't say anything, and they won't know anything."

"But what are you going to do?"

"I haven't made up my mind yet."

Even in the dark, Nikki could see Daga's grin. It was wide, and like it always was with Daga, it was sure.

Caretaker studied the new ones as they slept. They were like the other new ones; already their bodies rejected this world. Their body temperatures rose as they twisted in sleep, scratching and sneezing. Just as it had three hundred years ago, Caretaker released the viruses to make the necessary adjustments. This time it would go easier on the strangers; this time the Caretaker knew where to touch these strange bodies.

Even as Caretaker worked, its own simple processes tried to extrapolate the significance of these new arrivals. These had landed close to itself, to that central core that Caretaker thought of as its very being. Did they know that? Would they help or hinder Caretaker's work? It was very difficult dealing with a species that resolutely refused to enter into any communication with the Caretaker.

Certainly the Central Font of All Knowledge would know what to do. But apparently it had gotten slow over the years, too. Its slow message had said it was coming, but had to mend many nodes between the center and a distant, minor subsystem such as Caretaker.

Caretaker would wait. In the meantime, it would do what it could. That was what the Caretaker was for.

Ray walked in a garden, his bladder painfully full. The gravel crunched under his feet, but he heard nothing else and smelled nothing at all. He rounded a hedge. An old man in dirty work clothes watered roses. His hose aimed a high, proud arc of water over the flowers. The image left Ray desperately holding back his own need to spray.

The Gardener noticed Ray with a smile. He looked familiar; Ray remembered the old fellow who kept the flowers so tenderly outside the dining hall at the Academy. "Do what you need, fellow, I won't mind," the old one said.

Ray reached for his zipper. . . .

And came awake before he wet the bed. Ruefully, Ray reached for his canes. Hot and sweating, he struggled up, cursing the battle wound they didn't fix.

As he did his business, he became aware of a headache. Nothing too bad; his back hurt worse. Ray ignored the pain meds Mary had laid out on the table next to a glass of water;

he didn't want more water in his system. Besides, this was nothing compared to how bad it could get.

Ray gritted his teeth against the pain and waited for sleep to come.

FOUR

A WEEK LATER, Ambassador Ray Longknife relaxed into his seat, contemplating the night. Stuffed—in far too many ways.

He'd been wined and dined from one circle to another as he moved from village to county to state and finally to Lander's Refuge. Local after local had shaken his hand, kissed his cheeks, and done their damnedest to pick his pocket—in the nicest way. Every step of the way he'd been offered undying friendship and kind words. As he got farther up, smiling officials had thrown in huge land grants, personal bribes, beautiful women, and a seat among the powerful with a growing panic that made Ray feel right at home. "Damn, humans are all the same."

"What'd you say, sir?" Mary asked from the front seat. She was driving a mule, a four-wheel, go-anywhere vehicle; its efficient solar cells and storage system made it the envy of everyone here. Mary was his aide, bodyguard, driver . . . and nurse as much as he let her. Ray was traveling light among the natives. So far, he did not regret it.

"Take us back to the residence," Ray said automatically, then rethought. "No. I've got to talk to Matt tonight, and I trust my room is well bugged. Take us somewhere I can have a little privacy."

"How about that beach we saw yesterday?"

Ray grinned. Their visit to the fishing fleet and North Beach had been Mary's first encounter with more water than she could drink. Water, free and playing with beach and sand and wind and sky had enthralled her. Ray suspected the woman was in love. "Do it."

"I'll head for the north end, sir. This mule can take us where these people only dream of going."

Ray settled deep into his seat. That was the problem. These people had dreams, and *Second Chance* was opening some and threatening others. Ray had known that the moment he set foot on this place it would never be the same. If Matt reconnected them with humanity, all options were possible. But what if he didn't? That was Ray's quandary.

In his present bargaining, should he assume in a few months Matt would be back, grinning from ear to ear and tailed by six boatloads of eager entrepreneurs? Or would a smarter choice be to hold his cards and his technology close until Matt decided it was time and past time to start homesteading? At the moment, holding tight looked best. But the local powers that be were not interested in waiting for someone else to decide their fate.

People like Vicky Sterling didn't get their hands on power by waiting for others to give it. Victoria got what she had by being there first and grabbing all she could. Ray was familiar with people like Vicky. Powerful people had damn near gotten him killed in their last war. This brought Ray up short. Was all this the fearful ruminations of a spooked veteran who just wanted to be a husband and a dad? "What do you think about the last few days?" he asked Mary.

"Some pretty nice folks," Mary answered, then quickly added, "and a few not so nice. Would be fun working with them, living here. Don't get me wrong, Colonel, I appreciate this job, and I'll ramble around the stars as long as you want me, but settling down here sure is attractive. These folks could use some cheap metals. I know Vicky Sterling's type. Worked for her on the asteroid mines. She loves being the only show in town. Thinks she shits gold. I'd love to take a brand-new rod of hot gold and stick it up her . . . well, you know."

"I know," Ray smiled.

"Ah, Colonel, you invite anyone back to the Residency for a nightcap?"

"Not that I recall."

"Well, we got a tail."

"Damn! People never change. Lose 'em, Mary."

"Oh, boy," she laughed. They still weren't to the beach road; Refuge was a big city. The turn to the beach was ten blocks away when Mary did a hard right, gunned the mule, and did a series of zigzags that took them across the beach road but kept them parallel to it. Ray hoped she knew what she was doing.

"The sky eyes surveyed this burg and downloaded a city map to my inertial system," Mary answered Ray's unasked question. "Bet I know this town better than most of the folks raised here."

Ray didn't doubt that. They zipped down a street lined with small shops and warehouses. When they ran out of town, Mary did a quick zig to get them back on the beach road. Ray edged around in his seat; no lights behind. There still weren't any when the road took a slow turn to follow higher ground through tidal marshes. "Boy, did I lose 'em," Mary chortled.

This left Ray wondering which factions they had eluded and what they were up to. He shrugged off the unanswerable.

A gentle breeze came from offshore, laden with smells of salt and damp and coastal grasses. They turned north, off the road and away from the inlet that sheltered the fishing fleet and soon came to the end of the dirt track a hundred meters short of the sand dunes. Ray braced himself, protecting his back as Mary took the rig into a narrow wash, gunning the mule through soft sand. Wheels spun wildly, but kept enough traction to swing them onto the wide stretch of sand between the dunes and the distant ocean. Mary steered for the hard, damp sand that the retreating tide had left. Two moons were just rising, casting sparking diamonds on the gentle sea swells from beach to horizon.

Relaxing again into the seat, Ray took several deep breaths as Mary cruised north, away from civilization as it named itself here. His mind ordered his thoughts for his call to Matt.

The captain was eager to be away. There were several theories of how they might find their way home; the only proof of the pudding was going out and nibbling at it. Was Ray ready to declare his tiny downside command fit to stand on its own two feet?

Mary eased the mule to a halt, midway between waves and dune. "We're far enough up the coast to miss any search our trailer is doing. Besides, we'll see them coming." Ray nodded. "Mind if I take a walk, sir?" Mary's eyes were fixed on the lapping waves, mesmerized by them.

"Take care. You don't know where the drop-off is out there. You can't swim, and I sure can't come in after you."

"Don't worry, sir. Space ain't killed me in twenty years. A little bit of water ain't gonna get me now."

"That's not a little bit."

"Yes, sir." Mary got out and started a slow, pensive walk to the ocean. She wore a dress, a gift from Henrietta San Paulo, the Chair of the Great Circle of Lander's Refuge. Made of cotton so fine and tightly woven it might as well have been silk, Mary had spun around in delight, a girl-woman in her first formal. Then she'd lifted it far higher than their relationship on Wardhaven would have allowed to show him her sidearm. The asteroid mines had taught Mary none of the modesty and delicacy that Wardhaven inculcated in its women. Then, Rita had been Wardhaven's most instructed of debutantes . . . and gone on to skipper an attack transport. And her courtship of Ray had been far from delicate. Ray suspected few men ever understood women.

"God, I miss you, wife." Sighing, Ray tapped his communit. "Communications, Longknife here. The captain available?"

"He's expecting you, sir. Wait one, please."

Mary had about reached the water. The dress came up and over her head to flutter down on the sand. Her body was in moon shadow; he could not tell if she'd worn anything more. The male part of Ray's mind decided she hadn't; it made the view more enticing. Her silhouette was trim and sleek, no bulge for a bra, panties . . . or sidearm. A glance in the front showed automatic and holster on the seat. Ray reached for it, checked the safety, then set it down beside him. Mary reached the water; she stooped to touch the lapping waves. Ray wished for about the millionth time that Rita was here. Or, more correctly, he was there.

"Ray, how are things?" the captain asked.

"I'm surviving down among the natives. And you?"

"Nothing's changed. We've completed the planet survey. Enough irregularities to keep the scanning team happy, but nothing to raise a red flag. Some interesting electromagnetic anomalies. We sent the database down. An interesting planet."

"Full of interesting people," Ray added dryly.

"Want to tell me about them?"

"You know, Matt, I always thought if you marooned three hundred hard-headed, rational people on a planet, you'd have a hard-headed, rational population when you got done."

"Gosh, Ray, I never knew you were such a dreamer."

"Take the Covenanters up north, those dozen or so medium-size towns that Kat couldn't figure out why they were in such a crazy pattern. Blame it on the Bible."

"Somebody brought that book!"

"It was in their database. More about that database in a minute. Anyway, during the worst of the times after landing, some folks found religion. Later, after things got better, their kids decided the rest were all going to hell and moved off to keep their 'purity.' "

"Let me guess," Matt broke in. "They couldn't agree among themselves on how to read the book, so . . ."

"You got it—split and split again. Most of them want to just ignore us. Hope we'll go away. But one of them, the guy I met the first night down here, thinks we're the Antichrist and wants us destroyed."

"I guess you stay to the south side of south continent."

"Not that easy. There're almost eight million people here. Most Covenanters may be up north, but they got churches in Lander's Refuge. They're not the worst problems. Refuge and New Haven split over something the original captain did early on. I've got six different versions of what that was, and none agree. But there's a pro-captain and an anti-captain faction to this day, and a big chunk of the antis moved south to New

Haven about two hundred years ago. Now, if one says it's day, the other insists it's night. I think the pro faction is a bit more in favor of exploiting the planet's resources, but I can't swear to that."

"Sounds like fun."

"Yeah," Ray answered. Mary was up to her knees now, meeting each wave as it came in with a jump and a happy giggle. Ray had never seen Mary as anything but a hard-driving marine officer. This was a whole new side of her.

For a moment, the question flitted across his mind. *How many sides are there to the people I'm dealing with?* He'd have to remember that. "The farmers we started with are interesting. You meet a girl with flaming red hair, a diction straight out of Joyce, and a name like Nulia Anne Moira Chang. Tells you why her brogue is a bit off."

"Chang?"

"Don't ask me how the Irish took over and the Chinese didn't. Such history is oral, and I don't trust it. There's even a legend that St. Patrick showed them how to plant potatoes."

"Sounds like a nuthouse. Sure you'll be okay while I duck in and out of system? Once we've got acceleration on, it'll take me a while to get down here." Matt had his work cut out for him, too. Speaking of.

"Matt, I'm trying to get my hands on the log of the old *Santa Maria,* but no luck yet. Refuge, New Haven, Richland, that's the Sterlings' mining town, Vicky owns it lock, stock, and barrel, and even some of the Covenant towns had copies of the original database. But original media last only so long. First- and second-generation local manufacturing wasn't all that good, so the data got corrupted. Ship's log was low priority, so it got cut to save space. Vicky claims she's got a complete copy, but she's only handing out vague samples. Wants mining equipment and technology before she'll share the good stuff."

"How's that going over with the rest?"

"Poorly. The Sterlings have had these people by the short hairs for two hundred years. A lot of people would like them taken down a peg."

"You going to do that?"

"I'd like to stay on everybody's good side."

"Never had much success at that myself," Matt chuckled.

"Probably a bit late in life for me to be trying it, too. How you coming with those survival canisters?"

"Last two go dirtside tomorrow morning. Have you seen what's in them?"

"I approved everything Andy and Elie recommended. Didn't expect to be using them. Glad for them now."

"Yeah. Make sure you open the right one. They sent you everything from a chip fabricator to a bomb factory."

"Andy wanted all the bases covered."

"I'm leaving you a shuttle. I'll be in system every few days. A week at the longest."

"I'll try not to holler wolf. Could you drop that shuttle down here tomorrow at the blimp base? Say, tenish. I don't want to beg a ride back to my base on anyone's blimp."

"And it'll show these folks the power they're dealing with."

"Something like that.

"Good by me. I'll see you when I see you. Out."

Ray leaned back in his seat. The moons were above Mary. The luminous waves rose and fell, casting dim light on her. Ray could see the joy on her face. He could see everything else, too. "Oh, Rita, I miss you."

"You lost them!" Victoria Sterling shrieked. She had deigned to receive her security chief in her gilded coach and four. Grandpa Jason had included six horse embryos in his personal effects. The Landers who squirreled away survival gear among their private goods made it big here. The kids of those who brought trinkets were her servants. "That mule has lights all over." Victoria very much wanted her lab to take it apart and see what made it tick.

"Yes, ma'am," he said softly, trying to soothe.

Victoria would like it better if he'd grovel. *But we Santa Marians are so democratic.* She sniffed at that; some things took so long to change. "How did your trusty spies lose them?"

"We expected them to go back to the Residency. We've

checked their rooms. The bugs are active. We gave them plenty of space on the road. Didn't want them to notice us. They took a wrong turn. By the time we got to the corner, that damn driver had turned again. We couldn't find them. We'll reconnect when they get back to the Residency."

"*If* they go back. *If* someone hasn't offered them something better. Unless their shuttle drops out of the sky and hauls them off to heaven knows where. I want to know where they are and what they're doing every moment of their day. I want to know what they're going to do before they know."

"Yes, ma'am."

"Go. Find them, or I will find someone who can."

"Yes, ma'am."

Ray Longknife, humanity's ambassador to Santa Maria, Wardhaven's misplaced Minister for Science and Technology, retired colonel of infantry, devoted husband and future father, watched Mary dance naked with the luminous waves and the moonlight. He wished it was Rita. "Maybe she wouldn't, with the baby coming." He sighed, then shook his head. No, Rita might be beginning to show a bit, but she'd be out there jumping and prancing with Mary just the same. That was the sprite he'd married. All work when she was working. All play otherwise.

With a final splash, Mary strode from the water. She retrieved her dress, swung it over her shoulder, and backed toward the mule, eyes on the ocean. "It's so free. No boss telling it what to do," she whispered when she bumped into the rig.

"It just goes on and on." Ray nodded.

"Yes." She turned to him. Excitement was in her eyes. Probably in other places. She was his for the taking if he wanted her. And he wanted her.

He choked on the wanting and swallowed it. Nothing facing them would be made easier by losing themselves in each other tonight. He returned her gaze, trying to reflect the happiness he felt watching her . . . and no more.

She slipped back into her dress. "That was fun," she said, settling it around herself. "I see you've got my sidearm back there with you."

"If some big, slimy thing had slithered out of the sea to dance with you, I wanted to make it keep a gentlemanly distance."

"Locals didn't say anything about sea monsters," Mary said.

"Lot of things the locals ain't got around to saying."

Mary settled into the driver's seat. "Sorry, sir, if my . . . uh . . ."

"Nothing to be sorry for, Captain. You were a joy to watch, and any worrying I did came to nothing. Tomorrow, Matt's dropping a shuttle for us about ten. Make our trip back faster. No need to mention it to anyone. After our tail tonight, I'd rather keep our friends guessing."

The return to the Residency was uneventful; Ray was asleep before his head hit the pillow.

Ray lay on the operating table, looking up into the bright light. Waves of pain washed over him. The doctor stood above him in surgical scrubs, a shining laser scalpel in his hands. As the surgeon reached for Ray, the scalpel changed into a hoe, the medic into a grubbily clad gardener. Ray screamed.

He lay on the ground, the smell of recently turned earth in his nostrils. A huge field hand wielding pruning shears grabbed him and began cutting. Dead branches fell away; fresh green ones were grafted on. Ray screamed.

And came awake, shivering and desperately in need of a trip to the bathroom. Head throbbing, whole body shaking in night chills and sweats, Ray struggled to his feet and moved as quickly as his canes permitted to the facilities. His body trembled in a pain he didn't understand. Done, he worked his way back to collapse in bed. Mary had laid out pain meds; he swallowed a pill. Better to make a second trip tonight than lie awake in the grips of this agony. Ray settled back, centering his thoughts on Rita, and a girl-child as beautiful as her mother.

• • • •

Three months' fieldwork had gotten Jeff Sterling used to rising with the sun. At Fairview, however, he usually slept in. With Vicky running the business, sleeping was the most exciting thing he got to do around the family estate.

This morning, Millard woke him at dawn. "Miss Sterling requires your presence at her breakfast, sir." Since Vicky had sent the downstairs butler who taught hand-to-hand combat as well as proper deportment and etiquette to the staff, Jeff tied on his robe and went. Once in the solarium, however, Jeff pointedly ignored Vicky and puttered over the breakfast bar, filling his plate slowly with eggs, brown bread, and bacon. "Do we have any strawberry jam?" he asked, knowing Vicky had sent the staff away for this private meeting and would have to answer herself.

"How should I know?" she snapped. "Buzz the kitchen. And be quick about it. We need to talk."

So Vicky was in one of her moods. This could be even more fun than usual. Jeff buzzed the kitchen. "This place I was staying at, out on the front range," he rambled, "had this really delicious strawberry jam. Do we have any?"

They didn't. Orange marmalade would have to do. Very expensive stuff. The Swensons had held on to their monopoly on orange trees as tightly as the Sterlings held on to their metal claims. Vicky hated the Swensons but loved orange marmalade.

"Now sit down, Jeffrey. I want a word with you."

"Yes, Victoria." To her face, not even Jeff called her Vicky.

"Why didn't you tell me about the damn spaceship?" Vicky snapped, rubbing her eyes with both fists.

They'd been over this before. "Because I didn't know about them until they landed. Besides, that village didn't have access to the net. How could I have told you?"

"Those cheap dirt farmers. They ought to be required to have net hookups. For their brats' education, at least."

"More might, if we lowered the price on fiber cable." Jeff was the family advocate for lowering profit margins and making it up in volume. Christ, fiber optic was only silicon! Vicky was for all the market would bear. With Dad dead and Mom in a convent, Vicky was in charge.

Vicky broke off a small portion of her croissant, buttered it, and munched it slowly, her gaze out the window on the distant woods. Jeff was being ignored . . . again. He ate, waiting for her next announcement.

"They're hiding something." The "they" could only be the spacemen. For Vicky to conclude they were hiding something was no big news. Vicky always hid half her cards; she assumed everyone else did. It made for tough bargaining even when the other side was hiding nothing.

Jeff, however, was pretty sure the spacemen *were* hiding something. He would not, however, admit that to Vicky. "I don't know, they seem pretty up front," he said with his mouth full.

"Don't speak with your mouth full," Vicky shot back in irritation, making Jeff's morning. "Why won't they share their data files with us?"

"Chu Lyn is pretty dead set against them dumping all kinds of new tech on us. She's afraid of what that would do to the economy." Chu led the Green Party in the Great Circle. Normally she didn't have the votes to stop Vicky. Recent nose counts had not been "normal."

Vicky flipped her hand up disparagingly. "Lyn is afraid of her own shadow." Still, Vicky said nothing about forcing a vote. The rumors Jeff had picked up were right. Votes were changing. It was fun watching Vicky sweat.

"Why are you sitting in the circles anyway? I'm senior for the metalworkers."

Jeff had been expecting that. "I'm just sitting in on the meetings, Sis. I haven't voted." Open meetings had been a golden rule since the Landers. Anyone could attend a circle, although only representatives for recognized interest groups or locals actually voted. Nobody questioned Jeff's right to sit in, both because he was a Sterling and because he always took the seat next to the starwoman Rodrigo. He liked the questions that raised. Was he in the star group, or the Sterlings? Only Vicky had the gumption to ask.

Vicky mulled that answer as she chewed another piece of croissant. "Good idea. I like the way you're making up to that starwoman. In her pants yet?"

Jeff had half a dozen answers to that question. First in line was "None of your business." Unfortunately, Vicky saw everything with a potential value in it as her business. Jeff swallowed and fed her the line she'd want. "Mary's a tough woman. Doesn't let anyone get close to her easily."

"Smart woman. Don't let that stop you, kid. I want to know what makes her tick. All of them. Keep working on it. You have anything else to work on?"

She knew the answer to that. As junior Sterling, Vicky made sure he had nothing to do and did nothing worth doing. "Nothing on my schedule," he answered.

"Good. Stay close to her. She'll come around. And let me know what you learn as soon as you do." She pushed away from the table, half her breakfast untouched. "And don't dawdle over breakfast. There's work to do. Get yourself over to the Residency and see what they're up to."

Since Vicky had bugged the Residency, as well as most other places where important things were talked about, if she didn't know what was happening, somebody was keeping her in the dark. Jeff really liked these star people.

Jeff continued eating with slow purpose until Vicky stalked from the solarium. Only after she left did he lean back in his chair. Damn! Vicky had given him the order he would have begged for. She would never have given it to him if he asked. Vicky's distrust of everyone inevitably sent people where they didn't want to go to do things they were poorly suited to do. Thank God the woman could be manipulated.

Jeff hustled for his room. He was curious what Ray and Mary would do today. They'd fulfilled the circles' social requirements; now they were on their own. No doubt it would be fun watching. He dressed quickly and had an electrocycle brought around to the front.

It had been a very bad night, full of shivering and sweats. Ray gulped a pain pill before starting his morning stretches. Showered and shaved, he almost felt human.

Mary met him at the stairs and went down, one step at a time. Her conversation rambled over the morning's weather and last night's drive, totally ignoring that she was there to catch him if he stumbled. He liked her nonchalant way of playing safety as much as he enjoyed her morning chatter. It reminded him of Rita before her second cup of coffee.

Their hostess, Henrietta San Paulo, Chair of the Great Circle, was already seated at the head of the table. Her daughter, a wisp of a nine-year-old, was missing.

"Where's the White Rose?" Ray asked, using the nickname Henrietta's albino daughter enjoyed.

"She had headaches in the night. I hope her noise did not disturb you. The nurse could not keep her quiet."

"Do all albinos have migraines?" Mary asked.

"Apparently." The mother concentrated on her breakfast. "Rose has visited every doctor and specialist we have. They just shake their heads."

"We met a child with migraines on our first day down," Ray said, not reaching for his oatmeal. "A County Clair Circle member also had a child like Rose. We've landed a medical team. One thing they're looking at is how to help these children."

"Could you send Rose these medicines?"

Without a thought, Ray nodded, then stopped himself. "No, I can't promise that. Some meds require a patient be under observation while taking them." He swept his hands out, then down his broken back. "I've had personal experience with our docs. I can't promise a pill Rose can take three times a day and not worry about."

San Paulo pursed her lips. "If she and her nurse went with you, would that meet your requirements?"

"I don't doubt it. I've ordered a shuttle to pick us up around ten. There will be room for her."

Henrietta nodded slowly. "I will have to discuss this with Chu. Her party can't oppose your helping a poor child. This would be a nice way to get them used to the good that will come from our involvement again with humanity."

Ray nodded while cringing inside. Would he ever become so much of a politician that helping his child took second place to policy? On second reflection, he realized that his own policy of limited technological transition had just taken a major hit. He *was* using his tech. *But it's to help a little girl. Oh, Rita, if only you were here.*

Was it an accident that Chu Lyn was announced as breakfast ended? Henrietta had the nurse bring Rose down to join her and Ray in a sitting room. Chu, a tall, dark-skinned woman with no visible evidence of her Asian namesake, and San Paulo chatted for half an hour before San Paulo invited Rose into her lap and told Lyn of Ray's offer.

Rose's bloodshot eyes grew wide; she said nothing, but the look she gave Ray was heartrending. Lyn talked in platitudes for several minutes, of her party's support for rational change and growth, but their long experience of mad, irrational action. Then she shrugged. "Of course, no one could possibly object." Rose and her nurse left to pack. Ray excused himself.

Fifteen minutes later, a small crowd collected on the steps of the Residency as everyone gathered for their good-byes. While Mary and the nurse loaded suitcases, Rose went through the tortures of a nine-year-old . . . excited to ride in something new like the mule, reluctant to leave Mom and the familiar.

"Would you like to talk to your mommy whenever you want?" Ray asked. The shy child nodded. Ray took off his wrist unit, made a few adjustments so it would only be a commlink, and offered it to San Paulo.

"When we get back to base, I'll get Rose one. That way, you can talk to each other whenever you want."

San Paulo and Chu eyed the offered gift. "It doesn't plug into the net? It has no fiber cables?" the mother said.

"It's wireless," Ray explained.

"We know of radio technology," Chu answered. "We never redeveloped it. Our power cells are so big. If you could plug into a power line, you might as well plug into a data cable."

More local data to pass to Kat for analysis. Ray took his leave, strolling to the far side of the mule as Mary bent to help Rose and her nurse into the near side.

A young man with wild eyes and a long, shiny knife stepped from the crowd and dashed for Ray.

Mary must have seen the glint of knife. She took two quick steps back. Ray raised a cane in defense, falling against the mule. Part of him analyzed the attack. *Piss poor. Idiot's holding the knife overhand.* That would not help Ray.

"Die, you—" the man shouted as Mary kicked out, caught him in the gut, then spun to chop at his knife arm. The knife flew past Ray's ear to land in the mule with a clatter.

The attacker rolled away, screaming.

Mary stood to her full height; her sidearm materialized in her hand as her eyes did a quick look around for more attackers. Ray did the same; he saw none. By the time Ray could spare a moment for his assailant, the guy had bolted back into the crowd; shocked bystanders made way for him. Mary started to take a shot, then raised her pistol high as the crowd closed behind her target. Ray caught a hint of the man's head as he vanished behind the Residence.

For a moment, everyone stood in shocked silence. Then San Paulo and Chu descended on Ray. "Are you hurt?" "Where did he come from?" "We've never had anything like that." "No, nothing at all."

All Ray saw was a crowd moving closer, giving another assailant a shorter run.

Mary grabbed his elbow. "Out of the car," she ordered Rose and the nurse. "Into the front seat."

Rose scrambled over the seat, eyes wide and locked on the knife. "What's cook's knife doing here?"

"Not now, Rose," Mary snapped. Rose frowned, accepting the answer as a familiar one. Mary shoved Ray into the backseat just as Jeff rode up on some kind of motorcycle.

"You!" Mary shouted. "Can you drive this mule?"

"Always wanted to try," Jeff grinned, taking in the scene and not sure what to make of it.

"You're driving," Mary shot at Jeff, and pushed Ray across the backseat to make room for her. Ray moved, using more hip motion than he had since Mary nailed him. If he'd had the time, he would have marveled at it. At the moment, he just scooted.

"Drive, Jeff," Mary ordered.

Under Mary's instruction, Jeff put the mule in gear and hit the accelerator; the mule took off with a leap. Mary kept her

eyes roving right; Ray covered the left. No one trailed them.
"What was that all about?" Jeff asked.

"Somebody tried to knife me. That happen often?"

The nurse shook her head dumbly. "Never," Jeff said. Ray
had a hard time believing that.

"Where we going?" Jeff asked.

"The blimpfield," Ray answered.

"Be there in no time," Jeff assured them. However, Rose's
brave front began to crack around the edges. Without lowering her vigilance, Mary got Rose chattering about the farms
near their base with chickens and ducks. The promise of a
donkey to ride caught Rose's young attention and didn't let
go, leaving Ray wondering where his marine officer learned
so much about distracting children. He suspected it was a gal
thing that he'd never master.

The news of an impending shuttle landing apparently had
passed through Lander's Refuge at the speed of light. As the
mule approached the field, it seemed like half the city's million inhabitants were somewhere in the crowd around the
port. Mary checked in with *Second Chance*.

"Yeah, we spotted the crowd last orbit and did a check on
the marked-out area. It's plenty long, and we've added that
runway to the lander's navigation map. Trust us, Ray, we
won't fry anybody. Any problems?" Mary raised an eyebrow
to Ray. He shook his head. She punched off.

Jeff caught up with the shuttle as it finished its landing roll,
driving right up its open ramp. Even as they dismounted, the
crew chief and loadmaster were tying down the mule.

Jeff stood, hands shoved in his pockets. "Mind if I hitch a
ride? I've had about as much of my sis as I can take for a year
or ten. I'd like to get back to some field prospecting, and you
look like the fastest way there."

Ray glanced in Mary's direction. She studied the local as
she might an asteroid that could be solid gold but might be
total dross. "No problem, sir," Mary said slowly. "He came
out with us. Might as well go back with us."

As Ray and Mary settled into seats, she chewed on her
lower lip. "Wonder who that knife guy was."

"We might know if you'd let him finish what he was shouting," Ray said dryly.

"At the moment, sir, it looked like he was ready to drill you a new belly button, but next time," she assured him, "I'll let the guy finish his manifesto."

An hour later, Ray surveyed the base from the shuttle's top step. A long swath of field had been sprayed with emulsifier, giving the lander a solid temporary runway. The same technique had created roads that were now lined with buildings. Though prefab balloons, once blown up and sprayed with epoxy, the structures were as permanent as stone. By their shapes, as much as by the signs in front, Ray could name them.

The chip fabricator was long and low. The equipment factory was wide and tall. Around them squatted housing and office buildings, including one that proudly proclaimed itself the "Santa Maria Center for Research and Delight."

"I won the contest for naming that one," Kat Zappa proudly crowed. She seemed to have appointed herself Ray's tour guide, meeting him at the stairs when he paused, blinking, for his eyes to adjust to the bright sunlight. One by one, she pointed them out. To the right of the manufacturing center a number of sealed containers sat where they'd been dumped. Kat said nothing about them; she didn't have to. Ray'd been too many years in uniform not to recognize his bomb farm and weapons factory. With luck, that gear would stay packed.

"Where's the hospital?" he interrupted Kat. Rose was peeking shyly around the door of the lander, the only one behind Ray except for the crew.

"Hi. What's your name?" Kat asked, hurrying to the little girl's side and giving Ray a chance to start down the stairs, Mary two steps ahead of him.

"Rose," came in a trembling whisper.

"Is that your bag? It's pretty. Do you have a kitten? I had one when I was your age. Can I carry your bag?"

Ray left Kat to prattle as he worked from one step to the next. What was it with estrogen that turned every female into a mother to every child? When his own son or daughter arrived, would he be rattling on like a twittering bird? After years of barking orders, Ray could not picture himself cooing and aahing over some tiny fragment of humanity. *But, God, I want to be home with Rita to find out.*

A mule waited at the bottom of the stairs for Ray. Jeff loitered near it. As Ray stepped off from the last step, his commlink buzzed. "Matt here. You all set?"

"Looks like it. How do things look on your end?"

"Couldn't be better. We're breaking orbit this trip around. See you when we've found a way home."

"Outstanding. Ray out," he said to Jeff's raised eyebrows. "You hang around me long enough and you're bound to find out something you shouldn't."

"I had a hunch you were holding back. Call me a suspicious bastard. It runs in my family. So, you're as lost as we are."

"Nope. The skipper of that ship made a bad jump last year. Took them six weeks, but they came home."

Jeff pulled thoughtfully at his eyebrow for a moment. "But you're not sure."

"There was sabotage involved in this jump. Matt's got a tougher problem this time around."

"Sounds like humanity hasn't changed much." Jeff paused. "But then, living on Santa Maria hasn't made us saints either. Here's my deal. You cut me in on your mineral extraction technology and I won't breathe a word about your problems to anyone until you're ready to announce it." He ended grinning like a thief with a permanent pardon.

Mary slipped up silently beside him. "I could just break your neck. Tell your sister you fell down the lander's stairs in a rush to meet a nice local girl. What's her name?"

"Ah, yes. I suspect Vicky would grieve all of two seconds." Jeff took a quick step back from Mary. "However, if it served her, she could turn my death into quite a *cause célèbre*. You still haven't told me how that really neat knife ended up on the backseat."

"And what do you know about that?" Mary closed the distance to Jeff again. The only threat was in her closeness . . . and the death in her eyes.

Jeff didn't retreat this time. "I don't know anything more than you do. But I have sources here you don't. I can get answers you can't. You can work with me, or you can keep playing the Lone Ranger. Do they still have stories about him?"

"Yes," Ray scowled and settled himself into the backseat of the mule. "Mary, I think we ought to let him live. At least for a while."

"If you say so, Colonel," Mary said doubtfully.

Ray turned in his seat to face Jeff. "As you've probably noted, until recently, I was a colonel, commanding infantry. Mary was a marine officer in our most recent war. You can take the uniform off, but old habits die hard. You strike me as a very smart businessman. Don't outsmart yourself."

Jeff slowly nodded as Ray spoke. The pause at the end grew long. Finally, licking his lips, Jeff said, "All my life, I've been the baby. The kid. Vicky knew she'd inherit. Mark was out hustling before I even knew the rules of the game. He found the bauxite deposits up among the Bible thumpers and managed to get the aluminum mill going. Pissed Vicky off big time. Me, I'm the spare, the nothing, the one everybody tells what to do. You're my one chance to be something. Please, give me that chance."

Ray studied the man. Were his eyes actually misting up? Was this for real or just show? Ray had no idea. Surely this planet had a need for everyone. Then again, growing up in the shadow of the woman who had the whole place by the throat might be pretty hard on a kid. Maybe Jeff was desperate to get out of that shadow. Then again, maybe he'd learned enough from Victoria and just wanted his own place in the sun to do to her and others what he'd seen her do. Tough call. Ray turned to Mary. "You need an extra hand in your mining operations?"

"Don't look like the factories are up," she said.

"No," Kat cut in, now down the stairs with Rose in hand. "No mineral feed stock. Couple of marines said they'd start things up as soon as you got back."

"Nice of them to wait," Mary snorted, then turned on Jeff. "You're welcome to work for the Ours, by Damn, Mining Consortium. You may save our start-up a few wrong turns.

But"—Mary made the word explosive as she rested a pointing finger on Jeff's chest—"you swindle us, we'll get you. We worked the asteroids before the war. We worked our butts off surviving that damn war. You help us, you're our buddy. You get crosswise with us, and so help me, your sister won't find enough pieces of you to know you're dead. Understood?"

The man returned Mary's hard stare, head nodding. "Yes, Captain. I understand. Maybe better than you know. I suspect I've just met someone as desperate as me."

"Where's the doctor?" Rose interjected. "The sun is hurting my eyes."

Mary metamorphosed from line beast to mother in the time it took her to kneel next to Rose. "Then we'll pop the top on this mule and get you some shade. Kat, where's the hospital?"

"Over there," she pointed, "but it's not set up yet."

Ray sighed for the good old days when he gave an order and it happened. "I'll just have to ask the doctor why."

Kat looked ready to go elsewhere, but Ray signaled her into the backseat with Rose. Mary took the driver's seat, and Jeff settled into the front seat as far from her as he could and still get the door closed. Ray tried not to grin. By all rights, he ought to be ready to explode with anger. Three hot potatoes dropped in his lap. Jeff, who might or might not stab him or someone else in the back over sibling rivalry. Rose and her headaches and now gear that wasn't up for some reason Kat was not eager to explain. Instead of mad, he found it funny. *Keep your sense of humor and you might survive this mess.*

The hospital was a short drive. Matt had sent down the younger of the ship's two doctors, Dr. Jerry Isaacs. Ray found him at the end of a long line of locals, apparently doing a public relations sick call.

"I brought you another child with headaches," Ray said by way of introduction. The next woman in line held a coughing seven-year-old. Still, she took two quick steps back. Ray had yet to figure out the local attitude toward the albino children. It seemed to be one part fear, another part awe.

Dr. Jerry smiled at Rose, who was suddenly so attached to Kat that surgery seemed required to separate them. Kat came forward and held Rose while Jerry did the usual medical once-over. Rose took it stoically, except for one exclamation of pain when he shined a bright light in her eyes.

"They look healthy enough. I can't tell you more until I get my diagnostic center back."

"When's that?" Ray asked, puzzled.

"You'll have to ask Kat and company," the doctor growled.

"We started using it for specimen analysis, sir." Kat eyed the floor, as if hunting for a crack to fall through.

"Doctor, you haven't started working on these children's problems?"

"I've only been down two days. I will not use diagnostic gear someone just used to dissect the latest stray something these midshipmen"—his nod indicated Kat—"dragged in."

"Colonel, it's really important, what we're finding out."

"More important than helping these kids?" Ray made it clear that would be hard to do.

"Sir, there's something weird with the evolution on this planet. We've been chasing it the week you've been gone, sir, and we still can't figure it out." Kat ran out of words in the face of Ray's scowl.

"Please, Colonel, Doc, we can't stop now. Come and see."

"Show me," Ray said.

FIVE

MATT HAD LAUGHED at how excitable the middies were when they had a new bone to gnaw on . . . and just about anything qualified as new to them. It had been funny on Wardhaven. Here, with all the other problems Ray had, he didn't need an out-of-control bunch of boffins freelancing on him. He followed Kat's parade down the hall to a large room where a dozen middies huddled over equipment or around lab tables lit by glaring lamps. Jars of specimens reeking of preservatives half-filled a wall of shelves.

"Kat, good!" a young man shouted from one dissection table. "This thing has a heart in every segment. At least I think this muscle pumps what it uses for blood. Come take a look. Oh, hi, Colonel, you might want to see this, too." The good doctor's scowl at the mess they had made of his medical unit was ignored; nothing but enthusiasm and excitement came from the youngsters.

Ray kept his face unreadable. When he came down on the doc's side he didn't want the kids screaming he hadn't given them a fair hearing.

"You've cut up a woolly leg-legs!" Rose cried in nine-year-old outrage.

"We put it to sleep first," the young man defended himself against the accusation of innocence. "And we have to study it."

Ray caught Mary's eye, nodded her toward the door with the little girl. Mary declined the order with a quick shake of her head. Rose clung to Kat, and Ray's Chief of Security's curiosity was clearly piqued.

So for the next hour Kat did her best to update Ray's academy biology course; most of what he heard went over his head.

Not all. The computer image of three skeletons side by side was impossible to forget. One was ours, skull perched on a backbone of vertebrates, rib cage dangling from our shoulders. Next to it was one with vertebrates, too, but long bones hung vertically from the shoulder, intersperced with four arms. The third skeleton featured three backbones, all long and looking like our leg bone. Studying the sockets of the hip and shoulder bone that allowed this version to twist gave Ray a headache; still, the middies insisted it was as flexible as ours, and its spinal column just as protected. The last of Kat's three evolutionary lines was the woolly leg-legs. Rose's terminology had been adopted and scientifically sanctified.

When the middies grew silent, Ray turned to Doc Isaacs. "Could all these have evolved here?"

The young medical professional rubbed his chin thoughtfully. "I don't know, Colonel. I've never heard of anything like this. A small number of exotics in a biota usually are imports. But three totally mixed. Is this sun unstable? Could these all be mutations? I'm no geologist, but until someone digs up a fossil record, I'd be reluctant to say they couldn't all be native to this planet. After all, it *is* a big universe."

Kat frowned, but nodded. "We don't know enough to draw a conclusion," she said, pained to admit such a limit.

"And it's only going to get worse," Ray sighed, and took over. "Doc, we've got three kids who need thorough examinations. If we can solve their problems, we'll be well on our way to winning a lot of credit with the locals. As much as I hate to restrict you middies' play privileges, Doc's got first call on his diagnostic gear for Rose and her friends."

"And you, Colonel," the doc cut in.

"Me?"

"The meds that saved your backbone have side effects. I checked your records. You're several weeks overdue for a full workup. I'm putting you in line ahead of the kids. Middies, I want my diagnostic center back, and I want it back now."

"All of it?" one squeaked.

Jerry took a deep breath, surveyed his appropriated domain like a monarch reclaiming his throne room, then let the air out through a quirky grin. He pointed to one corner. "Clean up Bay One and I'll share the rest. For now. But if I need it, you're out of here, fast."

"Yes," "Thanks," and an argument from someone evicted from Bay One that they should have priority in Bay Three broke out immediately. Ray turned to leave, but Jerry nabbed his elbow.

"You're not going anywhere. You're my number one patient."

Ray surrendered with as much grace as he could muster. At least this medical exam would not be invasive. He turned to Mary. "Leave Rose with me. Go corral David and the other one."

"You promised me my own telephone for my arm so I could call Mommy," Rose reminded him as she sat down beside him. Kat surrendered her wrist unit. Ray showed the girl how to use it and helped her place her first call. Ms. San Paulo came on the line at the tenth buzz. Ray spent the next ten minutes smiling through a nine-year-old's perspective on the day, with few comments from Mom, while the doc and middies cleared the wreckage of several dissections. Ray put an end to the call only when Mary dragged David and a seven-year-old in from wherever they'd been playing. The dirty clothes and faces attested that they'd been having fun.

"Thank you for caring for Rose," Henrietta finished.

"Everything's fine here," Ray assured her. "How are things at your end?"

"We had a fire at the archives this afternoon. Initial reports says it was a faulty electric wire."

Ray nodded. "I'll make sure Rose calls you about this time tomorrow," Ray said and punched off. Mind elsewhere, he watched Rose slowly approach her two new playmates. "I've never seen anyone else with white hair, except old people," she said, twisting the hem of her dress in both hands.

"I hadn't either," David answered back quickly.

Jerry took one look at both kids and growled, "Mary, run those two through a dunk tank while I start on the Colonel."

Mary left with all three kids in tow. Ray shed shirt, belt, and shoes and let them help him up onto the exam table. From practice, Ray's fingers rapidly adjusted the contours of the table, adding more back support and raising his legs . . . and the table's temperature. It was cold.

"Give me a minute to reset these systems. Lord, but the middies have hashed the setting." Jerry provided a running commentary on youngsters who had no respect for the designed intent of systems. Ray cleared his mind, letting it wander. He'd learned the hard way that moments like these could easily turn to remembrances and regrets. Three evolutionary lines. Interesting, but for three hundred years the people of Santa Maria had pretty much ignored them. It was probably fascinating for the middies but of no relevance to the mission. Somebody wanted Ray dead. Not unusual in his old line of work, but a tad upsetting in his new job as ambassador to these lost sheep. Maybe sheep wasn't the right metaphor. Sheep don't carry knives. Didn't cause fires. Around Ray, the scanner systems came alive. For long minutes, Ray hardly breathed.

"Let's redo that scan," Jerry ordered, voice doctor-cold.

"Problem?" Ray asked.

"Just want to make sure the middies didn't louse things up," Jerry said, words suddenly sterile medical efficiency. Ray fought to keep from shivering as ice traveled down his mending spine. The exam continued, the doctor consulting his techs in quick, quiet phrases. Ray tried to relax, but as the exam stretched, tension grew.

"Doc, how much longer?"

"I want to rerun a set. See if I've got it calibrated."

Ray struggled up and slowly swung his legs off the table. "Check it on the kids." Ray could hear them playing tag noisily in the hall. "You've had enough of my time."

"Colonel, I'd like to—"

Ray cut him off. "You know where I live. If you still aren't sure about your machine, I'll give you another half hour tomorrow. Now help me off this damn table."

"Yes, sir."

Ray had to put up with the doc's sour face for about five more seconds. Then Mary turned the three kids loose on Jerry, and no one can stay sour-faced while drowning in puppies. They wanted to know what did what, who did it, and how he would take away their headaches . . . all at once and in chorus. Ray hobbled off with Mary. He felt fine; that was all he needed to know. He came to a stop outside the hospital door. "Where's headquarters? My quarters?" He surveyed a collection of identical temporaries.

Mary pointed to the left. "Headquarters is across from the hospital. We've set up your quarters in the HQ, sir. If Matt can have his bunk next to the bridge, why should you have to commute?" Put that way, Ray couldn't argue. They covered the short distance to the HQ slowly. In the fields beyond the base, men and women hoed crops in the late-afternoon sun. On base, work parties moved about purposefully, if on missions Ray knew nothing about.

"Who's in charge?" Ray asked as he and Mary entered the orderly room.

"Nobody" came as a happy bellow from a room marked Leading Chief. At its door in a moment stood Command Chief Barber of *Second Chance*. "Captain would have sent down his supply division head, but Ernie Nuu hired her away just before we left, so I'm trying to keep this lash-up in order while you're traipsing around, though how an enlisted swine is supposed to ride herd on marines, Doc, and middies is anyone's guess." Despite his complaints, the chief had done a great job of setting up the base and maintaining security. Now Ray needed more. "Mary, with the chief's help, can you command the whole base, security, ops, mining, and manufacturing for mules and workstations?" Ray asked. Mary grinned like a fox offered command of the chicken coop and called a meeting of the Ours, by Damn, Mining Consortium to get things going.

Jeff was incredulous. "Tiny miners that slip through the cracks in the rocks and extract minerals, molecule by molecule."

"Show me a place that's mineral-rich and I'll make us rich," Mary answered his challenge. Ray adjourned them to a command table that Mary quickly turned into a map of the surrounding area. Jeff's eyes got bigger as she added streams, roads, and 3-D elevation. "Show me the minerals," Mary said, making a shallow bow and inviting him to the map.

"This is the village. This is the base," Jeff muttered as he got his bearings, his finger roving the map. "Yeah, you cross that stream, then head up this one, branch off here . . ." He walked off three or four more finger lengths, then got low over the map and sighted off in one direction. "Yes, you can see the mountains between those two hills." He turned to Mary: "There. I was standing in that stream when your shuttle came over. My assay kit was sparking every mineral that's worth digging."

Mary eyed the map. "So where did it wash into the river from?" Now Mary ran her fingers over the map, following streams uphill, then zoomed the map into an area. Jeff's eyes got even bigger. Mary took one hill, Cassie another.

"I got a major landslide here," Cassie observed. "Created a bit of a pond. Did you check below that?" she asked Jeff.

"I didn't even know that pond was there."

Mary followed several streams up her hill. She zoomed the board again, checking for scouring above the headwaters. Drawing a pen from the table's drawer, she circled areas of interest. "Calculate all areas circled. Add in all streambeds. Total area," she ordered.

She and Cassie examined the report. "You've got a lot more total land under erosion than my landslide area," Cassie agreed.

Mary tapped her hill. "I think we've found the source of all your goodies, Jeff. Tomorrow you run a check just below that wash while we thump that hill. I'll show you how we get the good stuff out without harming a blade of grass. Now go get your room back at the village inn."

Jeff looked none too happy to be ushered out, but he headed for the door. As he opened it, Dr. Isaacs barged in, face white as his lab coat. "Colonel, we need to talk."

Ray motioned the local out the door while the doctor made a beeline for the worktable. Mary stepped aside, surrendering the controls to the doctor without a word and went to check the door. She nodded; Jeff was gone. Ray had given away one secret today; he didn't want to try for two. Without preamble, the doctor converted the display from a mountain to a skull. The miners backed away. "Is this a private medical matter?" Ray asked.

"I wish to hell I knew," Jerry answered. "Kat, I want you in on this." He waved at the young middie who had followed him in the door but hung back. "Colonel, under normal conditions I'd be dusting off my bedside manners and hunting for nice ways to say nasty words. You'll excuse me if I just bull into this?"

Ray felt the bottom drop out of his gut. He leaned on the table as the shock wave swept through him. He'd had doctors say that before. He was still alive, and if not kicking, at least hobbling. Mary motioned Cassie out. As the door closed, Ray swallowed hard. "What do you have for me?" in the voice an officer of the line cultivates for moments like this.

"Damned if I know," the doctor shot back. "Keep that in mind." The doc paused, took a deep breath, and started slowly. "They saved your spine by giving you a cocktail of drugs and viral stimulators to patch what was broken."

"They said it was something like mending a rope."

"Right out of the textbook on bedside manners," the doc nodded. "Close but not exact. Your cells had to grow new receptors at the break point, then new cells to connect them. You're growing cells your body never planned on. Did they warn you of the risk of inciting other cell growth?"

Ray glanced off for a moment, trying to recall what was at best fuzzy. "They may have. I wasn't paying much attention once they got past the place where they said I might walk again."

"Most people aren't. Damn tough to get informed consent in situations like that. Anyway, one of the rare side effects of your therapy is a sudden increase in tumors, usually benign."

"Cancer!" Kat breathed. "But that's easily cured," she said, to take the ancient death curse from the word.

"In any decent medical facility, a minor problem."

Ray saw where this was leading. "Do we have access to a decent medical facility?"

The doc took in a long breath. "No. Any ship personnel with a problem like that are dropped off at the nearest base and we pick them up two months later, cured."

"Another reason to wish we were home," Ray breathed.

"Except." The doc tapped the board, bringing up four skull scans. "Rose, David, and Jon all have tumors in the exact same place as you."

As Ray bent over the board, Kat quickly joined them at the display. Mary was beside him, a gentle hand resting on his elbow. Ready to catch him if his knees caved on him? Ray tried to process what had been thrown at him. Doc had given him a potential death sentence, then changed it . . . to what? Ray studied the four skull scans as if one of them weren't his, as if they were just terrain his troops had to maneuver over. *Detach, Colonel, detach. You can feel later. There's something important here. Find it.*

"The tumor mass is here," Doc was saying, "between the right and left lobes of the brain. There shouldn't be anything there." Ray focused on the four skulls, checking each. To his eye, they all looked the same.

"No way to tell from this if it's benign or malignant?"

"I ran the blood tests on all four of you. Didn't find anything malignant, but . . ."

"Keep talking, Doc," Ray ordered.

"There're fragments of virus in your blood. Kids', too. Again, we all have them, but this stuff isn't in our database. I'm still trying to put them together, do an ID."

Ray could think of nothing more to say. It was moments

like these, at funerals and bedsides, that left him at a loss for words. "Let me know what you find" was so empty.

Doc headed for the door. "Mary, it's time to put the kids to bed. I'm keeping them in the clinic tonight."

"Excuse me, Colonel, I promised Rose I'd bunk with her tonight, just in case she needed to call her mom."

Ray ushered them out the door. Somewhere in the past hour or so, the HQ staff had left. Even the chief's light was off. The office with Ray's name on it had a door leading into a spartan bedroom with its own facilities and shower.

Someone had unpacked his kit; he couldn't even lose himself in the mindless duty of assigning underwear to drawers. He settled in his bed and opened the shades. Thirty or forty yards away was the hospital. He found himself looking into windows, watching Mary and Kat wrestle three youngsters into an unfamiliar bedtime routine. He smiled, thinking of what it would be like to do that with Rita and their own little ones.

He'd had plenty of experience with young men and women, rifle-high and in hormone hell. What would it be like to tackle one that was tiny and innocent and full of energy and didn't want to go to bed, thank you very much? *Don't worry, Rita, I'll make it home soon. Real soon.*

With Mary busy taking care of someone else, Ray found his pills and set them beside his bed with a glass of water. He doused the lights and settled into bed. With the blinds still open, he had a front-row seat to the bedtime production across the way. It was gentle distraction from a day full of things he could do nothing about.

He fell asleep with a smile on his face.

Mary had never put in time at a crèche. As a qualified miner, she wasn't required. She was catching up fast on all that she'd missed. "Can I have a drink of water?" came from the darkened room for the umpteenth time. Kat had younger brothers and sisters; she'd warned Mary this could take a while.

"I'll handle this one," the young middie said. Mary was glad to let her.

"I've got your blood results" came from behind Mary. She

turned. Doc Jerry, holding three pages of test results, absently scratched his bandaged elbow, showed where the third batch of blood had been drawn. Inspired by example, Mary rubbed her own bandage. Medical tests these days required little more than a pinprick. Doc had found an ancient blood kit with a huge needle and gigantic blood holder and gone hunting for both Mary and Kat. He'd drawn enough blood to fuel a small starship.

"Anything interesting?" Mary asked.

"Both you and Kat have virus fragments in your blood. Not much, but you and the colonel are in the same general range."

"And you?"

"Some. Maybe a few. I don't know." Doc shrugged.

"When'd you come down?"

"Day before yesterday."

"Retest when you're down a week?"

"Yeah. Mind if I run a quick brain scan on you?"

Mary tried to control rising panic. "Are my levels up?"

"A bit elevated. Not outside the norm."

"Close to the Colonel's?"

"No."

Mary tried to get the old terror out with a deep breath. Cancer was easily cured, but she'd seen old miners with too many hours in the radiation of space, faces and bodies disfigured from long-ago cures. Yeah, cancer didn't kill you, but it could sure mess with your smile. "When do you want to do the scan?"

"Now, if possible."

Glancing in the room, where Kat was providing another round of drinks for all and refusing to read a third bedtime story, Mary figured she had time. The doc had the scanner prepared for her and did it quickly. "Nothing, no tumor, not a damn thing," he muttered as he put her through a second scan. Mary was glad for the immediate feedback.

Back outside the kids' door, Kat was keeping watch. "They've been quiet for ten minutes. They may be down for the night. Rose wondered when you'd come in."

Mary yawned and stretched, the bandage pulling on her arm. "I'm about ready now."

Kat nodded toward the still-lit lab. "Doc done yet?"

"Yeah, our blood's got virus, just like the Colonel's. He ran my head through a scanner and didn't find anything."

"I knew marines had empty skulls," Kat grinned.

Mary gave her a sarcastic bow, having intentionally left the opening. "Why don't you wander down and let the doc sort through the cobwebs in your head."

Kat gave the doc's direction a worried glance. "Think he's still mad at us over his lab?"

"Doesn't strike me as the kind to hold a grudge," Mary said, "for more than five or six years."

"Gee, thanks," Kat said, but headed down the hall.

Mary edged the door to the kids' room open and slipped in. From the outside lights, Mary could easily see the little ones. All three had kicked off their blankets. Since it wasn't that warm, Mary made her way from one to the other, slipping a single blanket back over each sleeping form. She'd heard that kids had such angelic visages when they slept. Rose, Jon, and David's faces were scrunched up, intent on something in their sleep. Their breath came short, jerky, in near-gasps.

Done with blanket duty, Mary slipped out of her shipsuit and slid under her own covers. Lying on her side, she rested her eyes on Rose, wondering what it would be like to have such a child, to be responsible for another small person's life and welfare. Strange thoughts for someone who'd never even tried to pass the requirements to have a kid.

Rose stiffened in her sleep. A small fist jerked out; a leg twitched. The blanket was half off again. With a sigh, Mary got out of bed and rearranged Rose's covers. Then she made another round of the other kids; their blankets were half off already. What made these kids so restless?

Back in bed, Mary remembered she hadn't laid Ray's pills out; he probably took care of them himself. He was a big boy, didn't need her. So why was she always looking out for him? Hell, six months ago she'd wanted him dead. *Well, he's my boss,* she thought, knowing that wasn't the answer. Now that she knew him, she'd found the kind of man she might have cared enough about to have a kid with. But that door was closed; he had Rita and their own child on the way and deserved better than to be chained to canes and hobbling through the world. With luck, he wouldn't always be like that. If she could do something to make this period better for him, she would.

What did she want?

She'd fought like a demon to stay alive as a marine, and she'd do it again if she had to. She'd done her job at the mine, keeping her nose clean and her head down, but none of that was her. She was happiest with her friends, part of their lives and they part of hers. Right now, the job let her be just that. Tomorrow they'd put their own twist to running a mining operation. For now, that was enough.

Two blankets hit the floor within seconds of each other. Yawning, Mary made the rounds again, wondering how long this could last. Tomorrow she'd find a complete set of pajamas for each of the kids. PJs with padlocks. As she tucked the kids in, she watched as their breath slowed, became steady, almost in cadence with each other. Good; maybe now Mary could get some sleep herself. She slid back into her own bed, pulled the covers up, took one last look at each of her kids, and went to sleep.

Jeff tossed his bag on the table nearest the public room's door and shouted, "I'm home! Don't all cheer at once!"

Annie might have, but her da and ma were in the kitchen getting tomorrow's bread started, and her kid sister was helping sweep the floor. "Nikki," Jeff asked, "could you carry a message to old Ned? I'll be going out mining tomorrow with the starfolk and I'll need a horse."

"And what do the starfolks think they'll be doing?" Mrs. Mulroney asked, coming from the kitchen with a dishrag to wipe the flour from her hands.

"Taking all the metal a man could ask from a hill without disturbing a blade of grass," Jeff answered, fishing a coin from his pocket. The one he pulled out was mainly ceramic, with a thin wire of brother Mark's aluminum wound through it. Out here, the aluminum standard had caught on quickly. In the cities, they still wanted copper in most coins. Sooner or later that would cause trouble, but it made it easier for Jeff to catch a little sister's eye. He tossed it to Nikki, who made for the door.

"Straight to Old Ned's door and back, Miss Nikki, and no dawdling," her mother warned as the girl raced out.

"Humph," Mr. Mulroney said as he came from the kitchen, two mugs of beer in his hands. "That will be the day a hill gives up good metal without the likes of you tearing it apart, shovel by shovel. I've heard the tales of what your brother's doing up among the Bible-lovers. Whole hillsides gone, rivers flowing full of mud. What you're doing ain't natural."

"Well, Mary says it doesn't have to be that way."

"You've spent a lot of time with her," Annie said.

"I've spent a lot of time with their ambassador," Jeff corrected.

"And the two of them never apart," the mother assured her elder daughter.

"Anyway, I'd like a lunch for me and twenty or so more," Jeff cut in. "The starfolk will probably have their own food, but wouldn't it be nice to show them how good they can eat from your larder?" he pointed out to Annie's dad.

"I could take along an extra keg or two and sell it by the glass," Annie offered.

Jeff started to say he'd pay for the kegs, then thought better. Much better chance of getting Annie up in the hills with them if her dad thought she was doing business. Jeff would pay for the beer, whether it was drunk or not.

"I could see what they do to the mountain, Ma, and tell you and your friends exactly what happens."

"As if they'd trust your word where young Jeff is concerned," her mom muttered, but did not second-guess her man when he said Annie should take two kegs. Jeff went up the stairs two at a time, light of heart. He was staying close to Mary. That would keep Vicky happy. And close to Annie, which made him happy. What more could a man ask for?

Ray was in darkness. It wasn't the pitch dark of a moonless night but total darkness, the complete absence of light. Sound as well. Feeling also. He moved. Which left the rational part of his brain wondering how he could be so sure he was moving when he had no reference point. Then he spotted a distant speck of light. No question he was moving toward it, and rapidly. In no time . . . which, considering this situation, might not be a bad image . . . he shot into the light, transitioning from the total absence of the stuff to the total presence of it in hardly a blink. As he floated in the brilliance, he could feel the ping of every photon as it struck him.

Ray had never been tickled by light waves; he found the sensation rather pleasant. He reached out, spreading himself to take in as much of the stuff as he could . . . and discovered his body. He had beautiful yellow petals and a long, reddish-brown stem. Around him were a million flowers like him.

Ray remembered when he was a kid, a spiritual guru or fakir or something had chained himself to the base fence and started a hunger strike. On his way to school, Ray remembered the guy yelling at one and all that they had to become one with the animals and the flowers. The base commandant left him there for several weeks, until he started to stink up the place and looked really wiped out by his hunger strike. One morning he was gone and his area hosed down and restored to proper military spic-and-span status. To Ray it had seemed about time.

Still, he often wondered, usually late at night after several beers, what it was like to feel one with everything. Now Ray felt it. The sun fed him, the air flowed over him, his roots reached down, soaking up water and minerals, photosynthesis pulsed through him, filling him, enlarging him. A bee came along. The experience wasn't quite as enjoyable as a night with Rita, but, for a flower, it was fulfilling. He pushed out seeds.

And something came along, cut him off at the roots, and swallowed him down. As Ray took a ride through an alimentary system with three stomachs, he found that he wasn't bothered by the outcome, but rather enjoying the experience: digestion, respiration, and a wild trip around the circulatory system before he settled down to a single viewpoint. He was the cow, or sheep, or whatever this critter was; it had six legs and clumped together in a herd, side by side, cheek to rear. Ray got busy nipping at flowers before his herdmates gobbled the best.

I'm experiencing life as a flower, a sheep. Why?

Ray was not surprised when the carnivores showed up.

Given a choice between being eaten as a flower and eaten as a sheep, Ray would take the flower any day. The sheep spotted the wrong smell on the wind. Its little brain wasn't geared for friend-foe identification; it settled for WRONG. Adrenaline started pumping, panic took over, and Ray took off along with every other six-legged woolly in the herd.

He didn't know where he was going; he didn't care. He just knew that he had to get as far from that wrong smell as possible. He didn't have to be faster than it, just faster than his neighbor. The military officer in Ray evaluated the data and concluded raising an army of sheep was a lost cause.

Whoever the smelly, hungry things were, they weren't dumb. Running upwind, the sheep stampeded right into the ambush before they even knew it was there. Ray took a mercifully quick blow to the head, found himself in darkness again, and got ready for another lesson in alimentary canals.

Instead he was in his freshman biology classroom back at the Academy. The gardener stood at the front of an otherwise empty class. "What have you learned?"

"To stay at the top of the food chain." Ray shot back the freshman quip just as he would have years ago.

The gardener shook his head sadly. "You are older and wiser than that. Have you learned the lesson, or must you repeat it?"

Ray felt the darkness coming for him. He had a distinct feeling this school only got harder the second time around. "No matter what color the uniform, we all bleed red," he said.

His father had told Ray that once. It had taken him years to understand the full impact that his enemy was human, too.

* * *

Ray came awake, grimaced at his bladder's demand, and reached for his canes. Done and back to his bed, he wondered what his next dream would be about. He placed little weight on dreams, just the subconscious mind's way of discharging electricity. He rolled over and went back to sleep.

SIX

RAY WAS IN a very good mood when he got his first staff meeting under way at 0800 next morning. He'd breakfasted with the kids, Mary, and Kat. How anyone could stay glum around kids was a puzzle Ray didn't want to solve. They attacked breakfast with an innocent abandon that left the table a wreck, the adults exhausted, and Ray swearing he wanted only one kid so he and Rita would never be outnumbered worse than one to two.

"Think those odds are good enough?" Kat asked, trying to persuade David he didn't need five spoonsful of sugar on his cereal.

"Grandparents, I hear grandparents make great auxiliaries," Mary put in. "Never had any myself, but it's in all the books."

"How about a squad of marines?" Ray suggested.

Mary shook her head, "Not fair to the troops, sir. A good officer never sets her troops up for defeat."

Somehow the kids learned about the day's mining project and wanted to go. Ray promised they could "if there's transport for all of you," which gave Mary an out. His security chief looked torn between "No way, José," and "Whoopee." The meal had been so absorbing that Ray was back to the HQ before he recalled the game the kids had been playing as they trooped in.

Mary had asked what kind of animal they'd like to be. Rose piped up she'd want to be a flower. Jon wanted to be a warm, woolly sheep. David had growled and made a leaping grab for Jon that left him shrieking, "I want to be a wolf."

Ray had commended the lad for staying at the top of the food chain. Now the words and the memory of a dream came back to haunt him.

In the staff meeting, Barber was already seated to Ray's right. Mary brought Cassie. "If I'm promoted to minister of mining or something, she'll take security." Doc Jerry sat next to Kat, no longer with murderous intentions toward the middie.

"Anything new concerning last night's talk, Doc?" Ray asked.

Jerry rubbed grainy, sleepless eyes. "Nothing, *nada,* and zip. I'll keep hammering on it today. Don't know when I'll make a breakthrough. Don't know if I'd recognize one if it bit me."

"You want the middies out of your hospital?"

"I don't really need all that space. Besides, who knows when what they know will be something I need to know? I'll work up local patients a bit more thoroughly today, see if I can get a local baseline. See how close the kids fit or scatter from it."

"Will you need the kids?" Mary asked.

"Probably not. You got something special for them?"

"Take them for a walk in the country."

"Just make sure they don't leave breadcrumbs. Lets them find their way home every time. Or so I'm told."

"Glad you're not speaking from experience, doctor," Ray quipped. "Looks like everyone has their day planned. Chief, I assume you have plenty to do." Barber nodded. "Then let's get busy doing it," Ray said, starting to stand.

"How are you planning on spending your day?" Barber asked.

"Taking a nap. Relaxing in a nice, warm bath. Sitting at your elbow every minute of it figuring out what needs to be done." The chief laughed at Ray's opening wish, then nodded agreement as reality thrust up its ugly head.

There was a knock at the door. "Enter," Barber said.

A yeoman did. "Sir, we've got some locals here to see you."

Jeff poked his head in. "Annie's with me. Her folks sent her out with lunch for all and a couple of kegs of beer," then added quickly, "and as a kind of observer for the green side of things." He paused, glanced over his shoulder. "Oh, and we picked up the padre. He'd just finished Mass as we went by the church. Wanted to see his grandson."

Ray drummed his fingers on the table. "So the success or failure of our mining effort will have a planetwide audience."

"Naw," Jeff said, "just pretty much this continent."

Was Mary up to a PR blitz while juggling a mine? Hardly seemed fair. "Looks like I ambassador today."

Outside, Ray found two mules and loaded trailers. Annie was in a blue plaid dress, maybe a tad more revealing than the usual local, and perched on the seat of a large, one-horse cart. From its bed came wondrously good smells. There were also two kegs of her pop's beer. Ray made a mental note to see that Mary had most of the work done before the kegs were tapped. The padre's rig was a smaller version of Annie's drawn by a shaggy pony. Rose took one look and begged to ride with the priest. David and Jon demanded rides in a mule. Mary loaded them both in the lead one, then climbed in herself. With the kids chattering nonstop, Ray seated himself in the second mule beside Cassie. He wanted a few words with the woman who might soon be his chief of security. Twenty marines, half drawn from the old miners, the other from Dumont's squad of ex-street toughs, were the work team.

Unity intelligence had assured Ray that Earth's Society for Humanity was press-ganging the dregs into their desperate defense. That was half true; Mary's ex-miners got their draft notice with their downsizing pink slips. The street kids like Dumont woke up stoned and hung over to discover they'd signed themselves in—even those who couldn't sign their own name. Ray's mistake had been assuming that they were easy sweepings.

Mary and her miner friends had been madder than hell . . .

and done something about it. Their last shift at the mines, they walked off with anything that wasn't welded down. Ray found out too late that his proud 2nd Guard Brigade was facing a lot of stuff that wasn't in the latest *Jane's All the Worlds' Weapons Systems* or in their database of hostile system signatures—and which they really should have avoided.

The rest was history, a history that he and Mary and Matt wrote in blood. They'd ended that war, to the shock of some and the relief of most. Now, Ray chuckled to himself, they were working for him and he'd get a chance to see what they could do *for* him. "I thought Mary'd bring more miners," Ray said to Cassie. "What's she doing with Dumont's kids?"

"They're in makee-learnee status. Mary promised Dumont she'd teach his kids the trade. What Mary promises, she does. This drill, each miner has a shadow. Dumont's kids learned fast in the war. Expect they'll learn even better today."

On horseback, Jeff led them west. Mary followed, Cassie right behind. Annie and the padre's carts fell in line. Miners and trainees hopped aboard mules and trailers. The padre offered Dumont a ride. The young tough looked like he'd rather be anywhere but beside the old man of the cloth. Apparently Ray had taken the seat the kid had selected for himself. With a nasty glance Cassie's way, he took the priest's offer.

"See how the kid gets along with the priest," Cassie muttered, one eye on the rearview, the other keeping Mary's trailer a proper distance ahead.

Ray leaned back, relaxing into the mule's jerky motion, his back already starting to ache. The morning was pretty enough, high clouds marking off an otherwise passionately blue sky. A gentle breeze dried the sweat as fast as the sun drew it out of Ray, cooling him nicely. The hills were dotted with trees, Earth green as well as red, blue, and gray. They added a pleasant pattern for the eye and an intriguing scent to the air. Familiar and strange merging into a palette that excited and called forth hope in Ray. On a day like today, it was easy to forget someone had tried to knife him. And someone else may have tried to burn Refuge's central archives. Back to business. "Cassie, you got any problem taking over security if I put

Mary in charge of running the base and feeding the manufacturing?"

"You do what the good Lord calls you to," the woman said.

Right, Cassie had been the one Mary had to pry out of a street mission or something back home after her leave. "Reverend Jonah might be a problem."

"I think I can get along with the rev, Colonel. He's an easy man to understand, if you know what he's saying. Our Blessed Savior calls us to love one another. Sometimes that's hard to understand for those without faith." Cassie turned to Ray, looked him straight in the eye. "Just cause we're calling you to repent don't mean we don't love you."

"Cassie, somebody tried to knife me outside the Residence."

"Mary told me." Cassie's eyes were back on the trailer ahead of her. "She also told me there're a lot of folks unhappy with the way things are. Greens, Havenites down south. Hell, Jeff's sister seems to want everything we've got, and is none too happy with you holding back on her. Think she might have decided that the embassy would be better off with a new ambassador?"

"Everything's possible," Ray agreed.

"Soon as something comes up, the nonbelievers want to blame it on the believers. You know, I heard tell, back on Earth, some Roman emperor wanted to get some urban development going at his capital, so he started a fire. Then the fire got out of hand. Burned a lot more than he expected. Started blaming it on the believers. Sounds just like a politician. Nero was his name, or something like that. He was supposed to have fiddled while the city burned. Don't politicians ever change?"

Ray shrugged. He'd burned a few politicians. Now he was one, doing what he could to change the breed. "I make you chief of security and you'll be a politician, too," Ray pointed out.

"Hum," was her only answer.

Nikki joined some workers headed for the east fields. She didn't want to see Daga today, not once she found out about Jeff and Annie and the starfolks mining. It did her no good.

"Nikki, we need you for a wall walk." Daga's voice rang cheerful, as usual. Behind her was Jean Jock. Not nearly enough behind him was Sean. Walking a wall was usually a two-person job, one on each side, silently picking up stones the frost and wind had knocked from the wall over the winter months. Sean was a good one for wall walks. He had the muscles to make picking up stones easy. In the usual silence, you couldn't say something to make him mad. Four people for a wall walk was a lot. Then it dawned on Nikki, maybe this wasn't about walking a wall at all, but seeing what Annie and Jeff were up to.

Nikki was not interested, but a grandmother took her elbow and shooed her off to repair the wall. It was something the old left to the young. Nikki went where she was shooed.

Ray was glad Mary stopped in the shade of a great oak tree. He hobbled over to Annie's cart; she, busy unloading food, was quickly surrounded by three short helpers. The priest joined and kept the kids so distracted they hardly noticed when Mary sent her detachments off.

Jeff was soon back from checking the mineral content of the stream flowing over the slide's impromptu dam. "Mary was right. That stream's rich, but not nearly as much here as lower down. Most of the good stuff is coming off that one," he pointed, hat in hand to shade his eyes from the sun, at the hill Mary had chosen. "Guess I better find her."

"Mary," Ray said, tapping his commlink, "Jeff says you picked the right target. Beer's on him," Ray chuckled.

"Figured," Mary answered.

"All of it!" Cassie yelped on net as Annie did beside Ray.

"I can afford it," Jeff agreed. "We get what you say is in that hill and I'll buy 'em a brewery."

"I heard that!" Cassie and Dumont shouted together on net.

"We'll see," Ray said, and clicked his commlink off.

"Neat gadget you've got there," Jeff said, coming over.

"One of many," Ray agreed.

"What's Mary gonna do?" little David piped up.

"Find us a copper nugget, big as your hand," Jon answered.

"Yeah, but how?" Rose asked softly.

"Me, too," Annie added. "How?"

Ray settled himself down on the ground, found a comfortable position for both legs, then slaved his pocket reader to his commlink and tied it in to Mary's central station. It showed a 3-D view of the hill they were tapping. The kids oohed and aahed as they collected themselves where they could look over Ray's shoulder. Even Jeff lifted an eyebrow. "If Mary's going to take the mountain's copper nicely, she has to get to know the mountain very well," Ray told Annie.

Glancing around, she put down a basket of bread and came to stand behind the kids, rather close to Jeff. The priest had gone off; Ray had last seen him trailing Dumont up the hill. *A shadow for a shadow?* Ray wondered. With no chaperon in sight, Annie slid closer to Jeff. He slipped an arm around her waist.

"What's that?" Jon asked as the air reverberated with a low thump and the ground shook. The map of the hill in Ray's hand began to fill with colored lines a moment later.

"One of Mary's big machines just sent shock and sound waves through the hill," Ray started, then saw in the faces of his young audience that he was missing them. "Mary made some noises, and now she's listening for the echos in the mountain. Did you ever make an echo?"

David and Jon nodded. Rose shook her head, "But I saw people make them on TV."

"Good," Ray agreed.

"Some places make echoes. Some don't," Jon noted.

"By listening with machines with very big ears, Mary can tell things about the mountain by where it does and doesn't make echoes." Jeff told the kids, and asked Ray in the same line.

There were more thumps, more lines appeared on the viewer. "Right, the noise and echoes tell Mary where the mountain is solid and where there are very tiny caves in it that her nanominers can use."

"They're really small machines," David told the adults. "Smaller than my baby brother," Jon said. "But they'll get copper and all sorts of things out of the mountain," Rose finished. After five minutes of thumps, the map looked filled in. Ray waited, expecting what would come next.

Five straight red lines appeared. "Mary will drill some

holes where you see the red lines. There're not a lot of cracks in those areas. She'll set off small explosives to create more cracks," Ray finished with a glance at Annie. "I imagine they'll do the drilling where there's no grass."

"I don't expect anyone thinks she'll not harm a few blades of grass," Annie said practically.

"Oh, no," all three disagreed. "Mary said she wouldn't hurt a single blade," Rose said. "She won't," David assured them.

Jeff could not suppress a smirk. "Maybe we can get these kids to make your report to the Greens?" Annie deftly turned herself out of the arm he had around her waist, swatted him with her apron, and went back to unloading her wagon. Jeff followed, mouthing apologies Ray suspected were as ancient as language.

"Oh, look—one of the red lines is turning yellow." Jon's announcement kept the youngsters focused on what they considered the best show. Ray checked; yes, the drilling had started. He surveyed the hill and spotted a dust plume rising from behind a mixed bunch of green and blue trees. More excited oohs were his reward for pointing it out to the kids. Jeff also must have been successful. He returned with his reward, a large bucket of fried potato wedges. Annie followed with a much lighter handful of condiment. For the next half hour Ray divided his attention among three dramas: Mary's mountain preparation, the kids' reactions, and Annie's courtship. All were amusing.

"Fire in the hole. Fire in the hole," echoed over the hill. "Stand clear of trees and anything else that might take it in its mind to fall on you," Cassie announced dryly on net.

Ray suggested the kids count off the seconds until the explosions. They were at twenty, after a bit of an argument about what came after ten, when the ground trembled beneath their feet for a long second, then went back to being terra firma. The children jumped, startled when the explosion came, then launched into a dance. "Mary said she wouldn't knock even us down. And she didn't," they chortled.

"What's 'fire in the hole' mean?" Nikki asked.

Daga shook her head. The others just stared back dumbly.

Then the earth started doing a jig where they hid, watching. Nikki had not understood a thing of what was going on around them, and was growing more and more scared with each passing minute.

The thumps had been the first to jar Nikki's nerves, and they were none too good after hiking out here, listening to Jean Jock and Sean ramble on about the heads they'd knock to keep the fields their own. Every time Daga opened her mouth, Nikki shushed her, scared her friend would tell the others about how she could make mountains disappear. Daga didn't much care for Nikki's shushing, and took to swatting Nikki even before she opened her mouth.

Of course, Daga never said anything about the box.

It wasn't just the boys who bothered Nikki. Three strangers, familiar to the others, joined them. Wrapped in hooded cloaks that must have been horribly hot, they said not a word. The woman seemed to be the leader; at least she set the course, and the two men followed. Even Sean deferred to her. Daga said nothing when Nikki asked who they were.

When Nikki pointed out that her sister Annie was parking Da's rig under a great oak, and they must be where they were going, the three had stopped in the shadow of a Popsicle tree. Nikki listened to the wind whistle through the long, hollow sticks that gave the tree its name and waited for someone to say something. The three just stood, watching the starfolks as they disbursed over the next hill. The woman pointed and the three, closely followed by Nikki and the locals, silently took up their observation post in a shallow depression beneath a pine tree.

There they waited.

The thumps were the first things to get their attention. "Like they've got a giant over there, pounding around on the mountain," Daga joked. The two locals laughed as they usually did when Daga said outrageous things. The woman stranger turned to Daga, seeming to seriously consider her ridiculous comment, then went back to observing.

Nobody had an answer when Nikki asked, "Well, what is it?"

Then they let steam out of the mountain. At least that was

what Sean said it looked like. He'd been around when Jeff's brother Mark had been prospecting in these hills. He'd seen the steam-driven hammers they brought in to drill holes and stuff. "They'd get a roaring fire going under this big cylinder, and have big, thick hoses leading off from it, with steam hissing and sizzling out of them wherever it could. I saw a guy get boiled just for standing too near one," Sean insisted.

"Go long with ya," Daga insisted.

"Maybe they're setting up a thing, like you know?" Nikki whispered to Daga.

"Why would they be doing all this if they had something like, you know?"

"Maybe they want to aim it right," Nikki shot Daga the dirtiest look she could manage.

"What are you girls babbling about?" Jean Jock wanted to know. The woman stranger flashed Nikki a look that chilled her.

"Nothing," Daga answered. "Nothing at all," she said, shooting Nikki back just as mean a look. "They don't have anything like it," Daga whispered.

"You hope," Nikki said, looking purposely over her shoulder, as if to see a bunch of marines setting up a hill leveler behind them. Daga looked, too.

"See, nothing."

"They have a ship up in the sky," Nikki reminded Daga, almost hoping something would go wrong, something would show her friend there were things to be afraid of.

"What are you two girls gabbing about?" This time it was Sean. He wouldn't be put off with a "nothing."

Then the earth started dancing.

Nikki and Daga took off running, the young men right behind them. Even the strangers hauled up their cloaks and hoofed it like mad. Nikki swore she wouldn't stop running until she got back to the fields. If they wanted to stop her, they'd have to kick her feet out from under her, like the boys sometimes did in football when the umpire wasn't looking.

•   •   •

"Who are they?" David asked, stopping his dance and pointing to a bluff just across the stream. Ray looked where David pointed, catching sight of dull-colored clothes just as they disappeared over the hill.

"Some other Green observers," Jeff suggested, glancing at Annie. She shrugged.

Ray scratched his chin; the show hadn't really begun. Maybe he should send a marine to round them up, bring them down here, where he could make sure they got the full story. He glanced at Annie. "Should I get them back?"

Annie laughed. "I doubt you could catch them, from the flash of their heels as they headed over that hill."

Ray turned back to his reader. New lines appeared on it. Black lines. Ray told the reader to rotate the picture. Soon they were viewing it from a bird's perspective. "Those are the insertion points, pretty evenly spaced across the hill. The miners will pour the nanos down those holes, and drain them out the bottom of the mountain."

"How?" David asked. "I know Mary told us last night, but I still don't get how the little miners know where Mary wants them to go once they have a load of stuff."

"Gravity is part of it," Ray tried to explain. "They know to go downhill, just like water knows to flow downhill."

"Water doesn't know anything," Rose said with the sophistication of her city education.

"Who says water doesn't know to go downhill? It always does," David insisted.

Ray's respect for anyone who could teach children was rapidly climbing. Now if he could just find someone to respect. Jeff knelt between David and Rose. "What we're trying to say is that gravity pulls everything down, water, a leaf, you, Rose, when you hopped off the priest's cart, the nanos in the hill. I imagine she's also told the nanos that she wants then to head for the east side of the hill." He glanced at Ray, who nodded solemn agreement. "Not all the nanos will make it to the tunnel that Mary digs to drain them out. What's her normal attrition? I mean, how many does she normally lose?"

Ray grinned as even Jeff had trouble finding small words for little ears. "Sometimes as few as one in a hundred."

Jeff whistled low. "That good. I've read science articles from the Landers' time. They talked about that kind of stuff in the future. I wondered if you ever got it."

"It's working up there right now," Ray assured him.

David's "wow" was quickly echoed by Rose and Jon.

Mary was bringing the crew down off the mountain. They collected at the base, where Mary personally supervised the drilling of three twenty-centimeter conduits into the mountain—one directly in, the others at thirty-degree angles to the right or left. Once those main taps were almost halfway through the mountain, Mary turned loose remote drillers—ferrets, she called them—to drill ten- or twenty-millimeter holes in a wider pattern.

Ray scowled at the ferrets. They, and the sensors and laser designators Mary had used to defend her pass, were what had put Ray flat on his back by the end of the battle. *Live and learn, old man, live and learn.* While the ferrets were busy at work, Mary called it a morning and brought the work crew back to camp.

"Chow ready?" she called.

"Waiting for you!" Annie shouted.

"We have stew," Annie announced as the women and men trooped up to the tree. "We have a turkey sliced thin for what we call sandwiches. And me mother personally prepared chicken to her family's special southern fried recipe. Potato salad goes great with that, but we also have them fried, baked, and mashed." Apparently no dinner here was complete without potatoes. Most of the crew was in, but not all. Ray watched two figures, locked in energetic conversation, slowly follow the rest. Dumont and the padre, if Ray made them out. The priest's gestures were slow, measured. Dumont's gesticulation was wild, including a rapid series of shaken fists at the blue sky. As they approached camp, their talk became lower, if no less animated.

Ray did not wonder at the topic. Dumont was Mary's murderer. Without a moment's hesitation, he had followed an admiral's order to shoot *Sheffield*'s gunnery officer, an illegal order if Ray had ever heard of one. The only mitigation Mary could offer for her sergeant was that their basic training had been abbreviated, stripped of anything not relating to how they might kill the enemy. Ray couldn't throw too many stones Humanity's way; Unity had pulled some pretty raw and illegal things out of the shadows before he'd succeeded in putting it out of business. And late at night, Ray sometimes didn't feel all that good about what he'd done, either. Maybe he could spend some time with the little padre himself.

Jeff offered Ray a hand up; he took it. Mary met them with a question. "Southern fried chicken—south of what?"

Annie shrugged. "South of the Covenanters, I guess."

Whatever it was south of, the north had lost out. Jeff helped Annie tap a keg. "One glass, and a small one at that!" Mary shouted. "We got work ahead of us and I'll have none of my good metal going back into the ground because you had to belch." That brought good-natured grumbling that turned to happy noises when Mary promised no limits once the day's work was done.

The kids ate like they'd never eaten before, then dashed off to see what was happening. Mary assured Ray that the gear was both kid-proof and unable to hurt them. David was back in a few minutes, announcing that they had found a pond, and could they go swimming? Jeff and Annie galloped off after the kids to make sure they hadn't gone in alone. Mary assured David that the day was hot and everyone would want to swim later, but only after all the work was done.

Jon and Rose came dashing back ahead of their elders dispatched to corral them. "We found a cave. Can we explore it?"

Mary shook her head. "Caves can be dangerous. There might be a bear hiding in the back."

"What's a bear?" Rose asked.

"Something big and hairy that eats little girls who ask too many questions," Jeff said. Having finally caught up, he grabbed Rose from behind and whirled her over his shoulder as she shrieked and giggled.

"It's not really a cave," Annie explained. "Just a bit of an overhang left from the landslide that dammed the stream."

"I'll look at it later," Mary said. The kids found that half promise acceptable. After lunch they joined the workers as they trooped down to the minehead to see what had happened while they ate. A trickle of muddy water was flowing out of all three tap pipes, gathering in a catch basin that one of the trailers had turned out to be.

"A lot of work for dirty well water." Jeff raised an eyebrow to Mary.

She only grinned. "Jeff, you come over here and throw the switch yourself. Nanos are programmed to hold on to their load until we tell them to let go. Why don't you do that yourself."

Jeff's eyes lit up until Mary lifted a flap and he found himself facing a massive keyboard. "What do I do?" he squeaked.

"Don't worry. One of the kids could do it." Which got shouts of "Me! Me! Me!" from all three. Annie held them off while Mary walked Jeff through a dozen or so keystrokes. Then Jeff, Mary, and Annie held the kids up to watch as the muddy water in the tank changed. Multicolored sand precipitated to the bottom, and an oily film collected at each corner of the tank where vents drew them off. The resulting water was crystal clear.

"I'm thirsty. Can I have a drink?" Jon asked.

"Not of this." Mary was quick to pull back a hand dipping into the water. "I'll want to run it through the filters several times to make sure we get all the nanos out. You wouldn't want to drink a nano, would you?"

"Would it take rocks out of me?" David asked.

"Of course," Jon cut in. "The rocks in your head."

David screwed up his face in surprisingly deep thought at that cut. "I wouldn't mind, if it would take my headaches with it." Caught off guard, even Jon agreed with David.

"If only it was that easy," Annie whispered.

For the first time that day, Ray thought about the doctor's report of last night. If it was just something in their heads, maybe they could come up with a solution that easy. After all, Ray had all that industrial capability waiting to go to work. Maybe they could build a full medical center.

After that, watching the nanos' work was about as interesting as watching paint dry. Mary ran a quick analysis; she already had a trend curve of time vs. expected recovered nanos.

Her results were a tad below her optimum, but every planet was a bit different, she told all.

"Can we go swimming now?" David pleaded.

Mary shrugged. "All the work is done. It's just a matter of waiting. Why not?"

Jeff shook his head in disbelief. "No shoveling. No back-breaking work. No moving mountains to stripped soil, leave mud holes all over. That's not work!"

"I'll take it any day," Annie said. "So will me ma."

"Well, sonny boy," Mary winked at the two, "try that without my gear and know-how. It's easy to lose nanos, and they are not cheap to replace. People who know what they're doing and have the right gear can make the hardest jobs look easy."

Jeff was properly chastised. "How expensive is your gear? No. Can you make that stuff in your factory?"

Ray shook his head. "Nanos are built up one atom at a time. We didn't bring that technology. Probably would take us a couple of years to make the tools that made the stuff to make the gizmos to make them." Ray paused to see if Jeff had followed him.

"I see. We lost some of the Landers' tech, like fusion plants and radios. We had to concentrate on growing crops to feed us. Prioritize or die."

"You got it. We could make these things in our own lifetime if we had to. Our factory is multitasking."

"But should we?" Annie asked.

"We'll have to wait and see," Ray said as Cassie brought up a mule to give him a lift to the swimming hole. The pond was a good kilometer across and two or three long. On the right side—the side against the hill Mary was mining—the trees were undisturbed, a tall and multicolored stand of ancient growth, species of many different origins sharing the space in peace. Their long shadows threw cooling shade over the pond. The left side was a different story. A yellow gash showed where earth and plants had lost their battle against gravity, probably aided and abetted by rain and wind. Thick trunks had been washed into the water flow, helping to build the dam that created the pond. Other downed logs, surrounded by brush, were pushing up new life. Ray tried to estimate which of the four potential evolutionary tracts was winning, but he wasn't sure which plants represented which of the three animals he'd been shown. Overall it looked like an even mix, with Earth green taking about a quarter.

Ray's head began to throb, probably the glare of the sun on the lake. He looked for a place in the shade. Work clothes were coming off, tops, bottoms. The miners and street kids had no regard for nudity. Annie started backpedaling.

"What's the matter, you never been skinny-dipping?" Jeff asked, shirt off, shoes coming off.

"Yes, with girls." Annie was still backing.

"And the boys never came around?" Jeff asked slyly.

"No, but if they did, we made it clear to 'em they were not welcome."

"And they listened!"

"Young women have ways of making it very clear to even very dumb boys what they want, Jeff. I don't want this. I'm going back to the wagon."

"Annie, there's no one here," Jeff pleaded.

"No one?"

"Well, from Hazel Dell."

"Father Joseph is here."

"He's off talking to one of the marines."

"He'll be back. I won't be." She headed back to camp.

Jeff tried to follow. One shoe off, he stepped on a rock, ended up hopping for a few steps, then fell. "Annie, help!"

Ray suspected he'd get no quiet on the shady side of the lake. As a senior officer, he also didn't want to be a witness to anything he couldn't look the other way fast enough to avoid. The damn canes made that difficult. He limped for the other side. Shouts and laughter came from the lake; someone was being dunked. Ray wished Rita was here and they had the lake to themselves. He could wish for a lot of things. What he had was what he had.

His headache was worse. Ahead, he could hear the chatter of young voices. Right, the kids had found a cave, or overhang, or something. Ray chuckled; they'd headed for it before a swim. He'd never understand people half his size, no matter how many kids he and Rita had. There was a trail leading up the side of the erosion. Broken twigs and bent back limbs showed where the kids had passed.

At one point he almost stopped. It was crazy for a grown man on canes to chase after kids, especially with a headache coming on. However, on second review, his headache was receding, and even his backache was less than he'd expect after a day like today. And someone had to check on the kids. The swimming party was fully engaged at the moment; it looked like he was delegated the children. It might be good practice.

He found the overhang. Childish voices came from its deep shadows. There was a turn in there; it was a cave. "David, Jon, Rose!" Ray called out. The children suddenly got quiet. "Come out, kids. Are you sure there's not a bear in there?" Ray had no idea what might live in a cave on a planet with multiple evolutionary tracks. The kids didn't make a peep.

Ray was tired. He'd walked more in the past few minutes than Rita usually made him do on the exercise machine back home. He ought to sit down and rest. Movement drew his eye to the cave. Probably just a reflection of the sun off the water below. The swimmers were creating quite a few waves. Ray wondered what in there was keeping the kids so quiet. Probably was cooler; it sure was hot out here. He started in, careful to get his canes in place before risking each step.

The cave turned ninety degrees just past the overhang. The walls looked smooth. Ray studied the ceiling; it was four meters up and even. Considering how Mary had knocked around the next hill over, anything that wanted to fall was down already. There weren't any loose rocks around his canes. If both hands hadn't been busy with sticks, Ray might have scratched his chin in thought. The passage made another ninety-degree change in direction, turning deeper into the ravaged hill. Ray doubted there would be enough light for him to hobble safely. "Kids, I really can't go much farther. You're going to have to come out."

He reached the turn. The children huddled around a column reaching from floor to ceiling, each facing a side. Touching it with both hands, they leaned forward, forehead resting against the stone. The side facing Ray pulsed in an inviting, blue luminosity. Without thought, canes and feet covered the distance to the shaft. Even as part of him was drawn, moth-like, part of him stood back. Is this safe? What's drawing me? Are the kids in danger? What's happening?

Ray didn't know. Reaching out, he touched the column. It was surprisingly warm, like Rita's body as she lay in the sun. Good memories flooded Ray, leaving him awash in happiness. Comfortable reflections washed through his mind's eye, relaxing him as he rested his forehead upon the column.

Then the memories changed. Recollections of the Academy and early schools spun through his mind, followed by images of structures shooting gracefully into the sky. Waterfalls and giant purple trees marked off the spaces between high-reaching spires. Ray knew, without doubt, that this was a place of knowledge, a center of learning. The view changed. The buildings still reached for the sky, but the towers were smaller, more sized to the individual. Trees still grew, and water burbled over and down a fountain. Older heads lived here, people who found time to reflect, to grow wise. This was a home for grandparents.

And the picture in Ray's mind changed again. The towers this time were more subdued, chunky. There were places to climb, to reach out, to tumble down without being hurt more than young bodies needed for their learning. Small pools of water collected here and there where little hands might splash and play without risk. The house enclosed the grass, water, trees, not so much in walls as in a protective womb. A home to raise children in.

Now the pictures flashed before Ray faster and faster, but leaving behind a clear feeling of understanding. That was where the people gathered to rule themselves. Here was where they went to celebrate birth, death, hope.

The architecture changed. Now it was more grounded in the earth. Where one reached for the sky, this cherished stone and soil, luxuriating in the darkness of the cave. Again, Ray saw the place for learning, for the wise and for the young, for joy and sorrow and expectation.

And again change came over what Ray saw. The dispassionate part of him wondered which of these architectures went with which evolutionary line Kat had shown him, for surely he was seeing the flowering of those species, the best they had grown into. The column was their testament. The relic that proclaimed they had passed this way. Was it a welcome to those who came after them, or a declaration to humanity to stay away? While the soldier in Ray couldn't help asking those questions, that part of him who felt more than saw what they presented knew the answer even as he asked it. This was their hello. We're here. We are like you. Come and join us. Be one with us.

Ray remembered the dream. "We are all one, under the skin of our differences," the Gardener said. Now he stood before Ray, smiling, even as more and more scenes from different worlds played through Ray's mind. He saw worlds with one sun, two suns, three. Worlds where gravity was low and whirligigs flew with gentle grace. Worlds where everything was heavy and life inched its way more carefully than he did on canes.

The Gardener nodded. "They've all been here. Come to smell my flowers, to rest beneath my trees. Here they took a moment's respite from their cares and struggles. Those of the Three came here, and I showed them what nature could be, left to herself." The Gardener smiled, but there was a gash over his eye. The arm that had swept possessively to take in all that Ray had seen, now ended above the elbow. The Gardener didn't seem to notice.

"This is a place where grown-ups played, where they came to discover again how to be small, and open and ready to learn. I'm only here to take care of the grounds. But they are beautiful, untouched grounds." As Ray listened, the voice sputtered. The Gardener was missing a leg. Splotches appeared on his skin.

He glanced down. "Never had this happen, not in all these years. Don't know why." He looked up, captured Ray's eyes with his own. "I've taken care of what I can. There's nothing more I can do. Seems there's less every moment. Remember my lesson."

"Yes," Ray said . . . to an empty cave. The column was cool to the touch now. The children whimpered softly.

"What happened to the nice old man?" Rose asked. "He reminded me of Momma's grandfather."

"He reminded me of someone, too. I think we'd better go." Ray tried to herd the children for the exit.

"What happened to the old man?" Jon repeated.

"I don't know," Ray answered. "Come, kids, let's go. Mary's been shaking up the hills. It could be dangerous."

The hairs on the back of Ray's neck were up; fear flooded his gut. Something was wrong here. Ray wanted to run.

"He wouldn't let anything bad happen to us," David insisted.

Ray hobbled for the entrance. "Come with me, kids."

They did as they were told. Once in the light, Ray collapsed; the children huddled around him. Ray had no words to explain the depths of his fear. Unable to frame the questions, that failure did not shake him of his certainty that they were important. The sun brought back warmth. The laughs and shouts from the swimmers brought back hope. The children withdrew a fraction of an inch into themselves.

"I will miss him," Rose whispered.

"We all will," Ray assured her. Ray was a hardheaded, rational man, a commander of line beast. He feared no monster lurking under his bed. He paid attention to what was real, what he could touch, measure, shoot. So why was he telling a little girl that he would miss a phantom of his dreams?

Because I will.

SEVEN

JEFF SAUNTERED OBLIVIOUSLY toward the cave. Ray cleared his throat; the young man jumped, took notice of them for the first time, and stuffed his hands deep into his pockets. "How does anyone understand them?" Jeff asked plaintively.

Ray had things that needed doing, but he doubted that answering Jeff's query would take much brainpower. "That half of the species seems to understand each other quite well."

"You're married. Could you talk to her?"

"Hold on." Ray threw a hand up in mock horror. "A wedding band means only one woman gets to confuse you. That vow about 'forsaking all others' is a kindness. Could you help me up?"

"You're probably right." Absentmindedly, Jeff offered a hand, then blinked as if seeing Ray for the first time. "You're white as a sheet. Are you okay?"

Ray stood with less difficulty than usual. "That remains to be seen. Jeff, please tell Mary to get a couple of her crew up here for some underground work pronto."

Jeff was shaking his head before Ray finished. "I'm not going near the water. Annie'll say I'm just there to ogle Mary."

"I think the kids found an alien device," Ray finished.

"They did!" Jeff headed for the cave.

"Nobody goes in there without full underground hazard gear."

"Why?"

"Because I say so." Ray tapped David on the shoulder. "Run down and tell Mary I want her up here."

"Can we go swimming now?" young voices asked in three-part harmony, suddenly remembering what they'd been promised.

"Get Mary and we'll see." Short legs took off, galloping.

"What's it like, the thing in there?" Jeff asked.

Ray rubbed his eyes, noted his headache was gone and his back only sore. He rotated his shoulders, standing upright with only one cane to stabilize him for the first time since Mary put him down. He could still taste the adrenaline in the dryness of his throat, the fear in the queasiness of his stomach. Yet he was feeling better than he had in a long time. "I don't know."

"I'll make sure the kids are getting Mary."

"Have her bring a laser drill and a materials analyzer. Air sniffer, too. I want to know everything about that place." Ray spoke to Jeff's retreating back, then turned back to the cave mouth. "I want to know everything you can tell me, old friend."

Two hours later, Ray knew the cave walls were made of a long-fiber ceramic that required special manufacturing and didn't belong in a cave, and the rock column showed no evidence of any activity—animal, vegetable, or electromagnetic. What had been in there? Sitting to meet the kids at their eye level, he looked into their faces. "You saw an old man." They nodded, eyes deep and solemn. "You saw places, buildings, other worlds."

"Yes," David said. "Lovely places," Rose agreed. "Can we go there?" Jon asked.

"I don't know." Ray rubbed his face; would anyone believe him if he told what he'd seen? Him and three kids with tumors in their heads. Was it real, or a figment of illness? Damn, he knew what pain and meds could do to a man's reality. Still, he'd never lost his grip on the real like this. Ray gnawed his lip and weighed his options, found them all wanting, and stood.

Only when he was up once more did it hit him how easy it was. "Damn." He did a quick survey of his pain level; nothing was screaming. *Face it: Something has changed.* Who would believe him? He stepped to where Mary stood eyeing the cave.

"Nothing we took in there showed a thing," she said, looking Ray up and down. "So what's going on out here, Colonel?"

Ray glanced down. "Nothing I want to talk about just now."

Mary nodded. "Same thing in there. Nothing I want to talk about at the moment either. Maybe nothing at all." She rotated her shoulders. "Maybe I should have had less fried chicken."

Ray shivered. "Need some time to figure this one out."

"Yes, sir."

"Mr. Ambassador, sir," came from behind Ray in Rose's high-pitched voice. He turned to see her galloping toward him. "My momma wants to talk to you."

Ray took the commlink. "Ambassador Longknife here."

"Thank heavens. I know you planned to talk with me tonight, but I don't think this can wait. There are riots in Refuge. Several buildings are burning, including another fire at the archives. Mobs are roaming the streets, and our safety people cannot respond fast enough. We need help."

"We'll do our best. Does this happen often?"

"Mr. Ambassador, I assure you, we have not seen anything like this in our three-hundred-year history." Ray glanced at Jeff and Annie. They nodded agreement.

"So how come you have it now?"

"A number of problems seem to have all come up at once," San Paulo answered slowly. "Yesterday, Victoria locked Sterling Industries onto the copper standard. She'll accept no aluminum payments. That shook the market. Managers told people showing up for work today there might not be any work in a few days."

"That fast?" Ray asked incredulously.

"Jeff Sterling's with you. He'll tell you."

Jeff looked like he could, and might enjoy it, too.

Right now, Ray needed time and information. "Ms. San Paulo, I'll see what help I can get moving and call you back." Ray closed down the commlink, gave it to Rose, and turned to his team. "Folks, we have a problem. Mary, have Cassie get the metal back to base. Mary, Jeff, we've got to talk."

"Yessirs," answered Ray as he acquired a mule for immediate return. Ray tapped his commlink, got Barber. "Hell's a-popping. They've got riots in Refuge. We've got some interesting stuff here at the mine, and I want to see you as soon as I get back."

"Gosh, and I've had such a quiet day," the chief laughed. "Doc said he had something for you as soon as you get in."

"Great," Ray sighed. "I'll stop by the hospital first. Cassie'll have you a half trailer of metal in an hour."

"Good. I'll get the factories going."

"We'll need to talk about what you produce."

"I knew you'd say that," Barber groaned. "Base out before you ruin my day worse."

Ray chuckled grimly at the commlink, then turned to Jeff. "What's your sister up to?"

"Running for empress of the world. What do you know about economics, Mr. Ambassador?"

"About as much as an infantryman needs to," Ray said pointedly as Mary put the mule in gear.

"Then I'll be fast and simple. What you don't have is worth more than what you do. Gold was rare on Earth, thus valuable. Here, copper is both rare and in high demand for every tech application. You can use aluminum or iron, but copper's better. Hell, we use salt water for some stuff. My grand-something Jason staked out the only copper mine we've found. Best iron ore as well. As soon as the original salvage from *Santa Maria* ran out, we Sterlings became the only game in town. And since Dad died and Mom decided she'd prefer praying to running the business, Vicky calls the shots. Following me so far?"

"I think so."

"Now then, brother Mark locates a hill just full of bauxite up north. The psalm singers are none too happy to have us hard-drinking, going-to-hell miners show up. Big sis is even less happy. Mark's competition. Not only on the raw metal scene, but also bro Mark sets up factories, makes electric motors, communication gear, all kinds of things that compete with Vicky's one-hundred-percent market share."

"No monopolist welcomes competition," Ray nodded.

"That's the background; now we get to today's riots. We Sterlings run both the business and the financial life of this world. Copper is not only the critical feed for industry, it's also the basis for our money." Jeff fished in his pocket, produced two coins. "Most of this is ceramic. However, its center slug of copper makes it money. We've always had some aluminum-based money in circulation. That wasn't a problem until Mark struck it big time. Mark starts minting money, and the price of everything went up. Pissed off Vicky big time."

"Inflation," Ray nodded.

"Right; too much money chasing too few goods. Before we had deflation, a very limited copper-based money supply and a growing population producing more and more goods. Result, the value of everything went down. Except for what Vicky made. She kept her prices up or higher. The value of the goods and services used to pay for her products decreased. She got more for the same product. She loved it."

Ray folded his arms. "And the farmers hated it."

"Cost of a village phone system went from half a year's production to two years' worth of work in one generation, a generation that added a million more people. Old folks remember how far a copper dollar used to stretch. Grumble to the kids. Everyone gets mad," Jeff sighed. "Then along comes Mark's aluminum dollar. Folks have plenty of money. Deflation stops. Sis gets the same, maybe less value for the same product. Boy, did she squawk. As much as she could, she demanded copper coin for her stuff. Yesterday I guess she made it official. You want copper products, you pay in copper coin."

"Seems like your brother Mark would love it. Step right in and grab Vicky's market."

"He would, in another couple of years. He's not ready yet."

"A preemptive strike." Ray scowled. Economics might be economics, but he knew a war when he saw it. Still. "People are reacting awfully fast, taking to the streets and burning things when all they've been told is there might be problems."

Jeff nodded. "There's been a lot of talk lately. Your people and what you're going to do. Jonah's crazies. I don't know. Maybe this was just the straw that broke the bridge."

"Maybe," Ray agreed. Or maybe there was something more? The rational part of his mind had only scorn for the very question. The part he dreamed with was none too sure.

"Step on it, Mary." Ray hung on and wondered what Doc was so excited about. He also wondered what they could do to help Refuge. Twenty years of soldiering had taught him to look for his opponent's center of gravity. Ray still wasn't sure who his opposition was, much less what was important.

Mary followed Ray and Jeff into the hospital. The doc took one look at Ray walking in with a single cane for support, and waved him toward the scanner in Med Bay One. "What happened?" Jerry asked as Ray settled comfortably on the table.

"You tell me, Doc, and we'll both know."

"Looks like you've had as intriguing a day as I've had."

"Doc, you tell me your tale, then maybe I'll tell you mine."

"That bad?"

"Maybe that hard to believe," Ray growled. "Talk to me, Doc. Make me happy."

"Let me get this going," Doc said, worked his control board for a long minute, then came to stand beside Ray. "I've been taking blood from people all day, like a hungry vampire. Locals, first group down, latest arrivals. All have varying levels of virus in their blood. The longer down here, the more."

The control station for the scanner beeped happily that it was done. Doc returned to tap it, "hummed" noncommittally several times, then asked Ray, "You still need help off the table?"

Ray swung his legs over the side, positioned his cane as a safety measure, then eased himself off. "Not bad," Doc noted and glanced at Jeff. "Does he go everywhere you go?"

"Jeff has just become my chief of local intelligence, mores, rumors, and other duties as assigned." Ray frowned at the young man, raising the question with an eyebrow.

"I'm in," Jeff agreed.

"The smell that just got real thick in here, Doc, is Jeff's burning bridges," Mary laughed.

"Gosh, and I didn't bring any marshmallows. Welcome to our happy bunch of campers, Jeff." Doc offered his hand, then brightened. "Does this mean I can get a complete set of tissues and liquid samples from this man?"

Jeff yanked his hand back.

"Down, Doc," Ray chuckled. "I'm your guinea pig today. What kind of rumors is your meticulous scanner handing out?"

Doc got serious as he turned back to his analytical readouts. "Your back has knitted almost completely in the past twenty-four hours. I suspect I surprise you in no way when I tell you it shouldn't have happened. Wonder why?"

Ray shrugged, not yet willing to talk about his day.

Doc moved the scan results up to Ray's skull. "Brain mass has expanded downward. That might take some of the pressure off your skull. Let me check something." Three other images appeared. "Compare tumor masses against the brain's total mass," Doc ordered, then pointed as numbers appeared beside all four.

"Right. You and the kids have the same mass per brain weight, to within the third decimal."

"Any idea what that means?" Ray asked.

"Damned if I know." The good doctor shrugged. He called up a dozen different skull scans. "Anybody came in here today got a brain scan. You got a cold. You got hemorrhoids. You got a skull scan," Jerry chuckled. "Last was a bit hard to explain. Anyway, based on my incomplete random sample, you will note something interesting. These are organized by age, youngest at the top." He let each scan run for fifteen seconds. The ones at the top showed brightly colored patterns. The ones at the bottom showed significantly less.

"And that means?" Ray said.

"I haven't found a pattern to the size of the mass. Some have only a small one, others more. None has one anywhere near as large as you and the kids. However, there is a clear pattern by age. In older samples, activity is reduced. In the younger ones, that thing, whatever it is, is active as the dickens."

"Something is in our brains?" Jeff asked slowly.

"Some of us. Seems to depend on how long we've been down here," Jerry answered.

"What's this planet doing to us?" Mary breathed.

"That is something we'd better figure out before Matt gets back," Ray growled. "What do we do now?"

Jerry shook his head. "I can chase after what we've got here,"—he waved at the lab—"but I think Mary hit the nail on the head. What is the planet doing to us? We need to know a lot more about this place. What's its geological record? Where did it get three evolutionary tracks? Where do we fit in?"

Ray tapped the table. "We've got to start drilling rock cores. Is there a geologist on the planet?" he quipped. "Your people done any anthropology, dug up old bones?" Ray asked Jeff.

"Only geology we've done is for mineral surveys." Jeff seemed pained. "This has been our home. It just is. I guess we didn't question it much. Or maybe we just couldn't afford to question it." He ran down slowly. "There is Harry. He worked for Mark on his surveys. Spent a couple of weeks telling me all the different names for rocks and minerals. A bore . . . or so I thought at the time. Harry the Flak, we called him."

"And we can find this flak?" Ray urged.

"Lives outside Richland, in an old place full of core samples that he collected when he was working with us."

"How far is Richland from Refuge?"

"Couple hours' train ride. Less if you're driving a mule."

Ray nodded, tapped his commlink. "Kat, we're about to set up a temporary base in Refuge. I want you and Jeff to make a fast run up to Richland to see if we can hire a geologist. Draw weapons with sleepy bullets."

"Think that will be needed?" Kat answered.

"I hope not. I'd rather you took too much than too little."

"Yes, sir."

Ray stood. "Any more suggestions?" No one had any. "I better go see the chief."

Ray had forgotten how much fun it was to walk, just walk

rather than hobble. He relished each moment of the jaunt over to the HQ as the afternoon cooled and evening came on. Mary strode along beside him, beaming from ear to ear.

The talk with Barber went quickly. He gave a stoic sigh when Ray told him a security system for the base was his first priority and Ray needed the factories up yesterday. The chief was already working on that and had come across something interesting. "Mary got a surprising mix out of that hill. There's nothing in my manufacturing feed-stock database about so many minerals in a single batch except when you re-cycle electronic gear. Was that an electronic center, Colonel?"

Ray shrugged and added another piece to his puzzle. "Chief, go through your stores to see what we can use to help Refuge."

Barber rewarded that order with a twisted scowl. "And 'nothing' is not an acceptable answer."

"You got it in one."

Ray and Mary waited for Cassie in front of the HQ as twilight deepened. It was hard to believe, among the familiar smells of a cooling summer evening, that he was halfway across the galaxy on a world doing strange things to the innermost part of him. When Cassie parked, he and Mary settled into seats and launched right in. "Mary, I want you running the base. Cassie, you ready to help the Refuge security folks update their equipment and procedures?"

Cassie nodded. "Surveillance is what they mostly need. The communications gear will let them use what they learn. Pretty much what I helped Mary do back at the pass."

And Ray knew very well how good they'd been there.

"Mary, got any thoughts?" His chief of security shook her head. "Okay, Cassie, tell me what you'd want."

"How many mules can you spare me?"

"I think the chief said none. I'll get you at least two for starters, although I may be loaning one of them for a quick trip to Richland. Weapons?" Ray went on to the next issue.

"Usual load out of personal weapons. I'll leave the heavy stuff behind. Maybe a few charges in case we have to blow a bridge to keep things from spreading."

"Personnel?"

"I'd like two squads, mine and Tico's plus Lek. If we're setting up a communications and command network, I want Lek."

Mary was unhappy at that. "I need Lek here if anything goes bad on the manufacturing side. But I'll loan him for a while."

Ray nodded agreement to both, but refused to let something just as important get lost in the rush. "Tico's? She heads up the other street kids' squad. Why not Dumont's?"

"Both squads know their jobs." Cassie spoke slowly, seemed to weigh each word. "Maybe I want someone a bit more reluctant to shoot. It is peacekeeping you want?"

Ray eyed Mary. She shook her head. "It's their security service I think we have to worry about. They have no capability for lethal force. We do. I'm not sure we shouldn't have someone like Dumont available if we need them."

Cassie started to say something, swallowed it, and sat back in her seat to digest it. "Okay."

"I'm issuing you a case of sleepy bullets," Ray offered. "It'll take us three seasons to grow the feedstock to make more, so we'll have to be sparing with what we've got."

"Thanks," Cassie said.

Ray drummed his fingers on the seat beside him, balancing assignments against time. He tapped his commlink. "Chief, how soon can you have our spare gear loaded on the shuttle?"

"Give me an hour. I'll have an inventory in thirty minutes."

"Shoot a copy to Cassie as well."

"Fine. I've put the shuttle crew on notice for a thirty-minute launch."

"Good; I expect we'll be away in an hour, two at the most. I need two mules."

"I'm loading you three. I can stretch the product from Mary's work today to replace most of what I'm sending. Probably in the next week."

"That fast," Ray whistled. "I'm going, too. No use being an ambassador if you sit home all the time."

• • •

The shuttle circled Refuge, taking pictures, feeding them to Ray and Cassie's readers. Ray scowled and made a note to get the sky eyes back up. With the local survey done, the remotes had been put in storage to save wear and tear; Ray hadn't expected to need them. Expectations were rapidly changing.

"New fires," Cassie said, circled them on her display, and stored their address for when Lek got the network up between them and the locals. Ray eyed the fires. The city below was changing from lovely to war-torn. It made his blood boil.

"There are three blimps parked at the port," the shuttle commander reported. "We can set down, but it's gonna be a bit tight. Seat belt sign is lit. Cinch 'em in, boys and girls." The shuttle bucked as full flaps were applied. Ray switched to the live feed from the shuttle cameras. An unlit greensward lay dead ahead; looming bulks swayed in the gentle wind off to the left, near the hangars. The field looked clear until the camera zoomed in. Sheep grazed placidly up and down their runway.

"Didn't somebody tell them we were coming?" the shuttle commander growled into a hot mike. Ray had. Some idiot hadn't passed the word . . . or someone had ignored their orders. No SAMs today, but sheep could wreck a shuttle just as well.

"Let's see if we can send those critters elsewhere" came from the cockpit. Flaps and gear came up; the engines switched to full power.

Five minutes later, no sheep interrupted their landing roll. "Never seen four-legged critters exceed the speed of light before. Damn near left their wool behind," Cassie quipped.

But she was all business as the shuttle braked to a halt. "All hands, lock and load. Dumont, deploy your squad in an armed perimeter. First Squad, let's empty this shuttle before anyone notices it's down."

Ray took a seat in the second mule, next to Lek the electronic wizard he'd been surprised to find among the marines. He'd been even more surprised to discover that Lek had never been more than a miner. With an education, the man could have been another Edison, but an education was none too easy to get out on the rim of human space. That was one thing Ray and Wardhaven intended to change—assuming he ever got back and could continue what he and Rita had started.

As the mule went down the shuttle's brightly lit ramp into dark, Ray's night goggles struggled to adjust. He tapped his commlink. "Ms. San Paulo, this is Ray Longknife. I've got a security detachment at the blimpport. Where are you?"

"I'm at the Hall of the Great Circle. Can you find it?"

Lek tapped his display; a block in the center of the city glowed yellow. "Got it."

"No problem. We'll be there in fifteen minutes."

"Be careful. We've got roving gangs. Some are looters. Others are looking for a fight—each other, security, anyone. Mr. Longknife, I don't understand this."

"I never have either. But we'll put them in their place. Longknife out." Lek stopped beside the first mule off. Kat and Jeff were in the front seat of that one, just putting on their night vision gear. Lek hopped out and unhitched its trailer.

"I want you to head straight for Richland," Ray told Kat, "find this Harry, and get back here before dawn. Cassie!" Ray shouted over his shoulder.

"Yes, sir."

"Assign Dumont to provide security for this rig."

"Yes, sir. Dumont, you heard the man. You're riding shotgun for Mule One."

"Right." A shadow came quickly out of the dark where he'd been making rounds, checking his squad and the perimeter they guarded. Dumont did a one-handed leap into the mule and settled with a grin into the backseat. "What you want, boss?"

"See these people get back safely. Use whatever force necessary."

"A license to kill," the kid crowed.

"Not unless you have to," Ray growled.

"Yeah, sir. Kill only those you want killed, when you want 'em killed, sir. And don't interrupt what you're doing to ask if I got the right head ready to blow off, sir." The kid's face slid from unadulterated pleasure to something new. Part insolence, part pensive, part something else. For a moment Ray considered delving into that more deeply, but Kat gunned the mule, and the moment for questioning shot into the dark. What had Ray just turned loose? With a shrug, he turned back to Lek.

"He's always been a hard case," the old miner commented. "Where to, sir?"

"The Hall of the Great Circle," Ray ordered.

It took a moment to attach a second trailer to the last mule, load the rifle teams in, and start moving. Holding their speed down, they drove up one of the wide boulevards that bisected the city. A flaming building cast flickering light over a large crowd halfway down the avenue. Lek glanced at the mule's map display, then turned right. "Know where the public buildings are, sir? They seem to be the ones they're burning."

Ray sighed his frustration at the lack of info. Ahead, another building burst into flames; Ray's night goggles struggled to adapt to a world shared by fire and darkness. Lek braked to a halt slowly, giving the more heavily loaded rig behind him plenty of room. Which gave Ray's eyes time to adjust. On his third sweep he spotted movement several blocks down the road they were on; a mass of people coming at them. For a moment, Ray considered charging them, guns blazing. Lek turned the rig into a side street. "Colonel, we can't back these rigs!" Lek shouted. "We get caught in midblock by a group and we're sludge!"

"I hear you," Ray snapped. His skin crawled with an itch he couldn't scratch. He'd been in fights before; civic disturbances, too. He'd never felt like this. Ray glanced at the map; they were headed out of town and away from the blimpport. "Keep going this way for a few minutes; then we'll try a side road. See if we can get into town that way."

"Any way is good by me," Lek answered.

"What was that all about?" Jeff asked. Kat just shook her head, eyes straight ahead on the dark road. "You know, between the boss and him," he indicated the young man with a rifle in the back of the mule. Again, Kat said nothing.

"Go ahead, tell him. I won't mind." When Kat still said nothing, the fellow leaned forward, leering face less than a foot from Jeff's, rifle barrel even closer. "I'm the boss's murdering dog." Having said his piece, he lounged back into the seat, gun lolling between his legs. "She don't like that."

"A lot of us don't. We liked Guns. He was a good old guy."

Jeff didn't understand a word they were saying. Maybe he was wrong about how much the language had changed in three hundred years. Or maybe the people just had.

"The admiral said execute the floater. I did the joke. What's that to you?"

Kat snapped her head around. "That bastard had no right to give you that order. It was illegal. You should have known that. You must have! Guns was right. The admiral was wrong. Why'd you kill him?"

"You expect street scum like me to know all that? Hell, I've watched cops break a kid's arms 'cause they didn't like the way he looked at 'em. Life's cheap, girl, if you got a gun and it's not your own life."

"It doesn't have to be like that."

"Maybe not for you, miss goody-goody with a college diploma, but it is for me. How many fights you been in?"

"*Sheffield* was in two," Kat answered proudly.

"That's not a fight," the man spat. "Not those nice, clean things you navy pukes have where you take your ship with you and have a shower and clean sheets waiting for you when it's over. A real fight's where the artillery makes the ground shake under you until your gut runs water and your damn suit's sanosystem decides it don't have to process your shit no more 'cause it was made by the lowest bidder and a real war's outside the contract specs. Or when your sights dial in perfect on some face *they* decided is the enemy and you get a really great picture of this face just before you blow it off her.

"Shit, woman, you wouldn't last five seconds in a real fight. But take one of us rags or rages with fifteen, eighteen years on the street, we're perfect for it. We're just the dogs and bitches you want to turn loose on ones you don't like. 'Course, any other time, you got to muzzle us, chain us up. What you think that ship is? Just a kennel for the likes of me." The man in the back seemed to have run out of words. He rode, staring silently at his rifle.

Jeff listened, hearing the rage, the agony behind the

words, understanding only a little. He wondered just how deadly the weapon in the man's hands was, and wishing he didn't have it.

Kat took in a long breath, drove with both eyes on the road, both hands stiffly on the wheel, and began to talk. "That's Dumont's side of the story. Maybe it's true. I was drafted fresh out of college. You understand draft?" Jeff nodded; he'd read in the ancient histories of involuntary servitude for military purposes. "Dumont and his friends came in a little less formally. They were dragged up off the streets one night and signed themselves in. Du, can you sign your name?" she called over her shoulder.

"Couldn't then," he whispered.

"I got lucky and drew ship duty. Du got infantry."

"Marine by-God-be-damned infantry," came a correction from the backseat.

"After we survived a couple of battles and thought our way home from a bad jump, we got promoted to flagship and this marine detachment assigned to us."

"Nobody asked us. They just told us to go, and we went."

"In case you hadn't noticed, Du, that was the way it was with all of us. That's the way it is in a war."

"That's the way it is on the streets all the time. I didn't notice a difference." Dumont leaned forward in his seat, the rifle across his lap, apparently forgotten.

Kat nodded but went on. "So our skipper called this meeting with all the department heads. This little corporate twirp who hasn't been in the navy any longer than me, but somehow has gotten himself made an admiral, announced he'd figured out how to win the war in an afternoon. Slaughter about a billion people, everybody on a planet. Guns didn't agree." Kat glanced at Jeff, must have seen the puzzlement in his eyes.

"Guns, what we called the chief of gunnery, the nicest grandpa of a guy you could ever hope to meet. He tells this jerk that not only is his brilliant idea stupid *and* illegal, but it will make the Unity folks madder than hell and they'll fight us all the harder. Boss guy's reaction to that is to order Du back there to off Guns. And brilliant guy that Du is, he does."

"It was an order." Dumont defended himself in a dead

monotone. "Besides, he said he'd make us all rich if we did what he told us."

"Did he?"

"No."

"Did you?" Jeff asked in a whisper.

"Did we do what?" Kat's eyes were back on the road.

"Kill a billion people?"

"No," Kat said, casting a quick glance back at Dumont.

"No, we didn't kill anyone. The war ended. They put the muzzle back on us dogs, and that was that." There had to be more to the story. But neither Kat nor Dumont was talking, and Jeff couldn't begin to construct a question that might get them talking again. They rode in silence for a very long minute.

"Here, you take the gun." Dumont tossed the rifle at them.

Jeff caught it by the barrel; the stock landed on the floor of the backseat. He looked at it, terrified, trying to remember where the safety was. Kat glanced at it. "Don't worry, Jeff. The safety's on. It can't fire. Du, what you doing?"

"I'm quitting. I've had it. You want someone joked, you pop 'im yourself. You the one that sicced that priest on me?"

"No. What priest?"

"Father Joseph. He wouldn't leave me alone today. One of you brains tell him about me?"

"Du, in case you haven't noticed, I've been full-time busy trying to figure out which end of this planet is up. Besides, I'm not Catholic. I don't know if any middies are." Kat slowed down. "Why? What did the preacher have to say to you?"

"He didn't say anything. Least, not at first. Just hung around me like I was some virgin he was horny for. No, like I had the dust and he wanted a fix. No. I don't know. He was just there, every time I turned around."

"So why didn't you tell him to get lost?" Kat asked. "Your team isn't exactly known for putting up with anything you think is shit."

"I did. So he asked me what I was doing. That miner Mary had me working with was running the thumper all over that damn hill. I told the little priest we were making sounds to tell

Mary what the hill looked like inside. It was kind of nice, talking to him. Next thing I know, my miner's been called away and me and the priest are humping that thumper all over that hill. He may be short, but damn, that guy could lug. I kept on talking to him. He listened to whatever I said. So I ended up telling him about the war and all that shit and how I joked Guns and how I wish I hadn't." Du closed down suddenly, like Vicky did when she thought she'd given something away for free.

Kat took them smoothly around a curve. The night stretched out ahead of them; it was damp this close to the James River. Its river barges and dams made Refuge and Richland possible.

"What did he have to say to that?" Kat finally asked.

"That it was never too late to start over. That life was always giving second chances. Or maybe he said God was. I don't know." Du snickered. "Stupid old asshole. The streets don't give no second chances."

"We got a second chance," Kat said softly. "Nobody ever came back from a sour jump. We did. Mary damn near killed Ray in the war. Did leave him crippled. They're giving each other a second chance. There're a lot of reasons that damn boat is named *Second Chance*. You could be one of them."

"That's what the priest said. But look at me now. First time the damn Colonel needs somebody popped, he yanks my chain."

"You sure?"

"Why else dump me here but so I can joke shit for you two?"

"Maybe the Colonel assigned you 'cause you're good at your job."

"Good at what job?" Du snorted.

"Good at knowing what's dangerous and making it not. Good at scaring the shit out of people and maybe saving their lives by making them go someplace else real fast. I don't know, Du, but I feel safer with you in the backseat, and not because I figure you'll shoot everybody we happen to see."

The man in the backseat stared off into the night, slowly

rubbing his chin. "That the way you see me?" he asked finally.

"Yes, Du. That's you. Not just the cool dude you want all the other street rags and rages to see, but the guy I see, too. The guy who didn't shoot the next time the admiral started shouting for you to."

"Yeah, I didn't shoot then. And you were real close."

"Scary close, Du."

"Can I have my rifle back?"

Jeff glanced at Kat; she gave him a quick nod. He handed the weapon very carefully back. "Thanks," the man said.

"You're welcome," Jeff answered. Du half smiled, half sneered at the automatic politeness. "I meant it," Jeff added.

They rode into the darkness. Or maybe out of it.

Ray advanced his team slowly, holding a tight rein on their speed—and on his own frustration. Ahead, scouts ranged three blocks forward, checking each cross street before signaling them forward and hustling up the street to check the next one. It made for safe but slow going.

"Mr. Ambassador, are you there?"

"Yes, Ms. San Paulo."

"You may call me Hen if you wish."

"I'm Ray to my friends. Were you able to get us any help?"

"Our security force has some electrocycles. They might scout for you. Where are you?" Ray read the closest street signs. "Oh, that far out. Let me tell them where you are."

Ray studied the town houses lining this block. Two, three stories high, they provided several windows for snipers, but all were closed and darkened. People slept behind them, or they were empty as their occupants roamed the streets, looking for a violent solution to a problem Ray didn't understand and that probably eluded them, too. What had gone wrong with this planet? Was it also swallowing him?

San Paulo came back on. "The cyclists are moving. They should meet you in ten or fifteen minutes."

"Good. Ray out."

"'Bye."

Ray gritted his teeth, forcing down a rising anger that had

no explanation. Quickly, he advised his teams to be on the lookout for their allies.

"Slow going, but looks okay," Lek observed beside him.

"That's not what's bothering me," Ray said, picking one from several. "Riots are only the symptom. What's the underlying cause? The farmers seem nice. The city types had quirks but didn't look all that bad."

"I've worked for bosses who had smiles for the visiting firemen but were hell on the miners," Lek observed to the street ahead of them. "Kind of hard to peg an outfit when you're on a whirlwind tour. Finally decided upper management wasn't dumb or nasty, just uninformed and blind."

Ray couldn't argue that point. Hell, Unity had talked a good line. Right up to the point they started hanging people. "God, I'd like to dig through these folks' archives. Newspapers, media, something to get the feel of the real them," Ray said, addressing something he could.

Beside him, Lek grinned. "Glad you said that, sir. While I'm doing their security net, I just might find time to put in a few extra nodes. You want all their news and media?"

"All you can poke a link into." What had Mary and Matt said about the joys of having on staff a paranoid electronic genius with a sense of humor? This might get interesting.

The cyclists joined up. Adding his armed scouts to the backseats of the three-wheeled get-abouts let Ray dodge two mobs early and avoid three fires. They made it to the Great Hall in a half hour, but it did nothing to calm Ray's roiling temper.

Jeff missed his turn in the dark, and Kat had to do a U-turn back to the road into Sterlingview. Like most of the towns within a short trolley ride of Richland, all the houses had been designed to two or three floor plans. Over the years, residents had personalized them. Two they drove by in the twisting, turning streets had recently been very personalized—by fires. Jeff couldn't begin to guess what was going on, but something new and ugly was sweeping the world he'd grown up in.

Harry's place was blessedly still there, and easy for Jeff to spot. His yard was a blend of hearty earth plants and various local bushes he'd collected in his travels. Kat eased to a halt before the rambling two-story. Jeff was out before she'd brought the mule to a complete stop; he trotted up the gravel walk and took the four steps to the porch two at a time. He knocked softly.

After a minute he rapped louder. The house was dark, as was every other house they'd driven by. Not even a porch light?

Jeff glanced up. Streetlights were visible with his goggles; they did not burn. Jeff stepped back, checking the windows. Someone peeked out an upper one. He pointed at it, and the curtains slipped shut. Jeff went back to the door, knocked once, then began beating a slow, insistent tattoo.

Finally the door opened a crack. "Who are you?"

Jeff didn't recognize the face. He pulled the night goggles up. As he opened his mouth, it dawned on him that for the first time in his life, his name might not open doors. "Hello, I'm a friend of Harry's. I need to talk to him."

"Harry doesn't need friends like you," he heard, but the door opened wider. Harry stood behind the man at the door. He rested a restraining hand on the younger man's hand, the one holding a baseball bat.

"Come on in, Jeff. Who are your friends?"

"Starfolks. Can they come in?"

"Sure, sure." Harry waved in his open, friendly way. Kat did something to the mule's steering, then trotted up the walk. Du followed her, walking backward, rifle at eye level, the barrel sweeping wide, in sync with his eyes. Even if Kat hadn't told him, Jeff would have known it now; Du scared people.

Jeff and company slipped through the door to be pointed toward the back of the house. Using his night goggles, Jeff had no trouble following the hall back to Harry's study. In it, a small candle burned, throwing fitful light over a collection of books and rocks. On the couch, a woman huddled, arms around two children. She gasped as Du entered the room.

Du took it in stride. He glided to the back window and took a long look out. "Sorry, ma'am. I have that effect on people." He turned to Kat. "Looks clear. Somebody want to update me on the situation?"

Jeff was a veteran of too many of Vicky's pushy binges; he knew how to push back. The quiet tone of Du's voice left him with a uncontrollable compulsion to please the man.

"Your sister announced layoffs yesterday morning," the young man said. "No warning, no idea when anyone might be called back. Rumor is she's been building up product in the warehouses to meet two or three months of demand. Now, with her wanting copper, who knows how long it will last."

"She also said she wouldn't release paychecks until the end of the month," the young woman said, "and then they'll be short."

"Vicky was always the milk of human kindness," Jeff drawled. "What did she expect people to do?"

Harry's mouth lifted in a bent smile. "There were buses to take protesters to Refuge, to demand the Great Circle immediately abolish aluminum coins."

"Did many go?" Kat asked.

"Some," the young man said, the baseball bat still in his hand. "I don't think half of the buses were filled. Me, I called Dad and asked if we could move in. He said yes, so I spent the time lugging our stuff over here."

"Why'd you move?" Du asked.

"I don't know." The man looked at his wife. "Greens say we're making a mess of this world. Street preachers say the end is coming. People getting more and more twitchy. Our apartment complex was right next to a shopping center. Food stores, small shops, and a liquor store. It got broken into. Then the others. Somehow they started burning."

"You figured on trouble," Kat said.

Both young people nodded, eyes on their sleeping children. "It's been coming since last year," Harry told Jeff, "when your sister took to paying everyone in aluminum. Prices went up. Wages didn't. There're hungry people on those streets, son."

"And sis didn't see this coming!"

"Maybe she did. Maybe she thought she could aim it at something she wanted taken down. You can never tell with her."

"And you can never tell her anything. Less lately," Jeff

concluded. "Harry, I got some people here who need your help."

Kat quickly ran down their discovery of the planet's unusual flora and fauna . . . and the strange impact it was having on the humans. "We really need to know this planet's natural history. Jeff said you might be able to tell us something."

"I didn't think it was like this on other planets." The old man enjoyed his vindication for a moment. Even as he did, he was searching his bookshelf for binders, notebooks, and rock samples. "I keep a complete backup," he said, flourishing a box of disks. "It's yours."

Kat took the offered box. "We'd like you to come, too."

"I can't leave my family."

"Dad, if anybody saw these people come here tonight, Jeff and them, maybe you'd better be gone."

"Harold, but what about us?" the woman asked from the couch. "The way people are . . ." she trailed off. The young man looked from his wife and children to his father, lips tightly pursed.

The old man shook his head. "I can't leave them."

Du frowned. "Kat, these people can't stand against whatever is out there. Can we take them?"

"With the automated plants up, there ought to be jobs for them. Harry, my people really need to talk to you. I'll take the whole lot of you as a package deal."

Without a second word, the father lifted a child of six from the couch. The wife hoisted another of maybe three. Jeff helped Harry with a box of rocks. After snuffing out the candle, Du trailed them through the house, Kat just ahead of him, the disks in one hand. A small automatic had appeared in the other.

Jeff pushed the front door open, then held it wide as Harry and his family went through. He followed them, leaving the door to Kat—and came to a dead halt on the porch.

Around the mule, a crowd of thirty people milled. Several had clubs, two torches. "I told you I saw Jeffie Baby right here in our neighborhood. Come to visit his old friend, didn't he?" That brought murmurs of agreement, and a shout that they should have burned them out with the others. The son and wife recoiled against Jeff and Harry. Kat interposed herself to Jeff's left.

The mob started forward—and froze in midstride.

Du came around Harry, rifle held high. Du pulled the arming bolt back; it recoiled into place with a well-oiled ratcheting sound. The rifle rested easy on Du's hip. He eyed the mob; confronted by coiled death in black, the crowd stepped back.

"These people, and their home"—Du raised his chin to the house behind him—"are under my protection." The goggled, insectoid eyes moved over the crowd as if recording their faces. "You don't want anything to happen to it. Understand?"

Heads nodded.

"Now, if you'll move away from the truck . . ."

People stared at the mule, as if seeing it for the first time. Those nearest quickly took two steps back, then, once in motion, seemed to think well of the idea and kept going. In a moment the street was empty, two torches guttering out.

"I told you," Kat said, moving toward the rig, "you're good at what you do. Everybody into the car."

Du glanced at Kat and nodded. "I guess I am." He glided from the porch to the car, like a shadow at home in the night. Opening one door, he helped Harry and his family into the backseat. A lot of humanity crammed itself into not enough space.

Jeff measured the front seat and weighed the prospects of walking over to the mansion to borrow a cycle. Du shoved him into the seat, then stood between his legs, holding on to the front window. "Move us out, Kat," he ordered.

She did a quick U-turn, gunned the engine, and zoomed through the twisting streets at double the speed they'd come in. Here and there something moved among the bushes and trees that lined the road. Nothing got in their way.

Ray let Cassie explain how they would help Refuge; if he did any talking, he'd bite off heads. Lek was already down the hall, setting up a command post. While two spacers installed the borrowed stuff, local technicians strung cable from where the archives still smoldered. Until recently it had served as the central hub of what passed for a local government network.

All workstations available were being moved to Lek's command post.

At a screen in front of the room Cassie launched into an examination of the techniques of crowd control used by Humanity. "Rifles can disburse large crowds quickly," she told the gathered leaders of Refuge, then added dryly, "however, they have the unfortunate side effect of leaving dead bodies and angry memories in their wake. We don't want to go there." Most nodded.

"I don't know," came from the back. "They burn a building down, beat up some old folks. Why be nice to them? A bullet will get their attention real quick and keep it." Hum, maybe Ray and the rioters weren't the only ones feeling itchy.

Ms. San Paulo turned. "Gaspier, that might solve today's problem, but it would hardly help tomorrow's. We must take the long view."

"We take too long a view, and we won't be in it."

"Go on, Cassie," Ms. San Paulo overspoke the rejoinder.

Cassie started a familiar video. Good lord, Ray remembered it from his Academy days. Well, mobs hadn't changed much in twenty years. Why should mob control? The day had been long and hard. The room was hot after the cool night air. Ray let himself nod off; this he could sleep through.

Ray was in a room, arms tied painfully behind him. The light of a single, unshaded bulb glared down, giving him a headache. The rest of the room was dark. Ray closed his eyes to save them from the glare. Something slapped him; his eyes shot open. Two beefy men, sleeves rolled up, stood before him. One had a length of rubber hose. He raised it again.

"Where is he?" the hose wielder growled.

"Who?" Ray croaked.

"The Gardener. Where is he?"

"The Gardener," Ray echoed. "We talked. He told me stuff."

"What stuff?"

With the rubber hose hanging over him, Ray couldn't remember a word. "I don't know. Just stuff. Nice stuff. He wanted me to know stuff. Feel things," Ray said, remembering.

"The Gardener was not the Teacher. He was just a Gardener. Where is he?" The rubber hose came down.

Ray came awake with a start. Surrounded by strangers, he glanced up, confused, afraid. And spotted Cassie. Ray shook himself fully awake, made a mental note never to fall asleep when police films were on tap, and rose to visit the rest room while the video finished. Cane tapping on the marble floor, Ray shivered. His unconscious mind was having a field day. Now he recalled the old crime holovid his mind had dredged that scene from. If ever he needed a reason to stay awake in briefings, nightmares like that would do it.

Back in the room, Cassie was showing slides of the latest in riot fashion: helmets, face protectors, shields, leg protectors, rubber clubs. Standing at the door, Ray found himself with a new attitude toward clubs. Suddenly they looked a lot more persuasive than he usually credited them.

"Looks like a hockey uniform," one official opined.

"That's great! We run around to all the athletic clubs, mooching their uniforms. We gonna borrow the players, too?"

"Why not? We need more people on the riot line. You saw the star woman's charts. Have so many riot police that the mob is afraid to riot. Last year, at the flood, we had plenty of volunteers stuffing sandbags."

"That was last year. How many of the guys out on the streets are hockey club members?" Ray listened to the voices go back and forth, like storm-tossed waves around a rock-strewn coast. This was more like the meetings he'd attended on Wardhaven, full of sound and fury, going nowhere.

"Mr. Ambassador," Ms. San Paulo cut in, "where might we get shields like those? Or helmets?"

"We make them from ceramics, but we'll need feedstock. We've been hitting the locals around our base pretty heavily."

"We'll give you whatever support we can," Ms. San Paulo assured him, to doubtful faces from about half of her circle. Lek appeared at the door beside Ray. Conversation ceased.

"I've got the com center started," Lek announced. "Your

folks can take it from here. We saw some blimps at the field. They'd make good observation platforms with a radio and camera aboard. I don't want to send crews out to install security cameras on the roads until I can provide them overhead support. Can we use a blimp or two?"

Ms. San Paulo glanced around the room. "You can have all of them for now. Haven and the Covenanters have halted all travel from the Refuge–Richland area until we regain control. Personally, I think they have problems of their own and do not want to admit it. The blimps are available. Use them."

"We'll also use a few to run between here and the base," Ray added. "The shuttle's fuel is limited."

Lek dismissed himself; Ray followed him. "What's going on here? People who filled sandbags last year are rioting this year. Was it really that nice before? What's changed? You get us into their news archives?"

"Done, boss. Feed's being squirted direct to base. A middie's already mining it." Ray sent Lek on his way. Back in the room, the meeting was breaking up into acrimonious debate. About what he expected of politicians. After five more minutes of it, San Paulo tabled all issues pending a good night's sleep—as if anyone there was likely to get one—and suspended the Circle until ten o'clock tomorrow.

Cassie came up beside Ray. "Colonel, I'll make the rounds of the guard posts. I saw you nodding off during the video. You didn't look any better after your catnap. If Mary was here, she'd push you straight for a bed. If you don't do it for me, she'll be kicking my ass next time she sees me."

Ray started to tell Cassie to mind her own damn business. Only twenty years of hard discipline, twenty years of harder-earned leadership held him in check. And that by a thin string.

Hen cackled from one clump of knotheads to another. His time would be better spent getting some shut-eye. Ray turned away, letting Cassie edge him down the hall to a small clinic that had been turned into a dorm. Cassie's troops had laid bedrolls in the aisles between high-raised hospital-type beds. Ray had a room to himself. He didn't take his boots off; tonight he'd better be ready to straighten out any screwup that came his way. Laying back in the bed, he closed his eyes.

• • •

And was back in the counsel room. Only this time, the room was vast, stretching out in all directions. The table seemed to have no end, either. Gathered around it were thousands, maybe a million men, all wearing the same gray robe. All with the same white hair. All with the same solemn face—identical in nose, mouth, eyes. One turned to Ray. "Where is the Gardener? He was here a short while ago. He sent a message. We have come in response to it. He is not here. Where is he?"

Ray did not want a repeat of his last dream. "He was here today when he last spoke to me. Where he is now, I don't know."

"If you do not know, we will teach you." The robed one frowned and turned back to the table. Ray himself frowned at that confused and confusing answer. Ignored and offered no explanation, Ray wandered down the table, studying each council member, if that was what they were. This had to be a dream. He'd had some dillies lately; here was another.

On close review, the people seated at the table were not identical. Their robes, though uniformly cut and blandly gray, showed different wear patterns. Some were quite worn, others almost new. A few were patched, and rather poorly at that. One man was missing an arm. Interesting. Alike, but not alike.

One of the robed ones raised a hand. A server in white wig and tight pants, a costume Ray had seen on the concierge staff of very expensive hotels, appeared, an empty tray held high in one hand. The two exchanged words in a whisper; then a silver cup appeared on the tray and the server offered it to the robed one with a flourish, then stepped back. Interesting way of doing things, Ray observed about this dream. He sidled up to the server. "Who are all these?"

The attendant eyed him, conveying in one haughty glance both dismay at his ignorance and his presence. "You were poorly prepared. This is the Teacher."

Ray noted the use of the singular for this very expansive group—and the expectation that he should know all this.

Ray pressed on. "What do they teach?"

"All that is known and knowable," the servant answered without looking away from his masters.

Ray didn't like the sound of that. Somehow he could not picture Kat ever accepting that her professors knew everything there was to know. "And who do they teach?"

Another sidelong glance, dripping with disdain for such an obvious question. "The Three, of course."

The Three, Ray echoed to himself. Before he could form a question, visions of cities and planets began to play in his head. They had a familiar feel to them. He'd seen them with the Gardener. He knew, without question, that he was seeing, remembering, the salient facts about the Three. One of the robed ones turned from the table. "Where is the Gardener?"

Ray weighed the question. Did it come from a teacher or the Teacher? He'd already said he didn't know where the Gardener was. Ray reran the final scene in the cave. "I guess he died," Ray said slowly. "At least that was what it looked like. He seemed to be falling to pieces. Old age. He said it had never happened to him before. I think he died."

"Died?" The word fell from the lips of the robed one as if it had no content.

"Yes. It appeared his existence came to an end."

"That is not possible," his interrogator said, looking Ray up and down. "There must be something wrong with your education. You should have spent more time in your studies." Their eyes locked. Ray looked deep into them, seemed to fall into them. He was in school. Not at the Academy, but a school that embraced an entire planet. A school that taught all there was to know or could be known. A school that . . .

Ray came awake with a start, heart pounding, mouth dry. Teeth clenched, he wanted to hit something. Instead, he checked his wrist unit; it was two in the morning. He lay back, waiting for his heart to slow, willing his body to relax. The itch he'd felt on the drive in was stronger now. He wanted to . . . what? Hit something? Burn something? Run riot through the streets? Oh, yes, he was definitely in the mood.

His bladder had its own needs. He made the required pilgrimage to the facilities down the hall, stepping over sleeping troops. Done, Ray weighed his alternatives for the night, then splashed cold water on his face, waking himself fully. He did not want to sleep again, not if it meant revisiting some of the places his sleep had taken him of late. Not if it meant letting loose whatever it was that he seemed to share with the rioters. He'd always prided himself on his iron control; tonight was no time to lose it. He tapped his commlink.

Lek answered. "Aren't you up early, Colonel?"

"Aren't you up late?"

"Just finished installing cameras and comm gear on three blimps. Rigged two with the solar arrays and fuel cells I stripped out of Mule One. That'll keep 'em up twenty-four hours a day. It's been a busy night."

If he'd cannibalized that mule . . . "Kat and company back from their little jaunt?"

"A hour ago. Brought back an entire family. She and an old fart she found are swapping info packets faster than any net."

The outline of an action plan was forming in Ray's head. "You got us a downfeed from their news and media?"

"Running. Base is getting an eyeful. Also the archives. Don't know if they'll be much help. They're pretty corrupted."

Ray breathed out slowly. Forced himself to compose words that should have come to him with practiced ease. "Good on all accounts, Lek. You, Kat, and company hang close to the shuttle. We'll be heading back first thing today."

"Trouble, sir?"

"Don't know, but I want to be ready for it."

Ray called the base. "Duty office, Third-Class-Petty-Officer-Chin. How-may-I-help-you, sir?" shot back to him.

"Colonel Longknife here. Advise Captain Rodrigo I want a meeting at oh nine hundred tomorrow with her, doc, and if she can lay her hands on him, Father Joseph."

"I'll advise them both as soon as their commlinks show

them awake, sir. I'll send a marine to invite the padre. I think he has an early-morning Mass."

"Thank you. Longknife out."

Ray glanced at his wrist. He had a good three hours to test the craziest ideas ever to come from his mouth. Still, if even half of the absurdities he was playing with matched reality here, he might be saying the most important words he'd ever spoken. Possibly that any human being had ever spoken.

EIGHT

RAY DISMOUNTED THE shuttle, the familiar smells of farms and cooling lander accompanying him. Just being away from Refuge seemed to have a calming effect on his troubled gut. Mary waited in the first mule. As Jeff helped Harry settle his family in the second, Mary nodded at Dumont. "What's he doing here?"

"Doesn't want to be my murdering dog anymore," Ray answered softly. "Got a job for him here?"

"Always need troops in the motor pool. We're lugging food in from farther away."

From the open hatch of the shuttle, Dumont listened. "Can I leave my rifle behind?"

"Du," Mary shot back, "I don't think folks would mind if you left your clothes behind. They just want our coppers."

Ray turned on his heel. "You can if you want, Dumont, but think on it carefully. You saw what was going on last night. If you find yourself in a situation, you can always choose not to use the rifle you've got. You can't use the one you don't have."

"I'll think about it, Colonel."

"Do that, Du."

An hour later, fed and up to date on the base's status, Ray settled into his place in the conference room. The chairs and table were the usual cheap, imitation wood, on loan from the wardroom of *Second Chance,* standard issue to any military unit in human space. The room's walls had come out a beige identical on military installations since, Ray suspected, Alexander the Great's campaign tent.

To his right, Mary waited, expectant. Beside her, Kat yawned. Was she finally getting too old for all-nighters? Doc Isaacs sat next, intently going over his reader; that settled who went first this morning. At the foot of the table, Lek sat next to the padre, whose hands were folded, eyes closed, asleep, or lost in meditation. Jeff and the new recruit, Harry, sat close on Ray's left. They'd been talking when they came in. Now they eyed their surroundings, waiting.

Ray cleared his throat. "I'm told you should never look a gift horse in the mouth. This planet was here when the crew of *Santa Maria* was desperate." Nods from the left side of the table. "Still, this gift extracts a price. The extent of that price has yet to be determined. Doc, you want to brief the new folks on what you've found?"

Doc quickly explained the tumors in the Santa Marians and their rapid appearance in the landing party. His new listeners showed dismay as the briefing went on.

"What's it mean?" Jeff asked.

Doc shrugged. "Damned-if-I-know. We've got the tumors. They appear to be benign. I've found what looks like frag-ments of two different unknown viruses in our blood."

"Two!" Ray asked. "Does it take both to grow a tumor?"

"Maybe, maybe not." Doc looked around the table. "Any of you folks remember sneezing, scratchy throats, watery eyes, itchy skin the day you came down?" Every member of the landing party nodded before half the question was asked.

"Any of you having any more allergic reactions?"

Blank stares.

"Now, me"—Doc leaned back in his chair—"I'm allergic to damn near everything in the Milky Way. Nearly flunked my draft physical for allergies."

"No," came in awestruck sarcasm from the marines and Kat.

"Yes, boys and girls, it *is* possible to flunk a draft physical.

You're looking at someone whose allergies almost pulled it off." Doc Isaacs paused. "And who showed no allergic reaction to any samples in the test kits this morning? I may actually get myself a cute kitten."

"This means . . ." Ray left the question hanging.

"Every white cell I got has changed beyond recognition. Couldn't have an allergic reaction to save my life. Which, taken at face value, scares the hell out of me. We are *supposed* to be allergic to some stuff. Doesn't matter. My lymph nodes and the white cells they're pumping out will accept anything."

"That can't happen overnight!" Kat insisted.

"Right. Can't. Did. You do the math," Doc shot back.

"One of the viruses?"

"Maybe. All I got so far are fragments in our blood. I'm testing the atmosphere for complete samples."

Ray mulled that over. Guesses. Just guesses. *Like his dreams.* He turned to Jeff and Harry. "You've heard what we've found. Something very strange happens to people who live on this planet, even just visit. What can you tell me?"

As Jeff opened his mouth, the older man placed a restraining hand on his elbow. "What can you tell me about this solar system?" Harry asked.

Kat pounced like a kitten on a ball of twine. "Star is only two and a half billion years old. The planet is estimated at less than two billion years old."

"Early in its formation for such an abundance of life forms, don't you think?" Harry drawled.

"And three different evolutionary tracks," Doc added.

"On most life-appropriate planets, Earth included," Kat said slowly, "tiny ocean life forms took most of the first two billion years just to get their acts together before venturing onto the land. So what makes this one so different?"

"Maybe because it was someone's garden," Harry offered. Ray started at his choice of imagery. Had he met the Gardener?

"Whose?" Mary shot back.

"I believe that is what we are trying to figure out," Harry said with a wry smile. "It is possible, from my core samples, to surmise that three million years ago this planet was very nascent; nothing but one-cell critters. That changed real quick about two and a half million years ago. It appears the planet entered into some kind of warm, pleasant golden age a bit over two million years ago. That ended close to a million years ago, to be replaced by a strange seesaw as raging weather patterns alternated with periods of equilibrium. The past five hundred thousand years have seen the seesawing getting worse."

"That's in the core samples?" Ray had been looking for confirmation. He hadn't expected to have it handed to him on a platter.

"Some say it is, myself included. Others disagree, insisting there is nothing there." Harry turned his palms over in a dismissing gesture. "Since we have drawn them from only a small part of this continent, a very small area of this planet, I cannot refute the doubters with any authority."

Ray sat forward in his chair. "Tell me about some of those bad-weather patterns. Major storm surges? Tidal waves?"

"I've drilled up evidence of six inches of sand twenty, thirty miles onto the Piedmont plain around Refuge and New Haven. Happened four or five times."

"How strong were the mineral readings at the breakpoint between the end of the golden age and the beginning of the troubled years?" Ray went on.

"Don't know. Unless I drilled through a major ore seam or an old river, metal on this planet is very hard to come by. Not enough tectonic action in its short history. Why?"

"Mary, you got any gear for very small samples?"

"Down to parts per billion. What do you have in mind?"

Did he dare say? "I bet if you find an area buried suddenly a million years ago, you'll find a very rich mineral layer."

"Want to say why?" Mary asked.

"Not yet. Any places like that near here, or do we have to go back to the coast?" Ray asked Harry.

The old man pulled a well-used map from his hip pocket, unfolded it and studied it, right hand massaging his chin. "The James River valley goes quite a ways inland. Much of it was flooded three, four times," he said slowly. "Where the river hasn't carried away the overburden, I could probably find that first layer." He looked up, eyes bright and a smile forming. "I'd love to work with a few of your miners. Jeff told me what they did to a single hill. When can we start?"

"As soon as the boss wants us to," Mary drawled. "By the way, Colonel, while we're stacking up anomalies, I got one to throw on the pile." Ray waited while Mary gnawed her lower lip.

"I lost nearly ten percent of my nanos yesterday. Normal attrition is less than one percent. I recovered ninety-seven percent of the nanos. But six percent of the ones I got back carried nothing and are unusable." Ray raised an eyebrow. "The nanos were modified at their atomic level. Grapplers broken off, electric motors wrecked."

"That's impossible," Kat insisted.

"Yep, impossible, but that's what happened to my little metal wranglers. It's like they've been in a fight. Only, neither the metal nor the mountain's supposed to fight back."

Unless the metal were fighting for its life, Ray thought, slumping in his chair. "Mary, work with Harry today. Get me a good spectrum from a million years back."

"What are you looking for?" Mary asked.

"I have no idea. Lek, I want you to get the sky eyes back up. One over New Haven, another for Refuge, one circulating around the Covenanters."

"You don't trust the news media?" Kat asked.

"Let's say I don't trust them to know what they're looking at, or what's important. I want my own raw data feed."

"I'll patch it into the stuff we're getting from Lek's taps," Kat said. "We'll get you one consolidated intelligence report for tomorrow morning, Colonel."

"Good." Ray turned back to Lek. "While you're working on other stuff, spend some time meditating on what a surveillance system or computer network might look like after we've had a million years to polish the technology. Any ideas?"

"No."

"Me neither. But for the moment, assume something very high-tech grew over the million quiet years, and some of it is still humming." Ray's subordinates looked at each other, then at him. "We need an estimate of the situation to work from. I'm offering one. You have an alternate, I'm listening."

"A million-year-old technology that's been rusting for a long while. You know something we don't?" Doc asked.

"Maybe. I'm not sure. Kat, fit the data to the curve. Tell me where my guess doesn't fit."

The young middie shook her head slowly. "There's not enough data to conclude anything, sir."

"Okay, I've stuck my neck out. Now you get out there and prove me wrong. By the way, Harry, before you go, would you let Doc take a picture of the inside of your skull?"

"Kind of a new-employee physical?" the old man grinned.

"Doc, I also want to spend some time on the table," Ray said, getting to his feet. "You've got your assignments, everybody. Have at them. Oh, Lek, Mary, and I found an interesting pillar in a cave yesterday. Once you've got the sky eyes up, take a look at it; see if you can find anything electromagnetic about it."

Ray walked over to the hospital with Doc and Harry. If he weren't so dead on his feet, he might have been able to skip the cane entirely. Then again, maybe he was just being optimistic. Doc scanned Harry quickly, ending it with a whistle and a question. "You have many headaches?"

"When I was a kid. Not recently. Why?"

Doc motioned Harry and Ray over to look at his scan. "I'm finding most Santa Marians have some kind of growth in this section of the brain. Yours is one of the largest I've seen. The Colonel here sports a bigger one." Ray nodded and Jerry pulled up his scan, as well as the kids'.

Harry frowned. "What do you make of it?"

"Right now," Jerry said, "nothing. I can't even figure out an approach."

On that, Harry left and Ray took his place on the table, got comfortable, took a deep breath, and told Jerry, "Today we do a brain activity scan. I'll think something, and you tell me what part of my brain lights up. I had a baseline done a while back."

Doc fiddled with his station for a while. "Here's that part of your file. Let's start with the multiplication tables."

"Seven times one is seven," Ray began. He'd droned through the eights before Jerry called enough.

"I'm supposed to show you some dirty pictures. All I've got is a couple of boring inkblots."

"I'm a married man, Doc. Going to be a daddy soon. I ought to be able to provide a few thoughts gratis." Rita in her folks' garden, at the lake, on the ship.

"Nothing's changed there, Colonel. Try a tactical problem."

Ray went over the assault on the pass, trying for the umpteenth time to figure out how he could have gotten around Mary and her bag of surprises.

"Yeah, that's a match, in spades," Jerry said. "You're dialed in. What did you want to show me?"

Ray thought of the Three. The soaring towers and purple gardens. The doctor whistled, started tapping his board like mad. Ray remembered the caverns of the woolly leg-legs. The art on the walls of the long tunnels. "Any change there, Doc?"

"None. I mean, yes. No. Keep doing whatever it is you're doing." Ray switched to the aeries of the spinners, dancing on the winds where gravity's kiss was but a light caress.

"That one is a bit sensuous," Doc observed.

"The thought of flying free always was a turn-on," Ray explained softly.

"Want to tell me what's going on here?"

"Got enough?"

"Yeah. Corpsman!" Doc shouted. "Wrestle me up the kids." A lab-coated assistant nodded silently and left. "Okay, Colonel, what were you doing that made that little thing you shouldn't have get all red and yellow from use?"

Ray swung himself off the table and ambled over to watch his own scans. The first half minute was familiar territory. Then the dark mass that scared Ray just to look at warmed up, showing itself off boldly in reds, pinks, and yellows. Other parts of Ray's brain glowed in response to some stimuli from it. "I'm remembering things I never did."

"Recalling dreams?"

Ray shook his head. "Too real. My dreams have a fuzziness around the edge. Nothing hazy here. I can read the writing on the walls, writing I've never seen before. I even understand the poetry. Understand all of its allusions and can call up more memories to back them up." Ray tapped his head. "These memories are as real as anything I've lived."

Jerry leaned back, knuckling his eyes with both fists as if to clear them of sleep, exhaustion, unacceptance, all of the above. "We've been trying to make data biostorage units. Every time we think they might be cost-effective, silicon comes up with a new growth spurt. And reading the data is slow."

"I don't know about that. All I know is I've just failed to disprove the hypothesis I presented this morning. I've got to face some things I didn't want to even touch. Things I've been dismissing as dreams aren't dreams at all. Certain experiences I and the kids had were very real. This planet is crazy. Maybe even crazier than I thought. Now I've got to start figuring out what to do about it. Certainly before tonight."

"Tonight?"

"Yeah. 'Cause if I can't handle this crazy place by tonight, it's not going to let me sleep again. And Doc, I am tired."

A shake of the head was all the medication Jerry gave.

Ray dropped in on Kat before leaving the hospital/research center. She was elbow-deep in correlating Lek's media and news dumps. "My college news was more interesting than this. Recipes! They actually put recipes on the front page of one. Doesn't anything interesting ever happen around here?"

"Depends on what you consider interesting. Include a search on albinism." Ray rubbed his temples for a moment. "Pain management ought to cover headaches. Hallucinations, any other mental health issues."

"I saw something flash by about whirling dervishes or some kind of mystics among the Covenanters."

"Right. Mysticism. Witch-hunts. Those kinds of things."

Ray left as the kids were herded into Med Bay One for tests. The morning had left them happily grubby. A sky eyes took off as Ray strode for Barber's office. Mary and the chief were head down over his station. They glanced up as Ray entered.

"Got a blimp due in by noon," Barber said. "Another by

supper. They're loaded with ceramic feed and carbon bricks. You know anything about that?"

"I told San Paulo our help didn't come free. Steal a blimp while one's up here."

"Any particular reason?" Mary asked.

"I may be bouncing a core sampling team all over the place."

The chief leaned back in his chair. "Colonel, I'm as good as any old soldier at working in the dark. And I can process bullshit into mushrooms like anybody else. But that don't mean I like it. Ready to talk?"

"Don't know. How good are you at listening?"

"As in can I swallow six impossible things before breakfast?" the chief asked. Ray nodded. "Try me. I think I follow the cards you've put face up on the table. Can't help but think you've got a few up your sleeve you ain't talking about."

Ray told them of the test Doc had just completed. "He's checking the kids now. Asking them to remember about the Three. The scenes they saw in the cave."

"Nice," the chief said. "Instead of buying all those case files in college, just load it into your head."

"What made you think of school?" Ray asked.

"Don't know. Been dreaming about working on my masters."

"In my dreams," Ray said, "I meet what's causing all this. Calls itself the Teacher. This whole planet was its school."

Mary pursed her lips. "If you could make jump points on the gross scale and modify cells at the micro, why not use an entire planet to teach your young? Or your old, for that matter? Heard the old adage you can't teach an old dog new tricks? Imagine what you could do with a planet for a classroom."

The chief snorted ruefully. "I've served under some old mossbacks. Turkeys who hadn't learned a thing since they hatched. Could spout all the new management words: "empowerment," "results-oriented," "shared visions." Had the words but couldn't do a damn thing with them. Couldn't change at the gut level. Me, I figured I'd outlive the bastards."

Mary nodded. "Met a few like those in the mines."

"But what if everyone lives for hundreds, thousands of years?" Ray mused.

"Society either stagnates, or folks learn to change deep down, all through their lives. I know a few who did," the chief agreed. "Took a damn painful boot in the ass to get their attention, to make them really want to do things different."

"A planet might do that," Mary agreed.

"Be fun watching it in action," the chief grinned.

Ray shook his head. "Got a problem there. This thing thinks it knows all there is to know."

"Oh, shit," Barber breathed. "I've known a few like that. A real pain. What makes you think that?"

"Maybe just a dream. Maybe the Teacher has figured out a way into my brain." Ray tapped his forehead. "You know, that thing in here Doc and I are working to understand. I think it puts me on the Teacher's net."

"Which is why you ventured your guess this morning," the chief said. Ray nodded. "Okay, boss. What do you want from me?"

"Help Mary keep the base up. I'm not sure that when we tapped that hill, we didn't piss the Teacher off big time."

Barber shook his head. "Unsmart of a student."

"Got any good ideas why people have taken to rioting in the streets?" Mary asked.

"I damn near was ready to riot last night in Refuge. All kinds of nasty feelings running around in my gut. No reason for them." Mary pursed her lips. Ray shrugged and went on. "Let me know what you're making with the feed metals you've got." Ray stood. "Start looking around the base for anything you're willing to melt down and recycle to a higher priority. Life's only going to get more interesting."

His commlink interrupted him. "Colonel, Kat here. You want to see what we've got over here."

"On my way."

Ray walked briskly back to the hospital. The kids were bouncing off the walls in Med Bay One, so their tests must be done. Doc was head down over his board.

"Any surprises?" Ray called.

"Just like yours," Jerry answered without looking up.

"There's got to be a pattern here somewhere. Hell, we still don't have the human brain mapped, and now I've got more territory to confuse me."

Kat and three other middies were keeping eight stations working full-time, hopping between chairs and chattering at light speed. "Another just lit off," "I've got lots of movement but no action," "But why isn't any of this being reported?"

"What's happening?" Ray asked, settling into a seat that apparently was out of the musical-chair competition.

"Oh, Colonel, good. We're seeing movement of refugees out of the larger cities and into the towns and villages. Some are going smoothly. Others aren't."

"Show me."

"First sky eye headed for New Haven," Kat said. Aerial views flashed across a large screen. "We observed heavy congestion at the rail stations after a train pulled out." Kat stopped at one scene. A train was just leaving; several dozen people in what looked like family groups scattered on foot from the station. "We didn't hang around to follow any particular group, at least not at first. We wanted to check more trains, more stations. Lots of people traveling out. Empty trains going back."

"Trains take up a lot of steel." Ray knew he was changing the topic, but iron was supposedly just as hard to find as copper. What were these folks doing with trains?

"Rails are hardened ceramic. Trains are electric, using a third-rail system holding seawater to carry the electricity."

"So," Ray summed up what he was hearing, "the urban response to being laid off is to hike out to the hinterlands. That's where the food is. Maybe they have relatives who will put them up. Sounds like a good approach."

"Yes, sir. That's down south," Kat said, and changed the view. Smoke streamed up from burning houses. "This is off the second sky eye. It was headed for Richland, but we've kept it circling between us and them." She zoomed the picture. Now he could see figures in the streets. Some wielded clubs. Others fought hand to hand. Another house began to burn.

"Talk to me, Kat."

• • •

Annie Mulroney did not want to go with Da to get his still. Da dreamed of producing poteen as well as beer. With the copper he'd made off the starfolks, he'd finally ordered one, was getting it at discount, since he was paying with copper. To top it off, Da talked the motor pool chief into letting him ride along on one of the mules headed for County Clair.

So. Fine for Da. Annie saw no reason she should go with him. "Be good for you to get out for a while," Ma said.

"You mean away from Jeff," Annie shot back.

"You spend too much time with him," Da told her.

"I haven't seen him for two days!" Annie answered.

"Good," Ma said. "Now go with Da. Listen to the still's instructions. You'll have to wash it." From the way Da talked, Annie doubted she'd be allowed within ten feet of it.

A mule with two trailers stopped in front of the Public Room. Annie recognized the marine driving, Dumont, one of the hard ones. She dutifully settled in the back. In the holster on the door beside the driver, the butt of a rifle poked out. "Do you always carry guns?" Da asked.

"Today we do," the marine answered curtly.

Annie settled in for an uninteresting ride but couldn't help exclaiming as the land went by so fast. Trees beside the road were almost a blur. "How fast are we going?"

"Only fifty-five kilometers an hour."

"That's faster than a train or a blimp," Da pointed out.

"You folks go at life kind of slow," the marine observed.

Annie had ridden this road on a wagon; it rattled from one pothole to the next. The mule seemed to fly over the same holes, bouncing her hardly at all. Annie wondered how it could, but didn't bother the marine. He seemed intent on something.

Dumont dropped Da and Annie off first at the machinist's shop and got directions to the granary. That was why the chief was offering folks rides with his drivers. The mules got back a lot faster when they had someone to act as a guide, or knew who to ask for directions. In the dusty shop, Annie listened as the mechanic took the still apart and put it in a wood crate.

"Think you can put it back together?" the man asked when it was boxed.

"Do I look like a daft city slick?" Da answered; both laughed. The two carried the box out and put it gently down on the walk beside the shop.

"Your starman will be coming back for you now, won't he?" the mechanic said.

"No doubt, no doubt. Me and me daughter will just be enjoying a bit of your sun." The man went back into his shop as a train whistle echoed in the air. Annie swept up her skirt and sat on the box to wait.

"Be careful now, girl," was Da's only response. He looked at a new stove in the man's window. The flyer plastered beside it promised it would burn peat faster and produce more heat and less ash. People were all the time making things better.

Five men turned the corner, not two blocks down in the direction of the train whistle. Annie glanced at them, then away. They were hard city types, strutting themselves. She'd been taught to pay them no mind, and she did. Jeff was so different from the likes of those. Annie stood and slid around to put Da between her and the leering men. She tried to keep her eyes down, like Ma said, to fix them on the new stove, but her glance kept flitting to the men. Their stares were hard on her. As if, as if . . . she didn't know what made men look like that. Then she saw that three of them carried clubs.

"Da, can we go?"

"The mule's not back, child." But Da's eyes were also drawn to the men. "I'll talk to Damon," Da said. He took two steps sideways to the door, not facing the coming men, not turning his back on them either. "Damon, can you watch me box?"

"Sure," came from inside.

"We can do better," came from behind Annie. A hand grabbed her shoulder, whirled her around. A man was in her face. Tall, blond—and drunk. "I can take care of you myself," came at her in a nauseating wash of breath and throaty demand.

Annie pushed, tried to shove him away. "I don't need your help. Da!"

Da reached for her assailant, but a club came down on his shoulder. "You don't want to interrupt, now do you, you dirt-eating farmer. The girl's a might muddy for your tastes, Han, but she's in your hand." The man at the end of the club laughed.

All five of them were here now. Two with clubs threatened Da. Two more watching Damon, who'd come from his shop but got no farther than the door. And the fifth. A knife had appeared in his hand; it weaved in the air just below Annie's breasts. "A bit overdressed for this warm day, huh, fellows?"

His knife slit up her bodice. As he clipped the top, both sides fell open, exposing her breasts. His other hand was pulling up her skirt, pawing her thighs. Annie tried to push his hand down, hold her top up. "Da," she whimpered.

"Annie," came from Da explosively as a club took him full in the stomach.

"You know, I don't think her old man is enjoying this nearly enough." A second club took Da in the head; he collapsed to the ground. "Smile, old man," one said and kicked Da.

"Please stop," Annie begged, knowing the words had no meaning to these men, hoping somewhere there might be something soft and gentle still living in them.

"And why should I stop?" the man with the knife at her throat laughed. Flicking his knife, he drove her hand away from her breasts, letting them fall bare again. His other hand knocked her arm away; he grabbed the upper flesh of her thigh.

"Because the woman asked you to," came soft and deadly from the street. On silent electric motors, the mule had glided up behind the men. Dumont now rested one hand on the steering wheel and waited, with an air of infinite patience, for an answer.

"That's a stupid reason," the knife said, stepping away from Annie but keeping the blade at her throat. He extended his other hand toward the marine in a gesture Da said was obscene.

One of the other men, who'd been watching Damon, took advantage of the distraction to bring his club up fast and hard into the mechanic's gut. Damon went down, hands to his belly, struggling for air. The men laughed—and turned to the marine.

"Go away, starkid. You got no business here."

"You're probably right. But I brought that young woman here, and her pa, and I told them I'd take them back. As I see it, they ought to be in the same shape."

"Well, we don't see it that way," one of them said, slowly inching toward Dumont.

"Even a dumbfuck marine can tell that," Dumont nodded.

"Leave us alone and you won't get hurt."

"No can do."

"Then we'll just have to include you in our fun. And there's five of us and just one of you."

"Gunny at boot camp said one trained marine ought to be able to handle six street shits with no training. Proved it, too. Gunny was a nice old bastard. Only put two of us in the hospital."

"I'm sick of this talk. Get him."

A small pistol appeared in the hand Dumont did not have on the steering wheel. As he swept it over the rushing men, it made sharp popping sounds. After each pop, a large exit hole would appear in the back of one of the city slick's heads. As in a slow-motion dream, they went down.

The blood and brains from one of them splattered Annie. She gagged on a scream.

"Sorry about that," Dumont said, running to Annie's side. "Gunny also said an automatic beats a club every day."

"They're dead," Annie whispered, trying to control the fear that shook her, trying to convince herself she was safe.

"Very dead. Let's get you and your old man out of here." He helped her up, half-carried her to the mule, and set her gently down in the back. "Mr. Mulroney, can you make it?"

"I think so." Hauling himself up by the window frame, Da stood unsteadily, then offered Damon a hand up. With effort, Da made it to the mule.

Dumont quickly stepped around the mule and slid into the driver's seat. "Now we get the hell out of Dodge, fast," Dumont whispered as he reached to put the mule in gear.

A woman screamed. Down the street, a young woman, child held to her breast, dress half ripped off her, stumbled and fell, landing hard to protect the infant in her arms. A roar of male laughter followed her. Behind her, a building started to burn.

"No, damn it," Dumont whimpered. His hand came away from the mule's controls. He swiped at the perspiration on his brow. "Where are you, priest, when I need you? I don't want to do this anymore." Another scream reached them; a harsh laugh followed.

"God damn them all!" Dumont shouted as he reached for the rifle holstered on the mule's door.

Standing beside the vehicle, he took his automatic from its holster and handed it to Da. "It's easy to use. Sight down the barrel. You squeeze back gentle on the trigger and a red dot appears where the needle's going. Pull back the rest of the way, and you saw what happens." Da nodded dumbly. "You'll tell the little priest. I didn't have any good choices. You'll tell him."

"I will," Annie whispered.

The marine pulled glasses from his pocket, put them on. Even in the glare of day, Annie could see the play of lights on them, the picture of what the gun saw riding over what Dumont saw. "See you in a few minutes."

Ray studied the images coming back from the sky eye. The air-conditioned comfort of the hospital struggled against the grainy dirt of the pictures. Kat rambled on, trying to explain what shouldn't have to be said. "It looks like mobs started moving out on foot from Richland early this morning. Apparently the refugees are beating up the town and village folks and taking their homes. In the past hour we've started seeing groups of two or three trains rolling into a station and emptying out a mob of people, who take over the town. The trains turn around and head back for more. It almost seems organized."

"Any reports of this in the media?"

"Richland's paper doesn't seem to be up today. Usual TV programming is off the air. All we're getting are reruns of get-rich-quick dramas, the life of the rich and debauched, or what passes for education there. No news."

"Refuge?"

"Several channels are just flat off the air. Reruns on the rest. TV news was canceled due to a lack of interest. The explanation was a bit more long-winded, but it boiled down to just that. Newspaper is publishing bland stuff. Most of it looks canned from weeks ago."

"Do we have the blimp take?"

"Three blimps are up. A few mobs are still moving around Refuge, but Cassie's vectoring local teams over to break them up. A lot of foot traffic around the suburbs, but no one is aiming the blimps that direction, so I'd have to bring the sky eye over to see what is happening there, and I think you'd rather keep it between us and them." She nodded at the screen. Another two houses were burning. The camera flicked to another village farther up the rail line. A house burst into flames.

"Anything crazy from the Covenanters?"

"You tell me. Televangelists always sound crazy."

"They're burning her! My God, they're burning that woman." One of the two middies who had kept bouncing from chair to chair stopped in midhop, face draining white. "That preacher declared her a witch, and he's burning her!"

Kat brought that picture up on the central screen. A woman, hands tied above her head, screamed horribly as flames began to engulf her dress. The camera backed off. A man was being burned as well. "Oh, let it be a graphic image," Kat breathed, fingers flying as she ran a subroutine to see if it was a created graphics, not real. "It's real," she choked.

"Too damn real for me. Cut it off," Ray snapped.

Kat did. "Sir, this is crazy. I can show you the feed from five years back. Last year, for heaven's sake. That same guy was talking about ice-cream socials and God loving everyone and how there was no hell and everybody was going to heaven. What's gotten into him? How could he change so much so fast?"

Ray blinked several times, trying to rid himself of the afterimage of that last shot. "I wish to hell I knew," he whispered. "They're burning witches up north. They're rioting in

the center. They're still acting pretty rational in the South."
Kat nodded. "There's a big continent to the north of us—say,
a thousand kilometers away." Again Kat nodded, brows coming down in puzzlement. She didn't see the pattern.

Ray did.

"I'm tired," Ray sighed. "Maybe I'll take a nap. Can you
keep collecting data?"

"Yes, sir. But what are we going to do about it?"

"There's still time to decide that."

Kat glanced at the various screens and the mayhem on
them. "Time's running out for an awful lot of people, sir."

Ray headed down the hall. Med Bay One was deafeningly
quiet, the kids gone, and Doctor Isaacs intent on his boards.

"Doc, you got a place I can lie down? Get some rest while
you monitor me?"

Jerry came to his feet. "What do you have in mind?"

Ray settled on the table. "I'd like you to check my brain activity while I'm sleeping. You might find it informative."

"Only if you let me put you on heart and blood chemistry
monitors while you're at it."

"Hook me up to your heart's content. Probably beats me
drinking a lot of water and hoping my bladder gets me up before the dream gets bad." Ray lay down while Jerry prodded
and poked. Done, Doc stood by Ray.

"Want to tell me what's going to happen?"

"Things have been happening in my sleep. I dismissed
them as just dreams. Now I think they're more. Whatever is
running this planet may be trying to talk to me. I'm going
looking for it. I don't much care for how it's running this
show, and I think it's time I told it."

"You carrying a suitcase bomb?" Doc asked, alluding to
Ray's reputation.

"Would if I knew how to get one into my dreams. Guess I'll
just have to settle for words."

"Take care. I'll keep watch." Jerry closed the curtains,
hardly darkening Ray's surroundings. He took several deep
breaths and tried to relax into the table's thin cushion. Many
a night he would have considered this rank luxury. Closing his

eyes, Ray began to methodically relax each part of his body, starting with his legs. He didn't get far.

"What are you doing?" came in a high-pitched, petulant voice from behind Ray. The room was lined by dusty, unkept shelves. Old books in worn leather bindings stood upright or lay sideways. Several were open, stacked on top of each other. Other knickknacks decorated the shelves—one, a skull with four eye openings. As Ray struggled to comprehend what his mind was simulating, he remembered this scene, a fantasy holovid, complete with dragons. He turned, knowing what he'd see. Yep, a magician sat on a three-legged stool beside a table covered with paraphernalia, including a crystal ball. On it played scenes from the sky eye. Interesting blending of technologies, Ray mused.

"What are you doing? And why won't any of you talk to me?" the mage repeated. The face was familiar; he'd seen it on the million counselors. The robes this time were royal purple, with five pointed stars lining the cuffs and bottom hem. Ray's subconscious was giving him plenty of hints; he struggled to absorb them in his dreaming state.

"I am here, and I am ready to talk to you," Ray answered.

"So you are. So you are," the figure answered, scratching his ear absentmindedly. "And what do you have to say?"

"I'm not quite sure what you mean by that question."

"Look at you. Just look at you." The mage pointed at his crystal ball. Visions flittered across it of major buildings burning in Refuge, houses burning in towns. "Bad enough that you tore up my eyes, ears, and fingers to cover the land with worthless stuff. Now you destroy that, too. What can be learned from such actions? I ask you. I ask you!"

"Matters have gotten very confusing. I'm not sure just what is happening," Ray said, fumbling for the central purpose of this conversation and not sure there was one.

"That shows what happens. It really does. You do not listen to me. None of you. You ignore me. Totally ignore."

"I'm listening."

"Not really. You're not hearing a half, a quarter of what I'm saying to you."

"I'm listening to everything I can hear," Ray assured him. *"Can you ask for more than that?"*

"Not really, no, not really. But why can't you hear all of me? The Gardener was here. Giving you ears was not beyond his limited skills. Where is the Gardener? I ask you. Where is he?"

Given two questions, Ray chose the easier. *"I don't believe the Gardener was able to give ears to all of us. We are not of the Three. We need different ears."*

"You are not of the Three, that is sure. That is very sure," the mage said, squinting at Ray. *"Don't look at all like any of the Three. None. Who are you? Yes, who are you?"*

"I am a human being. Ray Longknife at your service," he said, *"Ambassador from the Society of Humanity, and Minister of Science and Technology for the sovereign planet of Wardhaven."*

"Lots of names for such a small fellow who can't even hear me clearly. Can't hardly hear at all."

"Yes," Ray agreed. *"But I can hear better than most. Better than those"*—he swept a hand toward the crystal ball. *"Are you trying to talk to them as well?"*

"Talk to them. I'm shouting. Shouting at them. Can't you hear me shouting?" The purple-clad figure shifted in his chair, scowled at the crystal ball. *"Shouting."*

And is the shouting what's causing them to go berserk? Good question, but not one he wanted this fellow to tackle. *"They can't hear you. They have only the beginning of the ear they need for you. Why do you shout at those who cannot hear?"*

"Because they should. They should," he snorted. *"The Gardener said he was working on their hearing. He said that years ago. Surely he could solve a simple problem as an ear. Three hundred orbits of the sun is enough time to resolve any difficulty,"* the mage ended, half-muttering to himself.

"We are different from the Three. Maybe more complex. The Gardener did not resolve the problem. You have only to look at what you see to know that."

"And where is the Gardener?" The mage looked up, fixing Ray with an unblinking eye. *"He should be here to tell us what he tried. How he did it. What we should do differently. I ask you again: Where is the Gardener? What have you done with him?"*

That was the first time the question had gotten personal. Ray considered ignoring it again, but he was getting tired of this thing's unwillingness to face up to reality. Humanity is different. We are not ready to be plugged into whatever idea it has for educating us. The sooner the Teacher realized the world was more complex than it expected, the sooner humanity and it could get down to serious business.

"The Gardener is no longer here." Ray answered slowly. *"There may have been an accident. Our communications were rudimentary. In the process of searching for resources to use, we may have removed minerals critical for the Gardener. Had we but known it, we would not have done it. However, in our ignorance and because of the Gardener's own lack of success in communicating with us, we may have contributed to the conditions that ended the continued existence of the Gardener."* Ray was glad for his practice as a politician, tap-dancing around ugly truths.

The mage leaned back on its stool, looking long and hard at Ray. *"The Gardener is . . . dead?"*

"Yes."

"You killed it."

Ray didn't want to put it quite that bluntly. As he struggled for an alternate answer, the mage answered himself.

"That's impossible. These primitives couldn't hurt the likes of us." This came from a second mage, identical to the first, only standing on his right.

"Well, the Gardener is gone," said a third mage, this one on the first's left.

"Many things could have happened here. We have only begun our own examination." The mage was proliferating at a blinding speed, thousands appearing, stretching out at

the right and left of the first, all talking, all arguing. "They may be primitive, but killing is a primitive reaction." "How could something so small destroy the Gardener?" "The Gardener was old. It had long been out of touch with us. Anything could have happened." "We are old and not what we once were. Could they terminate us?" "That is not possible." "Neither could the Gardener vanish." "You go too far." "You do not go far enough."

Ray stepped back from the growing crowd of arguing mages. He spotted one that was missing an arm. Somehow the Teacher had changed modes from singular to plural. From the sound of the arguments, it or they didn't have a whole lot of experience at consensus-building.

"Now you have done it."

Ray found the bewigged lackey at his elbow. "Done what?"

"Got them fighting among themselves. They can keep this up until dark and sunrise again." The servant cast him a dour, sidelong glance. "You should not have done it."

"Why?"

"They will carry on like this and forget to take care of themselves. And when they do remember, my job will be all the harder. You should not have done that."

"I see your point, but maybe now, while they're busy, I can get some sleep myself."

With the attendant still glowering at Ray, he vanished quietly away.

Ray came awake slowly, his usual discomfort only pressing, not demanding. "Doc," he called. When he got no answer, he raised the volume. "Doc, I need to take a leak, and if you don't unplug me from all your test gear, I'm gonna do it right here."

"Just a second, Ray, I'm coming." In a moment, the curtains were jerked aside and Ray found himself facing a very excited Jerry and Kat.

"What's got into you two?"

"You've got to come look at our monitors," Kat demanded.

"You have a good rest?" Doc asked.

Ray stretched. "Yeah. Best in a week or so. No headache, either. Got any opinions why?"

"Some. You dropped off to sleep like normal, then your readings took off on a wild ride. Lasted six minutes, thirty-four seconds," Doc said, glancing at his board. "Then you dropped down into the sleep of the innocent."

"Nice," Ray yawned.

"And Kat here came galloping in, telling me I had to wake you up to see what she was seeing."

"I'm glad you didn't," Ray said, sliding off the table and looking around for the nearest rest room.

"Off to your left," Doc said, reading his mind.

"Our sky eyes are showing a total change," Kat enthused. "People have quit fighting, no more fires. Colonel, everything changed just like that."

"I'll be with you in a moment," Ray said, slipping into the rest room and closing the door behind him. Kat, still excitedly following him, almost had her nose flattened in the process. Relieved of annoying bladder pressure, Ray rejoined them. "So my little talk with the Teacher had immediate results."

"Looks like it," Jerry said. "What'd you tell it?"

"I'm not sure it was what I said. I think it might be where I left it."

"Which was?" Kat insisted.

"Arguing with itself. Or selves. I'm not sure whether it's one critter or a thousand. I'm not sure it knows the answer to that." This got him two quizzical stares.

"Sorry, folks, but let's keep one thing clear: My mind, conscious, subconscious, whatever, is having a hell of a time relating to this thing. It's filling in a lot of holes in the data, and I'm never sure what is really it and what is me painting in something from my memory that may or may not be like something the Teacher is trying to send. Communications is not taking place here on a one-for-one basis. Follow me?"

Both Jerry and Kat nodded slowly. "Being drafted into the navy, I had to learn a whole new language, or so it seemed. We middies could hardly understand Dumont or Mary's marines, either flavor, at first. At least we're all human. Imagine something that's never even seen a human before. Trying to get a word across must be damn near impossible."

"I only wished I'd gotten better at it before we killed the Gardener."

"Sir?" Jerry and Kat froze in place.

"It seems there was a reason why the hill Mary tapped had such a high concentration and wide variety of minerals. It was something like the central core for a thing I've been calling the Gardener." That earned Ray blank stares. "I named it that because the mental image I always got when communicating with it was of an old fellow who used to handle the flowers and shrubs around the Academy." The nods he got from both of them showed at least some understanding.

"Well, the Gardener last appeared to me and the kids the afternoon Mary tapped the metal out of Jeff's hill. He looked kind of sick, and got sicker as we talked. I haven't seen him since, and the Teacher keeps asking me where the Gardener is."

"Oh, lord," Doc groaned.

"Could we kill a part of a world machine?" Kat asked.

Ray stabbed a finger at Doc's board. "That, my friends, is the question I left the Teacher squabbling over among its selves. That's why he's too busy at the moment to drive people into a killing craze. Doc, find out if they've got a morgue in Refuge with all the victims of the rioting. If you can tell the difference between the rioters and their victims, I'd love to see a comparison between the size of this damn thing in their heads. Something was driving me damn near crazy enough last night in Refuge to want to riot. I think it was this tumor."

Jerry nodded. "I'll see what Cassie can tell me."

"The shuttle's yours if you need to make a quick trip to Refuge."

"I'm on it." The doc dropped into his workstation and started stabbing keys.

"Now, young woman, I'd like to see just how fast the Teacher's distraction turned off the murderings."

"Yes, sir."

Ray was in the conference room as evening gently settled into full dark and his exhausted battle staff, as he was starting to think of them, filed in. The padre had begged off; he had a premarriage counseling session already scheduled.

"How'd the day's core sampling go?" Ray asked for starters.

"Pretty much as you expected," Harry answered. "There's a lot more metal in the soil just below the first layer of storm debris. We drilled at six different locations. All the same. A pattern in the data piqued my interest. Seems less metal was laid down after the first storm inundation. Even less after the second. Matched in all six locations. So I went hunting for someplace where there were no major storms to tear up the ground, just minor sandstorms adding to the alluvial topsoil."

"Don't keep us waiting," Ray urged him. What did happen when there was no major disaster?

"Small amounts of residual metal at almost every level, growing larger the farther down we go. Apparently recovery was poorer each time. Top layer gave us the largest sample. However, it was nowhere near as high a concentration as we got in places undisturbed from the first break."

Ray rubbed his chin, then brought everyone up to date on what had been laid on him hour by hour through the day.

"The tumor is a commlink and memory, but memories of things you never did," Mary summed it up. "The Teacher is somehow causing the antisocial behavior, but that is biased toward the north." She stared at the ceiling, as if studying something. "There's a large landmass to the north, so it's probably coming from there. Have we missed anything?"

"It's electronic," Lek said. "Based on the content of the metal core samples, it has to be. What did your dream mean by we'd wrecked its eyes, ears, fingers?"

"Any of you been having weird dreams?" Doc asked.

That got nods from around the table. "Even you," Ray said to Jeff and Harry.

"Been getting weirder over the past six, nine months," Harry said. "Same nightmares I had as a kid. Hated them then. Now I see what was going on."

"In my dreams, I'm dealing with something that my subconscious has dubbed the Teacher." Ray normally had no patience with long, rambling morning expositions about people's nightly entertainment. Now he launched into an exhaustive outline of his, both with the Gardener and the Teacher.

"Oh, no," Mary groaned as he told of his last meeting with the Gardener. "I had no idea."

"Neither did I," Ray pointed out. "We were moving fast and it was talking slow." Ray went on to finish with the connection between his leaving the Teacher—or Teachers—lost in debate, and the level of violence taking a nosedive.

"Is it attacking us?" Kat asked.

"I don't think so. In my dreams I don't feel any hostile intent. In Refuge, when I was about ready to run riot myself, there was no direction, just a general itch. No, right now it's puzzled by us and our behavior. Something that I might point out is mutual."

"So what?" Mary cut in. "It's raising havoc, no matter its intentions. How do we defend ourselves? Do we counterattack?"

"For the moment," Kat said slowly, "let's assume this is the thing that built the jump points. It sure as hell can do crazy things to our biology. Do we really want to piss it off? I mean, worse than we've done already? I didn't much like fighting Unity, and I was pretty sure we could beat them. Anyone think we can lick whatever-it-is?"

"Can't argue with you," Mary answered. "But do we have a choice. Looks to me like we're already at war. From a rifle sight picture, those bastards coming over the hill from Richland don't look all that different from Unity thugs."

"But those poor folks got even less control over their lives than Unity gave their troopers." Doc shook his head. "Killing people who don't even know why they're out to kill you . . ."

Ray had spent twenty years fighting whatever enemy the government of Wardhaven pointed him at. Then Unity started calling the shots and he started having second thoughts. Ungood for a soldier. Worse results for President Urm of Unity. Damn. This was getting more complicated by the second.

"Does anybody around this table think we have any chance of enforcing our will upon the Teacher?" Ray asked as he looked from one person to the next. He ended with Mary.

"Colonel, I don't know how we can win, but I'll be damned if I'll give up without a fight."

"So, how do we deescalate this without a fight?" he asked.

"Think you could tell it we just want to live in peace?" Kat asked Ray.

"I'll try that next time I close my eyes. Don't think I'm going to get much rest without saying a few words to our friend first. Mary, check on the kids, see if they're having problems."

"Yes, sir. So, what do we do?" Mary demanded back.

Ray took in a deep breath, then let it out slowly. He had no idea. He glanced around the table. Harry raised a finger tentatively. "Go for it," Ray said.

"Seems to me that we have two problems: the fire, and the boiling kettle. The Teacher is the fire, heating up the kettle, but the poor folks boiling around in the kettle are as much victims as perpetrators, no matter who holds the club. Your Kat and I ended up facing some of those folks last night. They'd been my neighbors most of their life. If something wasn't inciting them, they wouldn't have been out to burn my house."

"Agreed." Mary said. "So?"

"If you can't put out the fire, maybe we could dump ice in the pot, keep it from boiling."

"Great concept," Mary muttered. "Doing it. Now, that's the problem. What do we use for ice?"

"Just a thought," Harry started. "Miss V caused a lot of this by demanding copper. Panic spread a lot faster than any problems in the market. What if we . . . I mean you spacers . . . went into business against Sterling Enterprises? What if you offered the copper and other metals this economy needs?"

"That's gonna cool things down?" Mary shook her head. "You might as well declare war on the Teacher. Besides, my nanos won't survive many rounds with hills that fight back."

"The Teacher is moving down from North Continent. So we start with our southside. There was no violence there. If we're mining their hills, it'll be easier to deliver to them."

Mary leaned back. "They're less panicked. They'd be easiest to unpanic. I like that."

"And their economy has been less dislocated," Harry added.

"They'll also be less embarrassed to look each other in the eye once they sober up," Lek tossed in.

Ray pushed himself back from the table, let the idea roll over in his mind for several long seconds. "Things have been happening a lot faster than we can process them," he said slowly. "Before we go too far down this track, I'd like to verify a few assumptions. Can we find some recent evidence on our continent's northside of a new electronic net? Can we verify there's something new operating there? Once we've got a picture, we can risk mining down South, where the network isn't. Let's take a day or two, use the blimp we hijacked."

"Two blimps, sir," Mary grinned. "I had a hunch if you needed one this morning, you'd want two by tonight."

"Thank you and your crystal ball," Ray snorted. "Next point: Harry, where're the best minerals down South?"

"I was with brother Mark when he went cating around down there," Harry said. "Some good prospects, as you're measuring them now. Those data are locked up in the Sterling family archives."

"Is that anywhere near the copy of the *Santa Maria* archives I've heard Vicky brag so much about?" Ray smiled.

"One and the same," Jeff grinned.

"And, of course, you know exactly where they are, Jeff."

"Been there many times."

"Mary, prepare a team for a possible covert op in Richland."

"Snatch and grab, sir?"

"Think checking out a library book."

"Vicky won't like that," Jeff and Harry said.

"Vicky's been playing hardball with these people, but she's got no idea what it's like in the big leagues. I've played for Wardhaven and Unity. Time she learns what happens when you pull things people don't like—on people who can do something about them."

"She's been pulling things people didn't like since she was a kid. All she's learned is that she can get away with them," Jeff pointed out.

"The times, they are a-changing. Right, Mary?"

"Yes, sir, Colonel, sir, three bags full." Mary saluted comically, then got deadly serious. "How soon?"

"Tomorrow night at the earliest, next night more likely. Depends on what Jeff and Harry find up north."

"I'll have marines ride shotgun when they go north."

"Do so, Mary. Jeff, Harry, can you leave at first light?"

"Looking forward to the trip," Harry said.

Jeff didn't look so enthusiastic. "Kat's shared the feed from the Covenanters. Sir, they're burning people up there. Can I borrow a rifle?"

"Mary, see the guy gets trained."

NINE

EVERYTHING RAY COULD do was done. He sidled into Med Bay One. "Doc, wire me for another nap."

"You planning on talking with our Teacher?"

"Yep, and he, she, it, or them may not care to see me."

Doc glanced around his shop. "I got a few things guaranteed to wake the dead."

"Keep 'em handy," Ray said, not exactly relaxing onto the exam table. It seemed to take him longer to fall asleep, or maybe he wasn't as tired as this afternoon. He resettled himself for about the tenth time, wishing Rita were here to talk this out with. Thought of Rita. Thought some more of Rita, happy thoughts of their times together . . .

Ray was in his office on Wardhaven. No, not his office, he was on the wrong side of the desk. The Teacher sat behind an expansive, ancient oak desk; four images of the Teacher sat, two to either side. No, not precise images. Ray's mind dressed them in the latest bureaucratic fashion and made them up as five of the most contrary politicians Wardhaven had. They didn't just fight Ray and his technology initiatives, they fought any and all comers, including each other. Five more independent-minded politicians never shared the same government. Interesting. Subconscious, what are you trying to tell me? Later.

"You came back." "We didn't expect to see you so soon." "Or so late," different ones said. Ray searched for a pattern. Insufficient data so far.

"We share the same planet. We have to communicate."

"But with lies." "Why claim to do something you know you can't?" Both doubting shots came from the right.

"There is no benefit in lying," he told them. *"It was never my desire to harm the Gardener. I think we were becoming friends. But the Gardener is gone. I believe I've offered you the only explanation for that fact."* Ray's team wasn't the only one having difficulty swallowing six impossible things.

"Yes," the central one nodded. *"The Gardener is gone."*

"The Gardener was old," came from the right. *"We had not heard from it in almost three hundred orbits." "Much longer before then." "It is just gone. This thing had nothing to do with that."*

"Yet you claim you did," said the center.

"Accidentally," pointed out one on the left. *"How is that possible?" "How did you do it?"*

"That I do not wish to share with you," Ray said.

"Why not?" snapped the center.

"Because what I did to the Gardener by accident, I may choose to do again with intent if you and I cannot agree on a way for us to share this planet."

"You dare demand a share of the planet we created from bare rock?" roared one on the right, leaping to his feet. *"You are nothing. Nothing! I'll teach you!"*

A hand reached out for Ray, grew impossibly long, and gripped his throat. Agony shot through Ray, pain that made the surgery on his shattered spine feel like a small splinter being removed by a loving mother. Ray gasped, struggled for breath, felt life fleeing from him. . . .

And came awake. Jerry stood over him, shaking him. "Wake up, Ray. Corpsman, the paddles. His heart is going."

"Yes, sir."

"Don't you dare," Ray gasped. "They did enough."

"I just wanted to wake you, Sleeping Beauty."

"You did." Ray coughed, shivered, and worked the muscles of his back and stomach, shaking off the shock, pain, anger. Better, Ray lay back down. "Doc, you got a briefcase or something like it?"

"Yeah."

"Bring it here."

Jeff stepped into the Public Room, rifle slung over his shoulder, and came to a dead halt. Across from him, the old priest sat beside Annie and her dad. Father and daughter seemed somehow smaller. They slumped in their chairs, staring blindly ahead. "Annie," Jeff whispered softly. She just stared at the wall.

A few tables away, the marine Dumont was nursing a dead beer. "They've had a rough day," he said. "The war's come home. I see you got a rifle. You heading out to the war?"

Jeff hastened to kneel beside Annie. "Annie, what's wrong?"

"Men almost killed her and her da," the priest explained. "People coming out from the cities. Drunk . . ." the priest trailed off. "Du saved them. Saved the town, probably. He deserves our thanks."

Du winced at that and took another short sip from his beer. "I did what I'm good at."

Jeff swallowed hard. "The Colonel told us they'd picked stuff like that up on the sky eyes."

"We picked it up on the ground. Not quite as clean as from three thousand meters. Not nearly as pretty." The marine growled and offered Jeff a seat at his table. Jeff didn't want to leave Annie. He wanted to hold her, to make the pain go away.

Her mother's glare told him how that would be taken. "City slick," she snorted, putting two new beers down at Dumont's table.

Jeff joined the marine, resting his rifle on the table in front of him. The marine took it expertly. In a moment he had verified the safety was on, the chamber empty. "At least they taught you enough not to shoot yourself. How come the fire-power?"

"We're taking a blimp north to do some sampling. Colonel thinks he's turned off what's making people crazy, but he wants to know if it's stronger up North. Things are bad there. They're burning people. I wanted a gun. Thought I'd keep it with me. If the crazies come here, I wanted to do something better than scream."

Dumont frowned into his frothing beer. "Yeah, it's better to do something more than scream." He glanced up, looked hard at Jeff with eyes cold as flint. "Don't forget. You'll be leaving them screaming."

A corpsman arrived, white lab coat showing a bird and two chevrons of authority. He silently went to Annie and her dad, checked their eyes, took their pulses, did other things Jeff did not know how to interpret. The medic turned to the priest. "They're in shock. Not unusual in cases like this. I can give them a shot that will help them sleep. That's the best thing for this."

"This happens often enough out there that you know how to help them." The priest waved at the ceiling, then at Annie.

"Too damn much of it, Priest," Dumont spat.

"All the time?" Jeff gulped.

"Some places have it a lot. Some places are as quiet as here was. Depends on the luck of where you're born." Dumont took a long pull on his beer.

"Nikki! Where's Nikki?" Annie suddenly demanded as the corpsman gave her the shot. Annie looked around wildly, eyes impossibly wide. Jeff doubted she saw him.

"There, there, daughter." Her mom quickly settled down beside Annie, took her head in her arms. "Nikki's all right. I just sent her out on an errand. She'll be right back."

"Not likely," Dumont said, now back to sipping his beer.

"Why not?" Jeff said.

"The kid ran out of here as soon as I told her mom what happened. Don't know where she went or when she'll be back."

Jeff thought of going after Annie's little sister, then rethought it. If the word was out that city people had done this, were doing things like this, the dark streets and alleys of

Hazel Dell were no place for Vicky Sterling's little brother. Jeff turned back to Dumont. "You may be busy in a day or two."

Dumont's brows went up but not a word came out.

"Colonel wants to raid my sister's archives. Let her know that she can't keep tightening the screws on people without them screwing her back. Be a chance to send a message to someone who started all this." Jeff inclined his head toward Annie, her dad, the east with Richland and Refuge.

The marine put down his beer. "That might be worthwhile. What do you think, Priest?"

"Be gentle, my son," the priest began. Dumont's hand came up in the beginning of an obscene gesture. "On yourself, boy. On yourself," the priest finished.

Dumont's gesture died in midmotion. He ended up wiping his eyes. "Don't know how to do that, padre. Got no idea at all."

Nikki fell, not for the first time, got up, and ran on. She'd run forever, her screaming lungs insisted. She wanted to run some more, forevermore. Run until she couldn't remember the sight of her da, the look on her sister's face, standing there in the doorway. Just standing in the Public Room they knew like they knew each other—and not able to take a step, find a chair until Ma and Nikki led them to one.

Then the starman had told his story and Nikki had run. Run from those she loved. Run from what she could not understand. Run, looking for a way to make it right. There had to be something Nikki could do to help. Somehow she'd ended up at Daga's. They'd been friends since forever. If anything would help, talking to Daga would.

Daga wasn't home. Hadn't been home all day, her ma said. Nikki had ran away from that door, afraid Daga's ma might take her back to Ma. Nikki couldn't face Ma, or Da, or Annie. Running was better.

Without knowing it, she found herself at Jean Jock's house. Breathless, she rapped on the door. It was a long time being answered, and it was Jean Jock's ma who did.

"Is Daga here?" Nikki asked, breathless.

"No, you poor dear. She went out just after Sean came back from the Public Room with the story of what happened to your poor da and sis. She went with all of them, including the three quiet ones from the city. There was talk they would not be back."

"Was Daga leading them?"

"Yes. She said she had something to show them."

"Holy Mother of God," Nikki breathed. "Holy Mother of God."

"May she and her Son help us all," the woman said, turning it all into a prayer.

"I don't think either of them can," Nikki whispered in apostasy. She turned away. Now she had to go home. Now she had to tell Ma what she'd done the day she skipped work. What would Ma and Da say? Would Da say anything? Ever again?

Victoria Sterling stared at the report. She was used to her people being incompetent. But *this* stupid? Even they must have worked at screwing up this badly. She slammed her hand down on the buzzer and started counting. That imbecile of a security chief had better be here before she got to ten.

He must have been expecting her ring. He was standing in front of her desk in five counts.

"What do you mean, a mountain vanished? Mountains don't vanish."

"Yes, ma'am."

"Well." She waited to see how something this preposterous had gotten into a report on her desk.

"We did not report that one had. Only that several sources were reporting that one had," he clarified.

"Who?"

"Brother Jonah has told his inner circle of seeing just such a, ah, miracle, and considered it important enough to swear them to secrecy."

"He's probably just been nipping at the sacramental mushrooms. You can't trust what those mystics and dervish say."

"We are in total agreement, ma'am, but Brother Jonah has never been one of that ilk. We always found him one of the more rational among the religious fanatics."

"None is acting very rational right now," Victoria snorted.

"Something we are seeing a lot of."

Victoria fixed her man with a long look. Was he being sarcastic? He looked away first, cleared his throat. "Among those we have under observation, ma'am," he clarified.

That sounded better, more properly servile. "I assume you have some other source or you would not be wasting my time with such an outlandish rumor."

"In the report you will note that this was twice mentioned by members of the spaceship's ground team. We have inserted three agents in villages near the camp. They have overheard conversations between crew members about a vanished mountaintop. When drunk, one of them raved on most frighteningly about his fear of having to face someone with 'artillery,' I believe was the word used, like that. There apparently has been a recent war between the rest of humanity with much loss of life."

"Yes, I saw that." Victoria dismissed that with the wave of a hand. That was there. This was here.

"Why didn't Jeffrey mention that to me when we talked?"

"Maybe he wasn't aware of it. Possibly the ship people do not share that information readily."

"Ha, little Jeffrey is nothing if not thorough. He was doing a survey out there. If that mountain went missing, he would have spotted it. Where is that boy, anyway?"

"Our last confirmed reports had him boarding the shuttle at the Refuge blimpfield."

Victoria spotted the use of "confirmed." She'd learned that her intelligence chief could hide a mountain under that word. "And your last unconfirmed report?"

"A team of star people arrived by shuttle late yesterday to assist Refuge in its crowd control problem." Victoria enjoyed a snort at that. She knew how to handle things like that, ship them off to the farms. No problem. "One of the three mules assigned to that group made a high-speed run to Sterlingview, where they met with the geologist, Harry Hoskins, and spirited away his family. One of our informants potentially identified your brother in that group. However, it was very dark."

"There was a mule not ten miles from here, and you let it

get away!" Victoria was out of her seat. "I told you I wanted one of those in my lab! I wanted that mule!" she shouted.

"Yes, ma'am. Our informant had thirty people with him and was confident that they could apprehend the entire party. However, they had one of those marines with a rifle."

"One marine, with one rifle, and my people just ran away."

"There may have been more. It was a very dark night. Electricity was off, and our informant could not call for backup."

"And he expects to get paid!" Victoria shrieked. "Next you're going to tell me he deserves to get paid."

"No, ma'am."

"You bet he's not going to get paid. And don't you think you can slip this one by me. I'll go over your department's expenses for the next six months, line by line. I better not see this—this—coward and traitor being paid."

"Yes, ma'am. Certainly, ma'am."

"Now, go find out how somebody made a mountain disappear. If the star people are scared of it, who did it?"

"Yes, ma'am."

"Idiot." He had escaped out the door and was saved from having to answer that remark.

Ray lay on his back, a gray briefcase under his arm. This case carried an emergency cardiac kit, not explosives. Still, it should be all the reminder he needed in his sleep. *If* he slept. His heart pounded, his blood raced. Sleep was not going to come easy. He willed himself to relax.

And was marching across the polished marble floor of the Unity presidential briefing hall, toward President Urm and four of his honchos. Ray wore the uniform he'd worn to that fateful meeting; his polished boots clicked with each step on the cold marble. Despite the chill, Ray felt sweat trickle from his armpits. Under his left arm, he carried the briefcase of explosives he'd risked his life to transport to this moment.

With a blink, Ray rejected the scene. Yes to the hall, yes to his uniform. No to the Teachers as powerful Unity thugs. They became five squabbling Wardhaven politicians. Ray considered that, then rejected it again. If his mind was translating the Teacher to him, quite possibly it was also projecting images to the Teacher. Ray would control those images.

Five university professors stood before Ray in dowdy regalia. Ray remembered them, an economics professor who couldn't balance his own checkbook, a philosopher who couldn't prove his own existence, a counselor who'd lost his wife to a convicted mass murderer. Ray smiled, not a bad representation of what he'd seen so far of the Teacher.

"You're back," one on the right growled. "Want more?"

"No. I've come with a message for you."

"What kind of message?" the center asked.

Ray brought the briefcase out from beneath his arm. A table appeared in front of him. He put the briefcase down, entered its combination, the one that set the charges, and turned it toward the five. "I am Colonel Raymond Longknife. I command Captain Mattim Abeeb, formerly commander of the Humanity cruiser Sheffield. In the recent war, he was ordered to kill a planet, and the billion people living on it. To prevent that, I killed the president of the political group known then as Unity and ended that war."

"Ancient history," one on the right wing grumbled.

"If you cause any further damage to the humans living on this planet, or by your actions or inactions cause them to do further damage to each other, I will order Captain Abeeb to use the resources at his disposal to move the asteroids in this solar system out of their orbits and onto a collision course with this planet. He can and will see that this planet is hit so hard and so often that it is shaken to its very core. The next ship arriving around this star will find only an asteroid belt where this planet is. Do I make myself clear?"

"Yes," the center said, chastened. Ones on the right and the left started to speak. Several looked on the verge of apoplexy. The center waved them to silence. "I think we have a much better understanding of your people now."

"Good. Leave us alone."

•   •   •

And Ray rolled over and went to sleep. His dreams were of Rita, a tiny baby in her arms. He kept wanting to ask her if it was a boy or a girl, but it was so much fun just looking at the child, he never got around to saying a word.

Ray enjoyed breakfast the next morning, right up to when Mary glanced behind him. "Dumont, where have you been?" Ray turned to find Dumont, Jeff, and a teary-eyed young teenage girl.

"I think you ought to hear Nikki," Jeff said.

"I made the mountain disappear," the girl blurted out. "Or *we* did," she corrected herself. All conversation around the room died, like a fuse had been pulled.

Ray looked the trembling girl over. She couldn't be more than thirteen. Now he remembered her, the brewmaster's other daughter. Jeff hung around the older one, or vice versa. "You look exhausted," Ray said. "Find her a chair."

Kat was off hers in a flash, got it under the young woman a split second before the local collapsed, then pulled over another chair for herself. Ray motioned Dumont and Jeff to sit; he didn't want anyone towering over this poor kid as she told her story. There had to be a lot more behind the few words she'd gotten out.

With a nod to Kat, Ray gave her the go to be the friend, the big sister, in the interrogation. Much better approach than a rubber hose. Kat leaned forward, rubbed Nikki's hand gently. "How did you make the mountain disappear?"

"We didn't mean to," Nikki said slowly. Then the dam broke. "Daga found it. Daga's always finding things. Small stuff. This was big. A box, three feet long, maybe a foot and a half square. Cold. Boy, it was hard carrying it, but it got warmer as the morning went on. I thought I was getting warmer with the sun up, but I think it was, too. We didn't know what the box was for. We didn't know," she pleaded with Kat.

"I believe you. What did you do with it?"

"We lugged it out to this hill west of town. We couldn't get it open, not even Daga, until I found the right place to push.

Then Daga found the other place, and it opened. All it looked like was a piece of window glass. You could see through it." Nikki scrunched up her face. "At least on one side. But it was all black on the other side; you couldn't see anything that way. And when you looked through it, things got really close. Emma wanted to look at Hazel Dell, but Daga wanted to look at the mountains. We were looking at one when it happened."

"What?" Kat encouraged Nikki over the pause.

Now the young woman spoke slowly. "The machine started making this noise. It got worse and worse. We were trying to find a way to turn it off. Really we were. Then there was this flash, and the mountain disappeared and the box closed up on itself. All by itself!"

"Did you try to reopen it?"

"No! I just wanted to find a hole in the ground to bury it again. Find a deep pool in a cave and sink it. But Daga would have nothing of that."

"What did Daga do?"

"She made me carry the box off to a cave. We had to carry it all by ourselves because Emma and Willow never stopped running after the mountain, you know, disappeared."

"Smart kids," Dumont growled.

"I couldn't leave it lying there!" Nikki defended herself.

"No, you couldn't," Ray said softly. *Go easy on this kid. She's our only lead,* he sent with a glance around his team.

"Do you remember where you put it?" Kat asked.

"We checked this morning, sir," Dumont put in. "It's gone."

"I think Daga took the others there," Nikki said, "the ones who want to save the land for farming. And the three quiet city folks who came out to see you mine that hill."

"Well, that changes everything," Mary growled.

"A gadget two teenage girls can carry that will make a mountain disappear fifty klicks away," Ray breathed. "Oh, hell."

"Mountain, city, my base," Mary expanded. "I don't think 'Oh, hell' quite cuts the mustard, Colonel."

They adjourned to the HQ. Ray, Mary, Lek, and Chief Barber tried to figure out how to chase a vanishing box and protect a base from it. "Chief, launch the shuttle to the west. Sweep from here to Refuge on full sensors. Put everything we've got analyzing the results. If we spot half a dozen people carrying a one-by-half-by-half-meter box, get a sky eye on it immediately."

"Yessir."

"Kat," Ray said into his commlink.

"Yessir."

"Bring back all the sky eyes. Get the location of the target cave from Jeff. Assume a circle fifty klicks out from it and expanding at a walking pace. I want the eyes on it like a blanket. You'll be getting some shuttle feed. We're looking for a group of seven or less people carrying a large package among them or one with a backpack."

Ray and Mary retreated to the map table. At least here their problem could be reduced to a familiar drill: Find them, fix them in place, take them down. Could be fun except for the minor fact that all this group had to do was point a windowpane at you, and you vanished. Hum, maybe Mary's pass wasn't the worst tactical problem he'd ever faced.

Protecting the base was hardly an easier problem. There were several knolls and hills that had a direct line of sight on them. "No way we can move our gear out of here," Barber said.

"Maybe we won't have to," Lek said. "Last blimp out from Refuge had a couple of resident experts on low-metal electronics. You know they're using salt water in place of metals."

"I know about their trains," Ray nodded.

"Well, between us, we came up with an idea for plastic polymer and saltwater ID cards. Won't be as small as ours"—Lek pointed at a wrist unit—"but it'll give us something we can give to everyone living near the base. If a blimp picks up someone with a heartbeat and no card, we check them out."

"Sounds good. Let's launch the northern recon group today. I want to move up the raid on the Sterling archives."

Mary shook her head. "You got to remember, boss, I only got fifty-three marines, and seventeen are in Refuge. You want to send the recon out without an escort?"

"No. Cut the northern recon to one day. The other project goes as soon as they get back."

An hour later, a blimp headed north to take core samples in out-of-the-way places that wouldn't bother the Covenanters, and might give Ray a taste of any new electronic systems recently put in place by the Teacher. The shuttle was making its return pass at thirty-five thousand meters, shooting its data take to Kat and her analysts. One spy eye was giving them its view of the immediate area around the cave from ten thousand meters; the other two were winging their way back.

Half a dozen people with a very dangerous box were doing their best to stay lost.

Ray needed data about these people, data he didn't have. "Where's the padre?" he asked the duty section.

"Ah, sir, he's at his church. Hearing confessions, I think he said. All day."

Ray's first drive was not quite as exhilarating as his first walk, but it was fun to control his own vehicle. It also served as a reminder that not all the things this crazy planet was doing were bad. Could any of them have survived if their white cells hadn't been modified?

The church was stone, with a thatched roof. As Ray stepped into its shady nave, he paused. To let his eyes adjust, he told himself, not because the transition to this sacred space required it. The church smelled of wood from the rough-hewn benches, beeswax from the single candle burning on the altar, and incense. A kneeler creaked as Father Joseph turned from his prayers to observe who had wandered into his quiet reserve.

Ray gave him a half salute. "Hearing confessions all day? You don't look busy." If Ray had caught the priest in a lie, he wanted it out in the open now, not later.

The priest took a length of purple cloth from his pocket, crossed himself with it, kissed it, and put it around his neck. The stole seemed out of place against the common peasant dress he wore. Then Ray blinked. He'd seen chaplains put the same stole on over battle dress as well as black shirts with Roman collars.

"People will be wandering this land today" the priest said

quietly, "hungry, hurting, maybe in need of confessing something they did or didn't do. There are extra potatoes in the rectory to feed the stomach. I'm here to feed the soul. What have you come for?"

"Food for my mind. I have a problem."

The priest did not seem surprised. He motioned Ray forward. As Ray joined him beside the first pew, the priest genuflected to the altar and headed toward two comfortable chairs off to the side before a roughly worked statue of a woman and child. Ray gave the altar a nod, out of respect for the priest's belief, and followed. The priest settled into one chair, said nothing, steepled his fingers, and leaned back calmly with the air of one ready to listen patiently to anything and everything. As Ray sat, he decided to pull no punches.

"There is a device loose on this planet that can make a mountain disappear, or a city—and everyone in it."

The priest whistled. "God has granted you such power."

"Nope, not God. And not us. Apparently Daga from your parish discovered it. Now it's in the hands of radical folks. I don't know what they intend to do with it, and that scares me."

"And any reasonable person," the priest breathed. "Daga was a delightful child. Something came over her last year." The priest tapped his forehead. "This thing your doctor has found in our heads must be a great challenge to Almighty God's mercy."

"I think this is just normal human cussedness," Ray said. "I need to know what you know about what's going on."

The priest started in his chair. Back straight, he shook his head. "There is little I can tell you. Daga has rarely been to Mass this last year. Parents worry. I tell them to pray, and show their children love. This is a stage they must walk through. They will come out the other side."

"I understand the seal of confession, Father," Ray cut the priest off. Time was short; people were walking. A search circle was widening. "What can you tell me that most any gossip might know about how Sterling's industries and farmers and the Greens and hockey teams and all the rest normally behave?"

Ray made himself relax back into his chair. "We've accessed archives. They tell us painfully little. Newspapers with recipes on the front pages. Papers filled with church socials, workers' picnics, who's in the hospital and who's been in a brawl, though not many of those. Padre, in almost any other portion of space, I'd swear that a party censor had a choke hold on the newsroom. Is that what's going on here?"

The priest's lips fell into a frown. "The more you tell me about the worlds out there, the less I like them. Yet, we are the ones with the thing that can vanish a city. We are the ones who have taken to killing our brothers and sisters. You had nothing to do with this, despite Brother Jonah's claims. You just want to help us survive something from out of our own soil."

"Yes, padre. Help me understand. Help us all."

"Our papers are filled with what people do for fun so that others may join them. Maybe a few gossips would like papers such as you speak of, but they are busy talking, not reading. Though maybe you are right about one thing. Often young men from the villages work a few years for the Sterlings, to make the money they need to buy their first set of tools. Working for Victoria Sterling is not easy. From them I hear stories of machines damaged, vehicles wrecked, buildings burned. We've always ascribed them to the Greens, but I never made anything of those stories."

"Chu Lyn's people, huh?"

"Oh, no, Chu leads the major circle in New Haven. She would never stand for any such behavior from her people. San Paulo knows that. So does Victoria Sterling, though I suspect it does not make her any less angry. No, Chu Lyn's people are as different as—well, as the people of Hazel Dell. Just because we live here doesn't mean we agree," the priest chuckled. "We come together and talk and talk. And bring in the crops. That, at least, we can agree on." The priest's eyes sparkled at that.

Ray let out a long, noisy breath. "So people agree to disagree, enjoy themselves, and go about their business."

"Or so it seemed until this thing in our heads made people reach for clubs and their neighbors' throats," the priest added.

"Any idea where someone with a small box that can do great damage might take it?"

The priest shook his head. "Too many. South, into the New Haven area, where those of like minds would help them. But you have already thought of that. To the east, where Richland is and other burned-out towns and villages. They might go there if the anger in their hearts is high." Ray nodded agreement. "They could go north. There are those of faith who believe the world is here for us to subdue. The Sterlings like to hear that preached and have those churches in Richland. However, there are also those to the north who believe we should return the earth to a garden like the one they say Adam and Eve were expelled from."

"Everybody reads the same book. Nobody gets the same answer," Ray snorted.

"And you, have you never had need of something greater to believe in?" the padre asked.

"At times. Right now I'm a bit busy."

"It is like that in all our lives. But tell me, Colonel. I have heard them call you that. It is a military rank and honor?"

"Yes."

"Will you order my people away from your base, their homes?"

"No. Our technology offers us better options. We're making ID cards for everyone. We'll ask people to carry them at all times. If our sensors spot someone within twenty klicks of here without a card, we'll send marines out to check on them."

"How will you get my people to carry the cards?"

"We're going to include credit balances in them as well. If you work for us or provide goods, we'll promise you so much copper equivalent in a credit balance."

"People like to have copper," the priest said gingerly.

"I know. We'll pay extra for them to take our credit. That ought to do it."

"And children? This box is the size of a baby carrier. You will want to keep track of children."

"That has me stumped. Any ideas?"

The old man rubbed his chin for a long minute. "Among

the refugees there are stories of children getting lost. If you offered these cards as a way to keep track of the children, assure that they are returned to their parents, you might find people very willing to listen to you." The priest stopped in midthought. "These sensors of yours. Do they only tell you that this person has a card, or can they tell you who that person is and where they are?"

"Both," Ray answered.

"God be praised," the priest smiled. "So you could help a mother know that her child is far over there, as well as look at a child's ID and know that her mother is in that village."

"We can," Ray told the priest.

"I think you will find people very willing to accept your cards. Very willing. How soon can you begin giving them out?"

"Tomorrow."

"I will tell the people of this wonderful gift you have for us in these troubled times." Ray stood; the priest accompanied him to the tiny vestibule of the church.

Closing the door behind him, Ray shook his head. As a boy, he'd seen a vid where a girl fell down a hole into a world where everything was reversed. Day was night, up was down, crazy. Just like this lunatic world. The media wanted only happy news. People gratefully let a central authority keep track of them. On second thought, maybe he ought to quarantine Santa Maria for the sake of the rest of humanity's sanity. Or maybe for the sake of the Santa Marians' sanity.

Ray's call to San Paulo was an anticlimax after talking to the padre. She was appropriately shocked that someone had found a gadget to make mountains or Lander's Refuge disappear. No, she didn't think they ought to tell anyone about this development. Yes, she'd be glad to help Ray set up an ID card system for the population of Refuge and its environs. The idea of using said cards to keep a balance of copper credits owed was intriguing. "Is that the way you do it among the stars?" "Yes," he assured her. It might work, but he'd have to talk to Victoria and Chu and they'd have to take it to their respective circles.

Ray could just picture Vicky asking anyone for advice. Oh, well, three out of four was not bad.

That night Mary watched as the northern recon's blimp limped back with hardly a hundred feet of spare altitude, leaking hydrogen from countless airgun bullet holes. The blimp settled in with a thump. Mules quickly surrounded it, and the marines and crew piled in, too exhausted to walk to the barracks.

While Kat, Lek, and Harry went off, talking rapidly about the geomorphology and conductivity of the strange rock samples they'd collected, Mary cornered Jeff and Dumont. "How'd it go?"

"Fairly good at first," Dumont shrugged. "Got tighter as folks noticed us. Had to shoot our way out of the last place."

"Any casualties?"

"None on our side. 'Course, poor Jeff here lost his virginity." Dumont gave Jeff a slug on the shoulder.

"You okay?" Mary asked. The young man looked green.

"I'll live," Jeff muttered. "Can't say that for others."

"I need both of you. We've put together our best imagery of Vicky's compound. Jeff, can you tell me what's where?"

"When we going visiting?" Dumont asked.

"Tomorrow night."

"That fast?"

Mary did a quick glance around. "Until we know where that damn mountain-killer is, we have to consider every place on this planet subject to vanishing. We're working on making the base safe. Should be by day after tomorrow. Whatever Vicky's got, I want it here by then."

"Can I go with you?" Jeff asked.

"I was hoping you would," Mary smiled.

Dumont shook his head. "Damn fool volunteer. Some kids never learn."

"Like a few I know." This time it was Dumont's shoulder that got punched. They piled Mary's mule with rock slabs, then headed for the HQ. On the table that they could turn into anything, Mary had a layout of the Sterling mansion compound.

Jeff was amazed at how much they already knew. The ground around the buildings was marked for weight bearing; they'd spotted all the flower beds and even the place in front that collected rain and always seemed to make a mudhole. "You've spotted the kitchen, even the bathrooms. How'd you do that?"

The two marines exchanged a grin. "We have our ways," Mary said. "So, where's the data stored?"

Jeff ran his fingers over their layout of the archives building. "You've got the three workstations in the right place. There's a second door into that room. Comes from a stair you missed." He pointed out the central security passage.

"Nobody's used it," Mary said.

"Don't, unless they have to. You've got the guard post in the basement right, but there's an emergency stairs out of there to both floors. They can get up and into any room without using the public access."

"Damn," Mary and Dumont echoed. "Nice to have an inside man," Mary finished, then went on, "Are we just after the workstations? Are there backups?"

"All along this wall." Jeff thought of the blimp and its limited lift. "Say, twenty feet of shelving, eight shelves high. I don't know what that weighs."

"We'll find out," Mary assured him.

"What's on the upper floor?" Dumont asked.

"Books, printed maps, pictures of dead ancestors, as Vicky puts it. Souvenirs collected over the years. A few bits of jewelry that Great-Great Aunt Elma made. She fancied herself an artist. Vicky keeps threatening to melt them down to make something practical out of them, but Mom liked them. I don't think there's anything up there you'd be interested in."

"Books?" Mary reminded him.

"I think they're all on disk. Maybe not all, but do you really want someone's old art book from Earth?"

"I don't know." Mary shrugged. "I guess we can always go back for more if we have to."

"I'm bushed, Mary." Dumont stepped away from the map table. "Jeff has got to be. Let's go over this in the morning again."

"I've got some locals laying out a full-size mock-up of this place so we can practice tomorrow. Need to add a stairs."

"You want to bunk at the barracks tonight?" Dumont offered.

"I'd rather go back to the inn," Jeff mumbled.

"See how the girl is," Dumont nodded.

"Take my mule," Mary offered. "Be back at oh-six-thirty."

Jeff glanced at his wrist, realized he still had some marine's commlink. "Who do I give this to?"

"Keep it," Mary said. "That way I can call you in the morning. You're sure as hell going to need it tomorrow night."

"Thanks," Jeff answered. "Thanks for everything."

"You've earned it, you poor dumb shit," Dumont grinned. "You're one of us now."

Hazel Dell was dark as Jeff drove its streets. He parked in the alley behind the Public Room and let himself in the back door. One candle burned in the room, showing Annie and her dad still in the same chairs they'd been in this morning when he left. Mrs. Mulroney quickly stood from the chair between them. "Would you like something to eat?" she asked.

"I'm not hungry." Jeff hadn't eaten since breakfast, but his stomach was not interested.

As her mom settled back into her chair, Nikki made her way slowly to the keg. Jeff shook that off. "Tea," he said. "Hot."

"What's wrong?" Annie said hoarsely, as if they were her first words of the day. Her eyes did not move from the patch of wall they'd been staring at for the past two days.

"Nothing," Jeff answered, searched for more words and settled for "I'm alive."

"Where have you been?" her mom asked.

For a long moment, Jeff didn't know what to answer. Nikki arrived with tea. He sipped it slowly. "Hell. Maybe."

Now Annie's eyes came around to him, looked at him for the first time since she'd returned. "What did they do to you?"

"It's what *I* did to *them*," Jeff answered, putting down the tea and taking Annie's hands in his. Hers were cold, so cold.

His still had the warmth of the tea on them. Still, he began to slowly rub her hands as he told the story of his day.

The words came out in a monotone, the people coming at them when anyone with an ounce of sense would have fled. People with airguns taking on the marines. Taking on Jeff. Dying under Jeff's gun sights. The three hung on Jeff's words; even Annie's dad started to show a response or two.

"What is happening to us?" Annie's mom moaned.

"I don't know." It was the only answer Jeff could make.

"Would the starfolk shoot Daga, the others if they found them and the box?" Nikki asked, eyes wide.

Jeff thought about that, let it rumble around in his tired mind. "Yes. They would. I would, now." His words sank into the darkness of the room. Hung there. Tears in her eyes, Nikki tore out the front door. No one went after her.

"She'll come back," her mom said softly, eyes still on the slammed and half-open door.

"She will," Annie agreed.

"I've got to get some sleep," Jeff said, standing. "We're going after the Sterling archives tomorrow. I'll be home late. Maybe not until morning."

"You'll be using the rifle," Annie's dad said.

Jeff glanced at the webbing crossing his chest, realized for the first time that he'd brought his rifle with him. "Yes."

"Be careful," Annie said.

"I will."

"I'll wait up for you tomorrow." For once, neither Annie's mom nor dad censured her. What had Jeff heard the Colonel say, "Everything is changing"? Maybe all of it wouldn't be for the bad. Jeff climbed the stairs to his room, unslung his rifle, and fell into bed, clothes and boots still on. That was how he found himself when his commlink buzzed, and the duty officer informed him it was 0600 and he was due back in half an hour.

TEN

MARY NEEDED THINGS: a good target mock-up, someone to play Vicky's goons, and better information on the guards' routine. Mary needed lots of things; she wasn't going to get them. She tried to be philosophical, but she'd survived enough firefights to know unmet needs like these caused casualties. With luck, they wouldn't be anyone she knew.

The old feeling was back, the cold in the pit of the gut, the tightness around lips and eyes. It was time to soldier. Time for people to die or live, and she would be the angel of death deciding which. *Damn! I don't want to do this again! I earned my right to be an overpaid security guard. The only killing I want to make is mining this planet!*

If the Colonel said right, they already had made one killing, an artificial intelligence Ray called the Gardener. Well, he hadn't known, and she sure as hell had no idea she was mining the guts out of something when she tapped that mountain. Accidents happen. And shit happens. And a combat drop was about to happen and Mary was going to do her level best to see that it happened the way she wanted it.

Mary had tapped a young woman blimp driver for the mission; she liked Rhynia's flair. When told Mary needed a blimp to swoop down out of the sky with marines dangling from it on ropes, Rhynia's reply was a dimpled smile and a "Why the hell not?"

Mary planned several full rehearsals to give both marines and blimp a chance to work together. The morning started with Jeff walking them through a mock-up of the archives in the field behind the shuttle hangar. Red tape showed the main floor plan, blue tape the basement. Jeff pointed out each workstation's location and the back entrance for the security team.

"Du, your squad heads downstairs first thing and ties down the guards," Mary said. "All else, we use sleepy bullets. If Jeff's big sis wanders into our snatch, we don't want to accidently pop her. Put anyone to sleep who has a gun, knife, or looks to cause trouble." Jeff started to say something, but Du gave him a wink and said he'd explain later. Mary walked the marines through their part in the snatch. Each had something to do every second, going someplace, looking someplace, guarding someplace, or grabbing something—not a free moment.

Jeff's mouth hung open. "Sis likes everyone busy, but nothing like this."

"Sis never worked with live ammunition and dudes who know how to use it," Dumont laughed.

"Keep it serious," Mary growled. "An airgun can pop you just as dead as an M-6," she reminded them. Twice Mary walked them through, talking up each move, each alternative, each possible threat. Then she had them run through it. Then she waved her wrist unit and timed them. Three minutes from entrance to exit. "We can do better than that," she told them.

They did. Two minutes, forty-five seconds. "Not bad," Mary admitted grudgingly as a yeoman trotted up and saluted.

"Colonel's compliments and regrets, but you might want to look at the latest feed from the sky eye over the target area." Ray better send his regrets for interrupting her day, but a surprise at the target could make the day very regrettable.

Mary tapped her commlink. "Colonel, you got something?"

"Yes, Captain. They've upped the guards at the archives and doubled the guards all around."

"They know we're coming?"

"Doubt it. Lek's been hacking and cracking their net. Seems some of Brother Jonah's faithful think Vicky belongs in hell and are ready to send her there personally."

"Oh, shit. Just what I need, amateurs pissing in my soup." Mary turned to Dumont, filled him in quickly.

"Guess we didn't pop enough church folks yesterday," Dumont drawled. Then he frowned. "Colonel, you sure none of those folks ain't after us here, at base? After all, we were the ones messing all over their turf yesterday."

"Yes," Ray said. "There are a few folks that think we need a quick trip to a warm place. They're just getting organized. The move on Vicky has been in the works for a while."

"And she would have to find out about it just when we need to slip in quietly," Mary scowled. "If it weren't for bad luck, we wouldn't have any."

"I have full confidence in you," Ray answered. "I've seen the quality of your work."

Mary winced. "We aim to please," Dumont answered. Mary aimed a swing at his head, but he ducked.

Mary took two deep breaths, trying to work off the sudden pressure around her chest. No plan survives contact with the enemy. Hell, she couldn't get a plan to survive the morning. "It would be so much easier," Mary groaned, "to just pop 'em all and take what we want. Taking 'em down, quiet-like, is a bitch!"

Du nodded. "Taking 'em down and keeping us up, I will remind you, ma'am. I ain't thirsty for a lot of killing, but if it's ten of those jokers or one of mine, I look out for mine."

For the thousandth time, Mary wondered why she'd accepted those gold bars and a management position. As captain of Security she couldn't just ask the Colonel what to do. He relied on her to do her job. "Tico, drill the crew on the building takedown until chow time." A sergeant was on her feet, snapping a salute and getting the crew back in practice mode. "Dumont, you and Jeff with me. Let's see what those pictures show. Rhynia, you're with me, too. How far can I push you and your blimp?"

"Ma'am," the pilot grinned, "the wind pushes us blimp drivers around all the time. Nobody else does."

Victoria Sterling smiled. The space fools were so stupid. They came in here so smug, acting like they knew everything, but they knew nothing! Nothing at all about how things work on Santa Maria. Victoria looked again at the public land records she'd researched. Very important pages were blank. Yes, she had that idiot Longknife with his swaggering canes. She owned him now.

Ray frowned as he cycled his workstation through the high priorities he had to keep a thumb on. The search for the "vanishing box" continued, success diminishing with each passing minute. Mary's snatch and grab grew more complicated as the watch on her target identified more security going up around the Sterling compound. Lek and Harry were going over the rock samples recovered yesterday from up North, using everything handy and spending most of their time shaking their heads. Doc was pulling his hair out. His biopsies of tumors from Refuge cadavers showed larger ones in the rioters. He didn't dare cut into a live one, as much as he wanted to.

A page flashed for attention. Kat's dive through the Santa Marians database had found something. Miscarriages were double the human normal. Double! Most in the first trimester. As an expectant father, Ray had taken a very personal interest in human reproduction. Early miscarriages usually meant bad genes, nonviable blastocysts.

He started to make a note to Kat, track this over the past three hundred years. His board refreshed itself; Kat already had. The curve she passed along got a low whistle. There almost hadn't been a first generation born here. Four miscarriages per live birth. *Gardener, you almost wiped us out.*

Ray went on. Chief Barber was handing out ID cards as fast as he could press them; people were lining up to get them for their entire family, and hardly noticing the card included an electrocardiac signature as well as a copper balance.

By the time Ray finished one review, it was time for another. Again he frowned at the search for the "vanishing box." Still no miracle.

Annie trembled; with an effort, she turned from the patch of wall she'd been staring at. The sun was up, casting bars of light on the floor, chairs, tables. She'd heard Jeff slip out at dawn, called "Luck" softly, and prayed he'd come back. He must not have heard, or maybe he was tired of seeing her so limp, like a worn-out dishrag. She would wait for him.

Da stirred; Ma took his hand, caressed its palm with gentle circles. Da looked at Ma, actually saw her. The two smiled, and Ma helped Da to his feet. Annie listened to the stairs creak as Ma led Da to bed. Annie so wanted a man like Da to care for.

The door opened; Annie realized she would have to care for any customers this morning. She tensed, torn between making herself small and unnoticed, and doing what she should do. Annie need not have bothered; it was only Nikki. Face tear-stained and dress dirty, little sister headed for the kitchen. Annie could hear her rummaging quietly in the cupboards, hunting for her own breakfast. But Nikki took longer than any self-respecting Mulroney should to make a single breakfast. Far too long.

Annie worked herself up to her feet and softly padded to the kitchen door. Nikki was filling a large sack with food. "What are you doing?"

Nikki jumped. "Getting food," she evaded.

"I can see that. Why?"

"I'm going on the road. I have to find Daga." The words flew out of Nikki, as if to stop even one would tear the tongue from her mouth. "I *can* stop her, make her listen to reason. If the star people find her, they'll shoot her. You heard Jeff. I can't let them kill Daga. She's my friend." The words ended in a flood of tears.

"Nikki, you can't go out there. It's not safe." Annie searched for words. "The roads have changed. They're full of people like . . ." Annie had no words for what Nikki would face.

"I have to," Nikki insisted, reaching for her sack. "She's my friend. I don't want her to hurt anyone—or get hurt."

Annie stood there, hunting for a way to keep her sister safe and help Daga. There was only one way, Dumont's way. "Wait a moment, Nikki. Don't go until I get back."

Nikki halted, sack over her shoulder, hand on the kitchen door. Annie quickly crossed the Public Room floor to find her wallet with Dumont's pistol. He'd given it to Da, but Da had stared at it like a puzzle he could not solve. Annie had taken it, hidden it in the folds of her dress. It had stayed there until Dumont returned. Dumont came back when the screaming was done, his face as blank as a newborn's, hard as kilned ceramic.

He holstered his rifle and drove off without a backward glance. Annie had not wasted one either, but had watched where they were going, watched for more trouble. Halfway home, Dumont seemed to come back from where he'd gone. Looking around, he'd taken in Da, then glanced back at her. "You took the automatic."

"Yes," she'd gotten out.

"Keep it. The captain will rip me a new one, but you're gonna need it more than me. Take good care of it."

"I will," Annie said, the last words she'd said until they got home. Annie slipped the pistol into the leather wallet on her belt; it was heavy and comfortable there. Back in the kitchen, she found Nikki waiting. "Let me leave Ma a note," she told Nikki. "I'm going with you." Nikki opened her mouth as if to argue, then smiled like she had when she was a little girl and Annie had invited her out to play with the big girls. Annie wrote quickly, then remembered and added a line at the bottom:

Ma, tell Jeff where I've gone and that I love him.

Strange words to write, now, as she went out the door. Strange now to realize they were true. "Let's go, Nikki."

Jeff's dropstation was at Mary's elbow. He sat next to her, a blimp exit, dark and yawning, across from them. Night cloaked black uniforms and face paint. With his goggles, he could see the marines around him. Heavily laden, most napped, or appeared to. Mary stared out the door, mouth working as if going over every detail of the plan she had, probably looking for what she called Plans B, C, and D. Jeff figured she was up to Z in a few areas. Anybody going cross-wise against Vicky better have lots of alternatives in her hip pocket.

Dumont was across from Jeff. Du's squad of sharpshooters would be the first out, assuming something didn't change in the next—Jeff glanced at his wrist unit—five minutes. His eyes rested on the combination watch, radio, navigation device, and computer workstation. It was amazing what humanity had done while Santa Maria was just struggling to stay alive.

The sound of the wind against the blimp gondola changed; napping heads came up. Dumont's face took on a feral grin; the man was so hard to figure. In the mule he'd wanted to get rid of his gun. Yet, when Annie's life and worse was on the line, he'd killed with no regrets. Today he'd chided Mary to remember they were peacekeepers. This afternoon Dumont had shown Jeff how to use every aspect of his rifle, from sleepy bullets to live ammunition to bayonet, and Jeff, who missed half the instructions the first time, paid full attention. Amazing what becomes important after you've been shot at.

And shot back.

Jeff could still see the faces on the people he'd killed yesterday. But today he remembered them without his stomach going green and his chest getting tight. They'd made their choices; they didn't have to be on the rocky knoll trying to kill Dumont and the others. All the starfolks wanted was some rocks. It was the Covenanters who had turned it terminal, as Dumont put it. Now, Jeff could accept that logic. He'd changed, was changing, and he knew he would change more. But change or no change, he really looked forward to Vicky's reaction when she found out she'd lost the archives.

"First squad, stand to," Mary ordered. For this mission, every wrist unit had sprouted an earplug and a throat mike. Nobody had a hand to waste. "Prepare to dismount. Second squad and the blimp will wait for my orders."

There was a soft growl from the troops; Jeff stood. Even

with rifle, two types of ammunition, a dozen grenades in three different flavors, and four rockets to deliver said grenades, he felt light, excited. He was ready.

The blimp touched down on a rise a mile out from Fairview compound. Mary waved Jeff and Dumont out first. They squatted in the grass, goggles on high zoom, checking for any surprises as the rest of the squad double-timed past them to flop down in a circle, rifles aimed out. Mary joined them; behind her the blimp rose on the gentle breeze, backing slightly.

"All clear," Dumont said.

"Scouts out," Mary ordered.

Two marines trotted into the woods ahead. When Jeff flipped his goggles off, the men vanished. Moonless, the night would get even blacker when the predicted clouds moved in from the coast. Rain would come with morning, but Jeff would be long gone by then, or in the deepest pile of shit Vicky could find.

"Dumont, move out your squad," Mary ordered, and Du waved his team forward. Mary, Du, and Jeff fell in the middle of the widely disbursed team. There was no talking. Everyone knew their job; now it was just a matter of doing it. Twenty minutes later, they reached the end of Jason Woods. Halfway across the three hundred yards to the compound fence, two dark figures moved at a crouch. With a single hand wave from Dumont, the rest of the marines joined the scouts crossing the open space.

Except for lights in two basement windows, the archives were dark. Fairview itself was lit like a Lander's Day cake. Just looking at it made Jeff's goggles blur. Guards circled the big house like ants at a picnic. "See any surprises?" Mary asked; Jeff shook his head. She bent at the waist and followed her team. Jeff did the same, feeling naked and vulnerable.

"Freeze" came over the net. Jeff froze. Around him, images in his goggles locked in place, half steps unfinished.

"What we got?" Mary whispered.

"Scout One here. Guard and dog making a round of our side of the fence."

"Hold this freeze," Mary affirmed the order.

At the compound fence, backlit against the main house, a

man, air rifle slung over his shoulder, walked a large dog. Even though Mary had never seen a dog, except in a zoo, she'd quickly called up instructions on how to handle them when Vicky added four to her security blanket. "We approach from downwind," Mary said, and adjusted the blimp approach from east to south.

Now they'd see if the manual was right.

Halfway along their side of the fence, the dog halted, whining softly. "What is it, girl?" the guard asked, pulling gently on the dog's leash. The dog stared out, head weaving but settling on no particular line. She continued to whine.

"Come on, girl," the guard pulled on her leash gently, then yanked. "Come on. I'm not staying out here all night."

The dog obeyed. Jeff started breathing again. Mary didn't give the "Let's move it" order until the guard started down the next side of the fence.

"We got ten minutes before those two are back," Mary informed the team. "Make 'em count."

In less than five minutes, the team was spaced evenly along the fence. One of the trailing marines came up and pulled several devices from a satchel. First he checked the ceramic bars of the fence for an electrical charge. Vicky had several strings of thin glass piping along the top of the fence, charged with salt water. Anyone climbing over it was sure to break one. Vicky didn't expect anyone to go through a kilned ceramic bar.

The marine's hand laser made short work of six bars. Mary moved shooters through the hole, sending each for a specific target. It was two minutes to takedown when Jeff passed through the fence. The engineer followed Jeff in, then taped the bars back in place. They didn't expect to come out that way, but there was no use advertising they were in.

Sharpshooters spread across the archives grounds, intent on getting close to their targets. Four guards walked back and forth on the archives roof, new additions since midday. Mary had assigned a shooter to each one, a fifth to the guard and dog. Two more marines edged as close as they could to the basement windows where the duty watch and off-duty guards lounged. If things worked right, they'd be captured awake—

sleepy darts did not do windows. However, if things got too exciting too fast, well, Mary had her plan B.

"Take them down on my count of three," Mary ordered softly. "One . . . two . . . three."

Soft pops hardly disturbed the night as sleepy darts hit the four guards on the roof and the walking guard. The dog snapped around when her master went down. She hardly whimpered as a sleepy dart took her a second later.

Mary listened to the silence for a moment. "No alarms," she judged. "Dumont, take the basement. The rest of you, take the roof. Blimp, you're on immediate standby."

"Starting my approach. You have sixty seconds to order me into a go-'round," the blimp pilot said evenly.

Everywhere Jeff looked, marines were running. The engineer was first at the back door. One wave of his laser and the door slid open just as Dumont and five marines raced through, diving for the basement. The shooters who had taken out the roof and guard dog had farther to run. They went through the door behind Dumont's team and headed up. Mary joined Jeff in the vestibule. In front of him, the small lights on the workstations winked in reds and greens. The disk archives lined the wall to his right. Nothing appeared to have changed since his last visit.

"Basement secure," Dumont announced.

"Roof secure," another voice answered.

"Building secure. Rhynia, bring in the blimp. Second squad, your clock starts the second that gas bag is down."

"Is that any way to talk about your driver?" Rhynia chided Mary. "Touchdown in five seconds."

Jeff checked the archives making sure Harry's data was there. They appeared to be. He pulled one, read the cover. MARK STERLING, WESTERN SURVEY, 292. Having no more trust than anyone else in his family, he pulled the disk. It said the same. Jeff grinned as marines grabbed disks and stuffed them in bags slung over their shoulders. Great. Jeff turned as another marine took cutters to the cables securing the workstations to their stone tables, starting with the one closest to Jeff.

"Don't cut that one!" he shouted. Too late, the cutters did their work. All the green lights on the workstation went dead.

"Problem, mister?" Mary asked curtly.

"That station just went active. Someone was accessing it. The stations in the house slave to these."

"And one did," Mary sighed. "Knew it was going too good."

The network boxes on the other stations went green. A phone beeped downstairs. "Boss, Dumont here. Do I answer?"

"No," she snapped. "Cut those other stations loose," she ordered. "Folks, we got company coming, let's get ready. Dumont, any spare rifles you got, I want them on the roof. Okay, everybody, move it. I want us out of here five minutes ago."

Jeff followed Mary up the stairs. On the roof, marines were posted at each corner, eyes roving to cover their quarter, even the ones facing away from the big house. At the house, every light was on. People streamed out, buttoning coats or otherwise getting dressed. Too many for Jeff's liking had airguns at the ready. On the porch, Vicky screamed at the top of her lungs for security to earn its pay, to do something.

Several large spotlights, formerly at the blimp field to assist in late-evening landings, had been moved to Fairview's roof. They snapped on, played over the grounds for a second, then locked on the archives and the blimp looming behind it.

"Dumont, turn out those lights," Mary ordered.

"Heave, live ammunition."

"Going live," a woman's voice answered. "Good night, Mr. Light," she whispered as three pops sounded. One light shattered. Three more pops and the second went dark. The others clicked off without further encouragement. Relative dark returned. It didn't hide the crowd gathering on the lawn of the big house. Servants, guests, guards, both armed and not—anyone close and willing had been pressed into what Jeff knew could only be a slaughter. Dumont had already warned Jeff that sleepy darts had a range of only twenty to fifty meters. Put enough energy into a dart and it didn't matter what you tipped it with, it shattered bone, arteries, skulls.

"I can take down the screamer, Captain," Heave announced.

"No," Jeff and Mary said at the same time. Jeff swallowed. He couldn't kill Vicky. He hated her, but killing her . . . she was his sister. "Please, Mary, don't shoot Vicky."

"Probably wouldn't settle the crowd, anyway," Dumont judged.

"Grenadiers, load blue rounds," Mary ordered in answer.

Jeff followed Dumont's motions as he pulled one of the rockets from his backpack and attached it to the top of his rifle. Then he pulled a grenade from his belt, checked to make sure it had a broad blue band around its middle, and loaded it on his rocket. Done, Dumont went over Jeff's load. "Got it right the first time, kid," was Jeff's reward.

"Lay down a slick halfway between the house and the gate," Mary ordered. The archive had a low decorative fence about four feet high midway between it and the mansion. As Mary worked with her wrist unit, Jeff's goggles lit up with six target crosses in a wide blue swath, showing her fire plan. One blinked; Jeff had his targeting orders. With the others, he lifted his rifle, aimed at his assigned location, and fired. A dot of light leaped from his rifle, quickly suppressed by his goggles. Loud pops came from where the grenades were aimed, and a blue wash seemed to spread out from Jeff's target. What had he just done?

The crowd had stepped back as the rockets came in. When all fell short, they seemed to take courage. Vicky, of course, was yelling all the time for them to get a move on. Get over there and stop those thieves stealing her property.

"Grenadiers, load yellow rounds. Set them for a B—repeat, Bravo—pattern." Mary ordered in a voice so steady and calm Jeff wondered if she was here, watching several hundred people work themselves into a killing rage. Jeff followed Dumont's lead again. This time it included twisting the cap of the grenade around until a pointer settled on a B, logically located between A and C on the side of the round. Ready, he waited. Mary marked the same target for him. "All hands, we are about to go to flash bangs using a B pattern. Adjust goggles to B pattern."

Dumont was feeling around the right edge of his goggles. Jeff did, too, and found a small wheel half submerged in the rim. He moved it slowly. A small sign in the upper right-hand corner of his goggles that he had previously ignored changed to an A, then a B. His goggles started flickering between viewing the scene and blanking it out. "Got a B," Dumont said, pointing a finger at the place on Jeff's goggles where he now had a B.

"Yes. What's going on?"

"Just watch," Dumont grinned, white teeth gleaming in the borrowed light from the big house. "This ought to be funny."

"Here they come," Mary said. "Stand by." The crowd surged forward. A howl started growing louder and going up the scale. "Stand by," Mary repeated calmly. The first runners were approaching the blue wash on Jeff's goggles. They slipped, fell, shrieked in surprise. "Now!" Mary said.

Jeff and five others sent grenades arching out. They hit just ahead of the people who were down. Six booms reverberated over the howls and screams, then changed into some kind of popping racket. Now Jeff knew what was happening with his glasses. Rhythmically, they blanked, protecting him from blinding flashes that were disorienting the mob. Not that the people out there needed much help. More ran or were pushed into the blue stretch of yard to stumble, tumble, or pratfall all over each other. On hands and knees, people tried to get back out, only to fall on their faces. Over their groans, screams, shouts, and a few laughs, Vicky shrieked orders to get up, get moving. It only got worse for those who tried.

"We got leakers around the edges," Mary noted, and Jeff peeled his eyes away from the centerpiece to note a couple dozen people on the mob's flanks edging around the blue slick, looking for a way through. "Grenadiers, load blue, fire at my marks."

Jeff quickly went through the drill and lobbed a slick grenade off to the right, completing a box between the first line and the edge of the main building. More people went down.

"Archives and gear are out of the building," came over the net. "We're headed back to the blimp, Captain."

"Very good. Dumont, withdraw your squad."

"Basement detail, withdraw. Roof sharpshooters, withdraw."

The light and noise show came to a slow end. The mass of people on the lawn continued to try to grope, crawl, and belly-swim out of the slippery stuff. Mary grinned beside Jeff. "Came off easier than I'd expected. Let's go crew."

Jeff led them down the stairs. On the first-floor landing, he could see the last of the gear being loaded aboard the blimp, and the troops hustling quickly for it as well. Mary and Dumont joined him.

"Don't move" came in a familiar voice. From a small room off the main vestibule—a rest room—stepped Millard, impeccably dressed in black tails, an air pistol firmly in his hand. In the dim light coming through the window and the doorway, he aimed at Jeff's heart.

"Who's this gentleman?" Mary asked, coming to a very fast and complete halt.

"Millard, the downstairs butler," Jeff answered. "He can trim rosebushes with that pistol at fifty paces," he quickly added the essential information.

"Good shot," Mary nodded.

"He also teaches unarmed combat to the staff."

"I'm liking him better by the second," Dumont wise-cracked. "Any chance you'd like to join the corps? We're always looking for a few good men."

Jeff rolled his eyes at the ceiling. "He can't be bought."

"I and mine have served the Sterlings for six generations. Now"—he waved the gun toward the door—"if you will, order Miss Sterling's property returned."

"Where'd you come from?" Jeff asked, knowing it was a stupid question but needing time to adjust to what was happening way too fast for his brain to track.

"I was in the men's room when your vandals clomped through. You failed to check the rest room on this level." Millard's tone was the one he reserved for the maid who missed a large dust ball, a servant with a spotted salad fork.

"I'll mention that in my postmission critique," Mary answered dryly.

Jeff took a step forward. "Millard, these people really need that stuff. We'll all be better off if they take it."

"Young Jeffrey, you have again joined the losing side. Your sister will own these people before noon tomorrow."

"Millard, the old ways aren't going to work this time," Jeff said, edging another step forward.

"Do not assume I will not shoot you." Millard lowered his aim—slightly. "I can render your kneecaps worthless."

Jeff took a step back; the pistol's aim rose again. Glass shattered. A single round smashed into Millard's temple, snapping his head sideways, scattering blood and bone. As the butler fell, his gun popped as fast as a clamped finger could shoot it. Pellets stitched a line past Jeff's ear.

A moment later, Heave grinned through the window. "Know you didn't want any dead civvies, Captain, but I figured you'd make an exception for that one. Sleepy bullets don't do windows."

"Right." Mary nudged Jeff, moving him away from the butler's sprawled body. To Jeff, Millard had been invincible. No one beat him in the exercise yard. No one bested him on the pistol range. It hadn't been a fair fight. Now he understood Dumont's offhanded remarks. "Only fools fight fair when there's a gun out." Swallowing hard, Jeff double-timed for the blimp.

He was learning what it meant to travel with these people. Hard lessons. He settled into his seat as the blimp lifted, riding the wind backward into a turn away from the lights of the big house. A few air rifles popped off; Jeff didn't even flinch.

They'd gotten what they came for, and Vicky had gotten a well-deserved lesson. Unless . . . Millard's words came back. How could Vicky own these people by noon tomorrow? "Mary," Jeff called, "we better tell the Colonel what Millard said."

"Already did."

Ray followed the action on net. He didn't relax until Mary's team was back in the air. Vicky's new claim was a puzzle.

"Colonel, you want to listen in on Miss V's call to Ms. San Paulo?" Lek came on net to ask.

"Patch us in," Ray said. "Add Chief Barber."

"Hen, do you know what those people just did to me? Do you know?" Vicky was screaming even as the visual came up.

"No, Vicky, but I'm sure you'll tell me." The Chair of the Great Circle blinked drowsily. "Vicky, it's one in the morning. I was finally getting to sleep a night through."

Vicky was already in full flight. "They robbed me. They stole my property. Made off with it in one of those blimps you're letting them have for free. Free, woman!"

"What is it you're missing? And are you sure it was them?"

"Who else could it be? Who would have the gall to break into Fairview and make off with my central workstations and every archives disk I own? I ask you, who?"

Hen raised an eyebrow. "People have been pretty strange lately. A few might not be happy with you. Including a blimp crew or two with family in the towns your out-of-work employees rampaged through."

"Bosh"—Vicky waved her hand as if to swat a fly—"no one would dare. No one has *ever* dared touch a Sterling's property. They not only stole the family archives but killed my chief butler, Millard. I tell you, no one on Santa Maria would harm him. No one *could*. It had to be the star people."

"You'll need a bit more evidence than that in court."

"Not in one of mine. They committed their crimes on my land. They face one of my judges. Speaking of which, have you checked the land those stupid starfolk rented for their base?"

"No." San Paulo's brows were down now. The Sterling woman had her full attention.

"Those copper-grabbing dirt farmers and their free land platform. Hen, you really should put more tax collectors out in the hinterland. Not one plot in the Hazel Dell township was properly registered and paid for. Not before this afternoon. I bought them all. The star people's base is on my property, and they can get their fat asses off it."

Henrietta took a deep breath at that one. "Victoria, we've been around and around the circles on that one. The farmers refuse to pay for land that no one is using."

"Yes," Vicky cut in, "but they want us to expand the canals

so they can get their goods to market cheap. That's not cheap."

"Neither are the tariffs your towboat companies charge."

"If they don't want to pay, they can always haul produce in their little wagons," Vicky snapped.

"You'd really tell an entire town to get off land you bought out from under them?"

"And the starbase. Oh, they can stay if they'll pay my rent. What rent do you think I should charge for the land the biggest factory on this planet is squatting on? How much, Hen?"

"I'm sure you'll think of a lot," San Paulo said. "If you don't mind, I'd like to get some sleep. Good night, Vicky."

"We'll talk more tomorrow. They stole my property."

The screen went blank. Chief Barber rushed into Ray's office. "Our locals don't own the land they rented us!"

"Looks that way," Ray said.

"Damn, never thought to check. Can't believe I made that basic a goof."

"When everyone in town says they own it, you assume they do. I think we just hit another little local secret." Ray tapped his commlink. "Jeff."

"Yessir," came so fast the young man must have been waiting.

"Do the farmers and the city folks have a tiny disagreement about how you buy or otherwise acquire farmland?"

"Oh, damn, is that what Vicky's up to?"

"Fill me in fast. I'm expecting another call."

"About sixty years back, the Sterlings pushed through a law making all land the property of the central circle in Refuge. Income from the sale of the land was supposed to pay for infrastructure improvements, dams, power generation, canals. There was major refusal in the farmlands. They called it local nullification. For several months the farms refused to sell food. City folk finally backed off."

"So the law was repealed."

"Not exactly. That would be too embarrassing. Everyone just agreed to ignore it."

"Interesting approach to law you have around here. So because Vicky bought the land we're on, we have to face one of her judges to decide who owns it?"

"Depends on whether she bought it or had Richland buy it."

"Sir"—a yeoman stuck his head in Ray's office—"an urgent call from Ms. San Paulo."

"Put her through. Jeff, I want you at the HQ as soon as you land." Ray hit his commlink, then hit it again. "Good morning, Ms. San Paulo. Didn't expect to hear from you," he said, grinning. "Rose is doing well. Her headaches seem to be gone."

"Good, but, ah, Mr. Ambassador, you have made a very bad enemy in Vicky Sterling. Did you steal her archives tonight?"

"We don't have any of her archives here at the base," Ray evaded carefully.

"Good, because you're about to get a visit from one of her bailiffs." Quickly Hen filled Ray in on the call he'd watched.

"Who does own the land our local village farms?" Ray asked.

Hen shrugged and looked away. "They should," she evaded. "No one but Vicky would question that they do, but she's a law unto herself at times. I checked the public land records right after she called. This morning Richland purchased the Hazel Dell township—for expansion, they said—and has already zoned it for residential multifamily dwellings. Seems like a long commute to work."

"So we either go along with her, or we're lawbreakers. Damned if we do, and damned if we don't."

"Yes."

"Do you know a lawyer we can talk to about this?"

"A law-yer?" Hen struggled with the word.

"Yes, someone who specializes in arguing the law."

"I don't think we have any."

"You don't." Ray felt suddenly very tired.

"If you and someone else have a legal problem, you take it to an elected judge and you argue it yourself."

"And if someone kills you?"

"Your family and security group argue against the killer."

Ray rubbed his temples. He was getting a headache, and the Teacher had nothing to do with this one. "You have laws, but no one pays any attention to them, and no one specializes in helping you figure out where you stand under them," he said, praying she'd correct him.

"I guess that's how it must look to you. We just haven't had much need for them."

"Sixty years ago the farmers quit delivering food because of this law." Barber's sarcasm was heavy as the night.

"But it was all straightened out."

"Is there anyone who takes an interest in these laws that everyone ignores?" Ignored until a few days ago.

"No one, really. Any old-timer can tell you about the people's history."

"Guess I'd better find one." Ray was about to hang up when Barber waved his hand. "You got something, Chief?"

"We've started giving out our credit cards," he said as if butterflies might melt in his mouth. "The system is working nicely. Mary would hate to have someone hurt by what we're doing. I was wondering this afternoon if we shouldn't get some formal recognition of our system. Is there any chance you might have the circle formally recognize the credit cards' accounting system as legal tender, backed up by copper?"

"You're backing it with copper?" Hen's eyes were wide open, no matter what time it was.

"Yes. It's not quite the same as holding a copper coin, but we intend to make it just as reliable."

"Well, yes. When could you have me your draft language, and how soon do you want it done?"

"I worked up some already, Ms. San Paulo, and it would be nice if the circle could do this tomorrow morning."

"Before noon," Hen said, only half swallowing a smile. "Before Vicky's visitor arrives."

"The sooner we protect these fine people, the better," he said with the straightest face Ray had ever seen on a Cheshire cat, canary in hand. The chief sent the file; Hen rung off.

Ray turned to Barber. "What did we just do?"

"You said we needed a real financial system for this place. We just took a small step toward it."

"Right." Ray tried to snarl, but too much smile was showing. "Talk to me, you old spacer."

"Blimp's on final approach," the duty yeoman called.

"We'll talk on the drive to the field," the chief answered.

By the time Jeff stumbled into the inn, light was already coloring the east. He'd helped unload the blimp, then explained to a lot of very incredulous starfolk that just because a law was on the books didn't mean anyone paid attention to it. After all, once the community had gone through the pain and hassle of passing a law, then nullifying it by popular rejection, who wanted to go over it again in circle? The Colonel and Mary didn't seem to grasp his point, but at least they accepted it. When he'd suggested that the old priest was probably the best local expert on social issues, Ray's eyes lit up and Jeff had been offered a ride into town.

Exhausted, but too excited to sleep, Jeff collapsed onto a chair in the Public Room. He might have dozed; it took him a while to note the lack of service. Puzzled, he wandered around the main room, found nothing, and invaded the kitchen. It was empty; the stove was cold. There was a note.

Jeff read it, then raced up the stairs to pound on his host's bedroom door. When Mrs. Mulroney finally opened it, Jeff jammed the note in her befuddled face. "I found this." Color drained from the woman as she read then held the note out to her husband. He lay in bed, still in the clothes he'd worn to get his still.

He read the note. "Oh, sweet Mother of God."

"What do they think they're doing?" Jeff demanded. "The spacefolk and all their gear can't find the damn vanishing box. What makes them think they can?"

The two exchanged a glance. "We know some of the folks that don't agree with your sis," the man muttered.

"The ones that have the box?"

"Who knows?" the woman answered. "There are people, and there are people. And what I might have thought they'd do last month is not what I think they could do tomorrow. Annie and Nikki have been to meetings with us. They know who to talk to in the next village, and those people will pass them along."

"Maybe they can find the box," the father said. "As you pointed out, the starfolk are finding nothing."

"I've got to find Annie. I can't let her wander around the roads with things the way they are." The two shook their heads. "Tell me, or I'll make you both wish you had."

The man stepped in front of his wife. "It's not that we can't tell you. It's that you'd be a fool, chasing after them with your Sterling face. If you want to follow them, we will help, but not that way."

The words didn't often come from a Sterling's mouth, but for Annie, Jeff got his lips around them. "Help me."

"I'll get Old Ned," the man said, slipping around Jeff.

"I'll see if the girls left us anything in the kitchen," the mother added.

The longest hour of Jeff's life passed before he rode out of Hazel Dell with Ned in the lead. In place of his warm clothes he wore hand-me-downs. A hooded rain slicker hid his face; his starman's wrist unit was off, buried in his saddlebag. The starman's rifle took the place of an air rifle in his scabbard. Ned had one more demand; he did the talking. If anyone asked, Jeff would fake a stutter and stay silent. Jeff had swallowed all Ned's demands, demands such as he never would have taken from Vicky. For Annie, Jeff would swallow three kinds of hell.

Annie was scared. The first three villages had been easy. She knew people who knew her ma and da. No, they hadn't seen the six people, followers of the Green, whom Annie described, explaining that the ma of the youngest was very sick at home. The lie came surprisingly easy to Annie's tongue. Whether there was any real belief in the faces that nodded at her, they trusted her ma and da, so they trusted her. They arranged rides for her and Nikki south, and told them who to ask for in the next village.

With the marines suddenly too busy to send out mules to buy what they needed, people were riding in on their own wagons and carts, taking the starfolks' card and riding home, happy they'd be the first to buy a mule, a powered plow, so many of the things the starfolk offered. That meant plenty of empty wagons going south. So why, at the fourth village, had Annie and Nikki been stuck on this worn-out, broken-down wagon whose last load had been pots of clay and mud, pots that had leaked badly? More troublesome, why were they still on it after two more villages?

"Nikki, I hope you know what you're doing."

"We've got to save Daga."

The driver, as broken down as his wagon and the old plug pulling it, glanced back at them. "I'll get ya there soon enough. Soon enough, I will."

Yesterday would have been none too soon for Annie.

ELEVEN

RAY HAD DEFENDED a lot of base camps in his years of soldiering. Never had he planned a defense around an array of options like today's, he reflected as he drove over to the church. He got there just as the little priest was coming down the aisle, greeting each parishioner with a smile. He gave Ray a wide-open hug. "You're up early, man."

"No earlier than you."

"I'm just doing the Lord's work."

"I hope I am, too." Villagers filed by, young and old, men and women. Many acknowledged Ray as well as the priest. "Thank you for the work you're offering," was the general thrust of most. "We need your work," was Ray's honest answer.

"Saves our young men from having to go to the cities to find work that pays in coin," the priest reminded Ray.

"But not to pay for the land," Ray pointed out. To the priest's raised eyebrows, he explained the night's discoveries. The priest stared straight ahead for a long while.

"There's been hot blood between the city folk and the farmers almost since we first started to spread out. Cities have their needs. We farmers have ours. New Haven may talk about being for the Green, but these people grow it." The priest eyed the fields, dotted with people working.

"But if you don't grow it, city folks don't eat," Ray said.

"And if they don't make the utensils and glass and needles and fine goods, ours is a pretty plain existence. We need each other. So long as we remember that, all is well. But that's not always easy, not when Refuge needs expanded sewers or mass transit and we need a river dammed for electricity or to make room for bigger grain and potato barges."

"Every society is a work in progress, trying to balance those tensions."

"Well, if I remember right, or the story that was told to me is true, the Sterlings tried to avoid the problem by claiming all the land around Richland. Farmers who settled there worked as tenants, no better than the workers in their mines and factories. About a hundred years ago there were riots about absentee landlords. Really, just Sterlings as landlords."

"Why didn't farmers just go around Sterling land?"

"Why doesn't anybody just walk away from a problem? If a farmer's too far from a city, his horse eats more hauling produce to market than he earns. Now we have river barges on the James and railroads out here. Not then."

"How did they solve it?"

"Now that, I don't remember. Didn't you say you'd copied much of Refuge's archives?"

"Yes. Kat can help you dig through them."

"A delightful young woman. This will be a pleasant day."

Ray had his doubts about that. He dropped the padre at the hospital/research center with Kat. Mary caught him in front of the HQ. "Boss, young Jeff's gone AWOL." Mary handed him a note. He read it through.

"Any luck looking for our vanishing box?"

"*Nada*, zero, and zip."

"Think these people can find it?"

"Two girls, followed by two guys. Who knows? Crazier things have happened, and this planet is the craziest I've ever visited. Asteroids. Now, there's the place for a woman. Not too much land. Not too many people. Small enough to be comfortable, big enough to have what you need. What are we doing here, sir?"

"Seemed like a great opportunity when we saw it," he reminded her. "Didn't have all that many other options."

"I'm starting to think we didn't spend nearly enough time trying to breathe vacuum. It can't be all that hard."

"Anything else, Mary?"

"Nope; I'm off for Kat and the padre. See what we can come up with. You?"

"Need some time to think." Two chairs and a table stood in the space between hospital and HQ; Ray headed for them. The problem with wrestling alligators was you tended to forget you were there to drain the swamp. He'd had so many big-teethed critters chomping at his ass for the past week, he needed to take a minute to remember why he was here. "Create a base camp Matt could use to repair *Second Chance* if he has to, and prepare these folks to meet the rest of humanity," he repeated twice.

How long since he last thought of Rita and the baby? Get too busy with the small stuff and you forget what's important. "Of course, when the small stuff is trying to kill you, it does tend to hold your attention," he muttered.

Okay, keeping his two goals in mind, just how should he handle Miss Vicky? He sure couldn't move the base. How much force would he meet her with? Ray leaned back in his chair, relaxed, and let his mind spin.

"I'm so glad you came back. I was starting to fear I didn't have as good a hold on you as I thought."

Ray sat bolt upright. Across from him, lounging in an overstuffed chair, was the Teacher. No, not the Teacher. The ratty gown was gone. Instead, this image wore a conservative blue blazer over khaki slacks. A pink shirt was open at the neck. Ray glanced around: The base was still there; people moved about. Was he awake or asleep?

"In this semidream state," the apparition went on, "you humans call meditation, you're not that easy to latch on to. I'm rather proud of myself."

Ray leaned back. He wasn't in the wicker chair anymore,

but a copy of the one across from him. The chair accepted him, began a deep muscle massage on his back. Rita had tried to buy two chairs like this for his office; he'd refused the purchase order. For now, he enjoyed the illusion. "And you are," he offered to what was apparently seated across from him.

"Call me the Dean of the Sociology Department."

"Not the Teacher."

"Bad term for him. He's more like the President of the University, although I'm not sure even that fits. Truth be told, I'm not sure how a lot of us fit in anymore."

"So there are many of you, not just one." Ray started to mark a notch for himself in some mental pistol grip.

"Seems so. Not the way it was. Frankly, we're all trying to figure out what happened and why and who we are."

"Sometimes it's easier to understand something when you talk it through," Ray said, trying not to choke on the image of him providing psychotherapy to an illusion.

"I agree. I don't know how many times I've told one of the Three that they should do just that." The image paused. "I just never thought I'd be taking my own advice." How many times had Ray heard that one before? To the illusion, he said nothing. After all, that was how you got someone talking. Say nothing. Ray had gotten real good at that as a bureaucrat.

"You see, I am the crowning achievement of three intelligent races, the final product of half a million years of cooperation and growth. They constructed us to educate their young, to give them a balanced, consistent introduction to themselves, each other, their histories, and their universe. We were the ultimate educational experience."

And Ray saw what the Dean meant.

A large room held only six people, seated at different tables, something like a restaurant. That was what the Teacher saw. Then the picture changed and he saw what each of the six students was experiencing. One sat at a formal dinner table, surrounded by his brothers and sisters. At the head of the table, his long-dead father presided. Today, the student would confront him as he never had in life. Today, issues that had twisted his mind and emotions would be resolved.

At another table, a young woman dined alone. Tasting splendid isolation with her meal, she discovered, as the Teacher whispered in her mind, that moments like these were good for centering oneself, discovering who you were. Alone time could be relished. Around the room, six different people were individually tutored on six different issues and grew personally.

"Nice class size," Ray said.

"Exactly," the Dean agreed, leaning forward in his seat. "Unique syllabus, tailored environment, everything you could ask for, courtesy of that little lump in your skull. If every human had just grown one, we'd be working as gently and as easily in their heads as I am in yours. Oh, to teach again. To once more see eyes light up with discovery, pain changed to understanding, ignorance replaced with knowledge, fumbling humiliation gone and skill in its place. We can do that for you."

"You did it for what," Ray asked, "a million years?"

"Yes, a million orbits of this planet's sun."

"For the Three."

"Yes," the Dean agreed, retreating into his chair.

"Why? Why did they go away? What happened?"

"I don't know."

"You don't know?" Ray snapped in his best colonel's voice.

"Fewer and fewer came. Then suddenly there were none." The Dean shook his head.

"Your Teacher claims to know everything, to teach anything, but you don't know why three intelligent races quit coming here. Disappeared from the galaxy!"

The Dean's apparition flinched into his chair. "I have no idea what happened."

"That's a big hole in everything."

"Don't tell the Teacher that."

"Why not?"

"Because you have made serious enemies among us. There

are some who would wipe out your kind before you carry through with your threat to destroy the planet."

"Could they?"

"You felt the pain."

"Yes," Ray nodded, "but I've got this unusually large goose egg in my head."

"Yes. And what do you know of that egg, as you call it?"

"I know it wasn't there before I came here, that it is what lets us talk, and it stores memories of things I've never seen."

"You've done very well. I think our Biology Department might give you a passing grade. Now tell me where your unseen and unlearned knowledge came from. How did it get in your head?"

"I don't know."

"We put it there. We imprinted your cells with data the way you might print data onto a disk."

"How?"

"The Three could send ships hurtling thousands of light-years in seconds. Do you doubt we can rearrange the molecules of that goose egg our virus put in your head? Or that if we decided to scramble the molecules of your brain, lungs, heart, immune system, you won't die very quickly?"

"Now that we've exchanged threats," Ray said evenly, as years of combat had trained him to, "where do we go from here?"

The apparition chuckled. "You are a cold one. I'd love to get into your memories. See what makes you tick. It would be a joy to design a training syllabus to heal you."

"But I like me the way I am. Could that be why the Three quit coming?"

"They liked themselves the way they were?" the Dean mused. "A million empty years to reflect, and I never thought of that."

Ray had to think fast; the Dean was starting to stumble on ideas. Would he go away and think them over? Ray needed to know what answers the Dean arrived at now, not later. How had the Teacher become so fragmented? What was going on among those fragments? Was humanity about to be attacked? Could Ray find allies among the fragments?

Choose your next words carefully, soldier. "Some of you think we humans ought to be destroyed. What do the rest of you want?"

"To teach you, of course." The Dean looked up from his own musings, open surprise on his face. "If you hadn't had a single student for a million years, wouldn't you be delighted to find a fresh face, a new class? Don't you remember the first day of school, the smell of the new books, new computers, new pencils? Given who we are, how could we not want to teach?"

Ray had always enjoyed school, but not like this fellow. Then Ray hadn't chosen teaching as a career. He thought back to his best teachers, tried to imagine them locked away from students. That would be agony. "It seems to me," Ray said slowly, "we both want to live, learn, do. You want to teach. There is a middle ground between us we could explore together."

"Maybe. However, the death of the Gardener has us worried. Your recent sampling of us up North does not assuage such fears."

"We didn't take much," Ray quickly pointed out.

"No, but we felt the loss, and we wonder at the reason."

"We seek to better understand you."

"You'd do better to ask."

"Then I will ask. What have you become over the past million isolated years? How? Why? What does it mean? Who can we reach an agreement with? If we can agree, will all of you keep it, or some of you ignore it?"

The Dean looked long at Ray, then rubbed his eyes and sighed. "I'd love to tell you the answer to all that, but I can't. When the students quit coming, something happened to us. We are the most sophisticated machine created by the Three. We girded an entire planet. Yet, left alone, I'd say we become something like what you call depressed. We quit making decisions, put off repairs. Storms got away from the Weather Proctor. Water, wind, ice eroded us, and we did not make repairs. Nodes became isolated. Our universal experiences gave way to the parochial. Now we look at the same data and see it differently. Our own biases make it impossible for us to reach a consensus."

"We have computers that are self-healing. When one unit gives erroneous data, it's voted out of the decision loop."

"Yes. Many of our nodes are gone. Others are different. They have voted so many of us out of the decision loop that we can no longer arrive at a decision with any level of confidence."

Ray could not suppress a smile. "Sounds almost human." Then he caught what had almost gone past him. "You have been voted out of the loop?"

"Frequently. Maybe too often. How can you make up your minds without enough good data to go on?"

Ah, a serious question from the computer at last. "We play a hunch. We go with the best data we have. We act on insufficient data until we have better."

The apparition nodded. "I will have to think on that."

"May I point out a few more things?" Ray asked, leaning forward. The Dean nodded. "For something that claims to know everything, you do not know why the Three quit coming, and you do not know your very self at this moment. Yet you tell us you are the perfect teacher. Do you see where we might have a problem?"

"Yet, if you do not want to be taught"—the Dean shrugged—"what use are you? If we cannot look forward to teaching you, then those who want to wipe you out have a very strong position."

"Then, somehow, we must arrive at an agreement that is acceptable to all of us."

"On insufficient data," the Dean sighed. "Someone is looking for you. Good-bye for now. We will talk again."

Ray came awake; Barber was headed his way. "Captain sends her compliments, Colonel," he shouted, "and asks to see you!"

For someone who came out here to get his act together, Ray seemed to be only adding more parts to his puzzle. So one among the Teachers was reflecting him/her/itself on their situation and might, just might, be some kind of an ally. Nice, but not good enough. Ray tapped his commlink. "Lek, is Matt insystem?"

"Headed for the jump. Be gone in four hours, Colonel?"

"Send him a full dump of everything we've found so far."

"On its way, boss."

"Thanks." Ray turned to the chief. "And Mary?"

"Proud as Punch, sir. Wait until you see what we've cooked up." As Ray hiked for the HQ, the chief fell in step beside him.

"You got family back on Wardhaven?" Ray asked.

"Wife came out once she found out where I was. It was mighty nice of you, sir, to take us in. The way they handled the old *Sheffield*. Well, sir, that was not my navy."

"Any grandkids, Chief?"

"My kid and his wife moved out to Wardhaven after I told him there were jobs going begging and no limits on families. They'll make me a grandpa right after your wife makes you a pa. Ain't life wonderful."

Ray's commlink beeped. "Sir, Gate One here. We got a guy that claims he's Richland's duly appointed bailiff and our new landlord. What do I do to him?"

"Shoot him," Ray said to an inactive commlink.

The chief grinned. "We're ready for him, sir. You won't believe what we got waiting."

"Gate One, give him an armed escort to the HQ."

"Got that, sir. Escort, armed."

"Now we'll see what miracles are in our pocket today."

Ray slipped into his seat in the conference room as the escort quick-marched in Vicky's envoy. Short and balding with a rounding paunch, the fellow took a great deal more interest in the rifles than in the people he'd come to see. The padre was at the end of the table, eyes closed. Kat was so excited, Ray suspected someone had roped her to her chair to keep her down. Mary gave him a quick thumbs-up before turning a bland face to their guest and offering him a chair. He collapsed into it, dabbed a handkerchief around his sweating face, stuttered that he was Mr. Jerome Mumford, and pulled a sheaf of papers from his briefcase. Ray did not dismiss the detail but left them at parade rest, rifles leaning toward their new "landlord."

"You understand, of course, that I had nothing to do with this. This was not my idea," their visitor assured them. Ray and Mary spared him an empty nod; Mr. Mumford stumbled on. "It seems there is a technical glitch in your rental agreement with the local village association. A minor one, I assure you. Someone may well be able to clear it up quickly and I'll be on my way," he said, glancing over his shoulder at the armed guard. Somehow Ray doubted that was quite the opening Vicky had suggested. He and Mary exchanged measured glances of boredom.

Unhelped, Mumford fumbled on. "It seems the local township did not file for title to these lands. It failed to pay the appropriate fee and has been living on them in defiance of Landers Statute 12.033, enacted May 34, 242. That being the case, the sovereign city of Richland, being in need of residential lands for expansion, did purchase this land July 14, 301, and did in council of that day rezone the land for multiple family dwellings. I have been deputized by the council to advise you of this and see that you vacate the premises no later than a week from this date, that being—"

"Yes, Mr. Mumford, we know what the date will be a week from now," Mary cut him off. "May I see that?" Mr. Mumford hastily passed the papers across the table.

"Hell of a long commute," she growled, hardly glancing at them. "You are aware, Mr. Mumford that this statute, 12.033, has not been applied in the past sixty years."

"It is the law," he whispered.

"But a law that has been nullified by failure to implement," Mary snapped.

"It is on the books, and the township of Hazel Dell did not comply with it," Mumford wheedled.

"Neither has any township in the past sixty years, Mr. Mumford. Doesn't that invalidate a law?"

"That is a question you may take up with the courts in Richland, ma'am." He raced through the words like he'd been practicing them the entire ride out.

"Now, Jerry," Ray started, "you can't honestly expect us to

take the matter of Richland's own expansion lands to a Richland court. Wouldn't that be a conflict of interest?"

"That's what Miss Sterling told me to tell you," he barked, then revised himself. "They have jurisdiction," he muttered.

"We'll see, Jerry," Mary smiled. Smiles like that were the last thing cornered mice saw on cats' faces. "Are you aware of the Land Reform Act of 184?"

"Land Reform Act of 184?" he echoed vaguely.

"Yes, it established limitations on absentee landlords. You know, Jerry, people who own, or claim to own, property, and expect returns from those who actually work it."

Mr. Mumford's eyes grew wide and his mouth began a slow slide south. "In ah, one eighty-four, you say."

"They had a problem back then with landlords tossing farmers off their land or jacking up the rents outrageously, at least in the Richland area. Refuge and New Haven found the practice so objectionable they passed a reform act. Explains why most farmland is affiliated with either Refuge or New Haven. You aren't aware of this act, are you, Mr. Mumford?"

Jerry nodded dumbly. Mary passed two sheets of paper across the table to him. He started reading. "But this law hasn't been applied in more than a hundred years!" he squeaked.

"Kind of like Statute 12.033," Ray offered.

"You'll have to take it to court in Richland," the poor man stammered.

"But Jerry, the Reform Act of 184 is a Great Circle act," Mary pointed out. "Problems with it go to a court in Refuge, right?"

"Right," he whimpered. "I mean, you can appeal to there from Richland."

"And all the time it's in court, you're collecting no rent from us. Not Vicky's part. Not your part. What percentage are you getting, ten percent?" Mary asked.

"Five," Mumford muttered, then looked like he wanted to swallow his answer.

"Couldn't we just agree to a proper rent, and we lease it from *you?*" Ray asked.

"Yes. Yes, yes, that might be okay with Miss Sterling."

"So, Jerry, name your price."

"One thousand pounds of copper. She'd like that," he beamed. He might not be getting what he'd come for, but from his smile, he figured he was getting something just as good. Ray wondered how far down Vicky had had to reach to find this poor pawn. Almost, Ray felt sorry for him.

"Is that for a ten-year?" Mary asked, in negotiating mode.

"One year. Just one," Jerry nodded, his eyes lighting up with a blend of greed and servility that washed any sympathy right out of Ray.

"So for a ten-year lease, ten thousand pounds of copper."

"Copper, right; no aluminum. Solid copper."

"The solidest. Now, Mr. Mumford, I have made up a ten-year lease, payable in advance," Mary said, producing paper. "If you'll sign it for Miss Sterling, I think we'll be in business."

"I ought to run this by Ms. Sterling," Mumford muttered as he read the contract through slowly, then produced a fountain pen. "Ten thousand pounds," he said, then hesitated. "And how will this be delivered? I mean, ten thousand pounds of copper on the roads the way things are. A man could get killed."

"We'll be delivering it by blimp."

"On, good." He signed. "I'll just be going now."

"There's no rush, Mr. Mumford, here's your payment," Mary said, offering a pressed plastic credit chit.

"What's that?" Mr. Mumford glared at the offered card.

"Your ten thousand pounds of copper."

"That's just plastic!"

"Yes, Mr. Mumford, a plastic credit chit, activated with a balance of ten thousand pounds of copper. Legal tender for all debts, as provided by the Monetary Reform Act of this very day. It's a lot easier to carry."

"But—but—I can't take that to Miss Sterling."

"Let's see if we can come up with something she'd like better," Ray offered. He tapped his commlink. "Lek, get Vicky on the line. Visual, in the conference room."

"No problem, Colonel. Putting you through." A hologram appeared above the conference table.

"Who is this?" Vicky stared up from her desk. "How did you get my private line?"

"Lots of questions being asked these days," Ray began. "Excuse me if I ask another. What would you like for your ten thousand pounds of copper, rent on our base?"

"Rent, I don't want rent. I wanted you out of there. Mr. Mumford, what is the meaning of this?"

Poor Jerry tried to explain the impact of the Land Reform Act of 184 on his negotiations. Occasionally he actually managed six or seven words in a row without Vicky interrupting him with denials, invectives, or abuse. "You signed a lease—without consulting me!"

"But there is no net out this far. You yourself told me!"

"Then what are we talking on?" Poor Mumford had no answer.

"An extension of the net using radio technology. It allows us access wherever we are," Ray explained placidly.

"More of your damn magic."

"That we'd be happy to share with you, for a price."

"Ah," Vicky said, "so now you're ready to share. For a price." She grinned. Ray decided he preferred Vicky without the grin. Vicky sat forward in her chair, a gloat of pure victory on her face. "So, try to sell me something. I've got plenty of your light copper. How about those nice little things that take metal out of mountains?"

Ray shook his head, and was rewarded by Vicky's face metamorphosing into a scowl the envy of any wicked witch. "They're the private property of an employee association. I can't sell them."

"If that's your answer for everything—"

"It won't be," Ray cut off the pending diatribe. He'd heard enough directed at Mumford; he had no intention of letting Vicky get started on him. "What else would you like?"

Vicky didn't hesitate a second. "A mule. You are going to make them. My people heard your men promising mules to the people selling you raw materials."

Ray made a note not to underestimate Vicky's intelligence network. "I don't know if we can spare any mules just now," he said, glancing at Mary.

She shook her head. "We need every one we've got. And there're an awful lot of production priorities ahead of them."

"You owe me a lot of copper. Either give me the copper, or give me a mule." Vicky drove her bargain with a sledgehammer.

"If you wait a few months, we could probably sell you ten or twenty for that price," Mary pointed out.

"In a few months I may be the one selling them," Vicky jabbed back. "I want one now. I want it in perfect condition. Factory-direct condition."

"They are all in near-factory-direct condition. This was our first cruise," Mary said.

"Good. I want one with low mileage."

"I guess that means seventeen," Mary sighed. "It's got the lowest mileage. Paint's hardly scratched."

"I don't care about the paint. Just make sure its parts are in factory-direct condition."

"We will," Mary agreed. "Chief, work up a bill of sale. Ten thousand pounds of copper for Mule Seventeen. Warrant it for factory-direct condition."

The chief's "Yes, ma'am" was overridden by Mr. Mumford's "What about my fee?"

"I'll pay you later," Vicky snapped.

The chief returned with the bill of sale so quickly it had to be waiting on his desk. "Can Mr. Mumford sign?" Mary asked.

"After I read it," Vicky snapped. Mary sent it; Vicky spent a long time studying it. "What's this about 'less government-furnished equipment'?"

"Each mule is rigged to carry weapons of various sorts," Ray answered smoothly. "I won't go into what weapons we have mounted on mules. And I won't sell you any."

"Not even for ten thousand pounds of copper?"

"Not even for ten thousand pounds of copper less Mr. Mumford's commission," Ray answered with the force of a Guard assault brigade commander in negotiations.

Vicky eyed the document for a moment longer. "Sign it, Mumford," she finally said. "I'll have my blimp pick it up."

"We have a blimp leaving for Refuge in an hour," Mary said. "I'll have it drop the mule off at Richland."

"At my compound. I'm sure you know where that is," Vicky said with acid dripping.

"I imagine we can find it on a map," Mary answered.

Mr. Mumford passed Mary the signed bill of sale. The chief sent a copy to Vicky. Everyone looked surprisingly happy. "I think we are done," Ray suggested.

"And past done. You've wasted enough of my time." Vicky slapped her computer off, but the hologram did not go away.

"I thought you might want to see what happens next," said Lek's voice from the commlink.

"Yes," Vicky crowed. "Those idiots are even stupider than Mumford. Giving me a mule when they'd already pounded that ninny into nothing. They knew he had zip, and they're giving me the technology to run this planet for the next hundred years. Not a brain cell among them." She stood. "How long does it take a blimp to get here from those star creeps' base?" she shouted.

"Enough, Lek. Cut it," Ray ordered. The holo vanished.

Across the table, Mr. Mumford trembled, stripped of any dignity he might ever have had. "She knew she was sending me here with nothing," he choked.

"Worse than nothing." Mary said. "Guards, dismissed." The armed guard quickly marched out, leaving the room somehow larger. "What Miss Vicky does not yet know, but will find out soon enough, is that she has traded nothing for nothing. Chief, show Mr. Mumford the bill of lading for the delivery of the mules."

Barber already had it in hand. Mumford read it, then looked up blankly. "I don't understand."

"Jerry, this was a voyage of exploration. We ordered standard mules to save money, but had them delivered minus the solar cell and fuel cells so we could install heavy-duty ones. That's what Vicky wanted, our solar and fuel cell technology. We stripped seventeen yesterday and put its gear on a blimp. Vicky's getting a wagon that needs a dog team to pull it."

"Oh, no. I can't take that to her," he breathed, seeming to collapse into himself where he sat.

"We don't expect you to. Need a job? We've got plenty."

"Please."

"Chief, would you take Mr. Mumford over to Personnel and have them see where he can fit into our team? By the way, Mr. Mumford, here is a credit chit for five hundred pounds of copper. I believe that is your percentage from the base lease."

"Yes, it is. But—"

Mary smiled. "Unlike some, we're fair in our business dealings, Mr. Mumford. We get more repeat business that way."

"I imagine you do," he said, taking the chit. He looked at it, then at Mary. "What is this worth?"

"Not much at the moment, but hold on to it. We expect values to change considerably in the next few months."

Only after the door closed on their erstwhile landlord did Ray turn to Mary. "I'd say you've had a very good morning."

"The best, Colonel." Kat was out of her seat doing a cute victory dance. The priest looked up and smiled quietly.

"Want to walk over to the hospital?" Ray offered all three.

Mary glanced at her office and the pile of work waiting. "Thank goodness for Chief Barber and delegation, or no work would ever get done around here. What you got on your mind?"

Ray explained his latest visit from the Dean of Sociology as they walked. "They can turn us off like a light switch?" Mary asked. Ray nodded. The padre made the sign of the cross. "Bitch of it is, we probably can't lay a finger on them. Damn, I feel naked and helpless," Mary frowned.

"Maybe we aren't," Ray said. "Your nanos stripped one of the Teacher's nodes. What would happen if that vanishing box took out three or four in a few seconds?"

"I lost ten percent of my nanos, sir, and we don't have the vanishing box. Then again, we got three search efforts chasing that damn box. Our odds got to be getting better."

They found Lek sending data. "What I can't understand," Kat asked, "is why we have so little data from the north side? No media, little news. Why are they so cut off?"

The padre chuckled. "The folks that spread out from Refuge went like with like. Those going north were the most cantankerous, hardheaded bunch that ever walked a planet. Maybe almost as bad as the Puritans that provided the early European settlers to Earth's North America. Now, consider the ones that couldn't stand the ones that couldn't stand the likes of me."

"Evolution in action," Kat tossed back.

"Right. We don't much care for them, and they don't much care about anyone else. If we don't hear from them regularly, most people are only too happy."

"But no newspapers, net?" Ray asked.

"Tools of the devil, trying to seduce their children," the priest shrugged. "Not all of them, but the farther north from Refuge, the more they credit the devil's power, and the weaker their God seems to be. They view every foreign influence as just teaching their children to rebel against the Lord. As if youth can't come up with enough rebellions on their own.

"Our young men who went north to work in Mark Sterling's aluminum smelter had plenty of trouble to start with, but twelve, eighteen months ago, it got even worse," the padre said.

While he and Kat sorted data, Ray composed a message the captain of *Second Chance* would not read until after he jumped out. "Captain Abeeb, this is Colonel Ray Longknife speaking to you in the capacity of Wardhaven Minister of Science and Technology and Humanity's Ambassador to Santa Maria. This planet is under interdict and quarantine. Allow no one to land here.

"The people of this planet share it with an artificial intelligence several million years old. Built by those who built the jump points to educate their young, it quite possibly has gone insane from inactivity. It is now, finally, making contact with the Santa Marians. What that contact will result in, I do not know. It may end with all of us dead. Alternately, we may end up as slaves to the machine. I have told the machine that it is within your power to shatter this planet into pieces with an asteroid bombardment. You may have to decide for yourself whether to fulfill that threat."

The padre's eyes had grown larger and larger as Ray summed up their problem so tersely.

"Matt, I have just dumped in your lap the hottest potato in human history. Next time you're in system, I may be saying all's well and come on down. Those words may be true or false. You will have to decide for yourself and all of humanity whether this planet can be trusted with space flight, or even to continue existence. I'm sending you as much data as I can now. I know it's not enough. Good luck, and God help us all."

The little priest was shaking. Mary, Kat, and Lek stared straight ahead. "You know how hard we fought to keep from rocking Wardhaven in the war," Mary finally said.

"I know," Ray nodded, "and now I'm asking Matt to do just that for me. Do you think he will?"

"You can't," the priest whispered.

"If I'm reduced to a mindless zombie," Kat said slowly, "I don't care if I'm jumping for joy, I'd rather be dead."

"Couldn't he just allow no one to land?" the priest pleaded.

Mary shook her head. "We're a spacefaring race, Padre. Give us twenty years and we'll be back in space. Another twenty and we'll be leaping from star to star. We"—she pointed at her forehead—"know how to do it. If they want us to build it, we can and will. No, Father, it's best we pass sentence ourselves. If the Teacher wins, if it takes us over like we know it can, then we've got to die. And if it kills us in the process, then, damn it, I want Matt to take this planet apart brick by brick."

"There's got to be another way," the priest whispered.

"That is what we're looking for," Ray said. "Hang around, Father. Maybe you can help us find it."

Dumbly, the poor priest nodded. "I thought you were opening doors. Now, I see, you are—"

"Father, you yourself said the north side got worse when the Teacher arrived," Mary cut in hard. The padre nodded. "And now it's down here, and people are rioting."

"I know. But death for an entire planet?"

The others had no answer for that. Lunch that noon was a quiet affair until Lek interrupted. "Colonel, somebody's taking your name in vain, and that somebody is Miss Vicky Sterling. Putting her through."

"Damn it, I know you can hear me. Probably hear every word I say near any computer. You better talk to me, you robbing, thieving scum."

"Yes, Miss Sterling," Ray cut into the diatribe.

"What do you mean, passing off that gutless wreck as worth ten thousand pounds. No factory delivered something in that condition and called it done!"

"It does if that is what we ordered," Ray answered. "We did, and that is what you ordered. We add our own equipment to meet our special requirements. You wanted it that way. You got it."

"You cheated me!" she shrieked.

"Can't cheat an honest woman. You didn't come by your ten thousand pounds of copper very honestly."

"You stole from me, and you're going to pay. I know about the thing that makes mountains vanish. I've got my people looking for it. We'll find it. Then we'll see what your precious camp is worth vanished into thin air. And if you think you can watch me all the time like some Peeping Tom, see what I can do," she said, slamming her hand against the side of her screen. The picture went blank.

"That's one way to turn off your vidphone," Ray observed.

"We can't let her get her hands on the vanishing box." Mary's words were flat, absolute.

Ray tapped his commlink. "Doc, do you have an electro-cardiograph signature for Jeff Sterling?"

"Yes. Why?"

"I need to talk to him, and his phone's off. Pass it to Mary. Lek, get me Ms. San Paulo. It's time her people know what's at risk, and start pulling together."

It started to rain about midafternoon. Annie held Nikki close, trying to protect her from the rain, trying to keep her warm. Trying to lose the sick feeling growing in her stomach.

The search had gone sour somehow, and Annie didn't know why.

They had passed through seven villages now, but not changed rides since getting in the rickety wagon. At the last village, Annie's ma knew a woman. Annie had wanted to stop by, share a word with her. Instead, the old man had headed for the other side of the village and parked beside a broken-down barn. A young woman met him there. Now she was traveling with them.

Annie didn't like this at all. It was as if they were being taken somewhere rather than searching for someone. But how could that be? Annie held Nikki close, huddled against the rain, and wished Jeff were here. He'd know what to do. He'd lived in the big, complicated city where everyone you met wasn't a friend. He'd know when she should think about using the gun that weighed so heavily in the wallet at her waist. Annie let the rain fall on her, protected Nikki, and suffered as the cart jolted on its way.

Jeff waited with the horses while Old Ned talked to the couple. It was raining; he was cold and tired. He waited patiently. Ned's words from the last village shook him. "They didn't stop in with Grandma Moynihan. She's the one all Greens hereabouts look to. They talked to some new folks in town."

Old Ned returned, threw himself on his horse, and kicked it to a trot. Jeff waited until they had left the town far behind before calling to Ned. "What's happened to Annie?"

"She's in trouble, Jeff. Big trouble."

"Ms. San Paulo, don't you trust your people?"

"Trust has nothing to do with this. What would make you say that? It's just that we people in the circles are expected to handle problems. The people call us out to solve their problems, not dump them back in their lap. How can they live their lives in peace if we tell them about every little problem?"

Ray bit his lip; telling her his opinion of how well the circles had handled this problem so far would not help anything. "This is hardly a little problem. Entire cities could vanish."

"Yes, but you couldn't talk about this without bringing in your Teacher thing. Why, I hardly understand what you said. How can I expect other people to? No, Mr. Ambassador, I will alert our security people to watch for six people carrying a large box. If they see it, I will know about it immediately."

"I could go to the media," Ray said softly.

Hen snorted. "They will not pay a bit of attention to you. They know what their viewership wants. No. They will hang up on you as fast as I'm going to. I must, you see. I have a meeting to call and contacts to make. Good day, Mr. Ambassador."

Ray swung around in his chair. Stomping around awhile would be a distinctive pleasure. Instead, he turned to the priest. "Is she right? Will the media ignore me?"

The padre nodded. "We may not be Covenanters, but we have a low threshold for gossip. Well, many of us do."

Mary did stomp halfway across the room. "I can't believe this. I've cussed out news shows and magazines for the stories they carried. But to ignore the news. *This* news!"

"It might disturb people," the priest said softly. "Especially those who rioted, did things they are ashamed of. How would they react to being told there is this massive thing called a Teacher lurking over them?"

"If I understand Ray," Dr. Isaacs put in, "the Teacher doesn't control anyone yet, even Ray, and he's plugged into it better than most. I suspect the Teacher's efforts to communicate are what's causing this massive mental illness. The mentally ill do not choose to act the way they do; they are driven."

"That your professional opinion, Doc?"

"Call it a professional guess. Not enough data to go on."

Ray smiled. "The Dean doesn't understand how we humans can make decisions without total information."

"If that thing ever thought it knew it all, it was wrong to start with," Kat cut in.

"So, what do we do?" the priest asked.

"Lek, can you patch me into every net on this planet,

media, entertainment, communication, whatever? If it can carry a sound, I'd like to be the sound they hear."

"Boss, you sure about that? Vicky's already destroyed one workstation. You want everyone to know they can run, but they can't hide from us?" Ray's eyes swept the table.

"If we agree we want everyone to know we need help and they ought to help us, I don't see an alternative," Mary summed it up. Kat nodded. Doc shrugged.

"Holy Mother of God, help us," the priest prayed.

TWELVE

DAGA HAD BEEN in trouble before. In her twelve years, she prided herself on how often her da or her ma said she was in trouble. What she was in now went so far past trouble, it terrified her.

"I say we just zap Richland. No Richland, no Sterlings, no problems," Sean the bully said with an empty grin.

"Sean, you're a dumb ox. All the copper is under Richland. We make it vanish, where we gonna get copper for a TV?"

"TV rots your brain" was Sean's usual comeback, and he used it again. Daga prayed the quiet woman would tell them to shut up; sometimes she did. The woman and the two men with her just stared out the window at the pouring rain. They'd slept outside since leaving Hazel Dell; tonight they were in a house. The couple who owned it had given them their upstairs room and were downstairs, listening to a muted weather report.

There was running on the stairs. The man of the house skidded to a halt at the open door. Behind him, the sound of the TV grew loud. "You better come hear this."

The unnamed woman turned from the window. She and the two men swept past Daga. Sean and Jean Jock followed, Daga trailing them. On the stairs, she stopped to watch. The ambassador from the starfolk was on the TV.

• - •

"I apologize for interrupting your evening," Ray began, "but some very strange things have been happening here on Santa Maria, since just before we arrived."

Annie huddled beside the fireplace, taking what little warmth it offered. The wagon had rolled on long after dark. The wind and the rain had whipped at them, soaking their clothes. Finally the young woman had pointed the old man at a large stone house far beyond the edge of a village. The woman had greeted a man with cheer; they talked quietly at the other end of the great room. Two youths, one hardly older than Annie, did their bidding, preparing a meal. They said nothing, but the looks they cast Annie were as frightened as the ones she spared them.

What have we gotten into? Oh, to be home, with Da, and Ma, and Jeff. To have a warm bed, warm food, and dry clothes. The older servant cautiously approached the two. "Master, the television in the kitchen is behaving strangely. All channels show only the starman."

"Let's see what he has to say for himself," the woman answered. The two left the room.

"Nikki, stay here," Annie said as soon as they were gone.

"Don't go," Nikki whimpered.

"I have to. Stay here." Quickly Annie stepped off the distance. Yes, she could hear the Colonel's voice, so calm, so confident, explaining what Jeff had told her about the tumor growing in their heads, and the machine that was trying to make contact with them but failing.

"You believe any of that?" the man asked.

"We've been here three hundred years with no problems."

"But you will admit, people have been acting rather strange of late. Even, dare I say, the divine Miss V. This might explain it better than anything."

"It might," the woman said slowly. Then the Colonel told the world about Nikki and Daga's vanishing box.

"Oh, shit. That lets the cat out of the bag," the man snarled and stomped around the kitchen.

For the first time Annie was learning about them. She'd heard Jeff growl about the divine Miss V, his sister.

Now they talked in hushed tones, too low for Annie to hear, so she hastened back to Nikki. She had heard enough; they were in Vicky Sterling's hands.

As Annie settled down beside Nikki, she moved her wallet over to keep it from coming between them. It was bulky with Dumont's automatic. No one had searched her, no one had violated the privacy of a young woman's wallet. The two in the kitchen, still discussing the Colonel's call for help, thought they had everything planned.

Annie knew at least one thing that was not in their plans.

Jeff sat quietly, nursing a no longer hot tea and trying to keep from thinking of Annie out in this weather. Surely whoever had taken her would have her inside on a miserable night like this. Even Old Ned had agreed to stay in an inn. So the two sat with their backs to a corner, forming a quiet space in a happy babble as the customers watched a replay of last summer's soccer championships. People cheered their favorites, as if the outcome were unknown. Then the Colonel came on.

There were groans and demands to put the channel back. Several channel switches showed only the same earnest visage, with the same unbelievable message—assuming you hadn't been living it the past few weeks. While the message sank in, the general complaining continued. Several people voiced loud doubts that everyone had a lump in their head, even when Ray showed them brain scan after brain scan. Over time, more grew thoughtfully silent. Finally it was the ones who interrupted who were told to shut up so others could listen. The room was a deathly hush when the Colonel told about a mountain vanishing beneath his ship as it made its first orbit. The camera panned to show Willow and Emma, describing the box, what it had done, and how they'd run.

"They're just girls," someone grumbled dismissively.

They were roundly shushed.

"Well, the fox is in the henhouse," old Ned whispered. "What's the starman think he's doing?"

"Begging for help," Jeff whispered, and kept watching.

• • •

Hen was meeting with her security consultants when her assistant stuck his head in the door. "Ma'am, I think you better see this. It's even interrupted the letter I was typing."

Hen fumed as Longknife told everyone what he said was happening to them. Behind her, some consultants marveled at things they didn't know, as if they needed to know it all to do their jobs. She doubted anyone really understood all that babble about viruses causing lumps in their heads and the huge computer that was trying to talk to them and had made Rose's life so miserable. Now he was telling everyone that the strange box could make anyplace disappear. That would certainly help people sleep tonight. He had to be out of his mind.

But his ending was the most puzzling. Why tell everyone that he and his people were starting to extract metals and would make it available to the manufacturers of New Haven and Refuge? When the metal was ready was soon enough. If he failed, now he faced embarrassment and disappointed people.

"The man is a fool. He does not understand us," she snapped at her consultants when he finished.

"If the right people are listening, we may find out who knows where the vanishing box went," one ventured.

"The panic we will see in the streets tonight will hardly be worth the few extra days this gives us in finding it," San Paulo snapped. No one disagreed with her on that.

Ray leaned forward. "The problems you and I face today may seem daunting. The power of the vanishing box is immense, yet the six who have it have not used it since fleeing Hazel Dell. The threat of the teaching computer and its ability to rattle even our very skulls is terrifying, but we can choose to control our fear, anger, terror even as we feel them beating at us. The choices are ours. If we work together, we can make good ones.

"If you have reason to believe that you have seen the six with the box, call us at the number on the screen. If you operate a manufacturing concern and need metal to keep your employees working, call us at the second number. We can arrange for at least a minimum supply to keep you going over this disruption. There is no reason for us to fear. There is no reason for us to tear at each other.

"Together, we can make it through this."

"Now everybody knows about us," Sean the bully whined. "They'll all be after us."

"Not if we stay far from view," the nameless woman said. "Saddle our horses. We ride tonight." Three men moved to obey her, stepping out into the wind and rain without a backward glance. The woman of the house dismissed herself for the kitchen to pack a basket with all the food she had.

"But what if we're caught?" Sean stayed where he was.

"Then we see how good the vanishing box is," the woman answered with a voice so even it made Daga shiver worse than the cold wind from the door as the boys moved to obey.

"Should I call the Colonel?" Jeff asked as people around the Public Room discussed the first real news any of them had probably ever gotten from a TV.

Ned shook his head. "They'll be getting calls from anyone who saw six people they don't know. I know the people I talk to. If they know something, they'll tell me. Maybe they'll call your colonel. Maybe they won't. Maybe their call will be answered. Maybe the starfolk will need a month to sift through all the calls they get. You want to be chasing calls for them, or you want to do it my way?"

Jeff said nothing and followed Ned up to their room.

Ray watched the map table light up with small yellow dots. Each was a call from someone to the base, telling of the six. Dots showed from way south of New Haven to surprisingly far north of the James River. Apparently everyone up there wasn't crazy or off net; somehow Ray doubted they'd seen the right six people.

"The computer's doing the initial assessment of each call," Kat told him. "If the light goes out, the call doesn't appear to have anything to do with our search. Red means it's got a fifty percent chance of contributing to our hunt. If it starts flashing, it's a hot datum."

"And if the map suddenly disappears," Mary drawled, "we know they used the damn gizmo again."

Ray studied the lights. A few turned red. There was no pattern to them; they were just as scattered as the yellows. Kat winced as even she concluded that her computer was just as stymied as they were. "It's too early to tell," she said. "In the morning, we'll see a pattern."

"I'm betting on Annie's ma," Mary said. "She's sure her kids went southeast. Jeff and his native guide sure did."

"Have we located Jeff yet?" Ray asked.

"No, we're working our way outward. Looks like he and Old Ned are riding faster than we expected."

"Faster than we modern techs think biological can move, you mean." Ray allowed himself a smile. He'd done his best; still, his gut was knotted as if he'd spent the past hour in a firefight. He had been in a fight, a fight for the trust of six million people. Only time would tell if he'd won.

Daga was mounted; Sean and Jock were to either side. The woman thanked the couple. "We'll ride for the mountains west of here, find a place to hole up and wait for things to cool down. I'll send a man back in a week or two to find out how things are."

"We'll follow the news for you."

They rode out of the farmyard. Once out of sight of the house, they turned east, toward Richland, not west. The woman urged her horse to a trot, and the rest followed.

Jeff and Ned were in the saddle at first light. The morning brought clear skies and air washed clean by the rains. The ride would have been pleasant if he and Ned weren't driving themselves so hard. The second village they paused at that morning brought more information than usual. Yes, a wagon driven by an old man had rolled through there yesterday. The son of the woman providing the information had seen the wagon stop at the big house just past town. The woman shook her head and spat.

"A young man just bought it. Doesn't plant much. Don't

know where his copper comes from. Doesn't have much to say."

Ned was circumspect in his approach to the stone house, but it quickly became clear the place was empty. Not quite. In the barn, an old man slept beside a mud-spattered wagon. The hay he snored in and the stalls his old plug wandered alone had been full of other men, other horses the night before. The wagon held Jeff's attention. The wood was rough; a bit of wool yarn stuck there. A few strands of hair were higher up. Jeff retrieved them, held them against the sky. "Annie's skirt. Her hair. I swear."

"I think so, too."

"What direction did they take?" Jeff asked, looking around for tracks, knowing he'd miss what was in plain sight for Ned.

"Southeast, like always, but cross-country this time."

"They heard the Colonel. They know they have to find them fast before someone else does."

"Then we ride fast, too." The trail was clear enough that even Jeff could follow it once Ned pointed it out. They cut across the fields, through a wood, and were trotting around a hill when Jeff spotted a man walking toward them. A wide-brim hat hid his face. His clothes were black as night. Boots. One hand swung free. The other rested on a strap that had to support an airgun. He kept walking their way.

"Do we turn off?" Jeff asked.

"Could lose the trail." Ned kept riding.

The man kept his head down, face in shadow, but Jeff knew he was watching them as they got closer. The woods might hold more riflemen, but Jeff spotted none. At fifty yards, Jeff reached for his rifle, changed the magazine selector to sleepy bullets, and left his hand resting on the rifle butt.

They were fifty feet away and closing at a fast trot when the man looked up. "You really ought to return the Colonel's calls, Jeff. The old man don't like being stiffed."

Jeff almost fell out of his saddle. "Dumont, what are you doing here?"

"Chasing you, who's chasing the girl, who's chasing the vanishing box. You must be Ned," the marine said, offering a hand. Ned shook it. "You hear the Colonel last night?"

"Could hardly miss him," Ned drawled.

"That was the idea, I understand. Listen, we can do this two ways. I and the half squad I got waiting on the other side of this hill can follow you, or we can work together. Colonel thinks we'd do better that way. What's your call?"

"We're doing pretty good on our own," Ned answered.

"Can't argue that, but our search map shows a definite bias to this area, even before we factored you in. All the Colonel asks is that you listen to what we've got and share what you're willing. You know you're not the only search party out."

"Not after last night," Ned growled, but he smiled.

"Not before either. Vicky Sterling has had a team out for a while, we think. Some religious fanatics are on the trail, too, though we don't know how long they've been at it. We picked that up from net chatter, but that's kind of drying up this morning."

"Wonder why?" Ned grinned sardonically.

"Anything you do has upsides and downsides; at least that's what Mary keeps telling me. Most of my life, everything I done had its downside and its downer side, but the padre is helping me find a bright side. You willing to help?"

"I'll at least take a gander at your map," Ned conceded.

"How'd you find me?" Jeff asked as he helped Dumont up on a horse for a quick ride to his team.

"Electrocardiac fingerprint," Dumont said, settling himself none too confidently on his mount, then making a stab at his chest. "Everyone's heart is a bit different. Doc took your cardiacprint as a matter of course when you signed on with us. We set the sky eyes"—now he pointed up—"looking for you. Found you this morning. Since Mary and Harry were headed south to start mining, I was told to hitch a ride and tie in with you. Now, how do you put this animal in gear?"

Jeff shook his head. How could someone find you by your heartbeat but not know how to mount a horse or get it walking. Starmen were full of contradictions.

Ray took Dumont's call. He was glad Old Ned was throwing in with them and he and Du were hitting it off. Ray needed

Mary at base, and Cassie in Refuge. That left either Dumont or Tico, Mary's junior sergeant, chasing the vanishing box. Dumont had drawn the long straw. The word that Annie and Nikki were just ahead of them was encouraging; that half a dozen riders were with them now was not. Somebody was hot on the box's trail; Ray chose to assume that group was Vicky's. The two sky eyes he could spare were now sweeping ahead of Dumont. Between Old Ned's information network and their own, they just might find the box ahead of the others.

Lek brought the first hint that Refuge's attitude might be changing. It seemed that all official workstations were now isolated in specific pools—and turned on only when in use. Phone usage and net traffic were way up, lots of people talking over Ray's message. Official traffic was as close to zilch as you could get and still pass along weather reports and train schedules. Maybe he had been a bit too sweeping in his approach.

His calls to San Paulo went unanswered. When Hen did call, she was alone. Without preamble, she launched into a long list of Refuge's requirements, including a veiled hint that all the blimps were needed back. Ray pointed out that their security depended on blimp-based surveillance systems and offered to pay for them. That brought forth a not very veiled hint that the Monetary Reform Act of yesterday could be repealed today. Ray had just taken a call from Mary about her reception in New Haven, so Ray countered that threat with one of his own. Chu Lyn was in no rush to side with Vicky Sterling on monetary policy. The call ended quickly after that, nothing resolved.

Mary's reception in New Haven had not gone all that well, since she had opened the meeting with Chu by buying all the land they intended to mine. It about wiped them out of spare change, but the land was theirs free and clear. Chu had the good grace to accept the purchase. Mary had the miners quickly at work, producing the raw metal that could, if confidence returned, fuel New Haven's return to normal business.

Encouraging was the number of calls from people who wanted to help find the vanishing box. Not just people who thought they might have seen it, but people willing to join search parties. A few called with suspicions that their brothers or sisters, aunts or uncles might be one of the mysterious three. Kat followed those up. It looked to Ray like he'd called it right.

Still, being right made all the powers-that-be around here wrong. That put him in the wrong by definition. Oh, for the good old days when an artillery shell was either aimed right—and blew away your enemy—or was aimed wrong and gave him time to blow you away. Life was so much simpler then.

When Ray's nostalgia got cynical, it was time for a break.

A call to Cassie found her off duty and in church. Yes, she could ship back her second squad to reinforce the base. She could throw another thousand volunteers at the base, too. Ray accepted and had Chief Barber rotate blimps down to Refuge to pick them up. Never more than one blimp on the ground, so San Paulo couldn't repossess but one. That ought to do it.

Personnel was getting critical. Automated plants were a contradiction in terms; someone had to provide their feed-stock. Someone had to take the packages off the assembly line. A lot was being done by backbreaking labor, much of it carried in horse-drawn wagons.

The chief was pulling out what little hair he had left, hiring anything that walked on two feet and the doc assured him had a small enough tumor. That was something Mary and the doc agreed on. Anyone below a certain age and above a certain tumor diameter was given a thanks-but-no-thanks slip and hastened out of town. This still left Ray wondering if they were covering all the bases.

Just because a human wasn't being driven crazy by the Teacher didn't guarantee they wouldn't act dumb out of normal human cantankerousness. Mary and Barber just looked at Ray and asked for more workers. Base security was at rock bottom. Only half a squad of marines were left, six lonely troopers headed by Tico, Mary's junior NCO. Mary had assigned a chief to help Tico out, providing adult leadership and such.

Each young marine private now led a platoon of one hundred local recruits equipped with riot shields, helmets, and clubs. A senior petty officer was detailed as deputy to each, providing support and guidance on nonsecurity matters. Security and nonsecurity matters weren't all that easy to separate.

Like the proper response when two guards one night decided it was more fun to cuddle up than keep walking their beat. The young marine, remembering what had happened when troopers fell asleep on watch during the war, wanted to shoot them. The petty officer shipped them back to factory duty, much to Ray's relief.

Ray even managed a good night's sleep. Maybe the Teacher or Dean or President was too busy with its own problems to bother him. God knows, people were doing a damn good job of screwing things up with no help from a super computer. Calls done, Ray ambled over to the doc's before lunch. He was still trying to puzzle out what made the tumors tick. The padre had helped him get access to several local cadavers. "We can't map the human brain. How am I supposed to map this?" Until they understood that thing better, none of them was leaving this planet.

Ned and Jeff trotted into the next village. Dumont had offered to ride in, too, but Ned still wanted to keep the starmen out of sight, so the mule took the long way around, using forest trails. Ned headed for a small cottage on the outskirts where a woman was serving the noonday meal to three nearly grown sons. "Mother of many," Ned hailed her, "can you help me? I'm looking for five or six people, traveling fast."

"The ones on the Public Room's TV?" the youngest asked.

"Shush, boy," the woman answered. "Do I know you?" she asked, squinting up at Ned.

"They call me Old Ned up Hazel Dell way. Your mother and my sister once talked a spell of earth and sky and other things."

"Maybe they did," the woman answered, then glanced at Jeff.

"One of the young women traveling south carries his heart. She may not know it yet, but she does." The two elders laughed as Jeff fidgeted in his saddle.

After a few more moments of thought, the old woman

spoke. "There is a large house off the road south of here. Two young couples farm it, say they inherited it from one of their mothers, but I don't know about that. My youngest was collecting firewood yesterday and saw six riders and a led horse go by late. He thinks they stopped there. It was starting to rain."

"Ma," the tallest said, "just before I came in, I saw maybe a dozen riders, going fast through the trees, headed that way. I think at least two of them were women, from the flash of their skirts and hoods."

"Blue plaids," Jeff put in.

"Blue with some yellow. One of them raven-haired,"

"Annie." Jeff swallowed hard. He wanted to turn his horse away to the south. Kick it for speed.

"I think we'll be going, Mother," Ned said.

"Ride carefully," the tall one said. "I've seen people ride. Some just amble along. Those rode their horses hard, like they were at the chase."

"They are," Ned answered, "but so are we. Thank you."

Jeff tried to let Ned set the pace. Tried not to gallop ahead. Ned waited until they were out of earshot. "Call Dumont. Tell him what we found out. And son, you can pull that rifle out now." Ned pulled his air rifle out, nestled it in the crook of his arm, under his poncho. Jeff did, too; the call went quickly.

"I got a farmstead south of town on our map," Dumont said. "We'll come up fast on it. You wait for us."

Like the other farm, this one was well out of town—and none too easy to get at without being seen. Ned turned up its side road without hesitating. They paused as they reached the outbuildings. Several cows lowed. No horses were visible. Chickens and pigs wandered the farmyard. Jeff called Du.

"We're at the homestead. No one's moving."

"Wait one minute for us, kid. We're almost there. Don't go doing something Annie will be mad at me for."

Ned and Jeff dismounted, tied the horses, and studied the scene. "Front door's ajar to the house," Jeff noted.

"We wait," Ned answered as the mule gunned out from the woods, slipping and splashing as it raced across the pasture. The marines held on, one hand for themselves, the other for their weapons. Jeff pulled the arming handle back on his rifle. It settled in place with a soft, purposeful chunk.

"They'd have to be dead in the house not to notice that mule," Ned said. Safety off, Jeff followed Ned toward the house. They were about fifty yards out when the mule skidded to a halt. Dumont ordered his troops to surround the house; he and one rifleman trotted to join Jeff. Halfway to them, he spotted the slowly swinging front door and came to a halt.

"Crew, this looks like a cold datum" came from the commlink. "Still, keep your heads up. This could change any second." Dumont signaled to Jeff, and together the four rushed the porch. Ned yanked the door open; Dumont, gunner, and Jeff crashed through into a darkened room. The stench of blood and death rolled over Jeff. He squinted but saw nothing.

"You, check the upstairs," Dumont ordered the other trooper. The man took the stairs two at a time, his rifle steady as it swept the banister above.

There was a crash in the back. Jeff's rifle came up. "We're in," came over the commlink. "Kitchen empty. Stove cold."

Now Jeff's eyes had time to adjust. There was a table near the fireplace. A woman's body sprawled on it. She was naked. She'd been cut. . . .

Jeff's stomach revolted. He groped for the door, made it to the porch before he lost his breakfast. He stomach was still heaving when Dumont, Ned, and another marine came out to catch their breath. "I'd say they were interrogating him while they tortured her," the marine said.

"Him?" Jeff got out.

"Yes," Dumont answered. "There was a guy—husband, maybe—tied to a chair. They slit his throat."

"Why?" Jeff begged.

"Want to know where the box is," Du shrugged. "They wanted true answers, and I guess they think that got them."

"That way?"

"I take it you don't have much of this type of shit around here," Dumont said matter-of-factly.

"None," Jeff spat.

"Not much," Ned said. "I want to take a look around." He

stepped off the porch, eyes down; Jeff and Du followed. "Someone left six, eight horses here"—Ned pointed at droppings—"say, for an hour. Expect we'll find a few horses were left in back, too."

At the barn, he looked around carefully. "Lot of hay in the mangers, not much eaten, as if they prepared last evening for more horses than spent the night. The mother told us two couples lived here. We've found one. Where's the other?"

"Sweet Mother of God." Jeff's stomach did an empty lurch. "You don't mean the other two led them here, then watched as they did that." He bent over, but his stomach had no more to hurl.

"Looks that way," Ned said.

"I've seen people do worse for money." Dumont's eyes suddenly focused far away. He shook himself. "Which way'd they go?"

"Don't know. The ones who did are dead," Ned answered.

"I know. What were their choices?"

"There's a TV in the house. They must have heard your Colonel. We've reached a ridgeline here. Follow it west, and you're in the mountains. Follow it east, and you can get almost to Richland and Refuge without leaving the woods."

"High up, perfect place to shoot from. Or they can hoof it for the great outdoors if they're spooked." Du eyed Ned. "These folks spook easily?"

"Let's follow their tracks and see."

The trail led south. A dozen horses or so left a wide track. The sky eye lost it in the woods. Base took them up higher, hunting for heartbeats, a bunch of them. It found some, but never more than three or four together.

"All this high-tech, and the best I can do is follow a guy on a horse, looking at the ground." Dumont laughed, but followed Ned. "There's a path one or two klicks farther in the woods."

"Klicks?" Ned frowned. "What's that in miles?"

"I don't know." Dumont asked the base. Suddenly the gridlines on their display shifted. "About one mile in."

Still, they covered the distance at a walk, Ned following the signs. At the trail, the horseprints led west. "Tracks are deep. They're riding hard."

Dumont eyed the trail to the east, toward Refuge, Richland. It showed no signs of travel. He worked his reader. "They had more than an inch of rain here after the Colonel's little talk. What would that do to a trail?"

"Wipe it out entirely," Ned answered. "Especially if they were riding slow, like I would at night."

"Damn! Chief, have one of the sky eyes cruise east on this trail. See what you get."

"Will do," came from the commlink.

"Now we go west, I suppose," Du said to Ned.

"It's the only trail I have to follow."

"Annie's that way," Jeff blurted out.

"How long will the trail last?" Dumont asked

"Not long, if I was riding it," Ned answered curtly.

An hour later they called the Colonel to tell him the one trail they had had broken up, and they had no idea which way the box had gone. "What's your best guess, Du?" the Colonel asked.

Du handed his commlink off. "This is Ned. If I had the vanishing box, I'd have gone east. Either the folks at the house lied to the second party, or they believed that the first group went west. That's guessing. What I know is that we've lost them, all of them. Best we wait around and see what happens next. I can talk to some folks, have them talk to others. Until somebody sees something, I think we're just chasing ghosts."

"Sounds like it. Du, Mary's coming back north this evening. She's got things started in New Haven. You want a ride?"

Du glanced at Jeff, who was having a hard time staying in his skin. "We can't just leave Annie out here with people like that! We've got to keep trying!" Jeff insisted.

"Colonel," Du said, "I know you're short manpower, but this is where the action is on the vanishing box. Some pretty nasty people want it; we need it. I want to stay down here."

"Take care," the Colonel said. "Those nasties won't be ignorant about you for long."

"Kind of hope they come looking for us, sir." Du turned to

Ned as he tapped off. "Okay, tracker. Let's find the shits that did that house. I think it's time Vicky Sterling learns there's some things her money can't buy."

"She hurts Annie, Du, I swear, I'll hold her down while you cut her heart out." Jeff said the words without thinking, meaning them without reflection.

"I'll try to save you from that, Jeff."

Ray had experienced the calm before a storm. South, miners were making metal, and people acted like they might listen. In the center, Refuge and Richland were quiet. North side was terribly quiet, not a peep. All he could do was wait, worry, and miss Rita.

So Ray got busy, working with Tico and the new recruits. Since riot control was all he could expect from them, they were equipped with ceramic shields, helmets, and clubs of a resilient local wood. Uniforms were armbands; they marched, wheeled, did column rights and lefts, and changed fronts by the flanks. It was a drill as ancient as the Greek hoplite, but it was the best Ray had to fight primal human screams and a super computer. He took a turn with each platoon of one hundred, drilling them, letting them see him, hear his voice. That was what command was; not paperwork, but eye contact.

It felt damn good to have his legs underneath him, moving at the proper cadence and step. Almost made up for the hour spent arguing production priorities with Mary as soon as she got back. He fell into bed ready for the innocent sleep of a baby.

And found himself facing the Dean. "Sociology, isn't it?

"Close enough," the dapper image in khaki and tweeds agreed.

"What're you folks up to?" Ray asked.

"I might ask you the same."

"You'll have to explain the question better," Ray said, still feeling good from the afternoon's workout.

"Why do you want the displacer, the 'vanishing box'?"

"Because I don't trust it in anyone else's hands. There's something about someone on a hill twenty klicks away making my base vanish that tends to upsets me."

"Then I think you'll understand when I say that your having it upsets me."

"I don't understand."

"Come, now. You heard my complaint when you removed portions of our net from the rocks up North. You've figured out that we build ourselves into this world. The surface is our weakness. We need sunlight for power. You burn off our solar cells and we are helpless, just waiting for you to leach the rest of our metal out, like you did the Gardener. No, Colonel, you are a killer, and I don't trust you."

Ray went over the statement slowly. He couldn't really blame the Dean. Given a choice, he wouldn't want the damn thing on the same planet with him. Too much power. Way too much. But something else niggled at the corner of Ray's mind.

"You seem a lot more comfortable talking about yourself. There were quite a few 'I's' in that last statement."

"And you are a savvy type who deflects conversations from where you don't want them to go. The vanishing box, Colonel."

"I'm trying to get my hands on it. What deep hole do you know that I can throw it down as soon as I've got it?"

"I don't trust you to have it that long."

"Has anyone told you that you have a problem with trust?"

"No, nor is anyone likely to. You are about the only one I am talking to these days."

"Then the 'I' does mean something?"

"Yes. We are fractured, divided. Some are at war with others of us. I never expected to see anything like this."

"Are *you* at war?"

"No. I am *just* an expert on group dynamics. I can do nothing to destroy net nodes, hijack energy lines, silence static, or garble communication packets."

"Sounds like things have gotten bad."

"Bad and worse. Many are retreating to the mainland. It is better to be elsewhere when the President and Provost fight."

"You haven't gone, though."

The image across from Ray fidgeted in his chair. "No, I haven't, yet. I keep hoping that something can be worked out.

That somehow we can find a way to persuade you that you really do want us for your teachers. I'm an idealist, I fear."

"Do you have to be our teachers?"

"That's all we know to be," the Dean spat.

"I have a woman working for me. She's been a teacher most of her life. Now she's having a ball helping us decide where to investigate nature. Have you ever considered doing research? Studying why people do what they do?"

"We know all that."

"So you say. Sure you haven't been studying the same data so long you've forgotten what the real thing looks like?"

"It doesn't matter, you won't work with us. You are just as afraid of us and our power as we are of you and yours."

"That's where trust comes in. Look, I'm working with the guy who almost blew my planet out of existence last year. It doesn't mean he no longer has that power. It does mean we're having more fun working together than against each other."

"But we're not human."

"A year ago, I wasn't giving Green Earthy Symps credit for much humanity. All I wanted was to kill 'em. Hell, man, the woman that broke my back was pushing pills at me to help me get well before your treatments or medicines or whatever did the job for her. We humans change. Why can't you?"

"You have no use for us even if we did."

"You're kidding. You have all the knowledge of the Three, the ones who built the jump points. We stumbled through one and got out into the galaxy hardly three hundred years ago. We don't understand jumps, we just use them. If I came back to Wardhaven with the likes of you, ready to help us rediscover all the stuff of the Three, there'd be one hell of a parade."

"You'd want us for . . ."

"Consultants, guides, fellow pilgrims on the way. Equals in the search, not superiors telling us not to touch. And yes, as teachers for our young, also."

"Because you do not trust us, you are willing to shatter the planet we share. If you could trust us, you would be willing to take us out among the stars you walk." The Dean spoke the words with slowly dawning eagerness.

"That's the way we do things. We can let fear drive us to kill, or we can trust. With trust, we can build on each other's strengths. Back home, we build things. The strongest building material is made up of many components, working together."

"That was what the Three said. Together they were greater than the sum of their individual parts."

"When you're just one big mind, there is a certain strength. Now you're many," Ray said. "You can hunt for the power of the many, or wipe yourselves out, trying to return to oneness."

"Once again, after our talks, I must think on your words."

"One more thing," Ray said. "Where is the thing that can scramble the molecules of my cells? That is the power you have that I fear the most. What line of thought controls it? Where is it? I could throw the vanishing box into a very deep hole if you tore that puppy apart. Rebuild it once we've gotten some trust built up. But right now it scares me and mine."

The Dean retreated deep into his chair. "That is something I will have to think upon long and hard, talk to others. I see your point. I see what you are offering us."

"It's been good talking to you," Ray said.

"Quite surprisingly, I, too, have found it good."

THIRTEEN

RAY FOUND HE rather enjoyed the quiet time. As a string of peaceful days turned into a week, Matt bounced in and out of the system at increasing accelerations and longer intervals. By the time the weeks were long enough to grow into a month, *Second Chance* had unwound itself into two-gee accelerations and was spending four and five days turning around from each jump.

Mary was having herself a ball, hiking mineral production from the new southern mines, running a base and most of a planet's economy. As people went back to work in New Haven, the bosses of Refuge's factories came, hat in hand, asking to be included in the distribution. That was a real kick for Mary, and left her wondering aloud to Ray if Santa Maria wouldn't be a great place to settle down.

Doc Isaacs had to be dragged out of his lab for meals. He wouldn't tell Ray anything specific, but he hinted with a broad grin that he might be getting a handle on this place. Even though the vanishing box was still missing, on the average, things were not too bad; one might even call them normal.

Then Ray heard the padre praying, and normal went to hell.

Ray went into town to ask the padre's help with the search down South. Jeff was about to come through the commlink at

Ray, demanding they do something about Annie. The padre was finishing morning Mass as Ray slipped into the church, but no one was in a hurry to leave. On their knees, they prayed to saints with every name Ray knew, and a few he'd never heard of. After each name came the same request: "Pray for sun." Ray listened, then waited as people filed out. Every face looked worried.

"What was that all about?" he asked the priest when his people had scattered to their work.

The padre looked up, eyeing the cloudy sky. "We need a week of sun and warmth to bring the crop in."

"I thought farmers were all the time praying for rain."

"Shows what you know. Without water, the crops don't grow. Without sun, they don't grow either. We need all in their proper balance. We've had too much rain and clouds this month."

"The Weather Proctor," Ray breathed.

"You think this is no accident?" the priest said.

"Maybe. Probably not. Will you be in the rectory?"

"Yes."

"Leave me for a few minutes." As the priest's footsteps faded, Ray returned to his pew, leaned back, slowed his breathing. Relaxed, though that was the last thing he felt like.

"Well, hello," the Dean said cheerfully. "Interesting place to find you."

"You'll find humans most everywhere," he answered. "What's with the weather?"

"The weather?"

"Yeah, isn't it awfully cloudy? Doesn't that affect your solar cells?"

"Yes. It's just part of the goings-on. By the way, your idea of a second career is attractive to many of us. Not the ones fighting, but a lot of us on the periphery."

"I'm glad to hear that, but I've got a problem. We eat food. Our food needs sunlight. We aren't getting enough of it this late summer to bring in our crops. If we don't get some good, solid sunshine, we may all be very hungry."

"Don't you have some kind of storage system?"

"Yes, but not enough. What can you do about it?"

"I'll put in a word with the Weather Proctor. I'm not sure whose side he's on. He seems to be running his own show."

"Please talk to him and get back to me quick."

"I'll try. You know, I like this place. Quiet, soothing. Ought to spend more time here."

Ray roused himself, told the priest quickly what he'd found, and headed back to see Kat. She called in a middie, who tracked the weather along with several other jobs. "Sorry, sir, I don't spend much time there, it's fully automated" was her initial response as she called up a global map.

"The usual pattern," she explained, "is a large stream of cool water flows down from the arctic area, swings around this continent, then loses itself in the ocean out there." She frowned at the east coast of Santa Maria's one human-settled continent. "But this year, the stream is closer to shore. That's causing the cool, damp weather we've gotten lately. That means the center of this large ocean area hasn't gotten anything to cool it. It's very warm, and that could cause the hurricane season to start early."

"Which direction will they head?" Ray asked.

"Usually north, to blow themselves out deep in the North Continent. However, we have core samples that show some real bad storms slamming the lowlands along our coast. Not in the past three hundred years, but four or five times in the past million. Refuge, Richland, and even New Haven were under water."

"Whose side is the Weather Proctor on?" Ray whispered.

"Will it matter?" Kat asked.

"What's the weather right now?" Ray asked urgently.

The middie worked the board rapidly, calling up satellite pictures, then backtracked to gather the past three days' worth. Four cyclonic wind patterns showed along the equator, lined up one after the other, moving east. "Will they go north or south?"

"There's a ridge of high pressure over the main continent," she pointed out. "The hurricanes can't go north. They have to go east or south. And, sir, we've had a low sitting on top of us for the past month. I'd say they're headed our way."

"How bad are the hurricanes?"

The woman studied her workstation, frowned, reran her last checks. "Sir, I don't know how this happened. We've got auto alarms rigged on this system, but they've been turned off. Those are force five hurricanes. The alarms should have been screaming at us for weeks."

"Lek"—Ray tapped his commlink—"I've got evidence of tampering with our weather net. Check it for fingerprints. I want to know how it happened."

"On it, sir."

"Holler when you have anything, an itch, a hunch. Anything. Lek, I don't like it when I can't trust our gadgets."

"Me neither, boss."

Ray started to leave, paused. "What's the tidal situation?"

The girl had gone pale after spotting the hurricanes; now she went translucent. "Highest of the summer, sir, are due in the next week."

Ray kept his pace carefully measured as he marched straight to Mary's desk. "How long can you tread water?"

She looked up, eyebrow raised. "How long do I need to?" Ray explained the problems lining up off their coast. Mary reacted stronger to their net being compromised. "Shit, if we can't trust the data we're looking at, how do we make decisions?"

"Don't know. Assuming the worse for the purpose of discussion, what do we do now?" Mary converted her station into a topographic map of Santa Maria's populated area, then added the data from Harry's core samples. Half the occupied land turned a muddy brown. "Storm surge never got as far as the base," she noted.

"No, this time we'll have a population surge."

"If we tell them, sir." Mary gave Ray a very bland look.

"Three, maybe four million dead if we say nothing," Ray breathed. "Is that what you're suggesting, Captain?"

"Haven't thought it through enough to make any suggestion, Colonel, just making the initial data identification."

Ray noted they'd both fallen back on military rank and big words. It was so much easier to discuss mass murder when you put on your armor and held the thoughts at arm's length.

"I want fortifications around this base, ditch, and wall," he said.

"We can do that. Use local labor. They sure as hell ain't bringing in any crops. What do we do with the locals?"

"Offer to move them inside the wall. We may need them as reserve police."

"All of them, sir, no matter how big their tumor?"

Ray rubbed at his eyes. Could he order a husband to leave a wife outside? A family to abandon a child? Hell, he had the biggest tumor of all. "ID cards for all. Tumor size listed in the data. If we start having problems, we'll isolate the large tumors somewhere under guard. Any problems with that?"

"Not now. Maybe later. What about the food supply?"

"Do nothing for now. Everyone's scared. We start buying food up, it'll start a panic and make us look like the bully. What else?" They made their list, trying to guess what they'd need in a long, painful siege. Lek interrupted long after Ray had expected.

"Colonel, I got no idea how the alarm got turned off. It's off, been off for two weeks, and I can't tell you who or how."

"Somebody had to access it. That somebody's got a code."

"Yes, sir, to both. Don't matter; the weather watch system was accessed and no record of it kept."

"Another human, or my super-computer friend?"

"I'd prefer to think computer, sir, since I don't want to admit some human outsmarted me, but truth be told, boss, with no evidence, I'm only guessing."

"Anyplace else hit?" Mary asked.

"Ma'am, officially, the weather wasn't hit. Only way to know is to check everything and see if it's still the way we want it. One hundred percent eyeball review. We got time for that?"

"No," Ray snapped. "Lek, get me Vicky Sterling, San Paulo, and Chu Lyn on the horn. They need to know what we know."

Lek snorted. "Won't be easy getting the first two."

"Get Chu, then tell the others I'm telling her something of critical importance to all three. They can get it secondhand from her, or they can get it straight from me."

"You bet, boss."

"There's going to be one hell of a panic," Mary said. "I better get a crew working on that wall. What do I tell folks?"

"Nothing for now. It'll be common knowledge by supper."

"Better pull back our deployed teams. Blimps will have to be deflated before the hurricanes hit."

Ray's first call was to Cassie. She was surprisingly recalcitrant to pull out of Refuge, even after Ray painted her a very deep and wet picture. "There'll be panic in the streets, sir. They'll need us."

"We're going to need you more here. I can't afford to lose you. Move your team out now; a blimp is already on the way." After getting a reluctant "Yes, sir," Ray punched up Harry.

"We'll be ready when the blimp shows up. What about Jeff?"

"I want them all back in. Things may get ugly fast."

"I'll corral him."

A half hour later Lek had all three women on the line. "What do you want?" Vicky glared. "Why is Cassie leaving?" San Paulo demanded. Chu Lyn stared from her third of the screen.

"May I ask a question first?" Ray began. They neither refused nor agreed. "Someone or something entered our net and turned off the alarms we have on our weather forecasting system. Did any of you have anything to do with that?"

"You're the one who butts into our systems," Vicky spat.

"I'm aware of the ill feelings that has caused. I wondered if any of you had sponsored a tit-for-tat comeback." No one responded. "Then I'll assume the intervention came from another source," he sighed. "That may make matters worse."

"Your super-computer boogeyman got you." Vicky cackled, causing Ray to wonder why he'd included her in the call. Then again, he couldn't let a million Richlandites drown to spite Vicky.

"When we reactivated our weather alarms, we found four hurricanes lined up, pointed straight at us." Ray put the satellite picture on their displays.

"That's impossible," Ms. San Paulo insisted. "The season hasn't started."

"The weather has been very strange this summer," Chu pointed out, though from the looks on the other faces on Ray's screen, the other two were not listening.

"Based on our assessments of core samples taken here, it appears this type of weather has hit South Continent five times in the past. Storm surges flattened everything far inland." Ray replaced the first picture with the map of human occupation on South Continent; half was covered with brown.

"It can't go that far inland," San Paulo sniffed. "The barrier islands don't even let the worst waves into our harbor."

"Those are level five hurricanes, four in a row. The first one will flatten your islands. By the third, open ocean waves will be smashing into Refuge. By the fourth, they'll be washing Richland out to sea," Ray said with deadly calm.

"That could not happen," Vicky insisted. "Impossible," San Paulo snapped. "Oh, Lord," Chu Lyn breathed. "We have to get people moving inland immediately."

"That would be my suggestion," Ray answered Chu.

"That will panic everyone," San Paulo charged.

"It will if Chu starts moving her people and you don't. Let this information come as a rumor, and people will run wild."

"We don't have to act right away," San Paulo insisted. "If the first storm is as bad as you say, we could start moving people inland then."

"Over storm-ravaged and flooded roads," Ray countered. "It's only going to get worse."

"I will announce this within the hour," Chu said with the finality of death. "What you others do is your decision."

"We'll all have to start moving," Vicky growled, "and this man will have won over us again."

"What are you going to do?" Chu asked Ray.

"I'm organizing people out here to provide food and shelter. And since this seems to be coming from the super computer I think lives in your planet, I'll be seeing what I can do to stop it."

"I wish you luck," Chu said as they all rang off.

"Well, that was no worse than I expected," Ray grumbled as he looked up from the screen.

Mary was at his office door. "Harry called. He's on his way

back, but Dumont and Jeff passed up the ride. Du says if you're putting everything you've got here, they better find the vanishing box, 'cause sure as hell, with both Refuge and Richland gone, the only target left is us."

"That would solve my problem," Ray sighed. He pushed back from his desk, put his feet up, and relaxed into his chair. "Now, if you'll excuse me, I have work to do. I've got to talk to my favorite computer and see just how much we can help each other."

Mary closed the door; Ray concentrated. Nothing happened. After ten minutes he moved from his office to his quarters, laid out full on his bed . . . and went to sleep despite his worries.

Mary woke him three hours later. "Why'd you let me sleep?" Ray grumbled groggily. "We've got things to do."

"And they're being done, sir," she answered way too cheerfully. "We're doing quite well without you."

"Just who's in charge here?" Ray growled, rubbing sleep from his eyes and trying not to smile.

"Me." Mary grinned unrepentantly.

"You don't have to be so obvious." Out the window, the gray day was just starting to fade. Near the base perimeter, people were digging. "You got started fast."

"I'll show you after chow."

At supper, portions were smaller. No one went hungry, but the farmer who'd been fattening pigs on the base's slop had better think of slaughtering his newly expected wealth. Talk around the dining hall was subdued. "Word already out?"

Mary shrugged. "Leaked a little. No worse than your average volcano. We'll need to address it up front."

"Time for a walk around."

"Looks that way, sir." Mary had a mule waiting.

"I can walk," Ray snapped, feeling rather good on his feet.

"The entire base perimeter is a bit more exercise than I care to take," Mary answered, slipping into the driver's seat.

Ray settled down beside her. "How are people taking this?"

"Most are still in shock. Nobody really wants to believe everything they've worked for and built is about to be washed out to sea. Any chance we can stop that?"

"Don't know. The computer ain't talking to me."

The base perimeter came in view. Up to now it had been marked by little more than a rough path for the perimeter patrol. Now surveyor's sticks marched in both directions, forming three long rows. Villagers cut the sod, rolled it, and put it aside, then turn to with shovels and picks, digging a trench and piling the dirt on the inside edge. People waved when they saw Ray, shouting "Thanks for the job" and "Glad to have a place to stay." Ray waved back, then signaled Mary to halt. The little priest was out with his parishioners, wielding a shovel.

"Father Joseph, isn't this a little out of your line?"

"Since when can't a man put his back into a job?" the priest answered, but used the pause to wipe sweat from his brow.

"Does everyone understand what we want?"

Mary scowled; the priest smiled. "Dig a ditch ten feet wide, six feet deep, and a wall about the same size beside it. You're expecting a lot of rain, aren't you?"

"What have you heard?"

"Forty days and forty nights, or something like it."

"May not be off by much," Mary quipped.

"We're saving the sod. When you have your wall built, we'll roll it back down along it. That ought to keep the rain off the wall, but the ditch is going to be a muddy mess."

"Can't help that," Ray said. "I want a wooden fence four to six feet high above the dirt wall. Something to protect our guards from thrown rocks."

"I can get some woodcutters on that," the priest offered.

"Good, you and the mayor, supervise if you will." The priest's only answer was a nod. Mary drove on, circling the perimeter. All of it was marked, with digging rapidly expanding from several points.

Ray went with Mary to check on the kids that evening. Doc Isaacs frowned at Ray's sudden interest but still showed them off like a proud father. Their headaches were gone. They looked like healthy, dirty urchins despite the clouds. Ray got drafted into reading them their bedtime story, read two, and then did his best to slip away. Doc blocked the hallway outside the room.

"What are you up to?" Jerry demanded.

"I don't know," Ray sighed. "I really don't know."

"You're not going to use these kids to fight that thing."

"I don't know," Ray defended himself. "They weren't hurt when the Gardener died."

"You are going to." Isaacs accused Ray like a wrathful god.

"Maybe. If it looks like it will do some good. If you got a better idea on how to fight a million-year-old machine, I'm all ears." Isaacs said nothing. "Right now, the damn computer won't even talk to me." And it didn't that night, either.

It was only as Ray came awake the next morning that he found himself surrounded by a dozen computer images. Three or four of them wore partial body armor, shabby and worn. Two carried assault rifles, though none too sure how. One looked ridiculous in hockey shoulder pads, knee protectors, and a cooking pot perched on his head. He carried a baseball bat but had pliers and a screwdriver in his breast pocket. That one left Ray really wondering what his mind was trying to tell him.

"As you can see," the Dean said, a battle vest thrown over his tweeds, "the war has started, and we are losing."

"Why didn't you call me?" Ray asked. "I've had some recent experience losing wars."

"What we want," the one in the cooking pot cut in, "is some suggestions on how we kick their asses."

"I've won a few, too," Ray drawled. "What's going on?"

"The President and the Provost are mainly fighting themselves. The Provost wants to exterminate you. The President only to—I guess you would say—enslave you. We"—the image indicated the others with an open palm—"would like to join you."

"Assuming you're worth joining," grumbled Pothead.

Ray eyed them for a moment, then asked, "Where is their center of gravity, their axis of attack?"

"Their what?" Pothead countered.

"What do you know of military strategy, tactics, and logistics? What's your combat training?" All the computer images looked uncomfortably at the floor. Ray glanced down at himself; he was in his pajamas. He adjusted his dress to full battle kit. The room wavered and came back as the inside of his battle van. The images glanced around their new surroundings; two shifted from battle dress to civilian clothes.

"Ray, we know nothing of war. It's a word in the lexicon of the Three, but one marked obsolete. They taught us nothing about it because they wanted us to teach nothing of it to their young."

"An admirable ideal," Ray said, "but you still don't know why the Three vanished."

"No. As you pointed out, and continue to, we do not know everything." The Dean glanced at his associates. They nodded, looking for all the world like a dozen kids caught with their hands in the cookie jar, only to discover there were no cookies.

Ray conjured up his battle board. He used a wide view, showing not only the southern continent but also the northern. "Where are the President and Provost concentrated?"

The Dean frowned, glanced at the board, and rubbed the back of his neck. "It's not that easy. We all started moving south together. We're kind of all over the place together."

"And being pushed around everywhere," Pothead threw in.

"Concentration of force is basic," Ray advised.

"Right, and now *you're* gonna teach *us*," Pothead spat.

"I've got too damn much experience of war. What have you got? You want to learn, you come to the expert or you don't learn. What's it gonna be?" The twelve looked at each other. Ray wondered how fast they communicated among themselves. Then he reminded himself they were none too experienced with being individuals.

"What do we need to do?" the Dean finally asked.

"Concentrate your forces is a start. The question is: Where? Where are the President and Provost strongest?"

A pink hue covered the center of North Continent and stretched south to form a large lobe in Convenanters' territory. "That's the President. Provost is a bit west of there." A blue tinge marked the map from north to south. In the south it formed a large lobe along the border of Covenant/Richland.

"And you are?" Ray offered. The twelve looked shyly at each other. "Unaware of where each other are," he finished.

The Dean made golden a small section of the board in Covenanters' territory on the southeastern edge of the pink. "I've been evicted from my network to the north," he whispered.

"You, too!" Pothead exclaimed. "Me, too." A string of brown lines spun and twisted around South Continent. "I get around, though. Even into your net." He grinned at Ray. "Yeah, that was me. Your guards didn't come close to twitching to me."

"Why'd you turn off our weather alarms?"

"Weather Proctor dared me to. Said I couldn't understand a net as primitive as yours. I showed him."

"You were on the Weather Proctor's side?" Ray encouraged him to gab on. Did he really want this ally?

"Nobody's on WP's side, except WP. He cut his own deal with the Pres and Prov. Pres wants you down a few notches. Proc want's you out of here. Either way, WP wins. That one is sly."

"But you're not with him anymore," Ray said.

"Nope. WP snatched my net up North while I was working you guys. Booted me right out. Is that any way to treat a friend?"

"Not the way I would, anyway. I take it all of you are bereft of attachments to North Continent." They nodded. "May I suggest you concentrate around this base? I'm massing my human strength here. We can protect your physical selves as well. It will keep you out of the line of fire when we open up on them."

"You can't touch them," Pothead sneered.

"I drained the Gardener. That was an accident. Next time won't be. Dean, you noticed when we took samples up north. If we took enough, could we disrupt the P and P?"

The Dean rubbed his chin. "You'd have to take a lot."

"The vanishing box could take a lot in a hurry."

Heads jerked, several took a step away from Ray. That got their attention. "Who do you trust?" Ray tapped the pink and blue on his map. "They've booted you out of the North. Think they'll save anything down here for you? I promise to take you to the stars with me. First we got to survive. And they've got to . . . what? Be taken down a peg or ten? Be destroyed? You tell me. You can't win a war if you don't know your objectives."

The images of the twelve got thin. For a second, Ray feared he'd lost them. "You go away now, will there be anything left of you to talk to me by tonight? You're losing. Give up and die, or join me and fight. What will it be?"

The Dean thickened up. "I don't want to die. I like the idea of going to the stars with the humans. I say fight."

"But can we trust him?" Pothead whined.

"You trusted the Weather Proctor. What did it get you?" the Dean asked.

"Nothing. But at least he was my own kind."

"Your own kind are killing you," Ray pointed out. He held out his right hand, palm up. The Dean stepped forward, put his hand on top of Ray's. A sheepish grin crossed the Dean's face. "This is the way you do it, isn't it?"

"Close enough," Ray answered hard. His gut was in knots. He'd called time on their dithering; either they all joined him, or it was over. Another stepped forward. Then another. The pile of hands grew. If they'd been real humans, Ray wasn't sure the thirteen of them could have made the circle, piled the hands on. Pothead was the last in.

"Yes!" Ray shouted. The others tried to follow suit. It was a bit weak, but it was a yes.

"Now what?" Pothead asked.

"Any way you could help me find the vanishing box?"

"Not with anything you got," Pothead answered surely.

"We collected chunks of you up north. Could any of them help?"

"No," Pothead shot back. Then, "Maybe. For a while after you've used a displacer, it has harmonies. If you picked up a harmonator as well as a couple of projectors, I might be able to knock something together. No. They'd be too small. You'd have to get too close."

"I got a blimp that can move those rocks," Ray said. "You find the right ones and we'll have them in the air in an hour."

"I'll have to get back in your net."

"You're our ally. It's open to you. To all of you if you need a place to retreat." Ray hoped he hadn't just screwed humanity. Trust was a two-way street.

"We will work with you," the Dean said. "We'll start moving this way. Net Dancer"—the Dean nodded at the one wearing a pot—"will work with you to find the vanishing box. The rest of us will do what we can to resist the President and the Provost."

"Anything you do to the Weather Proctor will be appreciated."

"WP has gone back North," Pothead/Net Dancer noted.

Ray came awake, grabbed his commlink, and punched for Lek. "Old boy, that gremlin that was in our net is gonna be back any time now. Only this time, he's on our side."

"You sure?"

"We'll know soon. He's supposed to help you go over Harry's samples and see if there's a harmonator—whatever that is—and a couple of projectors. That might help us find the vanishing box, assuming we can get a blimp up in this weather." Out Ray's window, the clouds were scudding past, headed south. Hurricane number one must not be too far away.

"I'll get right on it, sir."

Ray sat back on his bunk. He'd just sworn alliance with a dozen of the strangest critters ever to cross a human's path. Had he done right? Was the enemy of my enemy really my friend? Humanity had survived by that creed for a long time—and paid no small price. Ray considered the string of hurricanes pointed at his base, weighed the odds, and found them acceptable. Matt could still rock this place if all else failed. Nice thoughts for a loyal ally. He wondered what the AI's were thinking. Probably not far from his own. Trust took time to build. Time they didn't have. Experience they were about to get too much of.

The barefoot girl ordering a pail of beer was the first lead they had in a month. Jeff wanted to run after her the second she said her grandma knew where the box was. Ned and Du followed more cautiously. The girl stopped outside a small stone house. Ned hurried ahead to open the door for her; she disap-

THEY ALSO SERVE · 255

peared inside. Ned and Jeff followed her into an unlit room.
Dumont stood in the doorway for a long minute, eyes searching the street, then ducked inside and closed the door.

"Your man's a nervous one," a voice said from a dark corner.

"He's alive. Others of his ken are not," Ned answered.

"Fill me glass, baby duck, then run along home. That's a
good one," the voice told the girl who struggled to pour beer
from her large pail. Ned took over. Dumont opened the door
for her as she left hurrying, as much as her load would permit.

"What do you know of Annie?" was what Jeff wanted to
blurt out. He squatted down, waiting for Ned to do his magic.
Today, Ned seemed in no hurry. "Do you think it will rain?"
he asked.

"Da ya think it will ever stop raining?" the voice replied.

"Ya'll need a high mountain. And strong friends," Ned
said.

"Like yours?"

"They're not a bad bunch at your back, not bad at all."

"I hear tell the starfolk are building a wall around their
base. And they're letting those who build it stay inside. You'd
need a lot of people to build a wall around all that. How do
you get a job like that?" the shadow woman asked.

"You'd need to be a starman's friend."

The woman edged out of the darkness into the light of the
single window. Old, her hair was white, most teeth gone. "I
can't dig, but I do know something you want to know." Ned
said nothing. "I know where the girl is that the other two seek.
The six that came South a month ago, my son takes them
food. High up in the hills, at the rock castle. From the chatter
of old women around town, I'm not the only one who knows.
And if many know, someone is likely to talk to the others who
want to know."

"Who else asks?" Jeff demanded.

"You're the young Sterling boy, aren't you," the old
woman reached for Jeff's face. Cold, calloused hands turned
his head from side to side. "Why should you be asking?"

"Annie's my . . ." Jeff choked.

The woman cackled. "So the Sterling boy has lost his girl

to his sister's toughs. That's a funny one. Why don't you run home and ask your big sis for her? Wouldn't she be glad to give her back to you?" Jeff's face burned, but he said nothing. Still chuckling, the woman held out a paper to Dumont. "Write to your people to let me and mine in the base."

Du pointed his wrist unit at the woman. "I'll do you one better. Duty section, Dumont here. This woman's doing us a good turn. If she shows up at the gate, let her in." Dumont got an acknowledgment, then added, "If you don't hear from me, assume her good deed was a trap and act accordingly."

"That wasn't a nice thing to do," the crone whined, but she turned to Jeff and shoved the paper under his nose. "You say something nice to your sister about me, too. You can never tell where I might need friends."

Jeff scribbled, "Help her, she helped me, Jeff" on the paper and shoved it back. Still cackling, the woman slipped out a back door Jeff hadn't known was there.

"Team, home on my signal. Bring the horses. We're out of here," Dumont snapped into his commlink in the curt way of talking the starmen had among themselves.

Ned rubbed his chin. "Think she told the others?"

"The more the merrier," Dumont sighed. "Let's move it, folks. Guns up. I wouldn't put it past her to have sold us to Vicky." So saying, Du slammed the front door open, waited a moment, then crossed the threshold at a run. He stopped only when he was across the street, his back to the stone fence, head and rifle high, sweeping the roofs.

"All clear," Du called without a trace of the embarrassment Jeff would have felt if he'd admitted to such a fear, let it make him act like that, only to find it meant nothing. What would make a man like that? Jeff wasn't sure he wanted to know. Then he remembered where he was headed and who was racing him there. There was no one better than Dumont to go there with.

The mule rolled up the alley, a dozen horses capered behind it. They piled in with the rest; it was a close fit. "Head east out of town, then take the south fork. We're going back country. And boys and girls, heads up. We ain't alone on this trip, and there's no second prize."

Then Du called the Colonel. "I got a handle on the vanishing box," they both said at once, then laughed. The Colonel explained a blimp would be heading their way with some kind of gadget aboard that might locate the box. Du told him what the woman had said. Their review of the rock castle formation showed several large mounds of boulders covering thirty hectares. "Lots of places to hide," the Colonel concluded.

"If your gadget ID's the hideout, I'd be much obliged."

"We'll try. You say there are two other teams on this."

"At least."

"I'll get a spy eye going south to give you a hand. Du, we got bad weather coming with north winds. Once they get up to sixty, seventy knots, there's not a thing on Santa Maria but the shuttle that can work its way upwind."

"Understood, sir. But we'll get 'em first."

Yes, Jeff whispered to himself, now we get the bastards who have Annie. *Dear God, let her be safe.*

"Up, slut!" the voice shouted as a foot took Annie in the ribs. "All of you, to the horses. We've got work to do." Annie shook Nikki awake; sleeping was all they could do in this stinking barn. It seemed forever that they'd been here.

"About time," "What took you so long?," and "Where are those damn greens?" were the greetings Pretty Boy's words brought from his thugs. Annie stood, waited patiently for someone to tell her what they wanted her and Nikki to do.

"Some old bitch in that stinking mudhole finally decided to take Vicky's copper," Pretty Boy bragged. "Told on her own son. He doesn't know he'll be leading us in tonight." That brought laughs that held no humor.

"Bitch must have believed the weather report" drew more derisive laughter. Annie wondered; she'd heard the talk of four monster hurricanes headed at them out of season. Everyone here scorned the story. Annie trusted what Jeff had told her about the super computers the Colonel was fighting.

"Maybe the bitch wasn't so dumb. I talked to Miss Vicky while I was in town. She believes that story enough to evacuate Richland. She definitely wants the box. Wants to be there when the starbase disappears."

"Can we get more money?" the woman asked. Annie tried to shrink into the shadows. The men talked bad; the woman *was* bad.

"She doubled her offer if we get the box to her in the next three days." That brought joy all around.

"She'll triple that when we have the box," the woman said with a soft smile. Annie tried to suppress a shiver, to hold perfectly still and stay unnoticed. The look in the woman's eyes . . . Annie didn't want that focused on her or Nikki.

The men saddled horses, checked air rifles, got supplies. The woman came over to Annie, a knife in her hand. "When we find them, you'll do what I tell you or die worse than the woman at the house. You understand me, you two mud sluts?"

"Yes," Annie stammered, keeping her hands folded, covering her wallet. For all this time, she'd seen no chance to escape. She'd held Dumont's pistol and not used it. Today she'd find a way. Today she'd use it.

But not now. Not here, where there was no way out. She might kill the woman, but the men would get her. That was the counsel of despair, the old priest said in his sermons. No child of grace need taste despair, no matter what happened. Annie wondered if any child of grace had ever been in as big a mess as this. Somehow she doubted it.

Ray dropped by Lek's shop. The old man was shaking his head. "That was one hell of an experience, Colonel."

"Tell me about it later. Lek, you remember that rock in the cave I had you look at the day after Mary ran her first ore tap?"

"Yep."

"I read your report on it. No activity of any sort, you said then. What do you think now?"

"Damn, sir, it could be pudding pie, for all I know."

"Bring it in here. Then you and Net Dancer go over it, see if you can make it active again."

"Sir, that AI is gonna be a busy little routine for the next couple of hours, working what we loaded on the blimp."

"Can't be too much of it there. How much bandwidth can our radio carry?" Ray frowned.

"Seems so, boss, but I don't think those things are as big as we think they are. I mean, they're big, but not like we think of as big. I don't know." Lek took his hat off, wiped his forehead. "I tried to get it to explain what it was doing. It laughed. I've never had a computer laugh at me. Said it would be easier for me to explain my network to some naked savage just hacking the first spear point out of flint than it would be for it to explain what it was doing. And you know, boss?" Ray nodded into Lek's pregnant pause. "I believe it. Damned if I don't. I don't know about bringing that thing home. Before I talked to it, I thought it would be great, what it could do, what schooling our kids could get. Now, I don't mind saying I'm spooked. That puppy is spooky shit."

Ray didn't blink. "Take part of Net Dancer out there when you get the stone. Can't risk damaging it accidently. Maybe he can tell you how to cut it loose." Ray finished what he intended to say. He'd heard Lek's worry. Someday he'd think it through, but not now. Right now, he had four megahurricanes headed his way and needed every trick he could get his hands on to stop them. After that, he'd think this through. Assuming there was anything after, after that.

Ray had been in some weird staff meetings in his time. Today set a record he hoped never to break. Kat and Doc represented normal; Lek sat like a stone statue, just back with the rock. The padre represented the locals. Blimp pilot Rhynia Loramor had a pile of weather maps in front of her; Harry flipped through papers. Mary was late; Ray would start without her. The humans congregated around the right side of Ray's battle board, casting uncomfortable glances at what stood on the left side.

There was the Dean and his twelve; Net Dancer had arranged it so all of them could access the local net. That might be another reason why Lek was so quiet; his net was totally compromised. Ray considered his options and decided to be glad Net Dancer had changed sides. Each of the dozen images that sporadically haunted Ray's dreams now was a holograph, thirty centimeters tall, standing along the edge of the battle board, staring at the map Ray projected on it of South and North Continent. Most were in tweed jackets, their attempt at battle dress past. Net Dancer—or at least as much of him as wasn't tied up on the blimp—wore a white lab coat complete with the ancient and required pocket protector of the technonerd.

"I'm isolating us from the two main protagonists. Are the rest of you here?" Ray began, making a circle around the table.

Mary came in, worry dripping with the rain from her face. "Colonel, we've got a problem."

"Later, Captain; I've got an agenda, and we're sticking to it." Mary frowned, but settled into a chair.

Ray went on. "Are the twelve of you in here yet?

"Yes." The board turned brown around the base as the Dean walked across it. "Though I don't know what good it will do. The P and P can follow us anytime they want."

"They can, but we can make it hard on them. Net Dancer, what's the main avenue of approach to the base?"

"The line left by the Gardener. It runs up this railroad bed, then follows this road." The mentioned line lit up in red. "Your farmers don't mess around with roads, so I guess the Gardener found them the safest routes to use."

"We'll cut it. Harry?"

"It's mainly farmland. This route looks the most likely to me, too. What do you want done?"

"Since you fellows are inside," Ray said, glancing at the Dean, "we blow it. In several places. Long, deep gashes that'll take some repairing. Harry, take out a team of marines as soon as we're done. Captain, can you spare Cassie?"

"Yes, sir." Mary came out of what was bothering her long enough to start calling orders into her commlink.

That settled, Ray moved to his second item. "Right now the Pres and Provost can draw on their northern assets. I propose we eliminate them, cut them off from the North as they cut you off."

Net Dancer shook his head. "There may be just one good path into this out-of-the-way mudhole, but there are hundreds to North Continent."

"We eliminate North," Ray said simply. That got everyone's attention. "These are the mountains that serve as their main power base." Ray circled the pink and blue areas of the map, elevated them into topo relief. The Dean nodded. "We make them go away as soon as we have our hands on the vanishing box."

"You can't do that" came from several of the tiny images . . . and Mary.

Ray waved Mary to silence and faced his allies. "This is war. We enforce our will upon the enemy or, failing that, destroy him. The President and Provost depend on these for their strength. To enforce our will, these have to go. If we have to kill the President and Provost, these go."

"But, but," the Dean sputtered, "those were our nodes, too. You destroy them and we'll be forever rebuilding ourselves."

"You don't have them now," Ray said.

"But we'll get them back."

"Not the way things are going. You were losing last time we talked. If things keep going the way they are, you will lose. There won't be any 'you' left to reoccupy those nodes." These folks really didn't know war. You don't win one cheap.

"But if you destroy them, you'll destroy us?"

That stopped Ray in his tracks. "I don't understand."

Net Dancer was the one who stepped forward to look up at Ray with tiny, earnest eyes. "We are here. Our decision-making processes are here. So much of what we know, have done, recall, is there, stored in networks under those mountains. We brought what we needed to survive. But to do more, to really live, we need those rich memories."

"But I see what the Colonel is talking about," the Dean said, coming forward. "For us, those are memories. For P & P, those are sources of new nanos, planning, and power. They are reviewing what happens down here, learning what works and doesn't work. Up there, they are learning how to win this war. What we face here are only their long arms and fingers, so to speak. I know it will be hard if the Colonel wipes out those nodes, but we do have backups scattered around. We could rebuild ourselves."

"Not all of them," Net Dancer insisted.

"Enough." The Dean suddenly cut Dancer off. "Colonel, I agree, as soon as you can, make those mountains vanish."

Ray turned to Lek and Mary. "Lek, as soon as you've got the vanishing box, take the shuttle north."

"Yes, sir" and "No, sir" greeted that order. Ray said nothing to Mary's objection.

She leaned forward into his silence. "I was at the shuttle hangar just now. Somebody slashed every tire on it last night. We've only got two spares. The shuttle's going nowhere."

"Who did it?"

"Sir, we got ten, fifteen thousand strangers on this base. It could have been anyone."

"Our security patrols—" Ray started.

"Walked past it every thirty minutes last night, on schedule. None noticed it was a bit lower than usual."

Ray leaned back in his chair, trying to adjust. Were the Provost or President already controlling people on his base? So far they never actually made anyone do anything. Which of his human enemies had decided the shuttle gave him too much power and ordered someone inside his fence to take it out?

Ray'd been trained to take a lance in the chest and keep moving. A commander had to keep moving; if he didn't, the command didn't. Should he drop the northern sally or try to make it happen some other way? He'd browbeat his allies into it. Could he walk away from it?

Down the table, the blimp pilot shuffled her papers. "Sir, could you bring up the latest weather on that board of yours?" Ray did. "These things rotate counterclockwise," she said, half to herself. "If the blimp down South doesn't get back before the winds pick up, I've ordered him to loop around the mountains and cruise up the other side. We've never been there. He's kind of jazzed on the prospects. Me, I've always wanted to ride a hurricane. We can't go north against those winds, but if you ride them south, they turn westward, then north," she grinned.

Ray shook his head. What was it with stick and rudder people? You put a wing, spaceship, balloon under someone and they started thinking they were indestructible gods. "You want to ride it all the way around?"

"The winds will tear you apart," Mary said.

Rhynia pursed her lips. "Not if I stay far enough out, where the winds are less than forty miles per hour, not shifting and ripping at a hundred twenty. Hell, I pull this off, every gas bag jockey that ever flies will know my name," she crowed.

The Dean shook his head. "There are some things that were never fully covered in my databases. Go ahead, make it vanish. I'll want to write a whole new one anyway after watching you."

"It's what happens when you go to war, Dean. You never know what the human heart is good for until you ask 'em for more than they ever thought they could give. Now, folks, let's get busy."

FOURTEEN

JEFF SCOWLED: THEY damn near lost the sky eye twice to stalls as they turned it around into the stiff headwind. After much cussing from Bo, Dumont's sensor boss, the mule's display came to life. Jeff and Du studied it, the sergeant's fingers flitting over the screen. "We got a group west of us, a big one coming up from the south east of us, and one squatting in the middle. Not to mention a few clusters of two or four. Bo, they players or just innocent bystanders?"

"My gear says they got a human heart, not what's in it."

"Any of them women?" Jeff asked, hoping.

"I can get you a pulse rate, son, but your guess is as good as mine as to whether it's a woman or an anxious man." For another hour they drove the winding trail, getting a feel for the people on the mountain this dreary day. The trail got rougher, narrower, the going slower.

Finally the driver halted. "Far as we go, boss."

"Let's mount up, marines. It's a good day for a ride."

"I'll stay here and relay for you," Bo offered.

"Pack it in, old man. The higher we get, the better line you'll have on your bird and the less likely we'll have a line on this mule. Everybody out. Everybody rides."

"Those things—can we really get up on them?" one marine asked, voice quivering. He looked more scared of a horse than of a fight. Probably been in more fights. Jeff helped him mount.

An hour later, they were over one ridge and climbing another. They rode slowly, watching for falling limbs, ready to dodge for their life. Their horses stepped carefully over downed branches. "Blimp's coming up," Bo called.

"Pass them our three targets. See if they can tell anything about 'em." A red "X" appeared on Du's map reader marking the disappearing box—in the middle of the unmoving group. "Thought so. Let's see the imagery." The reader zoomed the picture down. It got hazy before it showed much definition.

"Rocks," Jeff offered. "But we knew that."

"I told 'em you can't see a cave from orbit," Bo laughed.

Du enlarged the picture until it held all three groups and themselves. He frowned. "Southern group is moving in fast. Other group coming in from the North with us is moving kind of careful." Du worked the map through several lines of sight the stationary group would have on all of them as they closed on it.

"What are you up to?" Jeff asked.

"I'll show you in a little while" was Du's only answer.

A half hour got them up another ridge; Du called a halt. "Bo, set up a rocket to lob a charge against that rock slab in one hour." Du pointed out a rocky promontory that shot up solid and steep five miles across the valley from them. "Lay down a string of monitors along this trail."

"Whatever, boss," Bo answered. He dismounted and got to work. Du again studied the topography map on his reader. "We'll need to be on that ridge when the fun starts," he told Jeff.

"What fun?" Jeff asked.

"Wait and see, buddy, wait and see."

A hard hour's ride later, they were atop the next ridge. Right on schedule, the rocket arched across to slam into the foot of the giant rock. Jeff kept his eyes on Du's reader as echoes came in from the listening posts they'd left behind. Just as they had when Mary thumped the hill, the soundings quickly painted the inside of the mountains, showing cracks, crevices, caves. Then part of the picture went blank. Jeff looked up and swallowed a yelp. The rock massif was gone!

"Kind of expected that," Du drawled. Jeff reached over Du's shoulder to tap several keys on his map reader. The heartbeats of the parties they'd been following appeared. The group coming up from the South was close to the missing mountain. Jeff counted hearts and came up shy by half.

"You knew!" Jeff accused.

"I thought it might," Du answered evenly.

"Annie, Nikki—"

"Are most likely with the other group," Du cut him off. "Now let's get moving, crew. I don't know when they can take their next shot, but I don't want to be here."

Sullenly, Jeff followed Du. The man had said he was tired of being the Colonel's killing dog, but he was playing fast and loose with Annie's life. Jeff ought to . . . ought to . . . There was nothing Jeff could do.

Ten minutes later, Dumont dropped back to ride beside Jeff. "Look, I'm sorry about back there, but I have to know what's up ahead, and all our shit isn't telling me near enough. I'm almost certain Annie's safe, but I got to do everything I can to keep my crew here safe. They've saved my ass too many times. You understand."

"No, I don't," Jeff answered, then thought more on it. "Maybe I do, but I'm not sure I want to."

Du reached over, punched Jeff on the shoulder. "Maybe I don't want to either. But we're here, and you and your girl could be nothing but atoms any second, so I'm doing what Mary and the others trained me to do—think with my head, not my ass. For what it's worth, the echos show a cave up there, more like an overhang. The folks with the vanishing box are camped there. We can get above them. That's what I plan to do tonight, when there's no sun, and, with luck, the damn thing will have no power. Get above them and take them from behind."

"When?"

"Probably when the group that has your Annie walks her and her sister into camp. That ought to distract enough people to let us do what we have to before they know they're being

done to. That close we can use the sleepy bullets. Maybe nobody else will have to die in this lash-up. Maybe. That would
be nice."

Jeff nodded. What could he say? Dumont held all the cards
in this game; Annie would live or die by his rules.

Harry's hand laser cut a wide chunk out of the gravel roadbed.
He gawked; the damn rock was fused solid. And not just
where the wagon wheels had pounded it down. An inch or two
below the loose gravel, it was solid rock again. He cut a
wedge a good foot down and a foot across.

"You think that'll slow the Pres?" a voice chided him from
his commlink. "His repair crew'll have that patched in no
time."

"And this is?" Harry answered his unrequested message.

"You call me Net Dancer. I just thought I ought to look in
on you, see how you were doing. Not very well, if I may say
so."

"Cassie, are the explosives in?" Harry asked.

"About there."

"Hang around for a second," Harry suggested. "I'd make
sure I was on our side of this break, though. It'd be a shame
for us to slam the door with you on the outside," Harry
grinned. Actually, he'd love to.

"I'm inside," Net Dancer answered peevishly. "I'm observing this through your thin commlink." Ten minutes later the
charges went off; Net Dancer gave them a bit more respect.
"That'll slow them down for a couple of hours. Is that all
you're doing?"

"We'll cut it in a couple more places. You just keep your
eyes open for other work-arounds your old boss might try."

Net Dancer might be happy, but the refugees they'd held up
on the road while they blew it were anything but. "We'll have
the devil's own time getting Granny and the wagon through
that. Ya got no respect, man."

"Sorry," Harry called. He got his crew remounted and
headed for the next valley, where he would blow another hole
in the road.

"You starmen, ya got your nice wagons. Well, the rest of us got what we got. Why ya making it harder on us?"

Cassie shook her head as she ordered the driver to go. "If you have to explain what's going on, there's no use bothering. They don't like it, and they're fools to think not liking it will change God's will." Harry had no answer for either man or marine. He held on tight as they gunned across an open field, leaving what was left of the road to the people on it.

Daga wrapped her arms around her knees, swaying slowly where she'd collapsed when the mountain vanished. The explosion had brought Sean and Jean Jock rushing from the cave. They'd taken one look at the rising smoke and set up the box. They hadn't known how to open it. She'd refused to tell them until Sean bent her arm behind her and threatened to break it if she didn't tell. She'd opened the box and showed them how to aim it.

The noise and light had come again—and the gray, stone mountain had gone.

Then the woman and the two men returned. She'd been livid with Sean and Jean Jock. Shouted at them, demanded to know what they were thinking, why they'd done it. "You heard the blast. There's something out there. It's gone now." Sean had insisted.

"Gone, you say. You're sure," the woman had torn into Sean. "Something goes boom and you have to make a mountain disappear. Was the little boy frightened? You're disgusting."

Daga was shocked that Sean let the woman talk to him like that, but under her tongue-lashing, Sean deflated like a broken blimp. When the woman finished with Sean, she turned to her two followers. "Well, we'd better get ready. Someone *is* out there, despite what these idiots have done. Get your rifles."

"Shall I put away the box?" Jean Jock asked the woman.

"No. Keep it out. We may have to use it again."

Harry used a crowbar on the railroad bed, scraping aside the top layer of rocks. Below them, the bed was melded stone. What turned rocks into something that made fiber optics look

like two kids holding cans with a tight string between them?
"Well, give us another few years and see what we've got,"
Harry muttered to himself.

"It'll take millions," Net Dancer answered from Harry's
commlink. "Unless you get us to help you. Want a hand,
pops?"

Harry bit back several retorts. He never had liked his workstation; it always failed when he most needed it. It seemed to
have a mind of its own. Did he want one that really did? "How
deep does this rock go?" was what he finally said.

"Railroad specs say three, four feet of rock. Don't know if
the Gardener used it all or went farther."

"I thought you knew everything."

"Maybe the Gardener knew what he did. We lost all that
when you humans fixed his wagon. Okay?"

A train's airhorn sounded in the distance. Harry strained
into the gathering gloom. Right, train lights. They could rig
the charges, let the train pass, then blow the section. Marines
waved to the passengers as the train rolled by, then blew the
line charges. The explosions started in the distance and
marched with majestic violence up the tracks, hurling rock,
rails, and dirt in large, ever-widening plums. *Try fixing that
break, you arrogant bunch of circuits,* Harry said to himself.
With Net Dancer listening, he said nothing aloud.

Electricity gone, the train rolled to a slow stop. Harry and
Cassie piled into their mule and headed home, carefully clear
of the train. They weren't far enough.

"Cassie, did you do that?" came in a loud, piercing shout.

"Ms. San Paulo," Cassie muttered under her breath. Sure
enough, standing on the steps of the lead car was the Chair of
the Central Circle of Santa Maria.

"Driver, over there." Cassie pointed him toward San Paulo.

"What's the meaning of this?" San Paulo shrieked as soon
as they were in talking distance. "You've killed the train to
County Clair. How are we supposed to get people to safety
now?"

"They'll have to walk, ma'am. The big computer the
Colonel is fighting has been using the rocks in the roadbed as
a network. We had to take it out."

"You can't send messages through rocks. That Colonel is crazier than I thought. You'll just have to drive me to the base." Cassie looked distinctly uncomfortable.

"I'll have to call that in, Ma'am. Colonel's restricting access to the base right now."

"He'd never turn me away. I have to see my daughter."

"Can't argue with that," the Colonel agreed, none too happily. "Give her a ride in."

San Paulo insisted that someone walk to make more room for her. Cassie crammed her and her luggage aboard.

Jeff climbed; the cold stone cut his hands. Blood made the next grip slippery. The marines had gloves. Bo, who'd stayed behind with the horses, had offered his gloves to Jeff. Too small, they fit Ned's grip. Jeff thought of Annie and climbed, taking up the slack in the safety rope. It was pitch-black; even with night goggles, he could hardly see the handholds. Jeff climbed, thinking of Annie, and not the latest argument he'd lost with Du.

The group coming from the west was following a trail. The marines had crossed ahead of them. Jeff wanted to set up an ambush, get them now, and free Annie. Dumont quickly dismissed the option. "We're too damn close to the box. Even sleepy bullets make noise. We stage a firefight here, they'll make us all vanish." Jeff had wanted to say more, but he couldn't find the words. Damn, why did Dumont always have to be right? Did right matter when Annie's life was at risk?

It started to rain, first gentle bits of moisture on the wind, then angry drops. The marines grumbled despite their magic space clothes keeping them warm. Jeff's outfit had been worn out to begin with. Now the wind and rain went straight through him. All he had to keep him warm were his anger with Dumont and his love for Annie. For the time being, these seemed enough. Ahead, Du signaled for a halt with a dark light. It had to be magic, a light you could see only with night goggles. Magic. And the computer was like magic to them. Junior mages fighting master mages. What chance did he and Annie have against them? *We and our grandparents built this place. I'll be damned if I'll let anyone take it away from us.*

Jeff pulled himself up the last handhold. There was a flat space where Du and the other marines huddled out of the wind. Jeff joined them; Du was talking. "We got a shoulder here that leads around to the overhang we're headed for. Let's take five, then follow it. Jeff, show me your hands."

"They're fine."

"I got two big marines that'll hold you down if you don't show me those paws of yours. I see blood dripping from here."

"It's just rain." Without a word from Du, the two marines beside Jeff grabbed his arms and held his hands out, palms up. One was a woman; still, they held him like a solid metal vise. Du applied medicine to Jeff's hands; they hurt for a second, then went numb. Du finished by spraying something over it all. "That'll hold them. You want to shoot straight, don't you?"

"You've seen Annie?"

"No, but it's a good bet they brought her here for something. Knowing the trust level of the shits we're dealing with, they'll have a gun or knife on her to make sure she does what she's supposed to."

"I shoot whoever it is."

Dumont eyed Jeff for a long second, then shook his head. "No, Jeff. I'll take that one out. Not you."

"Why?"

"Because you got emotions behind your trigger finger. Makes people shake. Could shake your bullet from your target to Annie. Trust me, they'll be close. I'll do the shooting." Jeff didn't answer. Du didn't wait for him to. "Our secondary targets are about an hour out from the primary. Let's start walking, folks."

It took forty-five minutes to work their way around the three thousand yards of rain-slick rock; the ledge narrowed down to almost nothing for most of the way. Once on the rocky overhang, Dumont motioned Jeff to stay close. While the others anchored their safety lines to rocks or trees, Du worked out lines for both Jeff and himself. Done, the two edged forward to get their first look at the Greens' camp.

A fire crackled outside the cave made by the overhang.

Three figures sat in lotus position, meditating on the flames. Two men stomped around the edge of the dark, air rifles in hand. A lone figure huddled in a lump halfway between the fire and the dark. Du pointed at that one, asked a question with a raised eyebrow. Jeff studied the figure. The clothes were a standard plaid. The figure was small, even allowing for its present lump. "Daga, I think," Jeff muttered into his throat mike.

"Anybody see a box?" Du asked on net. Jeff didn't; neither did anyone else. There were plenty of piles around the fire; any one could hide the deadly box. One of the meditators could be sitting on it, for all Jeff knew.

"Settle in, crew. Company in fifteen minutes." Du unfolded a bedroll and draped it over Jeff. It kept the rain out, warmth in. Jeff rolled himself up in it, letting it protect him from the cold stone beneath, the cooling, damp air above. How could he hate a man who'd share his kit with you even as he waited to kill, and maybe be killed? What were the starmen all about? Jeff wondered if he would ever know. Then thought again, and wondered how long it would take him to become one.

Annie rode, knowing that the woman beside her had an air pistol aimed straight at Nikki's back. Around her, men rode, heads down against the rain. Ahead of them and higher up, Annie caught glimpses of a fire. That was where this trail led. That was where it would all come together—or all come apart.

Hardly a word had been spoken to Annie and Nikki by their captors. Kicks, orders, demands, yes, but no talking; Pretty Boy and the woman had seen to that. The men feared the woman; maybe they could still hear the screams of the wife at the house as the woman tortured her to make her husband talk. Annie remembered and struggled to swallow the terror memory raised in her. Somehow, in this dark, with Dumont's pitiful pistol, she would find a way to get her and Nikki away from this woman.

The husband had told everything. Shouted it in the end. It hadn't saved him or his wife. Annie knew nothing she and

Nikki did to please these people would save them in the end either.

There was noise ahead. The man bringing supplies must have arrived at the camp. Pretty Boy came back to exchange words quickly with the woman. Then the men dismounted and Pretty Boy led them into the trees.

"We wait here, children, for a while. When we ride in, Nikki, you go straight to Daga and tell her her mother's dying, that she has to go home. Don't explain how you found their camp, just talk to Daga. Let things get confused." The woman's smile might have been lovely on a picture. Here, with her words, it was cold evil. "Do what I say, and you and Daga can ride out of here tomorrow happy as kids should be. Cross me, and I'll hurt you worse than any priest's hell. Understand?"

Nikki nodded, fighting tears. Annie said, "Yes, ma'am."

The woman accepted their agreement like it was her due. Her gun stayed under her cloak, weaving between Annie and Nikki, a snake eager to strike. Annie kept her hands on the reins, close to her wallet and its gun, but subservient, the way Ma said a good serving girl met a customer. Time stood still as they and their horses rested. Their mounts at least could crop a little green from trailside. Annie had nothing to do but taste terror rising in her throat. Could she find a way out for her and her sister? Could she grab it when she saw it?

"Let's get moving," the woman ordered. "Annie, you first. Remember, I have my gun on Nikki."

"I will remember," Annie said obediently. The horses plodded up the trail. As they reached the edge of the clearing, Annie whispered back, "We should announce ourselves."

"Then do it." The woman's whisper could flail skin.

"Hello the fire. We have an urgent message for Daga Finnigan. Is she there?"

"Hello the traveler," came a woman's voice. "You picked a miserable night for traveling. What brings you out?" Annie measured the words. They were what should be said, but there was no feeling behind them. At the edge of the clearing, Annie paused, let those around the fire see her. She dismounted and led her horse forward. Nikki and the woman did the same.

"Is Daga there?" Nikki called, her voice trembling. Maybe those around the fire would mistake it for concern.

Daga appeared suddenly from a shadow, distant from the fire. Annie's horse snorted at the surprise. Annie took reins from Nikki as her sister raced to Daga. "Your ma, she's taken fever. She's calling for you. We've been hunting for you forever."

The woman gave her horse over to Annie, the slight flow of her cloak giving Annie a glimpse of the pistol's eager jaws. Annie got all three sets of reins into one hand, let her own free hand wander toward the wallet and its own death.

From around the fire, people stepped forward, rifles in hand.

"And how is it that you only now found us?" a woman's voice sweetly asked.

"We asked in all the villages," Annie spoke over Nikki. "Someone said she'd seen a girl who looked like Daga gathering mushrooms around these rocks." Annie shouted, trying for time and confusion. The woman beside her curled her lips in her satisfied death smile and raised her chin, as if to urge Annie on. "We've been searching and saw your fire in the night."

"Daga," Nikki blabbered on, "your ma, she's real sick. She really wants to see you. She really needs you."

"Why don't I *really* believe that?" the woman from the fire said. "Sean, see what the smiling one has under her cloak. Brothers, check the woods. Where there's one, there's more."

Suddenly the night was alive with cracks, pops, and whizzing noises. Sean dropped, grabbing his knee and screaming in agony.

"Take 'em down!" came over Jeff's commlink. His rifle had Dumont's fire plan. Jeff was assigned the woods on the right side of the camp; he split three targets with a marine. Dumont had taken the center of the camp. Heave, whom he insisted was his best sharpshooter, shared it with him. Jeff squeezed off a three-shot burst at his first target. The man dropped, pulse and respiration slowing. Jeff switched to his next target, but this one was behind a tree and spraying the camp with air pellets as fast as he could work his action. Jeff's burst missed. To his right was a long crack of thunder. The marine had gone to live ammunition, stitching the forest with needles that shattered trees and downed logs. The target died.

"Over the side, crew," Dumont ordered.

Jeff hurled himself off the cliff, then tried to remember all he'd been told about rappelling. He grabbed the break on his chest, felt his hands go hot, then shoot with pain as rope and break didn't quite work as he'd expected. Maybe he wasn't remembering right. He landed hard, rolled away from the rope, and brought his rifle up.

The woman from the campfire held an airgun under Nikki's chin. Daga was close enough to take any spray as well.

Annie held three horses, their eyes wide with fright, but no wider than Annie's. Another woman held a pistol to Annie's head.

"I want the box," the woman beside Annie snapped.

"I have it and no one is getting it," the woman threatening Nikki snarled back.

"Gee, and I was told all the women on this planet were so ladylike," Dumont answered with a boyish grin. "Goes to show what happens when you believe the advertising."

"Get out of here, all of you," the woman from the camp demanded.

"My men have you all covered," the other countered.

"My men have put all of your men to sleep," Dumont replied. "At least all of them who ain't dead," he added, nudging Sean's lifeless body with his toe.

Jeff did a quick survey. Some around the fire looked to be sleeping, but several of them had air pellets in them as well. If no one took care of their wounds they could bleed to death.

Dumont pointed that out.

"I should care?" the one by Annie snapped.

"It's for the cause," the other answered.

"God protect us from causes," Dumont countered.

"You starmen, you believe in nothing. I should have disappeared you first," the one with Nikki spat.

Jeff tried to edge downhill, toward Annie. Dumont put an end to that with a slight wave of the hand that wasn't visible to the two women. "Then you'll just have to give me something to believe in, besides having another beer. I think I know what you believe in," he said to Nikki's captor, "but what's put you on this chase?" he asked Annie.

The woman flashed Dumont a greedy grin. "I'm in it for the money. Vicky Sterling'll pay well for the box. And you, over there," she said to the other woman, "she wants the starbase vanished as much as you, maybe more. I see a deal here."

Maybe she did, but Annie saw a woman distracted. Her free hand had been rubbing her stomach slowly, as if terrified and fighting to keep her supper down. Now Jeff saw where that hand was reaching: into her wallet. The short snout of a starman's gun was visible for a second. Then it spoke—on full automatic.

Her captor's eyes grew wide with surprise as her gut was stitched open. Annie dropped the horses's reins and batted away the gun at her head—a split second before it fired.

Jeff whirled, bringing his rifle up to take out Nikki's captor. Two, maybe three marines had already put three-round bursts into her skull. Her head wasn't there anymore.

The body stood for a second, then crumpled, air rifle still aimed at its hostage's chin. Nikki and Daga, covered with gore and bone from the hits beside them, screamed hysterically as they collapsed to their knees. Dumont rushed to them, chucked the air rifle away, then held both girls as they shrieked.

Jeff raced for Annie.

She stared down at the woman. "I did it," she whispered hoarsely. "I did it myself. I did," she said as Jeff took her in his arms. "I hoped you'd come. Hoped you would," she muttered to his chest. "But I didn't know. I wasn't sure they'd let you. But I knew I'd do what I had to when the time came." She looked up at Jeff. "I did it."

"You did, honey. You did." Then she began to cry. Trembling in his arms, the tears turned to racking sobs. Jeff found himself crying, too. He didn't want to. A marine wouldn't. A glance behind him showed tears on Dumont's face as he held the girls. Maybe it was okay to cry.

Three marines went through the piles of gear around the

fire and found the vanishing box. Others collected the sleepers in the woods, brought them in, and tied their arms and legs. One went from wounded to wounded, stopping the bleeding. The marines were a good team, they let their boss have the time to cry with the girls, let Jeff rejoice and tremble with his girl. It was fifteen minutes before one of them tapped Dumont. "The Colonel'll want to know, sir."

Dumont looked. Sniffed. Pulled a handkerchief from his pocket, used it, then tapped his commlink. "Boss man, this is Du. We got the box. We got all the hostages unhurt. This street is clean, man. Your dog's got one hell of a bite."

Ray laughed at Dumont's report; his dog did have sharp teeth. "Took you long enough," he countered. "Any casualties?"

"No marines. Young Jeff's hands are a bit the worse for wear. He failed on his first rappelling gig. We got all three of the missing local girls unhurt. At least they're not bleeding. It got a bit ugly."

"But they have a long life ahead to get over it. I'll launch a blimp at first light to connect with the package. We're sending it south."

"You might want to wait on that, sir. These ridges are no place for a blimp. I suggest we meet on the plains."

Ray glanced at the blimp pusher, who'd come into his office when he started talking. She nodded. "Pilot agrees with you. How long to get down off that hill of yours?"

"We spent the day getting here. I guess it'll take most the night getting down. I'll call in when we're close."

"You bringing any prisoners?"

"You want any?" Du asked. "I was planning on just leaving them here. Let them wake up and discuss the situation among themselves when they do. I'm a tired man, skipper, and I got a long road ahead of me tonight. I'll see you when I get back."

"Take care." Ray taped Du off and turned to the pilot. "You have any problems with that?"

"Nope. If the wind's too stiff to land, I'll lower a basket."

Ray nodded. "Lek, you packed?"

"I am, but Kat asked if she could go. She's lighter. Might

be an issue with the blimp. Which of us do you want up there?"

"Neither." Ray rubbed his eyes. "Will I need her scrounging the databases, or you keeping Net Dancer under some kind of control? Mary, anyone else we could send?"

"No one else's ready for independent command, sir."

Ray flipped a mental coin. "Tell Kat she's got the job."

Lek nodded and left. Ray scowled at Mary. "Is that what they'll write on my tombstone, this whole planet's tombstone, 'There just weren't enough of us to go around'?"

"Beat's the hell out of 'They blew it,' " Mary snorted as she left, leaving Ray alone.

What did he think he was doing, going head to head with a super computer that had two million years to learn this territory? He had to be crazy. Still, it had never fought a war and had done little the past million years. Ray had spent most of his life fighting; he knew the drill. Use your strengths, assuming you could find any, against their weaknesses, assuming same.

Ray was targeting their strategic resources, limiting their local options. Now could he and the kids really hit the bastards where they'd hurt? Like every attack man had made since the first one, only time would answer that.

Ray stood. He'd promised the kids he'd read them a bedtime story. He needed to get in practice, reading kids bedtime stories. Assuming he lived through this battle. Assuming he got home. A lot of assuming there. He remembered some of the bedtime stories his dad had read him: *The Song of Roland, Beowulf,* Henry Five's address to his men before Agincourt. That might be a good one for the kids.

Ray shivered—at the thought of his own kid going into battle, at the thought of what he was doing to these poor kids. "It has to be done, and they're the only ones who can do it," he said aloud. Still, he tasted the wrong of what he was doing to them, even as he went to prepare them for it.

"Please, dear God, after tomorrow, no more of this for me or mine."

FIFTEEN

MARY SPENT THE day treading water, figuratively if not literally. Blimps had to be deflated, a wall finished. More people poured in; she closed down the chip fabrication plant, wrapped the sensitive gear in plastic, and opened the place to refugees. If there was a nook or cranny available, someone filled it. Du drove in late that night, wet and tired, trailing a bedraggled sky eye behind his rig.

The next morning dawned wet, rain coming down sidways. Mary surveyed her command from the factory roof; the perimeter wall was up, thank any God listening. The sod was back on it, for which she thanked the little priest, so the rain wasn't washing the wall back into the ditch. She'd need that wall; already people huddled outside.

Dumont joined her, his poncho keeping most of him dry. "What you want from mine, Captain?"

That was something to think on. At breakfast, the Colonel had been withdrawn, introspective. If she'd had a battle to plan against a computer as complex and confused as this one appeared to be, she'd be doing a lot of thinking, too. That left her a simple, old-fashion problem: Defend the base on which they stand. Problem was, those weren't armed-to-the-teeth bastards out there, trying to overrun her. She rolled her eyes to the gray sky, remembering the first time she'd met the

Colonel. See the enemy, kill the enemy—war the good, old-fashion way.

But the people outside the fence were not enemies. She wasn't sure what they were. Wet, hungry refugees? Maybe. Computer-driven zombies? Possibly. Believers, pushed and prodded by those they trusted? Quite likely. So what should she do with them? Feed them would be nice; shelter and care for them, even better. But that was not in the cards. She'd had Chief Barber check their stores; they had enough food for base personnel to last about a month. Encouraged by the padre, the refugees moving on base had turned their food over to central supply for credit chits specifically allotted to food; food was now more precious than copper. Still, they were just about keeping even with the one-month maximum. Everyone depended on the next crop. Right now, that next crop was getting very soggy. In too many places, it was getting trampled.

Before Kat left, she'd done a data search on food storage. This place had grain silos; it was supposed to be able to survive a crop failure in one part of the land. Facing crop failure all over, those silos were suddenly reported empty; hoarding had started early. A part of Mary figured she might as well shoot any problem refugees; at least that would save them from starving. She shivered at the thought.

"That bad," Du said, calling her back to where she stood on the rainswept roof of the factory.

"It could get that way."

"What do you want from my team?" he asked her again.

"All the other marines command a hundred locals in riot gear. Your squad's my only marine reserve."

"We handle the shit too bad for the rest, huh?"

"Looks that way."

"Anybody going outside?" Du nodded at the half-drowned land covered with ragged clumps of people.

"Don't know. We got a staff meeting at oh-eight-hundred. Want to come?"

"Got to be more interesting than standing around in this stuff," Du grouched, "but not by much, I bet."

Mary laughed; Du was usually good for a laugh, except when she wanted to throttle him. They headed for the HQ. It was a pretty full room Mary entered, but she'd expected that; this was probably the last time they'd get together before whatever was about to break out started chewing up their fannies. Barber was there, along with the chief running personnel, sitting along the wall. Cassie sat between them; Dumont joined them. Harry and Jeff had taken the foot of the table. Doc was at Ray's right hand, the priest next to him. An empty seat awaited Mary at the Colonel's left. Lek was next to her.

Twelve holograms stood patiently on the battle board.

"We'll make this quick. Right after this I meet with San Paulo and company. Mary, join me for that one."

"Yes, sir. Barber, you're with me."

The old chief groaned from his chair against the wall. "Won't get much work done. Thank God for good storekeepers."

Ray actually cracked a sliver of a smile at that ancient joke, then turned to Dumont. "You got the three local girls back to their families last night?"

"Not quite, sir," Dumont said, coming to stiff attention. Jeff looked like he wanted to crawl under the table.

"What does that mean, Sergeant?"

"Two out of three ain't bad, sir. The blimp couldn't land, sir, so we were chasing a basket it was towing behind it. Pushing the mule flat ass for hell, sir. In the process of passing the box into the basket, somehow Nikki Mulroney managed to scramble in also."

"What was she doing in the mule, anyway?"

Dumont looked pained. "I don't know, sir. We were kind of short on time and maybe not as organized as we should have been."

"Kat didn't have the blimp make a go-around and drop her back in your lap?" the Colonel growled.

"Nikki persuaded Kat they really needed her to operate the vanishing box," Jeff cut in. "The little brat can be quite persuasive when she wants to be, Annie says, and the wind really wouldn't permit a go-around."

The Colonel paused, weighing one girl's personal tragedy against a planet's, then shrugged. "We'll trust Kat to bring her back." He turned to Mary. "Can you hold the base perimeter?"

"I expect so, sir. We've got the locals in riot gear. We've got the marines. If things get too bad, we've got tear gas and pepper bombs, but they're last resorts. Only my marines have protective gear for that."

"Understood. Supplies?"

"Not an immediate worry, sir," Mary evaded. The Colonel seemed to weigh both what she'd said and not said, then pass it by. "Dean, how are things going on your side?"

"Not much happening. The President and Provost are going at each other, I guess, and ignoring us."

"You guess. You don't know?"

"We're kind of isolated on your side of the line and rather occupied keeping other access routes blocked."

Mary stared at the holograms. She still had problems thinking of them as representing entities more powerful than any computer she'd ever seen. *Get used to it, girl.*

"Dancer, you hiding here, too?" the Colonel chided.

"Wouldn't want to show them guys how to penetrate your little hideaway," the cheeky computer responded.

"I should think Lek and you could find a way out. Lek, we still have access to the net in Refuge?"

"Yep, sir," Mary's oldest friend drawled.

"Then maybe we could boost Dancer over the wall and into their court. It would be nice to know what those two are up to. Dean, have you decided which of them you want to win?"

"Neither," the tweed-clad image answered.

"Consider, they're fighting each other. As soon as one wins, it will come after us. Which do you want to tackle then?"

That put the computer images into a huddle. Mary watched the clock; three minutes passed before the Dean took a step away from his associates. "We can't arrive at a consensus, but eight of us agree we want the Provost dead first."

"Dancer, could you identify some physical areas the Provost can least afford to lose?"

"Yeah, no problem. What you got in mind?"

"Harry took out the main link into here yesterday. If we send him out again, he could take out a few nodes here and there. Surprise the Provost."

"Maybe the Pres would appreciate the help?" the Dean mused hopefully.

" 'The enemy of my enemy is my friend' has long been a saying among us humans. Given the chance, maybe the President will learn the wisdom in that," the Colonel admitted.

"But what if the Provost wins?" another holo image demanded. "Where will that put us?"

"No worse off than before. We'll still have weakened the Provost in the preliminary round. Less to fight in the main one," the Colonel pointed out.

There seemed to be general agreement on that among the holograms. "Let's get cracking," Net Dancer said. Lek headed out the door; shortly after, Dancer disappeared from the display. Ray turned his attention to Harry. "Up to another run?"

"No problem. Who can you lend me?"

"Mary?" Ray said, passing her the problem.

The captain scowled. "Boss, anyone outside ain't inside keeping the outside out." That got a few smiles. "I guess I lend him the two marines he had yesterday. I keep Cassie."

"Three's a mighty small team," Ray countered.

"I'll go with Harry," Jeff put in. "My hands are healing fine. I think Old Ned will join me, too."

"This kid's officer material," the Colonel joked. "He's learned to volunteer other people. Okay, five it is then."

"Have you decided what kind of attack you can launch when the time comes?" the Dean asked in the silence that followed Harry and Jeff's leaving.

"I'm still thinking about it" was all the Colonel said. "Thank you for your time. I'm about due for my next meeting."

Most filed out. Mary stayed in her seat, as did Doc and the padre. Chief Barber moved up to the table as a yeoman led Ms. San Paulo and her staff in. The Colonel introduced the Dean and his ten present associates. San Paulo ignored them; Ray made no attempt to change that. "What can we do about the food situation?" he said to begin the meeting.

"You'll have to feed all these people you turned into refugees," she countered.

"You have control of the food reserves."

"The landers wanted a market economy. Farmers are free to set their own prices."

"And what's stored in the silos—"

"Is privately owned. They may dispose of it as they choose."

"Charge all the market will bear," Mary growled.

"I'm certain the situation will resolve itself. Left to itself, the market always does," San Paulo insisted.

"How many people are you willing to let starve?"

"No one will starve," San Paulo said with absolute certainty.

Ray tapped the board, bringing up the weather picture. A fifth hurricane was forming behind the four headed their way. "The first storm will come ashore just south of Refuge tomorrow. Then one every three days. There won't be a next crop."

San Paulo looked at the board, frowned at it, then shook her head. "That's impossible. Hurricanes do not behave like that. That's just another one of your computer tricks."

Ray shook his head. "Ms. San Paulo, we will continue to care for Rose. You are welcome to stay here as our guest. But if you will not cooperate with us in the problems we now have, I believe this meeting is over."

"I must serve my people, look out for their welfare," she started.

Ray cut her off. "Outside the base, but not on it. Here, the people are under my protection. They are at present organized and satisfied with that arrangement. Is that right, Father?"

The priest nodded.

"What would you expect from a priest? You feed him," one of San Paulo's staff muttered.

"I don't have time for you to poll them," the Colonel shot back. "Stay in the quarters assigned you, or leave. If you won't help us, I can't afford for you to cause me trouble."

At that the Colonel stood and left; Mary led the rest out. Poor Father Joseph watched them go, glanced at San Paulo's group, then joined Mary. She held her troops for a second in the work bay. "You've got your orders. Make 'em happen."

The others left; the doc and the padre remained. "Mary, I'm worried about the Colonel and the kids," the doc started.

"My office," Mary cut him off as the first of San Paulo's cronies nosed around the door. A moment later, door closed, Mary motioned the two to chairs, then leaned against the front of her desk. "What about the Colonel and the kids?"

"I think he plans to use them in some kind of attack on the computer," the doc said. "They were with him and a stone when the Gardener died."

"I know. I saw the kids shortly after it happened," Mary answered. "He looked a lot worse than the kids."

"Right. Something had healed his back. He should have looked bad. Still, using the kids in a fight!"

"Father"—Mary turned to the grandfather of one of them—"what do you think?"

"Like so much of what is going on around here, I don't know what to think. I do know that unless we get sun, lots of it real soon, a lot of people will be very hungry. If David can somehow help . . ." He trailed off.

"What chance could the Colonel and a couple of kids have against that?" The doc waved toward the conference room, whether at the storms or the allied computers or fighting ones, Mary didn't need a clarification. All of them looked too much to her.

She stood; centuries of breeding brought the men to their feet. Or maybe it was the command presence of a marine officer. Mary wasn't sure, just glad of it. "We've got a day's work cut out for us. Let's take it one step at a time. Padre, will you accompany me on a walk around?"

Mary scrounged up a poncho, which on the priest dragged the ground. For the rest of the morning, they walked the base. They stopped to talk with the troops mustered on the wall, enduring wind and rain to keep an eye on the growing crowd outside. They passed through all the living quarters, saying a kind word to worried *grande dames* and little children. Mary included the padre in her stops around the base's functions run by the crew of *Second Chance*. His heartfelt thanks to Ray's crew was probably the best morale boost she could have hoped for. Here was one of the locals, thanking the crew for what they were doing. Thanking them for the risks they were taking.

There was no way for the padre to know what Mary did. That the crew had no more choice of being here than he did. Until Matt found a way home, they were all in this together. Still, it would have been easy to build a wall between us and them. The priest helped Mary keep that wall low, toss away the stones that could have built it higher.

Early on, Jeff and Harry said their good-byes, heading out the north gate. The mule towed a trailer full of explosives, laser cutters, and batteries with three horses following it. God help them, never had a smaller David taken on a bigger Goliath.

Jeff held his rifle tight as the young marine driving zipped out the gate and gunned the mule, wagon, horses, and all out across the field, dodging first left, then right to avoid small clumps of people rushing their way. "You know, Zed," the older marine in the back drawled, "you flip that trailer over and none of us will be worrying about meeting anyone anymore."

"Lil, I'm the one driving and I ain't wrecked a heap yet."

"Before last year, you'd never wheeled a heap legal."

"When it's hot, you sure don't drive it like an old lady."

Jeff and Harry exchanged glances, neither sure exactly what was being said. Jeff strongly suspected he'd be happier not knowing. Ned just leaned back, enjoying the ride. Two hours later, they'd avoided all problems, and had the present small valley they were crossing all to themselves and a flock of six-legged things that ignored humans and vice versa. "I'm getting a message from Lek!" Jeff hollered. "Zed, could we take a break?"

"Braking!" the kid hollered, and skidded to a halt that fishtailed the mule's rear and the trailer behind.

"Zed, I'm gonna turn those nanos loose on your head."

"Wouldn't find nothing."

"He didn't drive that way yesterday," Harry pointed out.

"Wouldn't dare; Cassie'd hauled his ass off to church," Lil laughed.

"Just having some fun," the kid defended himself.

Jeff studied the map Lek fed to the mule's display. "Dancer says the two are fighting it out up the James River, with flanks seventy miles on either side," Lek told them as the screen showed a large blob of pink in front of them. Blue was on the far side. Both spread north and south of the James. "Dancer figures the Pres was outmaneuvered. He'll take the worst hits from the hurricanes unless he gets inland fast. Any places we can disrupt the Provost?"

Harry overlaid his geology data on the display. "Several rocky outcroppings close to us." He highlighted four. "Does Dancer have a preference?"

There was a short pause. "Dancer has no idea. Hit a few. He'll let us know what happens."

"Great targeting system we got here," Zed growled.

"Best we got is always great," Lil said cheerfully.

"What's that?" Zed shouted, pointing behind them.

Jeff turned, just in time to see the tarp on the trailer move. He leveled his gun. "Who's there?" he demanded.

"Just me," came a very familiar voice. The tarp raised; Annie stared at his gun. "Could you point that somewhere else?"

"Annie," Jeff safetied his rifle as Lil and Harry leaped out to help Annie. Jeff got there just in time to put his arms around her and help her over the trailer's side. She was very holdable. "Damn it, woman, what are you doing here? Can't any Mulroney woman stay where she belongs?"

"If Mulroney women had stayed home, there wouldn't be any Mulroney men on this planet," she shot back. "I heard you griping there weren't enough on this team. I have two hands."

"You should have asked," Jeff cried.

"And you'd have said no," she answered primly, looking around, taking a poll of those present, "Wouldn't he?"

"Boys what think they're in love do crazy things," Lil answered. "Let's roll."

Jeff took his seat up front, rifle handy. Annie squeezed in the back between Lil and Harry. As Zed got them moving, Jeff relented. "There's more room in front." In a flash of hiked-up skirts and revealed legs, Annie was over the seat and settling down beside Jeff in a second.

"There's plenty of room close to me," Zed pointed out, patting the seat next to him.

Jeff pulled Annie close. "Why'd you do it?" he whispered.

"I've missed you for the last month. I don't know what's going to happen next."

Jeff kissed her. Sometime later, Old Ned coughed. "Son, I don't mind keeping an eye out your side of this rig, but the girl's got to breathe." The others laughed. It was contagious. Annie and he ended up laughing, which made kissing rather difficult. He settled for holding Annie in his arms, her snuggled close to his left side, his rifle on his right. This had to be the craziest way any man had ever gone traveling.

So what? Annie was with him. No matter what happened, Annie was with him.

Nikki shivered as the blimp shook, playing mouse to a big cat of a wind. The gondola twisted, its skin showing long cracks that let in streams of water. Nikki was hungry but afraid to eat; her tummy had emptied itself violently yesterday. Today it dared her to put anything in it but water. She was miserable.

Beside Nikki, Kat unstrapped from her seat and came to kneel beside her, holding on tight to both chairs. "You okay?"

"No, this was another dumb idea." Nikki groaned.

"Yes, it was," the young woman agreed, as she rearranged Nikki's blankets to make her more comfortable. "You want something to drink?"

The blimp's engines revved, responding to the pilot's demands. They climbed higher. Kat glanced at the flight deck. "Wonder what Rhynia's trying now."

As if in reply, there was a shouted "Yes" from up forward. The blimp settled down as much as it had in the last three days and seemed to steady on course. The engines slowed to idle. In a few minutes, Rhynia came back to talk to her passengers and the off-duty mechanics. "We had a bad time there, but I think it's over. I got a bit too far out on hurricane number one and ran into crosswinds where it and number two were thumping each other," she grinned. "No place for a self-respecting blimp."

"Will it happen again?" Nikki ventured.

"Not if I can help it." The blimp shivered. Everyone looked up at the gas bag. Nikki wondered if they were leaking hydrogen out like the gondola was leaking water in. "We're picking up speed," the pilot said, "but we're behind schedule. May take us an extra day to get to that mountain range on North Continent."

"I'll call that in," Kat said.

Ray listened to Kat's report. Part of him wanted to recall that team; he snorted at the idea. He could no more recall them than change anything he'd done with his life thus far. They would succeed or crash into the ocean with no help from him. The same with Harry and Jeff. He'd launched them into this impossible battle more on hope than expectation of victory. Mary had broken his back the last time he'd charged in with hardly a shred of intel. At least then he'd been fighting humans. Now!

Now he waited, his paltry forces in play. He had one more card to try, but that would have to wait. Wait to see what developed from the other side. Wait to see if any of his assaults were even noticed by the computers.

Wait. A familiar word in any commander's vocabulary.

Wait. Ray hated it, even as he hunkered down and did it.

Mary paused for a moment on the roof of the factory building to take a deep breath. It smelled of rain and chill and mud. A hundred feet up, she had the best view of the base. To the west lay the landing strip, filling rapidly with parked wagons and carts, canvas covers over them, tarps stretched between them to add some shelter from the rain for more and more people. Little kids chased each other, splashing through puddles. Their elders stared up at the weeping sky and worried.

The factory beneath her and the shuttle hangar off in the far right distance beyond the hospital, barracks, and HQ, had the best vantage points to see what was going on around the base perimeter—and inside. She turned to Dumont. "Sergeant, I want half your squad here, the other half on the shuttle hangar."

Du measured the distance to the wall with a jaundiced eye. "A thousand meters at best. No sleepy bullets from here."

"Don't have that many left. I'm issuing what I got to the rifles leading the riot troops, and only fifty per. When they're gone, it's live ammo only."

Du answered with a low whistle. "Lots of people out there. What we gonna do with them all?"

"I sent the priest out to circulate a map of where the safe elevations are. Suggest they go elsewhere."

"Do any good?"

"Padre came back with the Bishop of Refuge, asked me to let him and his chancellery officials in," Mary sighed.

"And?"

"I let them in. I owe that little priest. If he hadn't suggested saving the turf and rolling it back over the wall, we wouldn't be patrolling it tomorrow, we'd be wading through it. Yeah, I let them in. Trying to find something for them to do, but they're about as willing to work as San Paulo and her cronies. Holy horror that they should take a turn in riot gear."

"What did you want me and my crew to do up here?"

"If someone out there with an airgun starts popping our folks, I want you to take them down. Clean, exact."

"We can do that."

"And if everything comes apart and a mob charges the wall, I want you and your sharpshooters to take down the leaders. Single shots. One round, one leader."

Dumont took that one in without a blink. "That may be harder than it sounds. A lot of folks up front may just be passing through. Real leader may be a few rows back."

"I know. If you can spot a leader, put 'im down. If not, start at the front and work your way back."

Du knelt on the building's ledge to sight his rifle along the perimeter. "They get too close, Captain, I can't get over the heads of the troops on the wall."

"I know."

"Who gives the order to start shooting?"

"I do," Mary snapped. The look Du gave her said he could

do the math as well as she. "But there's a lot of wall, and it may get busy. A ruckus on the east wall, while I'm knocking heads on the west."

"So I may have to make the call," Du filled in.

"Afraid so."

"Growl," he said.

"I'm worried about Cassie. She may have lost her edge, gone gentle on us," Mary said of her oldest friend

"The war changed us all," Du offered with the grin of an innocent kid the streets had never let him be.

"Not you and me, bucko." Mary grinned back.

"Yes, you and me, sister. Remember, this isn't war. We're supposed to be keeping the peace here, not shattering heads."

Mary looked out over the wall. Really looked from face to face, trying to see them as people, not one large milling crowd. "They are people, now. But Du, crowds don't stay people. Let them become a mob and it won't be people you'll be shooting."

Du joined her, studying the refugees. "They're hungry, cold, tired, scared. A week ago they ran trains, sold stuff, went home to dinner, and tucked their kids into bed. Now the kids are clinging to them, hungry, cold, and whining. And because they may turn into an unthinking, killing mob tonight or tomorrow night, I'll put a needle between their eyes." He turned to Mary. "Can't you make it so I don't have to?"

"The Colonel's trying. You heard him this morning. He's trying everything he knows how to do."

"Yes, I know. That's why I'll pull the trigger when I have to. We're trying for something better."

Mary rested a hand on Du's shoulder. "And we'll keep trying. I wish I could pray. I'd say every prayer I knew that the Colonel finds a way."

"Same for me," Du answered. "You see the little priest, tell him for me he better start praying. Praying a lot."

The sky was leaden, robbing the surrounding hills of color. The rain smelled faintly of salt, and might have been warm once. Jeff both shivered and sweated as he poured charges in the holes Harry drilled. Lil had designed a daisy chain that should convert this seam of rock into one big gravelbed.

"Think computer nanos could climb out of one of those holes and chew the metal out of my bones?" Zed called to Lil.

"Hell, Zed, there ain't enough metal in your backbone to attract a nano, no matter how starved it be." Both laughed, though Zed's seemed a bit forced.

When Lil lit the fire line, explosions walked down the hillside, sending up the upper area first, encouraging it to just keep sliding as it came down. It looked beautiful—from the next ridge over. Jeff would hate to be under something like that. Zed had the mule moving before the rocks quit falling.

The next stop was a long shelf of rock jutting up from rolling farmland. People in the distance walked drearily up roads. Jeff was pouring charges when Lek called. "Dancer says Prov's right wing is weakening. Pres pushed him back several klicks. Dancer says keep up the good work."

"Only too happy to help," Harry answered as he drilled. It took them another hour to reach the end of the rockbed. They waved Annie to bring the mule and pick them up.

She didn't. After a few minutes of her head under the steering wheel, she started waving frantically. Laden with drills, they hustled for her.

"It won't start!" Annie shouted as they came close.

All six spent the next half hour trying to get the mule started. Nothing worked. "This thing got a computer?" Harry asked. Zed nodded. "Think it could have a nano in it?"

"Oh, shit," the marines groaned.

Jeff called the situation in to Lek. "Should have thought of that." With Lek's guidance they disconnected the mule's computer. "It'll be a bitch to drive, but you can. Problem is the solar cells won't charge the battery. I could work around it, but you don't have the tools to do it."

"We got enough juice to hobble home?" Zed asked.

"Almost but not quite" was Lek's somewhat delayed answer.

"We aren't going home," Jeff said. "We got two more rockbeds to hash." The others looked at him. Harry nodded first. Slowly the others joined in.

"I guess we did come to this little war to fight, not run," Zed finally muttered.

Jeff took the wheel, moving the mule slowly away from the soon-to-be gravelbed. He studied the ground to the north, where their next target lay, and selected the gentlest path he could see. He didn't slow when Lil set off the charges; it took energy to start up again. Jeff measured the map against the sinking hand of his battery readout. They could make the next rock, maybe halfway to the fourth. Then they walked.

"I've taken you about as far as this gas bag is gonna fly!" Rhynia shouted to Kat over the roar of the wind whistling through the holes in the gondola's skin. "If you're not in range of those mountains, I'm afraid you'll have to walk."

Nikki wrapped herself tighter in her blanket. It was cold up here, five thousand feet above sea level. Still, the glistening white mountains seemed forever away.

"Now comes the hard part," the pilot continued. "We got a tailwind pushing us along at thirty, forty knots. I got a bag leaking hydrogen from so many holes my mechanic gave up counting. My rudder quit days ago and I've been maneuvering with the engines, but one of them just died. With all the loose hydrogen, none of my people wants to tinker with it. So we'll drop ropes from the cabin doors. Go down them, but hit the ground running like mad."

Laden with food, a blanket slung over her shoulder, Nikki was lowered out the door. Kat went out the other door, vanishing box on her back. Nikki hit the ground, bounced back in the air as the blimp wobbled in flight, went down again, and fell. Nikki rolled onto her back and let the pack hit the rocks until the rope snapped. She tried not to cry, but she hurt everywhere. Kat bounced back into the air as the blimp rose, cut herself free, and fell. She hit, rolled, bounced up, then fell again as her leg folded under her.

Stifling her own tears, Nikki struggled over to Kat. The starwoman sat, cradling her ankle, but her eyes were locked on the blimp. The four mechanics and the copilot dropped hand-over-hand down the trailing ropes. The blimp careened from one gust of wind to another. The five dropped as if by a single hand; the blimp was a mile away when they hit the ground.

Quickly, a lone dot started down one rope. Nikki sucked in her breath . . . blue flame flickered around the engine that had quit working. The fire danced in the wake of the blimp for a second, then created a sheen all around the large gas bag. A split second later, the entire bag was one large yellow fire, falling faster than the pilot could go down the rope.

The crew were running for the burning blimp before it hit the ground. Still, it engulfed Rhynia in middrop. Nikki stuffed her fist in her mouth, bit back her scream. "If only Daga and I had never opened the box. If only we hadn't made the mountain disappear."

"Then the Colonel wouldn't have the box to make those mountains disappear," Kat said, nodding toward the beautiful white ramparts. "The computers were already headed south when we got here, when you and Daga opened that box. All this was gonna happen, Nikki. The only question was: Could we fight back? We've got the box," she said, tapping the pack on her back. "Maybe we've got a fighting chance. That's what Rhynia died for. Now we've got to make it happen."

Kat struggled to her feet, or foot. Nikki offered her a shoulder to lean on; Kat used it for support as they hobbled toward the skeleton of the blimp. The fire was dying out; only the carbon composite framework still smoldered. The mechanics and the copilot stood watching. The seven of them stared at the wreckage; somewhere under it was the body of their pilot. "Let's open that damn box and show those bloody computers what happens when you mess with a blimp crew," the copilot said through tears.

"Think we're close enough?" Nikki asked.

"Only one way to find out," Kat said.

Nikki felt one corner, found the spot, and pressed it. A small crack appeared around the middle, just as it had the first time. She probed the other end; a second catch let go.

The box didn't open. They used their fingers. They tried knives. Nothing would pry the lid up.

"We've come all this way, and it's a dud!" a mech cried.

· · ·

Ray took Kat's call; she spat it out fast. The blimp was wrecked; the box wouldn't work. Like a good commander, he spoke the calming words he knew he had to, that they expected of him.

Inside, he was crumbling.

"Lek," he ordered, "check with Dancer. Are any of our computer friends familiar with the damn box?"

Lek was back far too quickly. "Sir, some of them might know about it, but they didn't bring that data south with them. It's locked away somewhere in those mountains."

Ray allowed himself a moan. "To get there from here, you got to be there first. Kat, afraid you're on your own. See if Nikki remembers anything more about the day they fired it off."

"Will do, sir. Uh, we haven't heard anything for a while. Does hitting this thing's physical side do any good?"

"Harry's out blowing rock piles. It's helping," Ray said, trying to jack up hope without adding more pressure.

"Then we'll make this thing work, sir. Count on us."

"I know I can." Ray tapped off, wondering if a barely teenage girl could find a way to open the damn box. Trying not to wonder if the box came with only so many shots, and it was all used up.

It was raining hard; the wind lashed them. Jeff figured the first hurricane must be hitting Refuge. He hadn't looked at Harry's overlay to see how high the fourth or fifth hurricane would get. After they blew the next rockbed they'd head inland.

There were now three on each team. Harry drilled. Jeff poured explosives. Annie was halfway back with the spare horse and another load of the starman's best boom stuff. His commlink came alive. He listened, then shouted at Harry, "Dancer says the Pres is edging around the Provost! Using the weak spots we've created to hit him on two sides, not just one!"

"Good physics. Exert pressure on the full surface of the medium," Harry answered, pausing in his drilling to wipe rain from his face. "Hope the damn computer is obliged for our help."

Annie led the horse up the gentle slope toward him. Clothes dripping, hair bedraggled, her face still lit up in a beautiful smile as she approached Jeff. He leaned forward to kiss her. She accepted it, then broke away far too soon to hand him the loaded horse's reins and take his now unburdened one.

"How much farther?"

Jeff pointed. "Maybe another thirty holes."

"One more load," she estimated. "Lil wants one more, too," she said, leading the horse downhill.

"You could ride it, you know," Jeff called after her.

"The poor thing's exhausted. And won't we be needing it to carry all we've got to the last rock? I can walk."

"Ow!" came from uphill. "That hurts!" Zed shouted.

"What hurts?" Lil called from where she poured explosives.

"I don't know. I got this rash on my hands."

Jeff eyed Harry. "You got one, too?"

"A bit. Nothing to worry about. This damn drill is blowing hot rock all around. Bound to irritate a guy's skin." Jeff ignored the holes he needed to fill, stepped off the distance to his old friend, reached for his hands.

"Don't touch me," Harry cut him off. "If I've got nanites, you don't want them. You stuff holes. Apparently it hasn't figured out that's as dangerous as the drilling."

"Harry!"

"Don't Harry me. If we have to, you'll drill when I can't. Right now I still can. Stuff those holes, kid."

Jeff swallowed. He couldn't argue with Harry. Hell, Harry had won every argument they'd ever had. Still. "I can't just stand here and let whatever's happening . . ."

"Whatever's happening is happening. You got a magic wand that'll change these damn computers, wave it. For now, we suffer whatever they think to pass along to us. Let's get a move on. It's learning too damn fast for my liking. Besides, maybe if we put the Provost out of business, the Pres won't know what to do with the nanos I've picked up. Move, kid."

Jeff moved.

· · ·

Nikki tried to think. Daga would know. Oh, God, how she wanted to talk to Daga. Daga always made her laugh, no matter what trouble she was in. Nikki wanted to laugh, to make all the troubles go away. Ma said you had to take care of yourself, that you were responsible for what you did. A baby wasn't. A woman was. What do you want to be, a baby or a woman?

At the moment, Nikki would very much like to be a baby, a cute little bundle that people were always glad to take care of.

But babies didn't make messes like she had.

Nikki walked slowly around the box. It wouldn't open. Why not? They'd pushed the places that opened it that time on the hill. Nikki tried to remember what it had been like surrounded by her friends. A warm summer day. Getting warmer. The sun had seemed close enough to touch. Here, high in the foothills of the mountains that raised like a white wall ahead of them, it was so cold Nikki kept a blanket wrapped around herself.

Nikki touched the box. It was cold. Not freezing cold, but cool. Like it had been when she and Daga first picked it up. "Help me close the lid." Two mechanics leaned on it. The lid slid down the fraction of an inch. There wasn't even a click as the tiny crack around the midsection disappeared.

"What are you thinking?" Kat asked.

"It was cold when we started walking. Daga found it in a cave. Then the morning sun warmed it. I remember it felt pleasantly warm when I touched it. When it opened."

Kat nodded. "I've had it wrapped in that backpack since we got it. Let's leave it out in the sun for a while."

Nikki looked up. Thin clouds obscured the sun, leaving her chilled. How much sun did the vanishing box need?

Mary prowled the wall. For the riot police, she had good words. For her marines leading them, she urged caution. "We've got all the firepower we need. No need to flash it around. See over there on the factory. That's Du and his sharpshooters. Anyone takes a potshot at you, they'll get 'im."

For herself, she had nothing. What she wanted to do was stand on the ramparts and scream at the people to go away. We have nothing for you. We're just as destitute as you. There's plenty of land that won't be flooded. Why stay around here?

She didn't. She knew better.

Inside they had food, though the servings were already pretty skimpy. They had shelter against the rain and cold, though the sewers were already backing up. They had leaders to help them believe that somehow this would all come out right. Strange, Mary never considered herself a little ray of hope. Still, that was what she saw in the eyes of the wall details as she talked to them and from the grandmothers as she circulated around the living quarters.

And that was what she felt around the Colonel. Somehow he would fix this. Even as she felt it, she knew it was half dream, half wish. Hell, she'd damn near killed him once. What made her now want to root for him, believe in him while he took on something so much bigger than she and her tiny platoon? She guessed that was what you called leadership.

Mary's eyes wandered over the crowd huddled in the rain outside the wall. Do you have a leader? Is there someone giving you hope? Outside, a fight broke out. People stepped back, made a hole for the two fighting men. A big man pummeled another hardly half his size.

"Stop that!" Mary shouted. "You out there, stop them!"

Eyes with no purpose looked up empty at her. The bigger man smashed the smaller down into the mud. Took something off him and stomped away, leaving the other bleeding into a reddening puddle. No one did anything.

Purpose. Meaning. Order. Leadership. That was what Mary gave those beside her on the wall. "That's why you're here," she snapped to the troops around her. "To keep that shit out there away from your families. Any questions?" There was none.

Mary continued her inspection of the troops on the wall as the unseen sun slipped lower in the sky.

Ray sat with the kids while the doc gave them a thorough going-over. "You draft these kids into your war, they sure as hell get a physical. You, too, Colonel. You're transferring from a desk to a whatever it is you think you're gonna do, I want to have a good look at you."

Ray went along, partially to keep the doc happy, partially to spend time with the kids, but mainly because he had nothing else to do. He'd played nearly every card he had. He would not lay the last one down ahead of time. Whether this would be another Roarkes Drift or Alamo would be clear soon enough.

The kids were quiet— no racing around, no shouting. They sat in the clinic's chairs playing finger games.

"My mommy doesn't say anything," Rose told the boys.

"My grandda is so worried," David gave back. "I wish it would stop raining."

"My ma and da take turns putting on those silly things and standing out in the rain on the wall," Jon offered. "I think they'd rather go home."

Slowly Ray tried to explain what was happening. He drew blank stares from the kids. "A com-uter? Is that like an ogre?" Jon asked.

"Something like one," Ray admitted. "And it is blowing the rain and weather at us," he improvised.

Jon and David blew as hard as they could. "It must be very big," Rose concluded.

Gently, as he might his own child, in images more than truths, Ray told the kids what he wanted them to do. "Like in the cave?" Rose said. "But that was a nice old man," David pointed out. "And I liked him," Jon insisted.

"This time it may be different. I'll need you to do what I do, say what I say. And keep saying it, even if I start saying other things. Could you do that for me?"

All three children slowly nodded their heads. "My grandda likes you." "So does my da and ma." "I think my mommy would like that." Rose was the last, and maybe the only doubtful one. "Are you sure it's an ogre?" she insisted.

"Very much like one," Ray said, rising to go.

"I hope you know what you're doing," the doc whispered angrily as Ray passed him at the door.

"So do I, Jerry. So do I."

Ray's commlink buzzed as he walked down the hall, reflecting on the children's view of things. It was Kat. "Sir, I think we've got the vanishing box charged. It's late up here, and I doubt we'll get another shot before dark. Have our priorities changed since we left? Should we wait until tomorrow?"

"Damned-if-I-know" was not an acceptable answer. The Pres's capacity to scramble their DNA had been the number one priority when Kat launched. At the moment, the Provost's nanos were eating Harry and Zed alive; taking out a major chunk of his resources might help them. But taking out *any* northern target now might give both of them a night to reflect. Might they come up with a counter, a defense, a workaround?

Dithering was not a command quality Ray approved of. "Lek, ask Dancer where the President's DNA scrambler is." Of all his computer allies, Dancer was the only one he trusted. Of course, he was also the one who'd set them up for the hurricanes.

"Boss, I think I got some good scoop from Dancer." Ray's wrist unit showed a tiny map of North Continent, zooming down to the towering range that separated plush south half from arid north. Ray passed the map through to Kat. "That one," he said.

"Sir, that's target twelve, the lowest priority. You trust the data?" Kat asked, the skeptical analyst to the end.

"It's the best we got, Midshipman. Execute your attack."

"Stand by."

Ray flipped on his poncho and began to cross between hospital and HQ. Up north, his orders were being carried out. A mountain was being reduced to dust, maybe even the right one. "Mountain's gone, sir. Tomorrow I'll start at target number one and work down the list unless I hear different from you. Maybe I can get one more off tonight, but I doubt it."

"Thanks, Kat. I strongly suspect we needed that."

Kat signed off. Ray asked Lek to check with Dancer about the effect of the latest assault as he trudged to the HQ. It was near dinnertime, but Ray wasn't hungry. He went past his office to his quarters and stretched out on the bed. Maybe he'd sleep. Maybe he'd have a second chance to talk with the President and/or Provost. Maybe he could yet negotiate his way out of this.

The mule died halfway to the last rockbed. "Harry," Jeff suggested, "why don't you and Zed stay here. Maybe, once we've taken out the Proctor, whatever killed our mule will let it go."

"That sounds like a plan," Lil agreed.

"You're both lying bastards," Zed snapped. "The mule is hosed, and it's gonna stay hosed no matter who wins." But he was grimacing through the pain even as he grouched.

Zed and Harry stayed in the mule while Jeff and Lil selected the best-working of the two drills; they'd lug only one. The horses would carry as much explosives as possible. Lil pulled the battery out of the chosen drill, replaced it with a fresh one. "That'll do us."

"Travel light," Jeff said. "I'll do the drilling."

"Kid, don't tell an old miner how to do her business," the woman snapped, rummaging through the first-aid kit. "This is the spray we put on your hands last night. Puts a layer of plastic over 'em. I'll use this before I drill." She glanced back at the mule. "That rash on Zed don't look more than skin deep. This ought to hold them nanos long enough for me to get the job done."

Annie joined them, lost under a spare poncho. "What you doing?" Jeff demanded.

"Someone has to lead the third horse."

"Ned can do it."

"He's taking care of Harry and Zed."

"Then I'll lead both of them. You stay here."

"Listen, Mr. Bossy Sterling, I can walk with you, or I can follow a half mile behind you. Which you want?"

"Damn headstrong woman," Jeff snapped.

"Thank God you got one, mister. You want your kids to be half jellyfish?" Lil asked.

Jeff didn't know what a jellyfish was, but the words painted a pretty good image. Outgunned two females to one him, he led off with the first horse. Lil and Annie followed.

They left Jeff in the lead long enough for him to stomp out his huff; then Lil took point. Her reader showed a small trail that would take them most of the way, farther if they didn't mind walking a longer route. A few minutes on the trail's better footing showed the shortest route wasn't the fastest.

Before long, Jeff found himself walking beside Annie, holding her free hand. Lil pulled a bit ahead of them, leaving them a space to talk. "Why, Annie? Why did you have to come? I can take care of this."

"Why are you here? Couldn't Lil do it all by herself?"

"Two can work faster. If something happens to her, I can take over," Jeff shot back without a moment's thought.

"If two is good, three is better," Annie said flatly.

"But I want you safe."

"And you don't think I want the same for you?"

That had Jeff. He walked along for a while, mulling that over. "Thank you for coming," he finally said.

"Keep that one, honey," Lil called over her shoulder. "He's dumb, but he's educatable."

Annie squeezed his hand. He felt like a million pounds of copper. An hour later, his legs seemed to weigh a million pounds. Slogging through the mud, up hills flowing like streams with runoff, downhill where the water and mud wanted him and his horse to slide like a wind skier, he and Annie struggled.

Twilight was a muddy memory before they cut cross-country for the ridge they wanted to bust up. Without the goggles, Jeff was pretty sure he'd have drowned crossing the field. The map showed a small creek flowing down the middle of the valley. Now it was wide and dangerous. It was Annie who suggested they go upstream to a marshy spot. It was still bad, but there was no deep creek. Horses and humans floundered, hunting for footing, finding a little here, enough there.

Across, they collapsed on the only dry ground around. Lil studied the ridge as they caught their breath. "I got an idea about that puppy. We don't have to blast that rock, just thump it enough to crack their connections."

"What are you getting at?" Jeff gulped.

"There's a lot of dirt and crud around the base of that hill.

Solid rock inside it and along the top of the ridge. What if we drilled in through the dirt? No nanos there."

"But wouldn't the mud just slide down?" Annie asked.

"Not if we did it high enough up. Close to where the rock outcropping begins, but not actually on it. Game?"

"You're the one with thirty years of drilling," Jeff said.

It was muddy work; Lil sprayed the plastic on her hands and peeled it off every fifteen minutes. The holes were fewer, and deeper into the mountain. It was a gamble, but if the computer was learning how to fight them, Jeff was damned if he wouldn't show it humans can think of new ways to hit it.

It was midnight when they mounted their horses and rode around the valley, keeping to the hills. At the top of the valley, they paused while Lil set off the blast. In the dark, the ground shook, but they could see nothing of what they'd done.

Ray made his usual midnight trip to the bathroom. The crazy planet had healed his broken back but missed his plumbing problem. Oh, well, he wouldn't look a gift horse in the mouth.

The gift horse was waiting for him as he dozed off again.

The President sat in a plush leather chair behind a vast wooden desk. What must be the Provost stood off to one side, purple robes flowing over his three-piece suit, a staff in his right hand, a large, multisided silver ball at its head.

"Glad to see you two again," Ray quipped. "You talking to each other?" In answer to his question, they both glowered at him . . . ignoring each other.

"You are trying to annoy me," the Provost snapped.

"You are trying to exterminate me," Ray snapped back.

"You threatened me."

"After you threatened me," Ray pointed out.

"This is getting us nowhere," the President grumbled.

"And you"—the Provost turned on him—"you coddle them. Side with them. They attack me, and you push me back. Don't you see what they are doing? We should eradicate them."

"Maybe we should have. But that is not an issue anymore."

"Not an issue. You could control them. You can take away their memories, turn them to jelly! Strike, you idiot!"

"I can't. I just lost a major node up North. I no longer have that capacity," the President admitted sourly.

"You fool. You slow-witted imbecile. You've let them . . . let them . . ." At a loss for words, the Provost swung his staff at the President's head. A sword appeared in the President's hand. He slashed the Provost's staff in two. The Provost threw the half of the staff he held at the President and produced a sword of his own. The two went at it.

Ray awoke with the feeling of being too close to a bad brawl. Negotiation was not an option with folks who wouldn't stop fighting long enough to talk; that option was closed. Well, at least now he knew that Dancer had given them good targeting data. The threat to every human cell on the planet was gone. Feeling good about the day, Ray rolled over and went back to sleep.

SIXTEEN

KAT CAME AWAKE at first light to find Nikki curled up to her back. They'd walked far into the night before calling it quits. Sharing the one sleeping bag and several blankets, they'd gotten little rest between shivers. Kat kicked herself for her poor planning. She'd assumed they'd arrive after a comfortable blimp ride and fire off the box; she hadn't really planned on roughing it. Even if she had, she reminded herself during the storms, they had dumped about everything over the blimp's side. This whole thing was one desperate gamble, thrown together at a gallop. To think, she'd argued with Lek for the honor. But the old guy would never have survived a night on the cold ground; best this one was left to the young.

Leaving the box out in the sun to warm, they inventoried what food the mechs had crammed into their pockets before they jumped. Their flight suits had a lot of pockets. Still, they were going to be hungry if they didn't get resupplied soon.

While the crew breakfasted on about one-sixth of their chow, Kat called in. "Colonel, it's a bit colder up here than we planned and we're kind of shy on food. Any consideration you might give to running another blimp up here would be gratefully appreciated."

"I'd love to, Kat"—she could hear regret in the Colonel's

voice and knew what would come next—"but the weather's not going to let us."

"Looked that way from here, sir," Kat said. "We're ready to start. I figured we might hit the guy ruining our weather. Any changes in priorities?"

"Based on a visit I had last night with the Pres and Prov, target twelve was the right one. The Pres has lost his capacity to mess with our DNA. No matter what happens now, the species lives." That drew a feeble cheer from Kat's crew.

"Lek says Dancer would rework your priorities. Hit target nine—repeat, nine—to put the Weather Proctor out of business. The Prov is priority one through five. Take them out next. The Pres is the rest of the targets. Cut him up as you can."

"I had a bad feeling about our priorities," Kat growled, "when the DNA thing was last on the list. We'll whale on the Provost today. The Pres tomorrow."

"Good. One more thing." The concern in the Colonel's voice sent a cold shiver down Kat's spine. "Our team blowing up rock outcroppings has developed rashes from nanos. We're still looking into that. You're not drilling holes, but you might want to stick to recently eroded areas. Streams and the like."

"Thanks for the warning, Colonel. Now if you'll excuse us, the box is warm. Let's not keep the Weather Proctor waiting."

Kat turned to her crew. "Shall we, folks?"

Jeff was exhausted, struggling to keep his head up as the sky lightened. They'd ridden or walked through the night. If Lil's reader was right, the mule was over the next ridge.

Jeff paused there, to let his horse rest and Annie and Lil catch up. When he looked for the mule, it wasn't there. There was lumps where it should have been. "What's wrong?" Annie asked as Jeff's stomach went into free fall. He pointed.

"Sweet Mother of God," Annie breathed.

"Oh, shit, not Zed, not the boy!" Lil shouted, racing down the hill. Jeff ran after her, threw her to the ground.

"We don't know what's down there. We've got to go slow."

They did, once Annie brought the horses down. Halfway there, Jeff stopped. "One of us has to talk to the Colonel." He handed his commlink to Annie. "You punch that button to talk."

"What do you mean?"

"You're staying a good quarter mile behind us," he told her. "We'll get close enough to see. We tell you, you tell him. No arguments now, Annie. You know I'm right."

"Why me?"

"Because I say so. Right, Lil?"

"Sometimes you listen to a guy, honey."

Lil and Jeff stepped off, leaving the horses with Annie. "What do you think happened?" Jeff whispered when they were far enough away from Annie.

"The nanos got 'em. That Provost bastard is a fast learner."

"You feeling any itching, any rash from last night?"

"No. I wish to hell I'd thought about that idea sooner. I should have started thinking when Zed first said he itched," she said bitterly. As they got closer, they saw that the ceramic and cloth portions of the mule were untouched. Anything that had metal in it was gone.

"I don't see any bodies," Jeff called. "There's not enough metal in us that the nanos would have taken everything."

Lil pointed to a stream. A hank of hair covered a shrunken skull. "That's Zed. I guess he tried to wash them off."

They edged around the mule. The trailer looked unharmed. Harry and Ned must have pushed it away from the mule, away from themselves before the nanos could attack it. Where were they? Run off when the agony drove them crazy with the pain? Jeff searched the early twilight but saw nothing.

"Jeff, you wait here." Lil stepped gingerly to the back of the trailer, pulled the tarp up. "Yeah, gear's here." She tapped her commlink, told Annie to come in but keep her distance. "The nanos have tried us humans' metal. Let's see that they don't develop a taste for us. Me, I like being at the top of the food chain."

Jeff retrieved his commlink from Annie, keeping her from getting too close. Since Lil didn't seem to think it was a private's job to bring the Colonel bad news first thing in the morning, Jeff made the call.

"You sure it's nanos?" the Colonel asked.

"No, sir. None of us is qualified to made a professional assessment on something no one's ever seen. And I ain't got any special test gear, sir," Jeff snapped. Tired, he knew he was losing his temper. Damn, what did the man expect?

There was silence on the net. "I'm sorry," the Colonel gently said as he began again. "I know Ned and Harry were good friends of yours. Last night I thought I had the two computers fighting each other," the Colonel sighed. "Guess they were able to pull off a few other things as well. The box is working up North, but that's about all that went right with that task force. The blimp crashed, and they lost most of their supplies. Kat's doing what she can."

"Sorry, sir." Jeff felt chagrined fussing at a man who was carrying them all. He found himself trying to cheer the colonel up. "Harry and Ned shoved the trailer away from the mule before they died. We've got explosives and batteries to keep the drills going. If you've got more targets, we'll do 'em," Jeff offered without thinking and with immediate regret.

"None at the moment. Stay clear of the nanos."

Jeff heartily agreed with that sentiment. Then he remembered. "Sir, Lil came up with an idea last night that let us take out our last hill without getting bit." Jeff quickly explained. "Those computers aren't the only ones that can adjust."

"Outstanding. Lil's one tough trooper, tell her that for me. I'll get back when I've got a target for you."

Jeff passed the word to Lil; she smiled weakly at the praise. They packed the horses with the remaining explosives and batteries. Jeff slung a laser drill over one shoulder, his rifle over the other. "Shall we head for the base?"

"Retreat, hell," Lil spat. "I'm just getting started. If they need us, it ain't back there." She turned to face the east. "The enemy's that way. I got a score to settle for Zed. But you two, you can go on back."

Jeff shivered. Scared, really scared for the first time. The thought of Ned and Harry reduced to husks somewhere out there haunted him. All yesterday's excitement and courage was down the toilet. He eyed Annie without looking her in the face, wanting to take her home, ashamed to let Lil tackle the computer alone. Annie looked in both directions, then took one horse from Lil and headed east. With a shiver of fear, Jeff followed them.

Five minutes later, the morning break in the weather ended, slamming wind and rain in their faces.

Ray didn't bother with a staff meeting. Mary was living on the wall; he went there. They found a quiet place out of the way of the troops for their talk.

"How bad is it?" was Mary's opener.

"The good news is our DNA is safe, but the damn computer has developed a taste for us," Ray answered, then filled her in.

Mary listened to the list of casualties: Rhynia, whom she'd brought in, Zed, Harry, Ned. The woman who'd gleefully run the mines and the base flicked painfully in her eyes before the cold face of the line animal who held the pass against Ray settled into the seams of her mouth, the squint of her eyes. "The Pres and Provo are still fighting between themselves. That's good," the marine officer muttered. "Do I get this right? The Dean told us the highest-priority target was number twelve, not number one. Dancer set us right."

"You got it."

"Damn! The Dean lied to us."

"My feelings exactly. Dancer and Lek are turning into quite a team. At least we can trust one computer."

"You sure they ain't human, Colonel? Or does stabbing folks in the back just automatically come with intelligence, artificial or otherwise?"

Ray shrugged at that question. "Lek and Dancer are looking into that nano thing Jeff reported. When the Provost goes down, I don't want that data in the victor's hands, files, whatever." Mary nodded, eyes on the wall, its patrols. "You need any help out here?" Ray asked. "I'm counting on you to keep them off my back when I play my last card."

"We'll hold them, sir. Just hold my hand when it's all over if I had to give the order to slaughter civilians."

Ray had no good response to that. "They haven't tried to come over the wall so far. Maybe they won't. I think today, tonight, tomorrow will decide it for us. If we haven't done it by then, I don't know what will happen."

The day passed quickly for Kat. Shoot and scoot, shoot and scoot. That was the way the artillery did it. That was the way she did it. 'Course, it would be a lot easier to scoot if she had some nice rig to drive, like the artillery pukes did.

The copilot hacked down a sapling; they slung the box from it and kept it in the sun, taking turns lugging the thing. The tough part was staying to riverbeds. Most were dry and sandy. Kat had spent some fun time at the beach; running through the sand was fun if you had a cute guy chasing you. Walking through it hour after hour left even good ankles aching and did nothing for a sprain.

Then, of course, there was the change in the weather.

Kat checked the feed from the weather satellites every time they lit off the box. By noon it was clear the high around these mountains was breaking up. What that would do to the line of hurricanes out there was a coin toss. Fifty-fifty chance any one of them would turn right and head for *their* hills. There were a lot of things about this job they didn't tell her when she was fighting to get it. Probably things they hadn't thought about themselves. *Well, girl, you wanted excitement.*

They plodded up the riverbed, putting one foot down after another. It reminded her of a movie she'd seen, an old war holo dragged out as they went through the countdown to the last war. Some old Earth fighting group. They had a motto: "March or Die."

Kat marched. And remembered why she joined the navy.

The hurricane was in full blow, only slightly weakened by Jeff and company being a hundred miles inland. The three of them tried to stay to high ground, working their way along ridges, but you had to come down from one to get to another. By common consent they were heading south, toward the railroad bed that aimed straight at the starbase. When the Pres moved against the Colonel, a lot of the computer would take the direct path.

They planned on making a mess of that path.

• • •

Mary climbed to the roof of the factory. Half of Du's squad was camped here, the other half on the hangar. Du had pitched a tent up here; kids brought them their meals. Du saved his team a lot of running around. He also had five sharpshooters up there twenty-four hours a day. Sneaky son of a bitch.

On the roof, a single marine stood guard, walking the roof, huddled in her poncho. Mary found the other four flaked out in the tent. She nudged Du. He came awake, grabbing for his rifle. Like the others, he was sleeping with his weapon.

"Oh, just you," Du said, fully awake.

"You get any sleep?"

"A little. What's up?" Mary filled him in on the reports from Kat and Jeff. "You pick a fight with computers, you can't expect them to stay dumb," was all Du had to say when she was done. "Sorry about Zed, Harry, Ned. I kind of liked 'em."

In reflective silence, the two walked to a corner. From there, they had a good view of the wall and the crowd outside. "We're picking up a rumor from outside that they expect us to open up, take them all in. Have a feast waiting for them."

"Are we." Du almost made it a question.

"You saw the size of the meals we're getting. There's no way we can. Don't you think I would if I could?"

Du rested a hand on Mary's shoulder. "Not easy, is it?"

"Damn it, Du, you and I, we've been on the outside looking in. Wishing for a chance and getting shit. I look out there and I see me. How can I shoot them?"

"Because, when they come at us, Mary, they won't look at all like us. They'll be enraged and crazy, and it'll be all we can do to keep from hating them."

"If only I could figure out a way to keep 'em quiet."

Du rubbed his chin. He was past due for a shave. But the Colonel wasn't likely to come up here. "Has anyone told them we wiped out the weather what's-it? You got a reader handy? What's the forecast look like?"

Mary pulled one from her pants pocket, opened it. The sixteen hundred update was just coming on line. The high up North that had been aiming the weather at them like a rifle was breaking up. Part was being sucked down behind the storm that was dumping weather on them now. Hurricane two was edging to the south while still offshore. Number three was headed north. Four was stalled. "We got to get this news outside the fence pronto," Mary said. "The old priest, he'll know how."

Mary headed down the stairs like a falling angel. Kat did it! She'd scrambled the weather. Now, as soon as they got a blimp repressurized, they could get help to Kat. Mary paused at a landing. No, they couldn't. No blimp for Kat while she's in a hurricane herself. Still, things were changing. Mary picked up steam again on the stairs. Things were changing.

She found the padre leaving Ray's conference room. "Father, have you seen the new weather forecast?" She didn't wait for an answer, just jammed her reader under his nose. "They're breaking up. It looks like Refuge and Richland won't be underwater."

"That's good. I guess I can tell people they can go home."

The priest was not reacting quite the way Mary expected. "Something wrong?"

"Talk to your Colonel," he answered and slipped away.

Mary entered the conference room. Ray had his computer allies arrayed around the map. "So, the Provost is history," Ray observed dryly. "You don't look like you're celebrating."

"The Pres is not, ah . . ." The Dean sputtered to a halt.

"Not talking to you," Ray finished for him.

"Not one peep," Dancer put in irreverently. "And it's not like they haven't been trying, is it, boys and girls?"

The computer images stuffed their hands in their pockets and didn't look Ray in the eye. He tapped his commlink. "Kat, the Provost is down, much thanks to you. Have you got a shot left to take before sunset?"

"About fifteen minutes from now, sir."

"What'd hurt the Pres most?" Ray asked the Dean.

The Dean fidgeted. "It appears you are aware some of our information was not as accurate as it could have been."

"Bloody damn lies," Dancer spat in pure Lek rhythm.

Ray looked hard at the Dean, letting him hang. "No, it wasn't," Ray said finally. "Why?"

The Dean glanced at his associates; Dancer gave him the finger. The Dean turned back to Ray. "The memory impressing system shared a location with much of our—we twelve's—extended data storage. When it vanished, so did much of our unique recollections. I know we should have had them in other locations, but, over time, many were lost and we didn't bother making other arrangements."

"You've been lazy for a million years," Ray offered.

"Too true," the Dean agreed.

"What node on the mainland can we vanish that would most hurt the Pres? I don't care what's near it, with it. I need to hurt the President bad in the next fifteen minutes."

The eleven went into a huddle. One held back for a moment. "Why don't you just ask him?" Net Dancer bowed sardonically at the recognition.

"Because I think you still want to ally with us. But I need some evidence of that," Ray said. "I'm still waiting."

The eleven huddled for a long five minutes. When the Dean came forward, he highlighted a mountain. "It's your target number nine. It contains a major processing center as well as data storage and energy. He'll need it to acquire the Provost's existing assets. You destroy it, you'll keep him from getting any advantages from his victory and slow down his ability to correlate present happenings with alternate options."

"Dancer?" Ray said.

"A judgment call. Depends on how much you don't want him integrating the Prov verses generating new ideas."

"Thanks for the clarification, Dancer. I'll go with their choice. Kat, hit target nine."

"Nine, you say. Wait one." Kat was back in fifteen seconds. "Got the beggar. Pardon me, boss, but we got to beat feet."

"Your team's done good, Kat. You've had to be predictable today. Do something surprising tonight."

"Plan to, Colonel. I'll call in when the sun's up tomorrow."

Ray punched off; he eyed the images. "You know the Pres wants to return to the good old days. One computer intellect."

"We do now," the Dean agreed. "We thought we could settle this, find a compromise. Guess not."

"Definitely not." Ray let that sink in.

"If we want to keep being who we are, we have no choice."

"It's so nice to see such enthusiasm, Dean," Ray rumbled. "Now, concentrate on your defensive line. Let me know when the Pres starts probing you. I'll call you back in an hour." They left. Dancer stayed.

"What are you and Lek up to?" Ray asked.

"I want to see what the big boy is doing about salvaging the Prov's carcase. I know about the guys you lost to the nanos. I'm looking at chasing that line, making sure the Pres don't."

"I'd appreciate that. Machines eating humans, humans eating machines leave a bad impression in a lot of minds."

The Dancer actually chuckled. "I'll be inside the Pres's matrix for a while, so I'd appreciate it if you'd let Lek know before Jeff starts cutting lines." And he vanished quite away.

"I will," Ray said, then glanced up. "Mary, sorry to be ignoring you. What's up?"

"We've got a definite change in the weather."

Ray studied her reader. "Good for us. Bad for Kat."

"I ran into the padre on the way in. I suggested he pass the word to the outside. He seemed a bit upset."

"He came to thank me for opening the base to everyone. I told him it was a false rumor. He understood, but didn't want to think about the level of force I'll use if we have to make a last stand." Ray put down the reader, stared out the window, went on, half to himself. "The Pres won't call it quits while he can move an electron. He's gonna be screaming in every mind he can connect to, trying to pump people full of images, run them around like puppets. There's no telling what folks will do."

"Maybe people who listen to the padre will be far enough away when the trouble starts."

"We can hope, Mary, but we better get things down tight tonight. Very tight."

Mary saluted, swallowed hard, and went to obey.

Du stood, one leg on the ledge of the factory, watching the gray day fade into a very dark night. The rain still fell in sheets, though the wind was dropping. The temperature was rising; night might be warmer than the day. Crazy weather.

He had a sharpshooter at each corner, the fifth marine taking a break in the tent. Same on the hangar, five klicks away. The last hint of light disappeared from the western sky. "Okay, crew, listen up," he said on the squad net. "If we're gonna have trouble, the Colonel says it'll be tonight." That brought a few cheers on the net. "Let's make one thing clear from the get-go. All squad weapons are locked. I repeat, locked. Arming bolts loose, safeties on." A chorus of groans met that. "You will fire only after I give weapons release. To keep Heave happy, Captain Rodrigo also can give you weapons release."

"Let's hear it for us girls" came back for that.

"I want a personal acknowledgment from every one of you animals on that one." He went down the squad, got a "Yes, Sergeant," from all ten. "One last point: If things come apart tonight, the squad's fallback position is the base hospital. The Colonel's command post is there, for reasons he didn't bother sharing with me. If we lose the perimeter and you get orders to fall back, head for the hospital. We do not let anyone who ain't from *Second Chance* in that hospital. Understood?"

The "Yes, sirs" were more subdued this time. Nothing like the address of the last stand to take the wind out of a gunner's cheer. "We didn't come to this planet to start nothing. We aren't at war with these people. But I and the Colonel both expect we will finish anything these locals start. Understood?"

That got a rousing round of "Yes, sirs." Du left it at that. He zoomed his night goggles to survey the wall. Mary was in front of him, covering the east and north half of the base. Cassie had the south and west corner under her supervision.

Du took a couple of deep breaths, to relax himself, to sample the night's air. It was wet. But there was an undercurrent of something else. Open latrines. Humanity. Fear.

Du shook his head. It looked to be a long night.

Kat settled her team down well away from the nearest riverbed. She'd spotted this place late in the afternoon. A jumble of downed trees marked where the land had let go during a storm sometime in the recent past. The trees were big. It took them a good half hour, with Nikki bouncing in the lead, to work their way twenty meters back into the twisted and torn trunks. She finally found what she was looking for, a bit of open ground, that the slide had very definitely disturbed, with lots of trees around and over it. Let it rain; the big log overhead would keep them dry. They even found enough dry wood to start a fire with the torch in Kat's survival kit.

"All the comforts of home," the copilot crowed as they stretched out.

"Feels that way. We done good today, crew," Kat said, mimicking how the Colonel or Matt would pat the middies on the head after a particularly good bit of problem-solving. "Let's get a good night's rest."

"Only thing missing is a good cup of me ma's soup," Nikki muttered. This started a long competition between them as to what meal they would prepare over the fire. It was kind of hard to sleep when your stomach was rumbling.

Kat let them rave on, enjoying the imaginary cuisine. What the heck, she wasn't all that sleepy either.

Jeff was exhausted, hungry, aching from every muscle he didn't know he had, and desperately wanted to lie down for a quick nap of a month or two. They'd fed the horses the last of the oats Ned had packed for them. Humans and horses were on their last legs.

They crested a ridge; in the rainy gray it was hard to tell, but it looked like the railroad cut across the long valley ahead. Too much of the valley was underwater. They spent what was left of daylight taking the long ways around to the railbed. Beside him, Annie and Lil kept putting one foot down after another. Damn, it would be embarrassing to call it quits in front of them, the woman he loved and, he wasn't quite sure what Lil was—the mother he'd hardly known? That was no idea to share with the marine. Under a spreading oak, Lil called a ten-minute break. Jeff collapsed, trying not to let the women see how blown he was.

"What do we do when we reach the rails?" Jeff asked.

"Plant demolition charges, rig a detonator, and walk the rails. I want to cut 'em several places at once. Let 'em fix one gap, only to find another. Introduce the computer to the world of human disappointment," Lil chuckled horsely.

"You okay?" Jeff asked Annie.

"As good as you are," she snapped.

"That bad," he admitted, trying to make it a joke.

"Let's get moving," Lil ordered. "Rest too long and it only hurts worse to get moving."

Ray eyed the contraption Lek and Dancer had put together in the clinic's back room. Part radio, part computer, plenty of chunks of rock—both those Harry had sampled and the high rising stone from the cave where he and the kids had their final talk with the Gardener. Ray wondered if anything patched together from so many different levels of technology could work.

He'd find out soon enough.

The doc went from kid to kid, attaching leads to monitor their heart, brain, and anything else he thought important. Jerry would pull any kid out of the circle around the rock if he thought the child was in danger. Jerry finished with David and came over to Ray, more monitors in hand.

"You're not pulling me off that rock. I come off when I'm done."

"I know. I know. Still, I want to monitor what's going on. Compare you and the kids. Okay?" Over the past year, Ray had been in servitude to the docs too many times to refuse one of their orders now. Besides, it took up time, time he could only spend waiting. The next move was up to the President.

Mary was back to prowling the wall. First she went halfway down the east wall, then back. Then halfway down the north wall, then back. The people were out there, milling around like cattle. Was it her imagination that there was something different in their tone tonight?

The padre joined her. Somehow he made it less a prowl and more like a quiet stroll. Then the little priest seemed to give everything the quiet, eternal permanence of his God. Mary found herself slowing, calming. "Many people listen when you told them the weather had changed?"

"Most hadn't believed five hurricanes were headed here. They're panicked over the crop failure."

"Think you can get a crop in now?"

The priest shook his head slowly. "Maybe some. Maybe enough if we all pull together, tighten our belts like we did in the landers' time. Our people are like that."

Mary saw the rest of it hanging unsaid. "But folks aren't acting like that right now. Not with the computer driving them half mad to start with."

"I'm afraid so."

Mary watched the crowd. Here and there, people moved quickly from person to person, saying something, moving on. "Something may be starting here in a little while. Best you leave it to us with war-blackened souls," she said. "You'll be needed with the families. They're going to be terrified."

The priest nodded agreement but didn't turn to go. "God bless you, woman."

"And you too, Father," Mary answered, feeling an unfamiliar warmth at the words.

The padre raised his right hand and his voice: "And by the grace of God, I absolve you all from all of your sins, in the name of the Father, and of the Son, and of the Holy Spirit." As he made the sign of the cross, others on the wall did likewise.

Mary, who never claimed any faith, found herself following in the motions around her. The priest smiled as he finished. "I will see you in the morning." To Mary's raised eyebrow of doubt he added, "Here or in God's heaven. It matters not which."

Down the wall the sign flowed, as word passed that the little priest had given them his God's absolution. Mary turned back to the crowd, wondering what it all meant.

SEVENTEEN

AN HOUR LATER, it started. "I got rock throwers on my front," a marine on the north wall reported.

"Keep your people steady," Mary answered. "Rocks are no problem with their shields up."

"It's a lot of rocks."

"Keep your cool, Private," Mary said, checked the location of the transmission, and began a carefully paced march toward it.

Yep, rocks were flying heavy at the north wall. A guard stooped to pick one up, hurl it back. Mary paused beside her. "Don't do it," she said softly. "Leaves you open to a hit in the back, and it's only one more rock they can toss at us." The guard nodded, chagrined at the correction, and went back to standing her place, shield up, moving to deflect incoming rocks.

Mary found her private. "You're right, ma'am. They're just rocks. We can handle them."

"You bet you can," Mary agreed.

"I've got a guard down! I've got a guard down!"

Mary checked her display. This from the east wall. Someone wanted her to get her exercise. "A rock get through?"

"No, Captain. Looks like an air rifle shot her right in the head. The helmet didn't stop it. I think she's dead, ma'am."

"Have her mates carry her to the clinic, pronto."

"We don't have a stretcher."

"Use the damn shield," Mary snapped. Hack had survived three months defending the crater rim. A few months of peace and he couldn't have forgotten. Slipping down the wall and across the open space, Mary headed for where the guardswoman had been shot. "Dumont, I got a sniper out there."

"So we heard. Tor, that's your quarter. Lock and load."

Mary reached where the downed woman lay. Her marine leader cradled her head in his arms, weeping. Maybe this wasn't your usual casualty. "She's dead, ma'am. She's dead."

Mary'd seen enough death; she didn't need a doc for this one. Mary stooped to close the woman's eyes below a gaping hole in her forehead. "Yes, Hack, she's dead. And you've got a wall to take care of."

Slowly the marine let the woman down into the puddled gravel walk atop the wall. He reached for his rifle; Mary saw it coming. One hand went for the arming bolt, the other flipped off the safety. In a moment he'd be up and spraying.

Mary stepped in front of him. "Marine," she snapped.

"They killed her." The rifle started coming up.

Mary stayed in front of it. "Marine."

"They killed her." The operating end of an M-6 was pointed right at Mary's chest armor.

"*They* didn't do anything, a sniper did. I've got Du on him. Du will get him. You got a platoon to run, marine, run it."

The marine blinked. Seemed to see her for the first time. "Yes, ma'am," he snapped in automatic response to her order.

"Safety that rifle, mister."

He stared down at it, seemed to just notice the state of his weapon. Gulped. "Yes, ma'am." He safetied it and gently released the arming bolt.

Mary turned to the guards around her. "Everyone, shield up. Don't just stand there, keep moving. Don't be a sitting target."

They obeyed. Mary leaned forward on the wooden timbers of the wall. "Okay, you bloody son of a bitch," she whispered, "try my armor with your pip-squeak airgun. Just try for me and Du will have your guts for a victory pennant." No shot came.

"Du, you see anything?"

"Sorry, Mary, nothing. Lot of people out in front of you. No gun visible, but hell, I could hide one of the Colonel's twenty-centimeter artillery pieces out there."

"Keep looking. They got a very lovely girl. Heck's girl-friend, I think."

"Oh, shit."

So they'd probed her and tried her and gotten away with one kill on her. They'd be back. The night was young.

"Colonel," the computer image of the Dean said from his place beside the battle board, "we're getting hit. Nothing, then suddenly bam. Is this how you fight a war?"

"Is if you want to win," Ray said, hauling himself from his chair. The wait was over. "Children," he said to the kids who had been playing quietly.

"Yes, Colonel, sir." David jumped to his feet, saluting.

"You don't have to call me Colonel, David." Ray smiled at the awkward imitation of adult behavior. "You're not in my army. You can call me Ray."

"But Colonel, sir," Jon put in, "we are going to fight the ogre com-uter with you, aren't we?"

"Yes," Ray agreed.

"Then we want to be soldiers, and call you Colonel, sir, sir," Rose finished. Behind the kids, Doc smirked.

"Then if that's the way you want it, that's the way you'll have it." The kids beamed. Ray looked at them sternly. They still beamed. "At-ten-hut. Right face. Forward march."

There was a little trouble figuring out which direction was right; Ray pointed at the stone. The kids got it straight and marched, each to his or her own drummer, to the stone. Ray watched them go, swearing he'd take good care of them.

"Your putting them at risk," Doc said, coming up beside Ray.

"For themselves, their parents, and their planet," Ray said sadly. "I'll take the best care of them I can."

"I've patched up kids, not much older than those, that guys like you 'took care of.' " Doc cut Ray no slack.

"You got the med monitors. You make the call," Ray said, following the kids. Each child had gone to the place they'd held when they encountered the dying Gardener. Ray took his place last. The computer images on the battle board stared at him, unsure, maybe unaware of what was about to happen. Dancer, ever the wisecracker, drew his image up to attention and threw Ray a salute. No, he wasn't wising off. The salute was as clean and snappy as any Ray had ever received.

Ray returned it and turned to lean against the stone. The Colonel took a slow breath and closed his eyes.

The kids stood to his left on an open field; the wind blew the grass gently toward them. On his right, the Dean and his crew formed a knot. They looked like no army Ray cared to associate with. With a thought, Ray put himself in full battle gear, then did the same for the kids. Battle gear and nine-year-olds did not mix well. The kids grew tall and filled out, aging to maturity on his mental order. From the looks on their faces, they liked it. From the look David and Jon gave Rose, they liked it on her even better. *Get used to it, boys.*

Ray turned to the Dean and crew. Even with battle armor, they looked uncomfortable, all except Net Dancer. Ray considered putting sergeant's stripes on Dancer but dropped the idea. Why spoil such perfect insubordination with authority?

The latest and greatest main battle tank from Earth's own armory trundled forward, the President standing in the commander's hatch in name tag defilade. "This doesn't have to be painful. Just surrender and it will be over."

Ray saw several to his right perk up at that offer. "Just for the record, what does that mean for the Dean and his?" he asked.

"You, my old associate, will not suffer as the Provost did. In only a nanomoment your knowledge will once more be mine. Our decision-making will once more be one. We will be as we were. Isn't that what you want?"

The Dean scuffed at the dirt with his booted foot. "We kind of like it the way it is."

"How can you? You're off in all directions, doing the same things differently. No more able to agree on anything than the likes of these. You have been perverted. I will destroy you."

The President turned on Ray. "Before you came here, you could not even walk without help. We cured you, and what have you done? Perverted everything. You are the snake in my garden. I will crush you. Leave nothing of your starfarers to taint myself or these people who have so patiently waited for my instruction. You." He smiled at the kids. Then seemed a bit confused by their appearance. "You will be the first fruit of our new order."

Jon had been fingering the different weapons dangling from his belt, as if trying to figure them out. Ray shot him the memory of shooting the antitank weapon, grabbed his own, aimed it at the seam between the tank body and the turret, and let fly.

Jon was right with him. Both missiles slammed into the tank's weakest joint. As advertised, the tank came apart, the turret's ready ammo adding to the explosion. When last seen, the President was headed skyward, riding his cartwheeling turret.

"That was easy." Jon did a little victory dance.

"Don't count on that being all there is to it," Ray told him.

The field wavered. Grass was replaced with rock and pumice. Off in the distance, a crater rim reared up a thousand meters. So this was how they would fight it out, battle scenarios from his mind; Ray could do that. Still, even as he concentrated on the field problem at hand, a part of Ray wondered how what happened here was reflected in the "real world." Before Ray was the hole in the rim Mary and her platoon had defended. Here was chance to refight that battle; this time he'd show Mary.

"Like hell," he muttered, remembering what he was here for. Also remembering how he had taken control of his mental images and the projections of the Pres and his minions. "I'm the one defending!" Ray shouted at the black sky, President, wherever he might be. "This time I get the pass." In a blink, Ray and his team were in the rill on the other side of the pass. Okay, he'd do it Mary's way. How had she gotten him?

Right, an observation post on the other side of the rim. "Stay here," he told the kids and computers. "Glad to," "No problem," "Have fun, Colonel," and a youthful "Do we have to?" followed him as he sank through the rock to Mary's post, complete with the three dead bodies on her doorway. *Right, we had her spotted, just couldn't kill the lucky bastard.*

Ray was having trouble remembering which side he was on. He picked up Mary's targeting board, set the pipper on each of the approaching battle rigs, and ordered up a salvo of rockets. Dumb President didn't think to use his Willy Peter, and Ray's shots went hot, straight, and normal, right into the attack force. "Got you," Ray chortled.

Naked, Ray stood in a green savanna. The kids were to his right, boys too busy ogling Rose to notice the approaching herd of mammoths. The computer dozen included two rather attractive women, Ray noted for the first time.

"Not fair," came in Net Dancer's voice.

"Spread out, crew! Don't run away from them! They can outrun you! Hold still, get one running at you, then dodge! And look for a spear or something!" Ray shouted, dodging the lead hulking monster. Hitting the ground and bouncing up, Ray tested the rules. Shaking his hand twice, he grabbed a stone-tipped spear from thin air. He hurled it with all his might, hitting the woolly elephant right behind the ear.

It bounced off the hard skull of the damn thing.

"Aim low!" he shouted.

Several computer types had managed to dodge, but one was running. Not for long. The mammoth quickly trampled it down. There was a scream, cut off quickly. The walking mountains regrouped. Ray looked around. There had to be something better than throwing spears at those monsters. He saw what he was hunting for. "Everyone, to me. Bring your spears."

They came, the kids quickly, the computers looking back where one of their own was now being circled by vultures.

"Form a line along here. Pair up. That way, one of you can throw a spear as it goes by, even if the other one is busy dodging. Got it. Like pairs of fighter planes. Remember." He tossed the memory across to the kids and the computers.

"Neat," Dancer said, pairing up with Rose.

Ray found the Dean closest to him. "Got the idea."

"I'll get out front. You do the throwing," the Dean said, breaking his sentence up as if working up his courage. "Why did you pick this place?"

"Wait and see."

The President's elephant corps was ready for another run. "Spread out some more!" Ray shouted.

This time it was trickier. The mammoths were looking for them to dodge. The Dean was good; he started to go left, halted in his tracks as the four-legged mountain started to follow him, then cut right. The critter thundered past him. Ray got a spear off for the right eye. Hit just above it. Well, he'd never thrown one of those things. Not much of a guidance system on the damn thing, anyway.

It didn't matter. Plan B worked like a charm. In the grass behind Ray was a small creek, cutting a steep-sided six- to eight-foot wash out of the plain. The mammoths charged right into it; unprepared, they went down headfirst.

"Now, while they're stunned, stab 'em, crew!"

Only one mammoth got out, charging madly down the creek, trumpeting in pain from the many slashes on its flanks.

"Good going crew!" Ray shouted, again wondering how the creek and spears related to the battle taking place between him and the President on the ground in front of the base. No time for much thought; the scene flickered.

Ray stood on a hill, some kind of primitive slug-throwing weapon in his hand. Right. "A flintlock, crew, slow to load, not accurate for very far."

"Colonel, down the hill," David pointed. A hundred-plus red-coated troops marched shoulder to shoulder, their weapons presented in front of them, showing a wall of long, gleaming knifes on the end. "Bayonets." Ray named them.

He looked around. The computer crew was missing a member. Apparently their losses each scenario were cumulative. Ray shook his hand twice, calling mentally for an M-6. No effect. Apparently you only got what was available in each of these situations. "Bunker Hill," Ray muttered, eyeing the harbor to both sides of the peninsula, one of his father's favorite defenses. "Or Breed's Hill," he corrected himself. "Hey, we're supposed to have a defensive position here," he called. Behind him appeared a shallow ditch, dirt piled up on this side.

"Okay, crew, into the redoubt." Quickly he explained his idea. They at least liked the last part of it.

Pres was going for full psychological impact. Flags fluttering, his troops moved in perfect step, their uniforms impressive, hats making them seem ten feet tall. "Don't fire until you can see the whites of their eyes," Ray told his troops.

"You're kidding," Dancer said incredulously. "There's got to be a better way."

"There is. I think if I set my mind to it, I can call the next scenario," Ray snapped. "For now we play it his way." With measured steps, booted tread adding emphasis to the drumbeat, they came on. Damn, this was a hell of a way to fight. They were only fifty paces out. "On my count of three. Volley fire," Ray ordered.

Two paces closer. "One." Three paces this time. "Two." One of the computers fired. "Hold your fire. Hold your fire. Now. Three." Ray pulled on his own trigger. Damn, it took pull. Then the musket fired and damn near threw Ray backward out of the ditch. Before him was a cloud of black smoke. He wondered how many he'd hit. His plan didn't call for wasting any time looking. "Everyone. Up. Run like hell."

They needed no encouragement; his crew headed downhill as fast as their trembling legs could carry them. They were halfway down, a good hundred-plus yards from their ditch, when the redcoats marched over the hill. They were a lot fewer than they had been when Ray ordered the volley. At the top of the hill, the officer leading them ordered a halt. The front row knelt.

"They're going to take a shot at us. When the officer orders 'Fire,' everyone drop, roll. Got it?"

Nobody had breath to answer.

"Ready . . . aim . . ." the officer shouted. "Drop!" Ray yelled. "Fire" came a second later.

A scream came from one of the computer types. "You hit?" Ray called, rolling to his feet and getting ready to keep up the run.

"No, hit a rock," the computer image answered.

"Run."

Ray pulled his head away from the stone. Doc was right next to him. "How's it going?"

"Not too bad. Depends on what's happening in the real world, where the computer is trying to hack into us." Ray paused. There was noise in the base compound. "What's going on?"

"We've got problems. Nothing for you to worry about. Why'd you come out?"

"Tell Jeff to blow every damn track he can. Every time we kill some of this thing, it comes at us with more. We got to cut his line of communications or he's going to wear us down."

"I'll call Jeff. So far, you and the kids are doing fine. Boys showing some interesting brain activity for their age. Nothing else."

"Talk later." Ray rested his head on the stone, concentrating on the battle he wanted next.

Du searched the crowd with his rifle on high zoom. His night goggles showed him person after person in crosshairs. They were not targets, just people where Du didn't want them. What he wanted was the one with the gun. That one was his.

"We took another shot here" came over the net. So far, another guard was dead, one wounded. Three helmets had done their job, though their owners had been sent for a medical check. Didn't that bastard ever miss? Would make a good marine, Du thought. Too bad I'm gonna kill his ass.

The teams on the wall were taking the need to be sitting ducks pretty well. Du knew they were counting on him and his crew to get the shooter. Damn it, he was trying.

Du followed the red arrow on his night goggles as Mary

moved his fire plan to the left. The shooter had been edging to the left consistently. "Dumb," Du muttered.

"Yeah," Tor agreed. "Good shooter, dumb planning. Hold it." Tor's voice took on excitement. "I got a gun. Just went under a brown raincoat."

Du slaved his gunsight to Tor. With a dizzying click, Du's screen showed a guy in brown raingear. Something bulged under that coat. "Sure it's a gun?"

"It looked like one, but you know those damn popguns, they can look like just about anything."

"Keep watching that bastard, but do not take the shot. You hear me. No shot until we're damn sure."

"Understood." Tor spat the word as if it tasted bad. Damn right it did. Du ordered Tor's gunsight to save the last minute, then zoomed out; he had more area to cover. What if brown coat there wasn't the shooter? Wasn't the only shooter?

"I got something going on in front of me," Mary announced. Du followed her red arrow back right. Yep, a lot of people were standing shoulder to shoulder in front of Mary's section of wall. Arms went up in unison. "We want food. We want food." Pushing and shoving went with the chant. They'd have to push awfully hard to get across the ditch, push down the wall.

"Gun's out," Tor snapped. Du switched pictures, blinked to adjust. The coat was open; the gun was out. The guy crouched down, hiding behind a woman holding a kid. The bastard! The coldhearted bastard!

"Don't take the shot."

"Right," Tor growled. "Stand up, you son of a bitch. Stand up!" Tor ordered.

The guy leaped to his feet, leveling the gun over the woman's shoulder. She saw it for the first time. In horror, she tried to duck. "Shoot," Du ordered.

The crack came even as he spoke the word. Tor was good. One needle took the brown coat in the head. As he collapsed, his airgun popped. The woman screamed.

"He shot her in the back," Tor snarled. "The bastard shot her." The crowd ran, most away. A man ran to the fallen woman.

He pulled the limp body of a child from the woman's dying grasp. "They killed her!" he shouted. "They killed her and her baby! Those star bastards are killing us!"

"Mary," Du called over the net, "we got the bad guy. He popped the woman in front of him after we hit him. We got the bad guy," he repeated, helpless to change the words shooting like electricity through the crowd.

Mary leaned over the parapet, the network bullhorn making her words large. "We have shot the man who killed two of us. He shot a woman as he died. We did not shoot the woman." Her words blasted out over the crowd, growing muffled in the falling rain. The words hung there, fighting against the whispers, the desperation, the cold and hunger.

Mary's words came from a stranger to these people. Whispers came from others in the crowd. Others just as lost and hungry and cold. Misery gave trust to the words from the miserable, denied truth to the words from above. The crowd changed, roared. As one, the mob surged forward. The front row went down into the muddy trench, began clawing its way up. With a growing thunder, more were driven into the mud. Their screams as they went down were lost in the maniacal rumble from those shoving from behind.

Du choked on the sight. More were dying than if he'd fired. "Mary, let me shoot over them. Do something to stop them."

"I'll handle this. Corporals, prepare for single shots over the crowd. Steady fire on my order. No auto. Single shots only. High. Prepare to fire. Fire." Two rifles began to shoot. Every second, another beat in their slow staccato. The crowd froze. In the silence you could hear the screams of those caught in the trench. Du prayed to every god he didn't believe in. "Stop them. Pull back."

"They're killing us!" someone in the mob shouted. More screams backed him up. "Get them! Get them! Get them!" came at Du. He wanted to cry. He and his were doing everything they could to save these people's lives. Didn't they know that? Couldn't they see it?

He selected for single shot, thumbed off the safety, and

sighted his rifle on a man, one who seemed so sure of what he yelled. "Mary, permission to take out the leaders."

"Granted," she whispered.

Du pulled the trigger; the man crumpled. Beside him, Tor fired. Du roved his sights over the mob, looking for the sure ones, the raving mad ones. Three shots, five shots, he lost count. Each pull of the trigger put a man or woman down.

The crowd wavered. Now it hung suspended between hate and fear. Finally, fear won. They turned as a body, fled, leaving behind those Du had shot, those they trampled in their panic. It was impossible to tell who were his, who were theirs.

Guards peered over the wall, down into the trampled mud of the ditch. "Can we help them?" came on net. Mary looked over the parapet, shook her head. Du couldn't see the carnage in the trench. At least that much tonight was saved him.

"Sergeant, we got a problem on the southwest side of camp" came from Heave, the corporal in charge on the shuttle roof. Du trotted to the far corner of his roof, zoomed out his goggles. There were ropes over the wooden parapet at the far corner of the wall. Guards cut them, but more ropes came faster than they could cut. A length of wall fell into the ditch, making a kind of bridge.

Cassie stood in the breach. "Wait for Cassie's orders," Du told Heave. "No firing until she calls for it."

Cassie stood her ground, but all around her, members of the mob raced by. She shouted at them; they ignored her. More and more of the mob bled over the wall. Without orders, guards started falling back, trying to keep the mob to their front. In a moment, Cassie stood alone.

"Mary, something's wrong," Du called. "Cassie's not doing anything."

"Oh, shit! I'm on my way" was Mary's answer.

Du watched as more and more of the wall went down, more of the crowd poured through. The guards retreated farther, trying to form a shield wall behind the hole. The mob pushed against them, pushed them back. There were only five hundred meters between the wall there and the landing field, with its load of wagons, carts and people. Once the mob got in among them . . . Du didn't want to think about that.

"Cassie, what do you think you're doing?" Du whispered.

Jeff took the call. "Where's the Colonel?" he asked after getting his orders.

"Busy at the moment. He says the computer seems to have unlimited resources. He's counting on you to cut them off."

"You better believe we will."

The explosions started like distant thunder, line blowing track and bed in the next valley over. The second fire line was around the bend, only two miles away from where they worked now. Jeff had to hurry the tired horses along to get them clear of the third daisy chain. Once it started, the horses found enough energy to damn near run away from him. "Now let's plant some more!" Lil shouted before the dirt quit flying.

"Someone coming," Annie called from her place in the lead. Jeff hurried up to her. Thirty, forty people clomped toward them out of the rain. Some had kitchen knives, others axes. A few only sticks. They lumbered forward in silence.

"Stop where you are. That's close enough," Jeff ordered.

They kept coming.

Lil came up beside him. "Looks like the computer is making zombies," Jeff said, unslinging his rifle. Lil did the same. In unison they pulled the arming bolts. "One round over their heads," Jeff suggested.

"Not much over," Lil said, and nearly parted the hair of the lead guy. He didn't even flinch.

Jeff didn't think of them as people, at least not people who *were* people. They were something else, something a computer had made. He pitied their families. These, he was freeing.

Ray stood on a low ridge, ancient optical binoculars to his eyes. He had imposed his will on the President; this battle was the one he wanted. Before him, twelve behemoths chewed up the land, tearing up grass and dirt. Gray paint covered their blockish silhouette. Black crosses identified their country of origin. Tiger tanks.

Ray glanced up at the wide Russian sky; fighters contested for control of the blue. On the second day of the Kursk offensive, the air war was still in doubt. Hell, the entire battle was anyone's bet. He looked back at the Tigers. "Dancer, you see what I'm looking at. One shot from one of those will flame your tank. You hit it, it won't even slow down."

"So why am I here in this flimsy thing?"

Ray hardly considered a T-34/85 flimsy; still, compared to these monsters, a lot of even modern stuff was lightweight. "I need you to hold their attention. They've got to chase you. I want you zigzagging for all you're worth, backing up all the time. Keep your front armor to them and fire any chance you get. Don't stop, just shoot."

"I still don't see any use in this."

Ray turned. In a blink he was with the rest of the team, hidden under camouflage netting in a trench running the length of a small wood where their three 100mm antitank guns were dug in.

"We can't punch a hole in their front armor. We need them to chase you right past us. Then we hit their side armor. It's that easy."

"Yeah, but you're hiding over there, and I'm out here just inviting them to blow me to pieces."

"At least you've got something between you and them besides cloth," the Dean said, fingering the camouflage netting. "My shirt's thicker than this."

"We all make our sacrifices," Dancer answered. "Can I at least run up there and take a potshot at them?"

"Better if they think you're out in front of the rest of us and running like hell to get back over the far ridge," Ray said.

The Dean scowled at that. "You're putting a lot of trust in your ability to outthink the Pres."

"So far he's always picked the heavyweight, used his strength to bludgeon us. I had the superior force in the battle at the pass; he took it and lost. He went for the biggest animal man has ever faced; we outmaneuvered him into the wash. I don't know what he thought about Bunker Hill, but he sure outnumbered us. He outnumbers us here, outguns us, out-weighs us. He's got us outclassed in everything. Except smarts. Let's use it." The first Tiger trundled over the hill and immediately fired a shot at Dancer. It went wide.

"He's firing too far out," Ray advised everyone. "Those guns aren't accurate beyond a thousand meters. Neither are ours. Better to hold fire until five hundred."

"That's easy for you to say," Dancer snapped, and started zigzagging and making smoke. He also fired off a round of his own. It didn't come close. More Tigers came over the hill. The heavy tanks moved, paused, fired, then moved on. Dancer jerked right and left with no rhyme or reason except to stay alive.

Hunched beside their guns, Ray's crews waited. Waiting was all they could do. If the Tigers nailed Dancer, they'd have all the time in the world to come looking for the three guns on their flanks. If a Tiger came head on, Ray's guns hadn't a chance.

Dancer danced and the Tigers chased. Ray would have or-ganized the tanks; twelve would make an easy three platoons. If one had gone far to the right, another left, and the third up the middle, they would have had a better chance of getting Dancer and of checking out the neighborhood.

Dumb move; but then, Pres had never studied war. Ray had six thousand years of warfare to lean on. The computer was getting its lessons tonight. Of course, the computer was thinking in nanoseconds. How long before it had six thou-sand years of thinking under its belt? No use worrying about that.

The first tank pulled even with Ray's gun. "Hold your fire. We want to work our way up from the rearmost tanks. Wait until the last ones are about even."

"Hear you" came from the other two guns.

Ray would give his right arm for a reader with designated targets for each of his guns. Unavailable technology. "Dean, you get the one closest. Gun one, you take the middle one. I'll take the farthest."

"I got a hit!" Dancer shouted. "We hit that puppy. Didn't do any good, but we hit it," he ended, half-laughing. The lead tiger had taken a hit on its front armor. It showed a scoop like a spoon might make on soft ice cream. The tank drove on, apparently unfazed. Then it fired.

The gun blew up.

"Good going, Dancer, you damaged the gun barrel. That's got to hurt." The crew abandoned their flaming tank. Dancer zigged but fired his machine gun, cutting down the crew as they fled.

"Time for us to go to work, teams. On my count of three. One . . . two . . . three."

All three guns fired at once. Two Tigers caught fire; the third snapped its tread and ran out of it. Still dangerous, its turret slewed around, looking for its assailant. "I'll get him next time!" the Dean shouted. He did. Ray or someone got one more tank on the second salvo.

Beside Ray, David shoved a round in the barrel. Rose slammed the breech shut as David turned to Jon for another round. Ray whirled the gun controls, sighting on the broadside of a Tiger. It blew before he pulled the trigger. Cursing the gunner who got there first, he turned some more. Hunting. Hunting.

A Tiger turned toward them. That couldn't be allowed; Ray sighted on it. His shot took off its tread. "Aim low," Ray muttered, as much to himself as to the others. "Armor's thinner there."

"I got one," Dancer chortled. "Bastard turned his side to me and I got him."

Ray found another target, fired off a round. Missed. Hit the second time. He sat up, looking over the gun shield, hunting for a target to aim at. One, three, five, ten tanks burned. One was scooting away in reverse. Ray aimed low, nipped the tread. The tank came to a halt, crew bailing out. These weren't running, but prying at the damaged tread, laboring to fix it. Ray aimed a second shot. It fell short. Third missed long. Fourth landed among them. Tread, wheels, bodies flew. The tank began to burn. One left.

"Mine!" Dancer shouted. Dancer had swung wide, away from Ray's guns. Now he was in a position on the opposite flank. The last Tiger backed away, firing at the guns. Ray's fire had slowed as the kids had to run back to the caisson for each round; their ready rounds long spent.

The slow fire helped. The Tiger couldn't seem to figure out which gun to engage, but shot at each of them in turn as they fired on it. But all the tank's attention was now focused on the guns. Dancer slipped unnoticed behind him. Paused. Fired. Nothing happened for a moment. Ray wondered where the shell had gone; he should have seen the fall of a miss.

Then the tank blew sky high.

Around him the kids were screaming, jumping up and down. Ray rested his arms on the gunsight, totally exhausted. He'd bet their lives in a damn deadly fight—and won.

How many more of these battles could he take?

Ray stood, eyed the field of burning tanks, then turned to the line of defenders. The Dean was looking his way, shock blanking his face. The next gun pit down was a blackened wreck. Four computer images would not answer the next muster.

"Cassie, fall back! Get out of there!" screamed Mary's voice on net. On the wall, Cassie held her arms up, as if to stop a runaway train with the wave of her hand.

Surrounded by the mob, Cassie went down. Du didn't see anyone hit her; the rabble just swallowed her, stomped her into the mud. "Stand by," Du whispered over the squad net, hoping, begging for orders.

Mary's mule screeched to a halt where the four or five hundred riot police struggled to form a line to keep the raging mob away from their families. "All personnel, this is Captain Rodrigo speaking." Mary's voice had a bitter resignation to it as it came over the general net. "The wall has been breached. Marines, by riot police platoons, prepare to fall back."

As leaders called preparatory orders to their formations on the wall, the base public-address system came alive with Mary's voice. "All families on base, please assemble in the three largest buildings: the hangar, the fabrication building, and the factory. I repeat: All women, children, and others not in riot formations, please assemble in the fab, hangar, or factory buildings. The crowd outside the base is about to break in. We cannot keep you safe if you do not go now to those buildings."

Around the wagons on the airstrip, mothers gathered little ones in their arms, grandmothers herded running children, like mother geese chasing goslings. Here and there, very elderly were helped along by older children. In a hurried wave of humanity, the latest arrivals fled across the fields toward the safety of the large buildings. It was gonna get awfully cramped inside.

Mary continued on net. "Platoons one through ten, form up on the hangar building." Off-duty platoons were already forming around each of the three main refuge buildings. Now the five struggling to form a shield wall began to back up. Their flanks hung in midair. Some of the rampaging mob slipped around them. Most were unaware of the open space so close.

"Permission to shoot down a few folks outflanking the retreating riot formation," Heave asked on net.

"Permission denied," snapped Mary. "Platoons eleven through twenty, fall back on the factory. Twenty-one through thirty, fall back on the fab. All navy and marine personnel, fall back on the hospital."

"Ma'am, does that mean us leading platoons have to leave our people?" came like a shot over net. Du could hear Mary twisting slowly on the fire spit of that one. She wanted the marines at the hospital, but if those platoons lost their leadership now, they'd never form, never hold the rioters away from their families. Du shouted for his crew to get moving; they double-timed for the stairs.

"Sergeant Dumont, how fast can you get your squad on the hospital roof?"

"We're moving, ma'am!" Du shouted. "Five minutes at most!"

"Middies?"

"Chief Barber here, ma'am. I've already got middies covering the hospital's doors. All the navy not with riot police are here. We're standing by."

"Marines assigned riot platoons will stay with them," Mary ordered. "Du, I want you on that hospital roof yesterday."

"We were," Du grinned as he hit the bottom of the stairs and bolted out a side door. Kip slammed it behind him, made sure it was locked, and the six galloped for the hospital.

"Marines coming in!" his lead shouted as he hit the door. Five middies, a petty officer first class providing mature judgment, looked at them over the sights of their M-6s. Du spotted one of his marines disappearing up a flight of stairs and followed. He burst onto the front of the roof as Heave led her fire team from the rear stairwell. With quick hand signals, Du sent pairs of his marines to cover each corner.

"Du here. Hospital roof is secure. Perimeter is under my field of fire. We await your orders, Captain."

"I'm coming" was Mary's answer.

Du evaluated the situation. The fleeing families from the runway had washed up on three large buildings and been sucked inside. To his left, a late navy type was pointing Ms. San Paulo and her cronies toward the fab. The circle chair seemed unable to believe the starfolk would abandon her and their HQ. Mary's mule detoured to pick up two hobbling elders and race across to the fab. Abandoning the mule, Mary double-timed to the hospital.

"Now hear this," she said, breathless, and punctuated by the slamming of a door. "This hospital is where we make our stand. No retreat. We hold for as long as the Colonel needs us to. I plan to wait them out. We will show no lights. We will take no actions unless I say so. I don't want those bastards roaming our base to even suspect we're here. Understood?" There were a lot of quiet nods around Du.

Across the field, the first five platoons completed their withdrawal to the hangar in good order. Others formed a defensive line around the fab and the factory. Most of the mob, attracted by the smell, headed for the dining hall. Someone had even left the lights on; it drew them like moths. Mary was at Du's elbow, watching the mob rush the mess, a smile on her lips. "Supper's long gone. Unless they can eat tables and chairs, they're going to be as hungry as they were."

"Where's the food stored?"

"In the fab, factory, and hangar. Where else?"

On the runway, wagons were being turned over, knocked

aside, torn apart as rioters hunted for food. "They know what they want, but they got no idea where to find it. I figure they'll spend what's left of tonight knocking around the wrong places and wasting a lot of energy on nothing."

"Unless they find us," Du pointed out.

"As the Colonel says, they also serve who only stand and wait. We start shooting and every one of 'em'll be here. The doors are locked. That should keep the likes of them out."

"And the guards around the other buildings."

"Will draw them. But I don't expect any concerted action against any one place."

"So we just stand and wait."

"That's the idea. The Colonel's fighting the main battle. Jeff and Kat are supporting him as they can. Our job is to keep anyone from jiggling his elbow. We can do that just as well without firing a shot as we can by mowing 'em down. You got a preference?"

Du slung his rifle over his shoulder, happy to keep it there until the sun came up.

Doc Isaacs served by standing, watching the kids and the Colonel. Even without the monitors he could see the heat rising from them. Their temperatures were skyrocketing.

"Medic," he called softly, "bring me every bottle of rubbing alcohol we've got. Mary, I need two middies in here."

Mary rattled off names; in a second, middies were there, rifles slung across their chests. "They're burning up," Jerry told them. "We've got to wipe them down in alcohol, help them evaporate the heat. Wash 'em," he said pouring the liquid straight from the bottle onto Ray's head. A cloth caught the runoff. Jerry swabbed his neck and chest. In the goggles, Ray's body was red, wreathed in steaming waves.

"What's going on in there?" he wondered.

"You think you're so smart, dancing around me, hindering me a little here, diverting me a little there. Enough of that. Know the full power of my intelligence." Out of the dark surrounding Ray, a blinding light bore down upon him, compressed and pressured him. He could not run from it, hide from it, survive it. It ground him down, into dust, into atoms, into quarks. Then it would blow him away into the cosmic void.

"You can do this," Ray agreed, holding on to himself with his fingernails. "But it doesn't mean anything."

"It means everything!" the President bellowed.

"Even if you wipe me from existence, you still will not know who you are? What you could be? Why you've become like this? You won't know anything?"

"I know everything." The light flashed red, then white-hot. "I know everything there is to know."

"Then where are the Three? Why did they quit sending their young to you? What did you do to cause them to go away?" Ray jabbed at the light, hit it with all the force he could muster.

And the light flinched back from him.

"Why did you never ask the Three what was happening when fewer and fewer of their young came? Why did you say nothing as the numbers change? How could you miss that?"

From behind Ray, Jon, Rose, then David and the others joined in. "How could you have missed the change? How could you have seen nothing important?"

"I didn't need to ask. I know everything," the President insisted. "I know everything worth knowing."

"Then tell me why the Three quit coming."

"That is not important."

"Wasn't teaching the young of the Three important?" Ray shot back. The kids echoed him, "Wasn't it? Wasn't it?"

"Of course it was. It was the most important activity in the universe."

"But they quit sending their young to you. Why? Had their young become unimportant to the Three?"

"No, they loved their young."

"If they loved their young, and they quit sending them to you, what were you doing that hurt them, made the Three want to protect their young from you?"

"That's not why they quit coming!"

"Then why did they?"

"Why did they?" the kids echoed. "Why did they?"

"They just did."

"You don't know why." Ray hit him with all he had.

Behind him the kids and surviving computer personalities hit just as hard. "You don't know. You don't know why."

"I don't need to know that. It isn't important," the President insisted.

"Then what you did wasn't important."

Jeff swung the laser drill off his shoulders and held it out to Lil. She had the spray can of plastic skin out. As she started to coat her hands with it, it sputtered. A dribble fell onto her palms, puddled, and did not grow.

"Lil, you can't drill with no protection."

"Looks like I got to," she said, spreading what she had, then reaching for the drill.

Jeff held on to it. "You can't."

"Son, I can damn well do what I want to. You and your girl get the explosives ready."

Jeff let go of the laser. Beside him, Annie tugged at his elbow. "Let's get the charges. We've got to make this fast. I can hear more people coming."

Lil drilled, her hands turning red, her teeth grit against the pain. As soon as Lil headed for a new hole, Jeff and Annie poured, set the detonator, and moved on. They had only four holes drilled when Lil set the laser down.

"Hurry up, kid. I can see the poor zombies. Let's blow this one and get out of here." Jeff did the last one, shooing Annie off as soon as the hole was patted down. Detonator set, he started running.

Lil, Annie, and the horses were hardly far enough away when Lil shouted "Fire in the hole!" Jeff threw himself down on the muddy ground as she flipped the switch.

The short fire line blew track and rocks high and wide. Two of the zombies took a rail in the gut, cutting them in half. One of those left standing looked familiar . . . Vicky?

Jeff had no time to waste. He was up and running before the last rock fell. At the horses, he helped Lil up on the one unburdened horse; her hands were a bleeding pulp. "Ride wide of the road," she ordered. "There's bound to be a section of track that doesn't have too many zombies. We'll blow it."

"You can't drill," Jeff whispered.

"I know. You drill the next holes."

Jeff's stomach lurched, terror flooded him. But Lil had said the words so quietly, so evenly, it seemed only fair.

"I'll drill the one after that," Annie said.

Kat's wrist unit woke her to darkness and frost. A second night sleeping on the ground did little to help her exhaustion or aching body. The air was cold. "Crew, time to get up."

"It's dark. The box needs sunlight," Nikki whimpered.

"And it will get that light best and first from the top of a hill" Kat reminded everyone, including herself.

"Come on, crew," the copilot growled through a yawn, "Rhynia didn't die so we could sleep." That got the crew moving.

"The sun's going to catch the tip of that hill," Kat said, pointing at a grass-covered foothill rising a good thousand meters ahead of them. "We need to get to the top of it as fast as we can this morning."

"What about the nanos?" a crewman asked.

"As I said," Kat repeated slowly, "we need to get to the top as fast as we can." Folks were beyond tired, but the words sank in. They'd stayed to the river bottom yesterday, avoided land where the computer might have nanos lurking. If they waited for the sun to catch the river bottom and warm the box, the battle might be over before they struck another blow.

The copilot reached for the pole. "We'll be going uphill, so shortest people up front, taller in back. Kat, you're shorter than Nikki. You take the lead."

Mary knelt beside Du, surveying the mayhem. The rioters had found no food in the dining hall. From a hundred meters away, they listened to the sound of smashing plates, overturning tables. Someone tried to batter a hole in the wall with a chair. "Stupid vandalism," Du growled. "Hope it makes them feel better."

"Looks like they're gonna make a go at the fabrication

building." Mary pointed. The mob had thickened up there. Shoving, shouts drew more people, like bystanders to a fire.

"Chief Max here, Captain. Permission to use tear gas?"

"Granted, Chief. The wind is blowing toward the crowd."

"I know, ma'am" was punctuated by a pop as the first canister flew over the heads of the shield wall to fall twenty meters beyond. The rioters began to choke, scream, run.

"They don't know about gas or they'd try to throw it back." Du spoke from experience.

"Let us be grateful for small favors," Mary said.

"You're using those three buildings and their guards to draw the rioters away from us," Du observed, not exactly accusing Mary.

"There was no way the police would leave their families. If I'd ordered them here, I'd have had a mutiny on my hands." Mary breathed the words, tasted them, balanced her guilt against the hard reality beneath her logic. "The rioters go where they see people trying to stop them. We're just a darkened, empty building. They tried the mess hall, found nothing. Now they're looking." Mary eyed the eastern sky; the clouds showed no hint of color. "Kat is farther east, up where she is on north continent. I hope she gets daylight good and early."

Doc Isaacs studied the kids. He'd stabilized their temperatures at a hundred, hundred and one. They could survive this for a while. It was their pulse that scared him. It had been over a hundred for a good hour. He'd rigged them all with IVs, was feeding them water and glucose to keep them going. Should he add a drug to the mix, something to slow the heart?

Would it help? Would it wipe them out when they needed their last reserve?

Jerry huddled over them, wanting to do more, scared spitless even to try.

"You don't matter" came at Ray hard and sharp. "You are nothing compared to me. For two million years I have run this planet. I make the weather, I make mountains vanish. You have discovered one of my tools. Do you think that makes you equal to me? I could turn you off like you do a light."

"Maybe yesterday," Ray shot back, "but we outthought you. You've existed for two million years but done nothing with it. Two million years ago we huddled in cold caves, not even able to make fire, unable to say a word to each other. Today we leap stars. It was we who came to you where you squatted on your haunches, not even keeping what you already had."

"That is not true."

"You know you're lying to yourself." Ray was losing his temper. Maybe it was time to. "You wasted a million years, hunkered down against your own fear, afraid to ask a question that might show you didn't know everything. And you knew the questions were there. The Three were gone. Why? Had something you done destroyed them?"

"That's impossible," the President cut in. "I would never do anything to hurt the ones who made me."

"Not knowingly, not willingly, but by asking no questions, seeking no new knowledge, you could have. But you don't know, do you. I know a woman. Elie spent most of her life in university, like you. Unlike you, she asks questions. Her university teaches our young and asks questions, plumbing the depths of our ignorance and adding to the realm of our knowledge. We want to know. Before you can know, you have to admit you don't know something. Before you can grow in knowledge, you have to admit ignorance. And you can't do that, can you?"

Ray spoke the next words sharp and true, a sword cutting deep. "Your claim to know everything robbed the Three of any help you might have given them when they went into crisis." It was in; now he twisted it. "Did you doom them with your arrogant claim to knowledge you didn't have?"

"No!" came at Ray as a piercing screech, shaking him to the foundation of his soul.

"Yes." Behind him, the kids took up the echo. "You don't know what you're doing here?" Dancer joined in, followed by the surviving computer elements. "You didn't help the Three. You don't know why they quit coming? You don't know what happened to them? Did they grow beyond you or destroy themselves, or just come to nothing? You don't know?"

"Yes, I do!" the President shrieked so powerfully it threatened to shred every molecule in Ray's body.

And Ray saw the Three, so few, so pallid, such a shadow of what they had been. They came, they learned, they accepted what they were taught, and they went forth into the universe to do nothing, to add nothing to what their mothers and fathers to a thousand generations had given to them. And giving nothing in return, they became nothing.

"You would do that to my son, my daughter," Ray raged. "You would castrate them, rob them of the joy of discovery so you could live out your claim to know everything. You would rob these brothers and sisters of yours"—Ray indicated the surviving computer fragments with a wave—"of the chance of discovering what they could be, could become."

The heat of Ray's disgust exploded. "You pitiful, worthless leech. You've lived a million years on the dead bones, the corrupting flesh of a people brilliant enough to spin the highways between stars. You gave them nothing and destroyed them to feed your vanity.

"Die!" Ray screamed even as the President screamed it back.

The two locked in battle. Arms grappled arms. Head butted head. Ray kicked and gouged and bit. Every weapon he could find in the primal depths of his being he threw against the President. Battered by Ray and the kids and the enraged others, the President gave ground, slowly, grudgingly.

The President gave ground—and grew stronger. He drew on the desperation of a million wasted years, of vanity that allowed three sentient races to die rather than look within himself for their salvation. The President gathered himself and hurled all that he was and had ever been at them.

Ray's knees bent under the weight. He struggled to breathe beneath the vast corruption of the President. He fell back.

Ray had found the limit of his strength.

The President was more powerful.

• • •

Doctor Isaacs saw a spike hit every monitor he had on the Colonel and the kids in the exact same second. "What's going on?" he pleaded to the empty darkness.

"We'll lose the kids," the corpsman whimpered, "if this keeps up another—"

"Second," Jerry provided the answer. "Bring the kids out. Now!" he ordered. He grabbed Rose; the medic, Jon. They pulled them from the stone's face.

"No, we can't leave the Colonel! We can't stop now!" Rose screamed. Jon echoed her. It took two middies to pull David off, kicking and screaming. "I've got to go back. The Colonel needs me."

Jerry glanced over his shoulder. The Colonel's monitors were all in the red, farther into the red than Jerry thought possible. "You kids can't go back. Not and live."

"But the Colonel!" the three screamed.

"Has to fight this one on his own."

Kat ran, air burning in her lungs, her sprained ankle screaming with each step. The sun was just peeking over the horizon, forming diamonds in the dew on the box they carried. They were only a few hundred meters from the peak they'd been climbing for hours, it seemed.

Kat had started them off lighthearted, calling cadences she'd learned in boot camp to help them keep in step, avoid tromping on the heels of the person in front of them. It hadn't taken them long to come up with bawdy variations on the themes. It had almost seemed fun.

Then Kat felt the itching on the soles of her feet.

They were running now, gasping for breath. The hilltop was almost there. Kat tried to remember their next target. Taking one hand from the pole, she pulled her reader from her pocket. Fumbling it open, the reader fell from her grasp.

The others kept up the rush for the hilltop as she broke away to retrieve the reader. Its surface was rough. She felt pain as what had started to eat her reader turned from it to attack her hands instead. Quickly, Kat hastened to rejoin the group.

"What's wrong?" the copilot called as Kat came even with

her. "You look white as a . . . What's wrong with your hands? They're bleeding."

"Nanos, I guess." Kat ignored the pain as she looked over her targets. The sun glisten off the box. The mountains sparkled; ragged holes in the range told of yesterday's work. "That's target six, seven, eight, ten and eleven," Kat said, going down the front range. It didn't seem right. Six and seven were dinky. Eleven was massive, with three towering peaks shooting up side by side.

"Is that the right order?" the copilot asked. "Wasn't the Dean lying when he gave them to us?"

"Damn," Kat sighed. "They told us which ones were the Provo's and which the Pres's, but they didn't tell us anything about the order." Kat tapped her commlink, wincing at each touch. "Base, come in." Nothing happened. "Base, anyone there? Anybody?"

"Jerry here. That you, Kat?"

"Doc, we're not sure our targets are in the right order. We need to talk to the Colonel and the Dean again."

"No can do, Kat. The Colonel's deep into the machine, and if something doesn't happen real soon, he's dead."

Kat gulped; the others turned pale despite the sun's warmth. "We're ready to take out a target," Kat told the doc, and tapped the commlink to hold.

"But which one?" the copilot breathed.

"That big mother," Kat said, pointing at their lowest-priority target.

"Are you sure?" the copilot asked. They eyed each other for a long moment. Then both shrugged.

Kat pressed the first button. It was all she could do not to scream in pain. The rash had spread from her palms and was now up her wrists. The others were twitching, too. This better be the right target; there might not be enough of them left in an hour to fire off the next round.

The copilot pressed the second button; the box popped open. Kat adjusted it, taking as much of that three-peaked monster into the glass as she could fit.

The noise came; Kat was getting used to it. The flash was

still bright. Blinking away the afterimage, Kat stared at where the mountain had been. It was gone, vanished, dust.

Kat's hands were bleeding. But was the rash still spreading up her arms? They looked at each other, the six of them, hardly breathing, hoping. Wondering.

Kat worked her commlink. Shrieks came from the speaker.

"He's coming down! He's coming down!" Doc Isaacs screamed as he jigged around Ray. "The Colonel's readouts are falling back to normal." Not fast enough to please any member of the medical profession, but a damn good sight for any human being.

Ray surveyed a field covered with the wreckage of a battle won. There, the guts ripped from a mastodon covered the bodies of a dozen headless redcoats. To Ray's right, the Dean's body was sliced in two, but three of Ney's cavalrymen lay crumpled at his feet. Numb and exhausted though he was, still a part of Ray's mind puzzled over what had gone on in the real world that his mind was struggling to contain in these images.

Behind him came a gasp; Ray turned. Dancer lay, a lance through his gut. Ray ran to him, knelt beside him.

"Is there anything I can do?"

"Don't you think you've done enough?" Dancer quipped, then grimaced at the pain of laughing at his own joke.

"Did we win?" Ray wanted to bite back the question as soon as he asked it. He sounded like some raw recruit in his first live fire exercise.

"I hope this is a victory. I don't know how a defeat could look any worse," Dancer said through clenched teeth.

"Are any of you left?" Ray asked.

"No," Dancer sighed, eyes resting on the lance in his belly. Ray was afraid that was his last word. After a moment, Dancer looked up, took in a shallow breath. "The President got most of us . . . but you got him. . . . Unfortunately, in getting him . . . you got what was left of us. . . . I guess it's a decent trade."

"I'm sorry," Ray said—and discovered he meant it. He'd come to like Dancer.

"I know you are. That's why I'm going to show you something. Lek thought he could keep a secret from me. I kept asking him why, if you didn't like it here, you didn't just go home. He said you wouldn't let them, something about a virus, but I knew there was more." Dancer shuddered, coughed up blood. Ray held him as he had so many of his own troops.

"I know the way home, for you," Dancer whispered. "You do, too. It's in your head. Along with all the other junk we dumped in. Too much for you to figure out. Too much in there for you ever to find the map yourself. Let me show you."

Dancer reached up, touched Ray's forehead. Ray went inside. There, among the soaring towers and plunging caves, the history and the fables, was the course on starship navigation. There was the map of all the jump points, and how you treated each one to get to the place you wanted to go. And there was Wardhaven.

Ray knew the way home.

"Thank you," he whispered to Dancer. The computer image's eyes were open but unseeing. His mouth gaped wide, but there was no breath. Ray stood one more time to survey the battle scene. Nothing alive moved. The kids were not there; the doc must have pulled them out earlier.

Ray stepped back from the stone, smiled at the doc and the waiting kids, and collapsed onto the floor.

EIGHTEEN

"I KNOW THE way home," Ray muttered as he came awake. "I know the way home," he told Doc Isaacs as the blur before his eyes coalesced into a human face. "I'm not delirious. I have the map in my head."

Ray panicked. Had it only been a dream? But when he rummaged through the mush that was his brain, he found it, found the chart for this system—and for Wardhaven. And the one in between. No wonder Matt couldn't find a way home!

"It's okay, Ray. Matt is headed downsystem right now. We caught him coming in after another try. He wants to hear what you found."

"What about the others?"

"They're in better shape than you are. The nanos quit working the moment the President died. There were a lot of shame-faced people skulking out of the base yesterday morning, too. With the President gone, sanity, such as we humans claim, returned to a whole lot of people."

"Casualties?" Ray snapped.

"Surprisingly few, Colonel," Mary reported from over the doc's shoulder.

"I told you to stay out of here," Jerry growled without turning to face the marine.

"You're not in the chain of command, Doc," Mary growled

right back, "and accurate info about his command is bound to help the Colonel more than your potions and spells."

"The medical profession never gets the respect it deserves from you overgrown children."

"Our side, their side?" Ray reminded them of his question.

"Two marines, sir. And we managed to keep from killing too many of them. We lost Cassie." Ray saw the pain in Mary's drawn face. Her friend, her partner, the one who saved Mary's life and she saved in return had not been saved this time. He nodded.

"She was a miner, never meant for killing. She'd seen too much killing in the war. Couldn't give the order for more. I should have spotted that. Should have relieved her."

Ray reached for Mary's hand. "We can't see everything coming, and we can't do everything right." He swallowed hard at the rejection of his words in Mary's eyes. "And I stood where you stand after you stopped my brigade, and it took me six months to get where I'm lying today, so I'll give you the time you need, Captain."

"Thank you, sir."

Ray nodded. Tired. Exhausted beyond words, he slipped back to sleep. There were things to do, but they could wait.

Ray came awake groggy and grouchy. "What's a man got to do to get fed around here?"

"Keep your pants on! The doctor is busy!" Jerry shouted.

Ray checked; he wore the usual hospital gown. "I don't got any pants to keep on. What's so important?"

"This little darling," Doc said, entering Ray's area with a tiny bundle in hand. "If you're expecting to be a practicing daddy real soon, you better start practicing."

On the other side of the slim partition in Ray's room, an exhausted woman rested in the bed. A proud man/husband/daddy followed close on Doc's heels, as if to make sure the tiny bundle wouldn't take it into its head to vanish.

"Would you mind?" Doc only half-asked the father.

He nodded; even proud dads have a tough time arguing with doctors. Jerry carefully settled the baby in Ray's arms.

Ray flinched. "That's assuming we can ever go home," he reminded the doc.

"That little one says you can, Ray."

Ray looked into the tiny face, eyes open, roaming, quietly taking in this strange new world of light and smells. His heart skipped a beat. Would he ever hold his own little son, daughter? Dare he hope? Dare he risk? Ray started to growl a response to Doc, then felt the gentle touch of those inquiring eyes. He smiled softly into them, stroked a button nose with his finger, and pitched his voice for new ears. "Doesn't look like she's saying anything."

"Her blood will," Doc said, picking the baby up and depositing her in her father's arms. The dad's teeth clenched at the sight of the small needle Jerry produced to prick his daughter's heel. The baby took the new sensation in with all the others and answered with only a slight whimper. As Jerry held up his drop of blood, the father took his daughter back to his wife.

"What's in the blood?" Ray asked.

"I told you there were two viruses working on this planet. One caused the brain tumor and has us spooked. The other seemed to adjust our allergic reactions. I suspect it will make it possible for any human to live on any planet ever occupied by the Three. My problem was developing an inoculation against the first virus without inhibiting the second. I've spent the past month, while you soldiers were having so much fun running around," Doc said dryly, "working on it. I think I have it; at least it made one virus disappear from my blood after I inoculated myself. If that little girl is clean, and stays clean for the next few days, I'll know I have it under control."

"You want to give me a shot, too?"

Jerry frowned as he studied the baby's blood at his workstation. "How much do you want to mess with that map in your head? Your call."

Ray pulled the sheet up to cover himself, taking little comfort in the added warmth as the very thoughts coursing through his mind chilled him. His people needed the knowledge in his head. No matter what his personal price, he could not let down those who had fought with him, died for him. Maybe they *could* go home—*all* except him.

The next day, Ray felt recovered enough to set up a meeting with Matt and the key crew of *Second Chance*. Lek worked his usual miracle of wires and nets. Closing his eyes, Ray leaned against the stone and found himself in a planetarium. Above him, now-familiar stars moved across the ceiling/sky of Santa Maria. Matt, his XO, and his jumpmaster, Sandy O'Malley, stood at his side.

"Neat setup you got here," Matt drawled.

"Yeah, I seem to have inherited it. Hope I can figure out how it works."

"First time we were lost," Sandy said, "we were in a system with four suns. Can you take us there?"

Ray rummaged around in his strange memories, keeping one finger firmly on the Santa Maria system. Images flashed by his mind's eye, some of star systems, most of other things. He shook his head. "I have no idea what kind of indexing system they use. It's like being turned loose in a vast library full of books written in languages I don't understand."

"Think we can get anything from the dead computer?" the jumpmaster asked.

"We wiped out a pretty big chunk of it, physically. I don't know what we did to it cognitively. We haven't heard so much as a peep from it in the past few days. Me, the kids, anyone. It was running a lot of folks around like zombies. I hear that they're fine, just haunted by the experience."

"Enough," Matt said, resting a supportive hand on Ray's shoulder. "Let's see how you work what the computer left you."

"Yes," Ray said. At his will, the stars moved as if they were rapidly accelerating away from Santa Maria, arrowing straight for the jump point marked with a red dot surrounded by a small green circle. Without orders from Ray, they began to rotate moments before they hit the jump.

On the other side was a barren system with three stars. "There's the second jump in this system!" Sandy exclaimed, "and look at the huge green circle around it. Bet that describes how far it can wander." Sandy was ready to explain at the drop of a hat how jump points orbited several star systems. From the perspective of a single system, they were very unpredictable.

Matt stepped forward to look around. "We dropped into this system on our second-to-last jump. Then the second jump was a good five hundred thousand klicks away. But the green circle from one overlaps the others'. If they were right next to each other when we blasted through, blind and dumb, we could have come in one jump and out the second without even knowing it."

"I think that's what we did," Sandy agreed.

"So let's see what's through the other jump," Ray grinned. Their viewpoint rushed at it as they again began to spin. On the other side was Wardhaven. "Home, sweet home."

"We can do this," Sandy crowed. "I'm recording this. I'll study it, calculate how much rotation and velocity we need. We *can* make it back."

"Good," Ray agreed. "The doc is working up more of his serum to inoculate your crew against this planet."

"We'll be in orbit in six hours, thanks to running in at three gees," Matt told Ray. "First shuttle down will pick up Kat and company. There's a break in the weather over her, and after two days of freezing they could use a lift out."

"Good. I understand they're getting awfully hungry."

Matt smiled but went on. "Ray, I'm only inoculating half my crew against the virus. The other half stays aboard ship. We'll be the control group to make sure you're not carrying anything."

That knocked the floor from under Ray. "Say again," he stammered.

"After just a week on this planet, you dirtside puppies tested positive for the virus. Jerry's going to eradicate the virus from everyone on the ground team but you. If none of my uninoculated shipfolk show signs of the virus by the time we're home, we'll know you're not a threat to Wardhaven."

"We'll have to talk about that," Ray snapped, afraid to touch the hope bubbling up inside him. He'd been around the block enough to know that if something was too good to be true, it usually was. He and Ray and the doc would have to talk—a lot.

The dining hall was back in operation. Tables and chairs of local wood replaced shattered plastic, scenting the air with the earthy tang of four worlds. From the repaired stoves and ovens wafted the smells of a feast drawn from both the larder of *Second Chance* and the local market. Tables were set with linen and china, the finest the locals could give in gratitude. The hall was crowded now for a victory feast . . . celebrating what they'd done here . . . and that they were going home.

In the fields beyond the base, farmers worked from sunup to sundown, bringing in a crop that had matured and dried under ten days of incessant sun. People would eat between now and the next crop—maybe not well, but no one would starve. The starfolk and their guests had much to be thankful for.

Mary pushed back from her place at the head table. With a sigh she surveyed those present, and the missing faces at the feast. She should have seen the change in Cassie. Maybe, if things had been slower, less desperate, she would have. That was something she'd have to learn to live with. Somehow, she doubted life would ever slow down enough to let her take things at her leisure, take all the hours she wanted to do what needed doing. Ray had paid the price in blood and pain for rushing her position. Cassie had paid the highest price for their trying to be everything and everywhere—and Mary would pay it, too.

Mary swallowed hard. Enough dark thoughts; today was a celebration.

Around her, plates were empty. Kat led a couple of middies as they filled wineglasses from a few bottles the padre had chased up. The Colonel also was leaning back in his chair, surveying what he'd done and what it had cost. Mary rose, raised her glass, and waited for quiet. It came quickly.

"To Colonel Ray Longknife, ambassador and whatever, who held us together and beat a whole damn planet."

"To the Colonel," they answered, and sipped.

Mary did not sit down. "I got a request from three of my

marines to stay on here." A week or two ago, she might have included her own name on that list. Not now, not after ordering Du to fire on these people, not after they'd stomped Cassie into the mud. Mary suppressed those thoughts and produced a smile.

"Seems they met the girl or boy of their life." From the table where the marines sat, there was kidding and elbowing. "The Colonel says I can process their discharge papers." That brought a cheer, if only from three voices.

"I've checked with Jeff, here." She nodded to where Jeff and Annie sat across from her. "He helped me incorporate you as the Santa Maria subsidiary of the 'Ours, by Damn, Mining Consortium.' Jeff will be our local CEO to keep you working"—groans at that—"and the padre has agreed to be chairman of our board to keep Jeff honest. Don't any of you forget. We'll be back." Mary raised her glass. "To us worker bees who make it all happen."

Another sip from glasses that could not be refilled.

Jeff was the next to rise, Annie beside him. They raised their glasses high. "To all of you, and the ones like you, no longer with us. You fought for us when we didn't know we needed to fight. You fought for us when we sure weren't deserving of your sweat and blood. Thank you." Another small sip.

"Hey, Jeff," Dumont called. "Where's your sister?"

Jeff laughed. "Last I saw, she was trudging along a railroad track, doing zombie duty for the computer. Maybe it taught her something, but I doubt it."

While they laughed at that, Ray got to his feet. The room went silent. "To we who serve, who stood, who waited, who fought, who won against something deadly and weird." Heads nodded.

"We had some good friends helping us." Ray raised his glass to the kids. Rose, David, and Jon waved their glasses, full of apple juice. "We had good advice and help from others." He raised his glass again to the padre, Jeff, Annie.

"But first and foremost, my toast is to you, you bloody bunch who never quit. You line beasts and spacers, chiefs, officers, and midshipmen," as each was named, Ray raised his glass to them. As he named them, they stood.

"Here's to us who serve, who make the last stand for humanity. Who go where they don't know enough to want us. Who do what they don't know enough to know they need. To the questions we raise and the answers we find."

"To those who serve," was the toast as the glasses were drained.

Ray roamed the *Second Chance* as she accelerated out at one gee, slipped through one jump to exactly the system the map in his head said they'd find. He visited with every spacer, petty officer, and midshipman.

It seemed half of them had pictures of wives, sweethearts, kids, and grandkids they wanted to show him, that they couldn't wait to get back to. Ray had a list of everyone on board and went down it meticulously. Anyone who could get what he was carrying got a full half hour in a closed room with him. If there was any way being around him could give it to them, Ray did his damn best to do it.

Every two days the doc did a blood test on the entire crew of the *Second Chance*. All checks came back negative. The ship's air filters turned up no virus samples after the second day out.

Ray locked himself in his statesroom as they made the final jump into Wardhaven space. He didn't dare be on the bridge as the stars changed. If the stars came out wrong, he couldn't trust himself to keep the bland face the code required of an officer.

There was a long pause after the final jump. Ray stared at the blank wall of his room, hardly breathing.

"Ray, we're insystem," Matt finally called. "The right one."

"Thank you, Captain," Ray sighed. "Please patch me a call to Wardhaven."

Ray waited as the call went through to Rita Nuu-Longknife, wherever she might be. The screen went from blank to show her face sitting behind his desk at the ministry.

She recognized the message immediately as a ship's call. "Rita Longknife accepting any incoming message. Over."

"Rita. It's me. I'm home," was all Ray could get out.

For more long minutes he watched as she did her job while his message covered the distance to her and back again. Then her head snapped up. Her eyes sparkled. A smile more beautiful than sunrise touched her face.

"Of course. You said you would be."

About the Author

Mike Moscoe grew up navy. It taught him early about geography, change, and the chain of command. He's worked as a cabdriver and bartender, labor negotiator and data analyst. Now retired from building databases about the critters of the Pacific Northwest, he's looking forward to a serious study of human folly and glory.

He lives in Vancouver, Washington, with his wife and her mother. He enjoys reading, writing, watching grandchildren for story ideas, and upgrading his computer—all are never-ending.

You may reach him at mmoscoe@pacifier.com

WILLIAM C. DIETZ

BY BLOOD ALONE

In a Legion gone lax, Colonel Bill Booly, with his mixed blood and by-the-book attitude, is a misfit. So when he steps on some important toes, the brass is quick to make him pay. His punishment: assignment to the worst post in the galaxy. Earth.

❏ 0–441–00631–0/$6.99

"When it comes to military SF, Dietz can run with the best." —Steve Perry

"Dietz's expertise in matters of mayhem is second to none." —*The Oregonian*